THE GHOSTS OF XICOTEPEC

BOOK THREE OF
THE ECHOES OF PANGAEA

James Tarr

Theogony Books
Coinjock, NC

Chris Kennedy/Theogony Books
1097 Waterlily Rd.
Coinjock, NC 27923
https://chriskennedypublishing.com/

Publisher's Note: This is a work of fiction. Names, characters, places, and incidents are a product of the author's imagination. Locales and public names are sometimes used for atmospheric purposes. Any resemblance to actual people, living or dead, or to businesses, companies, events, institutions, or locales is completely coincidental.

Cover Design by Shezaad Sudar.

Ordering Information:
Quantity sales. Special discounts are available on quantity purchases by corporations, associations, and others. For details, contact the "Special Sales Department" at the address above.

The Ghosts of Xicotepec/James Tarr -- 1st ed.
ISBN: 978-1648554933

Chapter One

"Esme, get up."

The girl buried her head deeper under the pillow. "No, Mama," she said, voice muffled.

She heard steps, and then the pillow was gone. "It is time to get up for school," her mother said, sternly but with a smile. Then she frowned in the dim room. "What did you do to your hair?"

"*¿Que?*" Esmerelda hadn't tried opening her eyes yet, but when she did, she realized she couldn't see anything, and there was hair in her mouth. She brushed some hair away with a small hand and spit the hair in her mouth out.

"You look like you got attacked by a badger. You look like a badger," her mother said, frowning, hands on her bony hips. "Get out of bed. I will brush your hair when you are dressed. And a bath tonight. No arguments. Now, out of bed. *Ahora*," she growled when the girl didn't move. Esme knew that tone, and knew if she didn't do what she was told, her mother would follow up the growl by hitting her on the backside with her sandal.

With a groan, Esme rolled over and sat up. She yawned and blinked, then finally stood up. Her mother gave her a look, then left the room.

Half-asleep, Esme dressed in the faint light coming in through the open door. Once she had her school uniform on—white blouse over knee-length, pleated gray skirt and white stockings—she turned and looked out her window for the first time—and blinked in surprise.

"Is that what snow looks like?" she asked her mother as she came into the small kitchen. Her father, short and squat, was sitting at the table, also blinking away sleep, a steaming cup of coffee in front of him. Her mother was at the stove, frying tortillas.

"Is what what snow looks like?" her mother responded without looking up.

"Outside."

"*¿Que? ¿Nieve?*" her father said. He stood up and looked out the kitchen window. He laughed. "*Si*, almost. Except thicker. And whiter. And colder." He sat back down at the table, wrapped his thick, scarred fingers around the cup, and took a sip.

Esme's mother put the hot *tortilla*, wrapped around a thin layer of refried beans, on Esme's plate on the table before looking to see what had her family's attention. Fog, thick fog, outside the window. So dense, there was nothing visible beyond the curtain of white, not even the big bush at the edge of the property, ten meters away. Xicotepec de Juarez often had fog, usually in the mornings, rolling down out of the surrounding hills, ridgelines of the Sierra Madre Oriental mountains, but this was perhaps the thickest fog she'd ever seen. In the winter, it usually got down into the 40s, sometimes even the 30s, but the eight-year-old had yet to see more than a thick morning frost on the ground.

"Sit down and eat, and I will brush your hair," Esme's mother told her and went in search of a hairbrush.

"Will we ever get snow?" Esme asked around a mouthful of food, wincing as her mother worked out a tangle.

Her father shrugged. "We have. And we will again. Last winter we had ice on the streets, remember?" Xicotepec de Juarez was in central Mexico, located on Highway 132, which ran from Mexico City northeast all the way to the Gulf Coast. Like Mexico City, it had some elevation, so the temperatures remained moderate all year 'round. Mexico City had twice as much elevation, but it was on an arid plateau, whereas Xicotepec was in a valley deep in the Sierra Madre Orientals that saw much rain—which meant the possibility of snow in winter, if the temperatures dipped low enough.

"When will it snow?"

Her parents laughed. "Am I a fortune teller now?" her father asked. "Where did I put my crystal ball? I should play *la lotería* if I could see the future. Maybe next winter. Maybe not for ten years."

Her father downed the last of the coffee, grabbed his tool bag with a familiar *clank*, kissed his daughter on the forehead and his wife on the lips (while giving her a discreet squeeze), then started out on his ten-minute walk to work. He was the head mechanic at Tino's Mofles, where they repaired transmissions, brakes, radiators, suspensions, engines, and yes, even mufflers.

"Make sure you walk with Cara this morning," her mother told her as she helped Esme into her pink backpack stuffed with books and papers. The girls almost always walked together, but the fog was so thick, it made her mother nervous.

"*Sí, mama.*"

"And stay out of the street. Cars won't see you until it's too late."

"*Sí, mama.*"

With a kiss, her mother sent her out the door. Esme stopped at the curb and looked all around her at the white filling the air. She'd seen fog before, but nothing like this—the house next door was fuzzy, as if someone had draped it with the cottony insides of one of her stuffed animals, and the house beyond that was just a blurry blob. She could feel the faint moisture on her skin as she waved her hand around and laughed with delight. "Esme, don't be late!" she heard her mother call from inside the house.

She started down the sidewalk, and after thirty steps, stopped and turned. Her low house was painted light blue, with a tin roof, and it had nearly disappeared from view. There was just a hint of its color through the fog, which seemed to be moving, slowly, sideways across the ground, like it was alive.

Her house was on the outside corner of a sharp bend in the narrow street, on the edge of town. Beyond it wasn't much, just a few vacant lots filled with chunks of concrete, before the jungle began, the green thick on the steep slopes around the valley in which the small town sat. She wondered if the fog would be as thick in town, near the school. She hoped so. It was wonderful.

Esme continued walking, the heels of her fancy, black, slightly uncomfortable school shoes echoing oddly in the thick air. It was dim, almost dark. If the sun was up—and it had to be—she couldn't tell where it might be above her. The brightly colored buildings to either side—squat, with nearly flat roofs—came in and out of focus, the fog sometimes sliding past her in visible wisps. She thought, chewing at the inside of her cheek as she walked, it was like tiny clouds. No, like waves on an ocean—she'd never been to the ocean, but she'd seen it on TV.

The sidewalk was cracked and old, but somewhat level. The street, on the other hand, was in poor condition. Many of the narrow streets on the periphery of Xicotepec de Juarez were dirt, or in such poor condition the asphalt had crumbled to gravel, and there were frequent potholes.

She reached the corner and waited for her friend. Esme was a few minutes early, but she thought it might take longer to get to school, walking through the fog. The familiar corner seemed foreign in the gloomy haze, strange, an island inside a cloud, floating, isolated and murky. And chilly. She hugged herself, thinking she should have worn her jacket, and looked around.

Ahead of her, an ancient VW Beetle squatted at the curb, its rounded edges blurred even more by the heavy morning fog. Past it was Boba's small store. Its white walls disappeared into the fog, and the words hand-painted across the front in bold black and red— Cerveza Tecate, Tacos de Asada, ATM—seemed to hover in the air.

She'd heard there used to be a bus to take the children to school, at least the ones who lived on the edge of town like her, but now everyone walked. Maybe now that the war was ending, the buses would come back. She'd never seen the war, not in her small town, but the adults often talked about it. They said the town used to be busy and full of people. To Esme, it still seemed as if it was, especially downtown around the square, but her parents said Xicotepec had lost three-quarters of its population during the twenty years of war. In that way, it was no different than many cities throughout Mexico. There were a lot of empty and crumbling buildings in town—maybe the people moving back would fix them up.

The moisture in the air made sound behave strangely. She could hear a car in the distance, hissing along pavement, but up close, everything was muffled, as if she had cotton stuffed in her ears. The fog soaked up the sound, and what she did hear seemed to be coming from every direction at once, like the sound of someone approaching quietly.

Esme turned and peered down the connecting street. She couldn't see anything but the post of a street sign, and the shadowed, grayed-out bulk of a house on the far side of the street that she knew was abandoned. "Cara?" The way her voice echoed and then fell flat was disconcerting in a way she didn't understand. "*¿Cara, hola, eres tu?*" It made her briefly nervous, and she thought about the stories of blood-thirsty "ghosts" the kids at school would tell. That made her mad at herself. She wasn't a little girl anymore. She was almost nine years old, far too old to believe in ghosts, or monsters, that snatched little children.

Immediately back from the corner on her side of the street was a small vacant lot. A house had once stood there years ago, but after a fire, the remains had been bulldozed off, and the space had been left bare, full of weeds and chunks of concrete. The weeds seemed especially tall, and Esme was frowning at them when one low, dark form detached, then another, creeping forward.

* * *

Cara was skipping along the sidewalk, humming to herself, when she heard the scream. It seemed to be coming from everywhere at once, and she spun around in circles. It went on and on—and then cut off sharply. She couldn't see anything but the vague shapes of the houses lining the street. "Help!" she shouted reflexively, but then she froze. She'd... had she recognized the voice? The scream? "Esme?" she said. "Esme!" she shouted, and then started running.

She reached the corner at the same time as an adult, and she looked up to see Esme's mother, who was staring at something, eyes big and bulging, hand over her mouth. Then Esme's mother screamed too.

Cara looked down. There, right in front of her, was a huge spray of blood across the sidewalk and into the street, so fresh it was steaming in the cold morning air. So thick and bright and red, so very red it seemed fake, but she knew it wasn't. Beside it, on its side, was one of Esme's shoes.

There was no sign of her best friend as Esme's mother screamed and screamed and screamed.

* * * * *

Chapter Two

As "rustic cabins" went, it was ridiculous. Obscene. For a mansion belonging to Hollywood's current number one box office draw, it was actually rather modest. Sure, there was a six-car garage and a helipad, and it was set in the middle of more than a hundred hilly, wooded acres, but the house itself was just three thousand square feet and change.

By Hollywood mansion standards, it was an outhouse, but by any other standards—especially those of Carbon County, Wyoming—it was fabulous. Especially for a guy there alone most of the time.

The house was all exposed, stained hardwood walls and thick beams, more southwestern than country, with hints of log cabin, but nothing too kitschy. The antelope, elk, and buffalo heads mounted on the walls would have been props in Hollywood, and considered in poor taste by just about everyone he worked with, which was why it was rare for him to invite anyone in the business to this retreat. They were all, in fact, real, and he'd shot the animals himself, something doubly unacceptable to the Hollywood crowd, half of whom were vegans.

He hadn't built the house; he'd bought it from the man who had, a guy who'd made a fortune putting up next-gen cellsat towers then retreated from the high-tech world he'd helped create. Randy liked it because it was isolated. He had to drive an hour just to reach a town big enough to have a traffic light. Grocery shopping was an all-day adventure. Sometimes he did, and if he wore a ratty baseball cap and acted normal, more often than not no one recognized him. It was... weird. And awesome.

Once you'd made it, you didn't *have* to live in LA, or Hollywood, or even in California. Not with videoconferencing and worldwide satellite highspeed data services. The famous people who lived there did so because they liked it. They loved being recognized everywhere they went—loved being seen—alone and with all the other beautiful people. He'd had quite enough of Los Angeles.

Sure, he spent a lot of time in big cities, promoting himself and his latest movies, doing interviews, walking red carpets, and hitting a few of the "right" parties—though fewer and fewer of those. But he loved being able to retreat to his Fortress of Solitude as one interviewer had called it. He couldn't see or hear his neighbors unless they were out shooting on their property, and maybe not even then.

He was sitting at his big burlwood desk, staring out the window, daydreaming, when his phone rang. He checked the number then answered.

"Hi, Bob, what's up?" Bob Goldberg was a long-time collaborator and was currently the co-executive producer on Randy Max's next movie project, *Glass Man.* It was an espionage thriller based on the best-selling book, and a bit more cerebral than many of his recent movies. It was currently in "pre-production"—they'd decided on most of the filming locations and had cast most of the supporting roles. Principal photography was four months out.

"Randy! My man!"

Randy had to pull the phone away from his ear, and he snorted. "Bob, how many coffees is that for you already?"

"Who can count that high?" his manic producer said. "Who would want to? Why deny yourself one of the true joys in life?" His voice was booming.

"Coffee?"

"*Indulging,*" the man said, his voice a growl.

Randy snorted again. "Which is why you're on wife number four."

"Who's keeping count? Never look back. Listen, I wanted to call and let you know, I secured final studio funding for *Glass Man*. We're now 100 percent funded for the proposed shooting budget. Now we just have to work on funding the marketing."

"I have ultimate faith in you." It wouldn't be much work. Of the 27 projects Randy had been involved in since he'd gotten his big break, 22 of them had made a profit, and 15 of those had been blockbusters. His pictures were as much of a safe bet as was possible in Tinseltown.

"As well you should. Listen, ah... when I was calling around, working my magic, I was talking with a number of big names—BIG names, huge names—who indicated they were just dying to throw container ships full of cash our way, your way, if you ever finally decide to make a movie about your time in Oman."

"Bob—"

"I know, I know, but just listen: what better way to honor the men who were there with you? The guys who didn't make it back. Tell their story."

"Bob—"

"You know how huge it would be? You know how long people have been waiting for the full story? The true story? The real story. Hollywood legend Randy Max, on tour with the USO in Oman, when suddenly the compound he's in comes under fire. He has to grab a rifle and defend it like the Alamo, saving the lives of a dozen men."

"That's not quite—"

"And killing terrorists. How many? Five? Fifty? You've never said, but some of the guys there made it sound like you shot a lot. What was the official enemy body count after that attack? Wasn't it eighty-seven? I mean, Jesus, Randy, how many of those were you? You know how many actors at your level have ever done anything like that? None, zero, zip, zilch, nada."

"Lee Marvin was a Marine Corps Scout Sniper wounded in combat in the Pacific."

"Was he a world-famous actor at the time?"

"No, this was before he got into acting."

"Exactly, you're making my point."

Randy took a slow, deep breath. "I made a promise to the guys around me," he said, "that I wouldn't do that. That if we lived, I wouldn't make a bullshit movie about it. I've always tried not to break my promises, and for LA, I've got an exceptional track record, but that is one I *will not* break. Ever. And you need to stop asking."

Goldberg gave an expansive, theatrical sigh. "Fine. You're leaving fifty, probably a hundred million on the table, but whatever, who cares about money? Not me. See you next Wednesday for that final casting call?"

"I'll be there."

After the phone call, Randy's mind drifted back to the Oman incident, first, then to the adventure he'd had in Mexico a few months earlier that almost nobody knew about. That had been even more thrilling and exciting than his brush with death in Oman, and just as true. He was still dealing with a little PTSD from it, as he had the Oman firefight, which was why he'd been spending so much time alone at the "ranch," as he called it. Working through it—which mostly meant waiting for the nightmares to stop. It wasn't often that you got into an extended, running gunbattle with Mexican guerrillas… and then watched them get stomped to jelly by a pair of enraged brachiosaurs, wondering every second if they were going to turn on you next.

After sitting at his desk for almost half an hour, staring out the window, hardly moving but to breathe, he wiggled his mouse to wake his computer, then opened a fresh document. He pulled the keyboard close, hesitated a second, and began typing. He'd never actually written a screenplay before, not from scratch, but after reading thousands of them, the words flew from his fingers.

EXT - HILLTOP - MORNING
The sun is low above the Mexican jungle. Steam is rising, making the light waver, showing just how hot and humid it is. A dirt road is visible below, winding through the dense, green jungle into the hazy distance.

Camera moves down slowly toward the road, where a large vehicle built for offroad sits. Gear is piled on the roof rack and rear door—cases and spare tires and dusty red gas cans—oversize, knobby tires squatting on the ochre mud. Dirty diesel exhaust spews from the tailpipe in a low growl.

POV swings down, behind the vehicle, TIGHT on the big spare tire, then around the side, moving forward, slowly revealing a mud-spattered logo on the driver's door, PALE-OSAFARI, INC., and the half-visible roaring maw of a T. rex. Door suddenly swings open, and a muddy boot appears in the footwell. The owner steps out, TIGHT ON THE LEG—well-worn, muddy boot, and above that a tanned, muscular leg. Camera pans up and pulls back, and we see an athletic, outdoorsy man in a faded khaki shirt, a few huge cartridges stuck in loops at his belt, the image of a professional hunter. He puts on a bush hat, places one hand on the top of the door, the other on the roof of the 4x4, and one boot on the running board of the vehicle, then stares into the distance.

Randy leaned back, reread his intro, nodded, then leaned forward once more and resumed typing.

* * * * *

Chapter Three

Seamus O'Malley stood before the tall open window, the sheer, white curtains waving gently in the light breeze, then decided to step out onto the narrow balcony. Just past his toes was an ornate, black, wrought-iron railing that reached nearly to his waist. He leaned over and looked down. The street four floors below was narrow, and it seemed even more so lined with the six-story Haussmanian apartment buildings that were quintessentially Paris. With that thought, he looked to the left. The top third of the Eiffel Tower was visible above the apartment buildings sitting shoulder-to-shoulder across the connecting street. The city was still waking up, the sun not quite over the horizon, and the street before him was dim. Lights were glowing warmly on Gustave Eiffel's amazing construction.

Not a bad view. Far better than any he'd had while working—most military bases tended to be very utilitarian. Even if they were located somewhere scenic, the views were usually ruined by turrets, shipping containers, the constant roar of aircraft, or the occasional incoming enemy fire. Warzones were always dicey when it came to sightseeing.

He shifted his gaze across the apartment buildings that lined nearly every street in the area. Most of them were older, displaying the classic Parisian look of apartment buildings designed and constructed by Baron Haussmann right around the time of the American Civil War. High ceilings with big windows kept the apartments bright. Built in a time when class meant something, the first two floors were for the rich, the third and fourth floors for the middle class, and the smaller, low-ceilinged apartments at the top for the servants. The wood floors of the apartment still showed the original herringbone motif. There were fine moldings at every corner, and around every door and window. He'd learned the street-facing sides of the buildings featured cut stone from one of two famous quarries, and they'd held up very well.

"Beautiful," he heard from behind him.

"Aye, I was thinking the same thing," Seamus agreed. He turned and stepped back in, off the balcony. Sadie was in the big old bed, giving him a lazy, sleepy smile, sheet pulled down to her waist.

"I think we are talking about two different things." She twitched her chin toward him. "Giving my neighbors a show?"

Seamus glanced down. He'd slept nude, put on clothes for his morning run, then stripped down afterward. "I've got nothing they haven't seen before."

"Oh, *mon cher*, I beg to differ. After all, you are so old…"

He snorted. It had become a running joke with them, after he'd learned he was the first man she'd been with since high school who wasn't her junior. Still, he was starting to feel the years.

He smiled, then sniffed, and sniffed again. "I think I'm due for a shower," he announced. "I smell like… well, what you'd expect, given your demands last night."

She blinked, and her mouth opened wide in mock outrage. "*Mes demandes?*"

"'Tis no shame in being a woman with appetites," he said with a smile, walking to the side of the bed, where he took her hand. She was smart, which wasn't so common among the women he'd had in his life, and he found it a refreshing change. Under the beauty was the steel of will. That was why she'd been so successful in her work, and why she was still alive. His fingers gently traced the scar on her arm, fully healed after six months, but still pink and shiny, not yet beginning to fade. She had them all over her arms and sides, but none as bad as the one on her thigh, an indented divot marking the injury that had nearly killed her. Bite marks. Smart, beautiful, and like him, one of a scant few people in the world who'd fought dinosaurs hand-to-hand and lived. In her case, a pack of Coelophysis, two-legged carnivores the size of large dogs, brought back from the Triassic courtesy of the now-defunct Pangaea amusement park/zoo. He knew what she'd gone through—what she was still going through—and he hoped he was helping.

At first, she hadn't liked him touching her scars. She could barely stand to look at them herself. They were a reminder of the attack. Of Karl, who'd died defending her life. But Seamus reminded her of what he'd said when they'd first met in the hospital—"You did well just to survive. Wear your scars proudly." Then he'd added, "They'll always be with you, a part of you. Make your peace with them." She was trying.

He bent down to give her a quick kiss, then padded into the bathroom, which she'd redone herself after moving into the apartment several years before. It had a large, modern, enclosed shower stall. When she heard the water running, she threw off the sheet and headed in after him. With the new heater, it was almost impossible to run out of hot water, and the stall was more than big enough for the two of them; they'd proven that several times over.

Afterward, Seamus dressed beside the bed in some of the last clean clothes he had. He'd already done laundry once. "They say fish and family grow ripe after three days, and I've been here for ten," he told her as she pulled a flowered dress over her head. "I know my visit here has been killing you slowly."

She frowned, that cute little line appearing between her eyebrows. She opened her mouth, but before she could say anything, he added, "*La petite mort.* Dozens of them. Hundreds. It's a wonder you're still alive."

"Shite," she said, in a passable Irish accent. "Shite and bollocks." Which made him burst into laughter. She'd taken time off to be with him, but was quite busy with something at work. Something she found very exciting, something sciencey and incomprehensible when she'd tried to explain it to him, but he was happy for her. When she'd had to sit down with her laptop for hours at a time, typing or on video conference calls, he'd fit in a workout or a quick jaunt to some new corner of the city. He'd been to the Louvre three times, twice on his own. He grabbed his Walther off the bedside table and stuffed it into the holster inside his waistband.

"I still don't understand how you were allowed to bring that into the country."

He let the shirt fall to cover the gun. "I didn't fly commercial, luv. Raven's got their own terminal at de Gaulle, thanks to all the work we're doing for and with France in North Africa and along the border with Germany. Being allowed to go heavy in-country is part of the fine print. Although the local *gendarmerie* might take a bit of convincing of that if it's spotted. Might have to get an officer or an embassy involved. So I do my best to blend in, like a native. Speak the language. *Madame, vous avez un beau derrière,*" he said, bowing to her.

Sadie laughed out loud. "Oh, your accent," she said, looking pained.

"Maybe you can do the talking, then, and I'll be the pretty one." He smiled and shrugged. "Plus, technically, I still have a bounty on my head. I've been ordered to go armed everywhere and at all times." He had serious doubts about whether FRAP would, or could, even pay the sizable bounty at this point. They didn't seem to be a functioning organization, just isolated pockets of armed men without a cause, making trouble around the country, operating more like the criminals from which *La Fraternidad Progresista para un México Nuevo* had sprung. Raven had been letting the Mexican military handle most of it, drawing down its forces in-country, shuffling them around the world to other hotspots. After twenty years, it was the end of an era. The thought made him… sad. He shook it off and smiled at Sadie.

"Should I shave my disguise?" He gestured at his beard.

"I like it, but I don't know how you can wear it in that heat."

"You should try armor and a helmet. I don't even notice this fur ascot."

It had been a lovely week, and then some, but he was heading back to Mexico that evening. He hated to leave, but he was antsy to get back in-country. There was still much to do. FRAP had been crushed as a functioning entity, but there were still die-hard groups all around the country, causing trouble and/or hiding, but doing a bodge job of it. Maybe there always would be, but the widespread violence, after more than twenty years—the war itself—seemed to be over. The people running the country were talking about rebuilding. Foreign corporations and governments were talking about investing, repairing the infrastructure. For a profit, of course, a tidy percentage of Mexico's oil production or some such, but money made the world go round, along with sex and violence. Three of his favorite things.

The isolated guerrilla attacks were giving Raven something to do, but they were still steadily reducing their numbers, moving people and materiel elsewhere around the globe. He'd been fighting in Mexico for so long—almost his entire career as a contractor—and the conflict had been going on before he'd joined in. He wasn't sure what the future held for him. Did he want to start all over in a new theater of war? Maybe have to learn a new language? He didn't have that many years left in him—war was a young man's game, and he hadn't been a young man in over a decade. With his seniority and his record, he could go anywhere he wanted, anywhere Raven had a presence, but he didn't want to get stuck behind a desk. Better to retire, get out of the game entirely, than have to watch the young men heading to war without him. There was always private security, executive protection, but it wasn't the same thing, would never be the same thing, as war. Nothing else was.

"What are you thinking about?" she asked softly, seeing the expression on his face.

"The meaning of life."

"Oh, well, if that's all... did you want to go to the café again for breakfast? We've gone there almost every day..."

"Their coffee is brilliant, and their pastries are better. I love Paris, in spite of all the Parisians." He'd visited the city once, over a decade before, and had fallen in love with it. That was how he'd known the Paris motto—*Fluctuât nec mergitur*, "She is rocked by the waves, but does not sink." He'd always wanted to go back, and when Sadie had made the offer... "And I don't know when I'll be back."

She flashed a quick smile at that and nodded. She'd had a great time with him, fabulous in every way. He was smart and funny, and had a breadth of knowledge on subjects she knew little about. He was handsome. He was a tender and ferocious lover. She tried not to think beyond the immediate. Was it more than just a fling between two consenting adults with shared trauma? How could it be? She was staying in Paris, doing her work at university, still deep into the griffinflies and butterflies she was categorizing; he was a professional soldier, flying back to a warzone. She might go into the field again, but not to Mexico. Never to Mexico. There were too many bad memories.

"And when we get back, if you want, you can go for your run."

He'd taken a few days off but didn't want to lose too much of his edge. He'd been working out in her apartment when she'd had work to do, simple bodyweight exercises, pushups, sit-ups, squats, high reps, and been running around the city. When given the opportunity to take your morning run around the Eiffel Tower and the Arc de Triomphe, you took it. They were 2.4 kilometers apart. If he went early enough, traffic wasn't an issue.

"I already had my run, luv, while you were snoring so cutely."

"I do not snore."

"Of course. My mistake. Must've been the cat." She had no pets.

"How long were you gone?" She'd never noticed his departure.

He shrugged. "Did my usual ten kilometers." Pushing it as fast and hard as he could. Anytime he'd felt himself start to flag, all he had to do was picture the T. rex roaring in his face, teeth coated in fresh human blood. The Allosaur, running flat out toward him, soaking up bullets like raindrops. The Brachis, tall as buildings, in a berserker killing rage, crushing people and vehicles alike. Dinosaurs. Too many bloody dinos.

* * * * *

Chapter Four

It had been a week, and finally Edgar—Gar to everyone who knew him—could take it no longer. They were on their morning break, in one of the spacious supply closets only the maintenance and cleaning crews seemed to know about. He grabbed a fresh roll of toilet paper and threw it at the new guy. The roll bounced off the young man's head. Carlos and David didn't say anything; they knew better than to get involved when Gar was in one of his moods. In fact, they were shocked he'd waited a full week. For Gar, that was forever.

"So what are you doing?" Gar demanded.

The new guy blinked. "What?"

"Why is a *pinche gringo* emptying garbage cans and cleaning toilets in Mexico City?" The modern "self-cleaning" toilets only did so much—you always needed a person there, with a mop and a brush, to clean up the inevitable disasters.

Mike had been studying a lot, but still, the rapid-fire Spanish was hard to follow. But he got the gist of it. "*Alguien tiene que hacerlo,*" he said. "Somebody has to do it."

"*Alguien tiene que hacerlo,*" Gar repeated, mocking his words and accent. He jabbed a finger at Mike. "Your Spanish is shit, but that can't hide the fact that you're a college boy. Smart, big words. Are you an undercover boss or something?"

"He's twenty," Carlos said. It was an accurate guess. "He's not boss of shit."

David laughed. "Yes he is. He spent all morning cleaning toilets. He is the boss of shit. *El Jefe de Mierda.*"

The three cleaning men laughed long and hard at that, then Gar glared at Mike again. "Why?" he demanded.

Mike told him the truth. "I don't know what to do. Whether I want to go to school, go to work, go into the Army." He'd dropped out of school. Probably not the Army, but...

"So you're doing this?" David said, pointing at the service cart. "You joined the EstrellaCorp *Bandidos de Baño?*" It was a nickname they had for themselves, Gar, David, Carlos, and two of the other men who helped keep the 65-story building, *Torre Cielo*, clean and fresh. One thing Mike had been surprised by was the sheer number of people required to keep 65 floors of bathrooms, wastebaskets, and kitchens clean. The *Bandidos de Baño* was just one of four cleaning squads. The remaining three were staffed with women. Then there was the maintenance and physical services personnel, security, grounds people, and the kitchen staff who kept the cafeteria running...

"I've never done it before. I knew I'd learn something, even if it was just that I didn't like the job."

He really was at a loss. A crossroads. He had no idea what he wanted to do with his life. He didn't really care about business or making money. He was smart, and his dad said he could be successful if he applied himself, but how motivated would he be to succeed in a career he didn't care about?

His father had always said, if you want to know a company, wanted to know a business, the best way to accomplish that was to do as many of the jobs inside that company you possibly could. There was no better way to know a company, inside and out, than doing every job in it from the bottom to the top. Which was why so many CEOs who'd come in at the ground floor of their companies had been so successful over the long term. They had a breadth of knowledge earned from real world experience.

Thinking about it, Mike had realized he didn't really know anything about... anything. He hadn't had to work during high school. His father had given him spending money if he'd needed it, but never insisted Mike get a job. Mike suspected it was out of guilt for working so many hours and for Mike's mother being dead—not that his father'd had anything to do with that, or that Mike had ever blamed him for it, or for remarrying. In retrospect, he wished his father *had* made him get a job. But you couldn't change the past; he'd learned that the hard way, working through the nightmares and stress of being chased and shot at by guerrillas. Twice.

Maybe he was being ridiculous, taking his father's suggestion to an extreme, starting out literally scrubbing toilets, but if so, neither his father nor the man who might—maybe, possibly, someday—be his father-in-law had said a bad thing about his decision. Maybe assuming he'd learn something valuable from the experience. Like not wanting to scrub toilets for the rest of his life; he'd figured that out real quick. At least he'd learned what the job was, what it entailed.

"You didn't know cleaning toilets would be a shitty job?" Gar roared, laughing. "*Pinche estúpido.* Maybe you're not as smart as I thought." He checked the time on his EstrellaCorp palmpad—the company provided them free to all employees—then stood up. "Break's over. Get off your lazy asses. Next up is thirty-three. Accounting."

Carlos and David groaned. "*¿Que?*" Mike said.

David just sighed and rolled his eyes. Carlos told him, "Accounting is mostly women. They don't like touching their *culos* to the toilets—they think it's dirty—so they hover and make a mess, everywhere. It'd be so much cleaner if they just plopped their *culatas grandes* on the seats."

"One of those 'self-fulfilling prophecies,'" Gar barked as he opened the door and pulled his cart out into the hallway. When he turned around, there was an older man standing there. He was short and thick, in an expensive gray suit, maroon silk tie, and matching pocket square. Gar's eyes went wide, and he froze.

The older man watched the rest of the cleaning crew wrestling their carts out of the storeroom. Mike didn't notice when their constant chatter stopped dead until he turned around and saw their visitor.

"So, how has the week gone?" the older man asked Mike in English, a twinkle in his eye. He looked the young man up and down. Mike was wearing a dark blue jumpsuit with his name over one chest pocket, and the EstrellaCorp logo over the other. He gave the other three men nods.

"It's been… educational," Mike said, being honest. Gar looked back and forth between them, not daring to move a muscle.

Eddie nodded. "Good. That was the point, after all. The first five years I had jobs, I worked like a dog. I didn't clean toilets, but I did just about every other dirty job. Now when I get my hands dirty, it is just figuratively. Anyway, my lovely and gracious daughter Margarita has informed me that we are all going out to dinner this evening. Her mother and I, and you. Salcedo's, which she knows is my favorite. I find that concerning. Do you know the reason? The occasion?" David was squinting, trying to follow the English. Carlos' mouth was hanging open.

"This is the first I've heard about it."

Eddie chuckled. "Just when you think you're in charge…" he said to himself. Then he peered into Mike's eyes. "You're sure? She's not announcing an engagement, finally? Or perhaps a pregnancy?" Mike's eyes bulged. "I…" He cleared his throat. "Not that I…" Eddie laughed and clapped him on the arm. "Well, I suppose we will find out tonight, yes? Come to my office after work. I'll fly you back to the house, and you can change there. You'll want to shower too, I imagine. Honest work makes a man sweat." He looked at the other three men and nodded at them. "*Caballeros*." Then he turned on the heel of his expensive loafers and strode off.

"Who was that guy?" David asked. "He looked familiar." Gar cuffed him on the shoulder, staring at Mike.

"He should," Carlos. "He signs your checks."

"No, he's the boss of the boss of the boss of the boss who signs your checks," Gar corrected him. "*No mames. Estás pero si bien pendejo. Madre de Dios. Eso fue* Gordito*, hijo de puta.* He owns this building—" he waved his hand around them, "—and half of the city." He glared at Mike, angry at being lied to. "You *are* Undercover Boss, *puta madre.*" Which meant he was probably being fired.

Mike shook his head. "No, I'm not. Really."

"Bullshit," Gar said in English. His accent gave the word flavor and character.

"No, seriously. I just wanted to do the job. See what it was like. I'm no boss."

"Then who are you? How do you know Gordito?" Carlos demanded.

"My father is a CEO and knows him." He saw that wasn't going to satisfy them. "And… I'm dating his daughter."

"Which daughter? The one with the *chi-chis?*" Carlos asked.

"No, the one married to the attorney general, *coño,*" Gar spat at him. He looked at Mike. "*¿De verdad, la chica Echevarria de las grandes tetas?*"

He had to nod. There was no way he could answer no to that question without lying.

"*Puta madre,*" Gar cursed, then whistled. "Rich and looking like that? And you, looking like you? Marry her before she changes her mind. Propose, tonight, at this dinner. *No seas gilipollas.*"

David had pulled out his palm, and he and Carlos were looking at photos of Tina. Perhaps the most famous was the one of her in a bikini beside a pool when she was eighteen. "Are those real?"

"Yes, they're real; have you seen her mother?" Carlos said, then looked at Mike. "Are they real?"

Mike hung his head at the turn the conversation had taken, shook it, then admitted, "Yes."

"Are they as big as they look?" David asked.

Mike blew out a big breath, then shook his head again. "Bigger." She dressed to minimize them, in fact, but you could only do so much. Actually, he was pretty sure they'd gotten bigger since then.

Gar stared daggers at him. "Asshole," he said in English, equal parts jealous and angry.

"Come on," Mike told them. "Don't we have toilets to clean?"

"*Sí,* okay, Undercover Boss," Gar said.

"I liked *Jefe de Mierda* better," Mike told him.

* * *

Mike rode with Eddie Echevarria in his personal helicopter from the helipad atop the EstrellaCorp building to his newly purchased house in the hills west of Mexico City. A personal helicopter was a ridiculous extravagance—conspicuous consumption—unless you were a billionaire who'd been targeted by the guerrillas of *La Fuerza*. Their attack on Echevarria's mountainside home had left it a smoking ruin and a number of his staff dead. The house was currently being rebuilt. The new "house" was more of a compound, really, a *hacienda* with a large main house, a guest house, a helipad, a tennis court, a pool, and a huge garage, all of it enclosed by tall walls, guarded by a number of passive and active security systems, and armed men. Echevarria had doubled the size of his security force after the attack that had nearly killed him and his wife, and armed it even more heavily. Even though *La Fuerza* seemed to be in its death throes, that didn't mean it couldn't or wouldn't strike out one last time. Even in times of peace, rich men were juicy targets, and he was the richest man in Mexico.

Mike and Tina were currently staying in the guest house, a temporary arrangement that had gone on longer than he'd expected. Then again, his relationship with Margarita "Tina" Echevarria had gone on longer than he'd expected. He was head over heels in love with her, but he wasn't sure she felt the same way about him. How could she?

She was beautiful, smart, had finished her graduate degree in biology, and was looking for a job. He was five years her junior... and cleaning toilets. Sure, they'd been through trying times, been in actual combat together, but how much of what she felt for him was simply due to shared trauma? He worried about it every day. It wasn't like he was actually poor; his father was the CEO of the Pearl Sapphire hotel chain and could give him a middle-management position (at least) any time he asked, but...

He showered and put on clean clothes, a polo shirt over khakis, and rode with Tina to the restaurant in one of three large, armored SUVs staffed by heavily armed security personnel. Her parents were in one SUV, he and Tina were in another, and a third led the way. The lead vehicle was equipped with a pedestal-mounted M134D electric Gatling gun located in the exact center of the large SUV, hidden inside. The turret took the place of the second row of seats. At rest, the conical, six-barreled muzzle was pointed at the ceiling, and when needed, it popped out the roof. A similar vehicle and gun had saved their lives during their escape from the now-famous guerrilla attack on Cancún.

Tina was wearing a white silk blouse over black slacks, and just looking at her took Mike's breath away. He'd known her less than a year, and they'd been intimate for just over six months, but it seemed like he'd known her his whole life. Yet every glance at her was like he was seeing her for the first time.

She was being closemouthed and secretive about this dinner she'd arranged, and she held his hand in the back of the vehicle as they rode over, a small smile on her face. Possibilities ran through his mind, but he'd learned to keep his mouth shut, as his capacity for asking stupid questions was apparently infinite. "Better to keep your mouth closed and be thought a fool, than to open it and remove all doubt." He was pretty sure that was how the quote went.

Salcedo's was a high-end steakhouse, and Tina had reserved the entire restaurant. Not that she was expecting that many people, but for security purposes, it was far safer and easier. The staff had pushed a number of tables together in the center of the restaurant.

Ted Billings, the Echevarrias' personal pilot, was already waiting at the table.

"Now, what's this all about?" her father demanded as soon as he'd placed a drink order with the uniformed server. He glanced at Billings. He liked the man but wasn't quite sure why the pilot had been invited to what he'd thought was a family event. "You know how I hate surprises."

"Hush, Papa, this is not for you, or about you. We're a bit early. Wait and you'll see." The titan of industry, chastened as a man of power could only be by a daughter, sat down with a bemused grin on his face.

The two SUVs remained outside, parked near the front of the restaurant, one man remaining with each. A man was posted at the front door of the restaurant, another at the rear door inside the kitchen, and two inside with them—Beni, the chief of security, and Manuel, who'd been with them for years and, with Beni, had been part of the effort to rescue Tina when she'd been kidnapped by *La Fuerza*. Mike had been kidnapped with her and knew the men very well. They knew him, too, and had seen him carrying a rifle and covered in blood that wasn't his own. No matter age or life experience, shared combat made brothers of men. Soft drink in hand, he walked over to Manuel.

"Do you know what's going on?" he asked the thickly muscled man. He didn't bother asking Beni. You could light him on fire, and he wouldn't ask for water.

Manuel shrugged his big shoulders. "A dinner; that is all I know."

Mike looked past Manuel, and then did a double take. "Dad? What the hell are you doing here?"

Roger Rudd made his way across the restaurant and hugged his son. "What, I'm not allowed to go out to eat with my son?"

"Well, sure, but… what, you just flew down to Mexico City for dinner?" His father's offices were in Houston. Pearl Sapphire had its own fleet of executive jets, but still, Houston was a thousand miles from Mexico City. Tina came up.

"It's a little more than that."

"It is?" Mike looked from Tina to his father and back. "Is there something I should know?" he asked her.

"If there was, I would tell you," she told him, mouth twisted in a private smile. She and Roger hugged. He hadn't seen her in months, but they'd talked on the phone more than a few times. Roger gave her a kiss on the cheek, then went to say hello to her parents. He and her father had become friends as well as business partners since Roger had found himself in the same crashed helicopter as Tina, fleeing the guerrillas chasing them cross-country.

Next to arrive was Arturo Paul Morales, *fiscalía general de la República*, the Attorney General of Mexico, and his wife Marisela… who just happened to be Tina's oldest sister. Tina's mother, Rosita, jumped up from the table with a happy cry when she saw them. Tina's other sister Rosalia arrived next, with her husband Umberto, who'd inherited a construction empire and was doing his best not to bankrupt it before the post-war boom kicked off. The Echevarrias were the closest thing to royalty Mexico had at the moment. Mike still couldn't believe his luck.

Mike looked around at all the family. His father was being introduced to the Echevarrias he'd never met before. "What is this?" he hissed to Beni and Manny. "Did someone die? Is someone getting married? Is someone pregnant?" Manny shrugged. Beni just stared at him. To anyone else, it would have appeared that the slender, well-groomed man was stone-faced, without expression, but Mike knew him well enough to see that he was hiding a smile. "*Que te folle un pez*," Mike growled, which got no reaction out of Beni, but made Manny bark with laughter.

"Your Spanish, it is much better now," Manny said.

"*Que te den*," Mike told him, frowning.

"*Sí*, yes, good," Manny said, clapping Mike on the shoulder hard enough to rock him. Then he was pushing past Mike, shouting and waving. Everyone in the room looked over, then stood up.

Antonio had been the youngest member of the Echevarria security detail, helping to guard Tina in Cancún. In addition to getting slightly banged up when the Tahoe he was piloting at speed took a nosedive into a quarry—with Mike and Tina in the back—he'd been shot in the hip during the subsequent firefight with the pursuing guerrillas. The injury had been quite bad, and his pelvis had required reconstruction, followed by intensive physical therapy. He'd finally been cleared to return to work, and he was beaming as he walked across the restaurant unassisted, displaying just a faint limp. Beni shook his hand, then Mike, with a big smile. Manny hugged him, and then Eddie and Rosita were there, smiling and talking and hugging the young man.

"Get this man a beer!" Eddie told one of the waiters.

"*Señor*, please, no," Antonio protested.

Eddie would hear none of it. "Tonight, you are a guest. Tomorrow you can work—you can stand there and look like you're sucking a lemon like Beni—but now you drink and relax. That is an order," Eddie said with a smile.

"Yes, sir."

Appetizers were set out across the tables. The voices grew in volume as the alcohol flowed. It was the first time the entire Echevarria family had been together in six months, since shortly after the attack on the estate.

"Sir, I have a question," Mike asked Eddie. The older man leaned back in his chair. One of his eyebrows rose. "How did you know where we were? Where I was? In the storage closet?"

"Your phone," Eddie said simply. "EstrellaCorp palmpad. You think after everything that's happened—with you, with my daughter—that I don't track you everywhere you go? Both of you?"

"Oh." That made sense, and Mike didn't blame him, though he didn't much like it.

Mike noticed a few chairs were still empty, but didn't bother asking, knowing he'd get no answers. Manny seemed nervous and kept checking his watch. Then a few minutes later, Manny jumped up, looking toward the door. Mike followed his gaze and saw a very pretty blonde walking their way. She looked familiar, and several people called out to her, but it took Mike a few seconds to place her. The issue was the hair. As soon as he pictured her blonde mane tucked inside a helmet, he recognized her—Chris Evers, copilot of the Peregrine (piloted by Ted Billings) that had been involved in the rescue mission outside Zaragoza, and pilot of the aircraft that had tried to rescue them in Cancún before being shot down. She and Manny had been an item since Zaragoza.

Chris greeted everyone, and Tina made sure she got a drink, then gestured to everyone to sit. Tina stood near the head of the table, near her parents. "I wanted to get us all together tonight for several reasons," she said. "One, to Antonio coming back."

"Antonio!" everyone shouted, hoisting drinks in his direction. He looked embarrassed.

"We've lost so many to this war, seen so much death and destruction, that it is nice to have something positive to celebrate." She smiled at him. He'd been shot defending her, and while that was his job, she also knew it was a debt she could never repay.

"Second, I wanted to announce to everyone—even Mike doesn't know this yet—that I was offered a job as a research scientist with Kenmore-Garcia." There was clapping, and cries of happiness and congratulations. "They have offices right here in Mexico City, but I would be spending some time out in the field, which is what I wanted. This country has suffered horribly in the war, and for a number of reasons, our agricultural productivity has dropped dramatically. Kenmore-Garcia is one of the firms trying to reverse that, increasing production while having no negative effect on the land, which has been damaged by war in so many ways. Their dream is to reach industrial farming production levels while using organic methods that can be easily employed by local farmers, and they have some fascinating ideas on how to do that. I honestly don't know if that goal is fully attainable, or long-term sustainable, but they seem to be one of the leading voices in helping to rebuild Mexico, and I'm happy to be a part of it." The announcement earned her applause, and she waved it down.

Her sisters clapped politely, but they'd never understood her obsession with science… or work. Attracting—and keeping—a wealthy husband was the only kind of work they'd ever been interested in. Rosalia had already failed once at that. Her first marriage, to an architect, had been a disaster, but thankfully a brief one. She seemed happier with her current husband who, while not especially smart, was a hard worker and seemed determined to make her happy. Marisela, on the other hand, wasn't about to let the *fiscalía general de la República* get away and used everything from sex to threats of violence to maintain control. He seemed happily married, if slightly terrified of his wife. They assumed Tina was only interested in Mike because his father was a wealthy CEO.

Tina smiled, then turned and looked at Chris and Manny. "And finally, we're here because of Chris Evers joining the family, so to speak." Chris smiled, and Manny's face broke into a huge grin. "I believe they have something to say?"

Chris looked at Manny. He opened and closed his mouth twice, then his face darkened, and he lost the power of speech. For a strong, tough guy who'd seen more than his share of fights and combat, he was shockingly shy. After watching him struggle for a few seconds, Chris took pity on him and stood up. She placed a hand on his arm.

"First, I'd like to thank you, *Señor* Echevarria, for the kind job offer." She nodded at Eddie, then at Ted Billings, who'd vouched for her. "When my contract is up with Raven next month, I'll be joining the EstrellaCorp executive fleet, and I'm looking forward to not getting shot at while I'm in the air." Everyone laughed at that. She'd learned to fly in the Air Force, and had gone to Raven for the lucrative money. "After eight years with Raven—" *had it really been that long?* The time had literally flown by "—I decided it was time to move on." She'd also be working shorter hours and getting paid twice as much while, presumably, not getting shot at.

The war seemed to be winding down, but that'd had little to nothing to do with her decision. The spark leading to her retirement had been the death of Josie Williams, her friend and fellow pilot, during an attack the year before. Josie had left no one behind but her aging mother. Chris wasn't getting any younger. While she'd never been much interested in a husband or a family, after the devastating attack on Joint Base Sapphire and Josie's death, she'd been rethinking a lot of things, and spending more time with Manny. She'd felt something that, for her, had been extremely strange. The desire to start a family. She wasn't too old for children, not yet, but she wasn't getting any younger...

She took his hand in hers and faced the room with a big smile. "I guess I'm here tonight to, well... Manny and I would like to announce..." She was getting embarrassed as well. "We're engaged," she said finally, lifting and turning her hand to reveal the ring she'd been trying to hide. The diamond was modest but sparkled brilliantly in the light.

All the women in the room jumped up and crowded around her, congratulating her, and covertly evaluating the size and likely cost of the ring. Manny stood off to the side, looking pleased and embarrassed at the same time. Ted Billings looked proud as a father. Manny had literally jumped out the open door of his Peregrine onto a roof, under fire, to rescue Tina, while Chris had been pumping rockets and chaingun fire into the guerrillas running around the compound.

During dinner, Mike spoke with Tina. "You could have told me. Why didn't you tell me? About the job."

"I didn't want to tell anyone," she admitted. She glanced at her father, then lowered her voice. "If Papa knew where I'd applied, he would have called them. Exerted influence. You know he wouldn't be able to stop himself."

"Yes, but… Margarita Echevarria. The name is not exactly anonymous."

"Maybe, maybe not, but if my father knew, there would be no maybe about it."

"You're right," he had to admit. He kissed her. "I'm proud of you. Now I just have to figure out what the hell I'm doing."

"You will," she said confidently. She was unconcerned with money, as only the truly rich could be.

After dinner, many of them got up from the table to stretch their legs and talk. "So," Roger asked his son as they stood against a wall, "learning anything?" He puffed on a thick cigar. Mike didn't smoke, but weirdly enough, he liked the smell of cigar smoke.

Roger had been less than happy when Mike had dropped out of college, but Mike had been adamant that he didn't want to take classes just to take classes. Until he had some clue what he wanted to do, he felt like he was just wasting his time. Then he'd asked to be put to work, doing something. Anything.

"Yeah, actually, a lot," Mike admitted. "I never knew just how much work it took, behind the scenes, to keep an office building running."

Roger nodded knowingly. "Support staff," he said. "Facilities maintenance. They're the people who actually keep the ship of industry afloat. In the military, it takes ten guys to support every one in the field, in combat. In business, it's no different, whether you're talking about the guys who implement the decisions made in the boardroom, or the guys keeping the toilets in the executive bathrooms from overflowing."

"Wizard of Oz," Mike said. "The man behind the curtain."

"Something like that."

"The whole supply chain, no, support structure. I never thought of it before, but it's… fascinating."

Roger nodded, watching his son, puffing at the cigar to hide his smile.

After the amazing dessert, individual marbled *tres leches* cakes, Eddie and Arturo were off to the side, puffing at the Cuban cigars Roger Rudd had brought. "You are busy?" Eddie asked his son-in-law, the attorney general.

Arturo snorted. "I have the work of three men. Even with another assistant, I seem further behind every day. What is the American phrase, 'One step forward, two steps back?' But I've been spending a lot of time on a side project."

"Which is?"

"You remember, last year I led the raid on the casino in Cancún owned by *La Fuerza*? We seized some cash, but the importance was that it shut down the casino, which was used to launder money, usually for foreign purchases. Not that many of the countries they were in business with cared, but some did—at least on paper; they wanted the money to be clean. Then less than a month later, General Ramos led that attack on the other casinos, looting them of cash. Which honestly seemed petty. When we killed him and General Davis, they had the money from the casinos there with them, millions of dollars." When speaking of money outside the budget, they usually spoke in dollars, as it was a far more stable currency than the Mexican *peso*. "Almost as if they needed the money." The drone footage had nearly been comical. After the thousand-pound bomb had landed right on target, the air had been filled with confetti, except the confetti had been green American dollars. The Special Forces troopers who'd called in the airstrike hadn't known whether to collect it or leave it on the ground.

"Didn't they?"

"*La Fuerza* has had iron fist control over the drug trade in Mexico since before the start of the war, twenty-five years. That's billions of dollars a year. *Hundreds* of billions. Every year. So where is it?"

"Haven't you been seizing overseas accounts? I thought the news report last month said you'd frozen over a trillion dollars in assets."

"Yes, a trillion dollars. An almost incomprehensible sum of money. But *La Fuerza* should have been pulling in that much every few years."

"They had expenses. There was a war on," Eddie said with a smile, waving his cigar expansively.

"I've been looking into their expenditures. We found reams of documents, records, after the raids on their Zaragoza and Tenosique compounds, transcripts of intercepted radio communications, even receipts. Incomplete, some of it garbage or out of date, or written by semi-literate *campesinos*, comparing it to lists of seized and destroyed enemy assets, including combat equipment provided by our military. Additional intelligence provided by CNI." CNI was Mexico's version of the CIA. "After two months, maybe three, I was finally able to make some sense of it, produce some order. And I might know something about the great Timotéo that even his generals didn't."

"He had a tiny *penito*?"

Arturo laughed. He'd seen the photo, the "selfie" of Timotéo taken by the *escara*, the private contractor who'd killed him, O'Malley. The great Timotéo, sprawled on the floor, dead and bloody from multiple stab wounds. For some reason, his pants were around his ankles… revealing remarkably diminutive equipment. "*Sí*, that too, but no. I learned… that he was a thief."

Eddie blinked. "*¿Que?*"

"Stealing. Skimming off the top. Taking a percentage for himself since the very beginning. He used various excuses, when he bothered to explain himself at all, but it was a constant pattern. More some years, less in others. I still have no hard evidence, it's all circumstantial… but it's very compelling. I'm convinced."

Eddie sat up a little straighter. "Cash? We are talking about cash?"

"Yes, I believe so, most of it. I found that one personal numbered account of his in Bermuda, but there was only ninety million dollars in it."

Only ninety million dollars… Eddie frowned. "How much money are we talking about?"

The attorney general took a sip of his beer. "Well, see, that's the problem. The amount of money it *could* be… would be enough for *La Fuerza* to get back on their feet, buy a fleet of jets or tanks, or the services of another mercenary company like Raven for a year. Longer."

Eddie cursed, colorfully and at length. Arturo took another drink, then leaned forward. "But that's one problem, the possible existence of that money. There is one other." His eyes twinkled. He lowered his voice. "I think I've found it."

* * * * *

Chapter Five

Raven PMC wasn't military, not officially, but commercial airports didn't like—and weren't set up to receive—heavily armed aircraft carrying armed personnel. So inside the US borders, Raven usually leased space at military airfields.

Seamus rode a C-7 Zeus, a midsize—by military standards—cargo plane with extended range, from Paris to an air base somewhere outside New York City. He slept most of the way, sitting up in an uncomfortable webbed seat with earplugs stuffed into place. The big, loud plane was built for range and cargo, not speed, comfort, or passengers. He switched planes at the dark airfield, getting on a C-130J Super Hercules heading south. That plane made two brief stops en route to load and unload cargo before depositing him at Eglin Air Force Base in Florida. From Eglin, it was less than a thousand miles straight shot across the Gulf of Mexico to Joint Air Base Carmela, the main destination for inbound Raven personnel. He had to wait four hours before he could jump on a battered C-25 Airlifter heading in the right direction.

JAB Carmela occupied a large chunk of land adjacent to the Mexican International Airport—officially *Aeropuerto Internacional de la Ciudad de México*—outside Mexico City. After most of a day riding around in bumpy, noisy military aircraft, Seamus was tired and cranky. As the cargo ramp of the plane cycled down, he was more than ready to climb into a spare bunk, as he wasn't due to report for six hours. The mid-afternoon sun was bright on the tarmac, and the air was ripe with the smells of diesel fuel and overheated metal.

Seamus had his backpack over one shoulder, his big clothes bag in his opposite hand, and was just starting down the ramp when he saw the figure waiting at the bottom of it. For him, apparently, as he was the only passenger on a plane filled with pallets of hardware.

Seamus trudged the length of the ramp, dropped his bags, and saluted. "Sir," he said, curiosity plain in his face. Colonel Richard Kresge was the second-highest ranking member of Raven in Mexico. He wore a navy-blue suit with a black tie and white shirt. His black leather dress shoes gleamed. Seamus was pretty sure it was the first time he'd ever seen the man in purely civilian attire. Hands on his hips, he gave Seamus a dirty look.

"Took your time getting back, O'Malley."

"Yes, sir. Absence makes the heart grow fonder, as they say. I'm chuffed you missed me. It's the personal touches like this, a heartfelt meeting on the tarmac, that make the men so fond of you."

Kresge sighed and rolled his eyes, then glanced at his watch. "Do you have a locker here? Clothes?"

Seamus shook his head. "Just what I brought in with me, and it's all dirty. I've got a locker at Victoria Base with civvies and an old uniform, and one at Joint Base Sapphire stuffed with armor and toys."

"Okay. Check with a supply sergeant and tell him you need civilian clothes. Preferably something without a Raven logo. We should have what you need. Shower and…" He'd been going to say 'shave,' but he realized Seamus still wore the beard he'd grown in an attempt to disguise his features. "And meet me in front of Building A in forty-five minutes. We're going for a ride." Kresge turned and headed off before the sergeant could throw any more witticisms his way. He was sure there'd be enough of them in the coming hours.

Seamus stared after him, then grabbed his bag off the pavement and stomped toward the Raven building. He didn't know what was going on, but he'd learned not to ask or worry. He was back in-country on schedule, and hadn't done anything in France to cause an international incident, so whatever was going on, it wasn't his fault.

When he arrived, freshly showered, teeth brushed, and clad a dark green polo shirt over khakis, there was a large, unmarked SUV idling in front of the building. Seamus didn't recognize the man behind the wheel. The rear door opened, and Kresge beckoned. "Come around and get in." He couldn't roll the windows down in the armored vehicle.

Seamus walked around, opened the rear door, and climbed in beside the colonel. The big vehicle pulled away, heading for the front gate. Kresge eyed the pistol on Seamus' hip. "You won't need the pistol."

"FRAP still has a million-dollar bounty on my head," Seamus reminded his superior. "Two million if it arrives still attached to my breathing body. You gave standing orders for me to be armed at all times, sir. Not that I needed the encouragement."

"Yes, well, try to keep it in your pants."

"As always, sir. I am the picture of discretion."

The SUV cruised into the city. Seamus had been through Mexico City a number of times, but had never spent any serious time there. He recognized a few landmarks, as well as the building the SUV ultimately pulled up beside. Still, he had to ask. "Is this the bleedin' Presidential Palace?"

"Technically, the National Palace," Kresge said, peering out the heavily tinted windows. He gestured out the opposite window. "That's the Supreme Court Building." He gave Seamus a look. "You were requested, personally, for this operation. Try not to embarrass yourself. Or Raven."

Now Seamus was seriously intrigued. "I always *try*, sir," he said helpfully.

Kresge blew a lungful of air out and opened the door. There were two uniformed soldiers framing an entrance at the side of the building, and three more standing nearby, rifles slung. The colonel approached them, Seamus in tow. Kresge identified the two of them. One of the soldiers got on a radio, then told Kresge, "Wait."

They only had a minute to wait. A functionary in a bland, gray suit arrived. He was about to usher the two Raven men inside when the soldiers stopped him and pointed at Seamus' pistol. Whatever the man said in reply made the soldier clamp his lips shut and nod. "This way, please," the government official said.

Seamus stayed a step behind Kresge as they were led through the opulent halls of the palace, some of which dated to the 16th century. They went up a wide staircase, down a hall, and then were led into a mid-sized conference room with an oval table. There were two men already inside. "Please wait," their guide said to them, then he shut the door behind himself as he left.

Seamus studied the two men in the room, both Mexican. One was an inch shorter than him but thick with muscle, in civilian clothes but obviously military. The other was taller, older, and slender, in a suit. With a familiar face. Seamus stepped over to him. He snapped his fingers a few times. "I know we've met, but…"

"You were naked," Inspector Ramon Torres said drily. He'd recognized the contractor immediately.

Seamus shook his head. "Sorry, mate, you'll have to narrow it down."

"There was a Tyrannosaurus Rex running around."

"Ah, yes, the salad days. You were part of the rescue crew that dropped onto the roof. *¿Un fedérale, no?*"

"*Sí*, Inspector Ramon Torres." They shook hands.

The other Mexican man stepped up. He was so thick with muscle it made him seem shorter than he was. He had dark skin and close-cropped hair. "That photo was real?" he demanded. His English had only the trace of an accent. He'd seen the photo. Everyone had seen it. A naked man, brandishing a machete and screaming in the face of a T. rex. Who could believe such a thing wasn't faked? But this was the man in the blurry photo; that much was clear.

"Aye," Seamus said with a nod, "and I have the nightmares to prove it." The soldier frowned and looked at Torres, who nodded to confirm the tale. He'd seen the juvenile T. rex with his own eyes. He'd been in the aircraft that had taken the now-famous and much-disputed gun camera photo.

"How did you survive?" the soldier asked.

"Nobody likes getting hit in the conk *con un machete*. I think I hurt his feelings. While he was trying to pull it out with those little arms of his," Seamus demonstrated, tucking his arms into his armpits and waving his hands wildly, "I ran like a little girl." He smiled innocently.

"You ran into a *hacienda* filled with *La Fuerza* and killed a dozen men to get to *la señorita*," Torres corrected him, wanting to give the man his due. "While naked."

"A screaming, naked man charging at you does tend to freeze the blood of even the hardiest souls, so I had a wee advantage. Oh, that doesn't sound… I mean, I had a huge, swinging advantage," Seamus corrected himself with a big smile.

"And then you killed Timotéo," the soldier said, suddenly realizing this was also the same man in *that* photo. The *escara*, giving the V for victory sign, while behind him the leader of the communist insurgency lay dead and bloody. And pantsless, for whatever reason.

Seamus looked at him and gave him a small smile. "It was a good day," he said with feeling. The soldier nodded in understanding.

They heard approaching voices, and the double doors to the room opened. Two men walked in, their heads bowed together, deep in conversation, followed by a third. A fourth, obviously an aide, stopped by the door. Seamus blinked, and he, like everyone else in the room, jerked to attention. Well, this day had just gotten even more interesting.

"Gentlemen!" the president of Mexico said, beaming. As usual, his suit was magnificent—a fine, gray weave with the faintest hints of purple that were set off by a matching tie and pocket square. "Thank you for waiting. I can't stay for more than a minute or two, I'm between three meetings at once, but I wanted to make the introductions. Make sure you understood how important this mission was. Colonel Kresge, so glad to see you again." He reached out to shake his hand.

"Mr. President," Kresge said stiffly.

The president moved to the next man in line, the dark, muscled soldier. "Sergeant," he said, heartily shaking the man's hand. "Have you introduced yourself? No? Well, this is Eddie Echevarria," he said, introducing his companion. "I think you're the only man here who hasn't met him." Eddie, smiling, moved in for a handshake. Everyone knew the two were very close, and while Echevarria wasn't technically an elected official, he had the influence of one. The president announced, "And behind him is Arturo Morales, *fiscalía general de la República,* my attorney general." The president gestured at the soldier before him. "Gentlemen, this is Sergeant Miguel Alvarez of our *Cuerpo de Fuerzas Especiales,* our Special Forces. He led the raid, the airstrike that took out *Generales Ramon y Davis* last year. Just the latest addition to a long and distinguished career."

"Good show," Seamus said with a nod. He'd seen the drone footage of the strike. Quite satisfying, that, especially the stolen cash filling the air afterward like confetti.

The president turned to him. "Ah, Sergeant O'Malley, so good to see you again. And wearing clothes, even better." Seamus had to laugh, and the room relaxed as they saw the president was in quite a mood. The president extended a hand to Torres and told the room, "For those of you who don't know, this is Inspector Ramon Torres, *División de Inteligencia, Policía Federal,* and *El Centro Nacional de Inteligencia,* our CIA; he is a liaison between the two. He and Arturo have quite a presentation for you. A mission." He pointed at Torres, Seamus, and Sergeant Alvarez.

"You men have been chosen, not just because you have proven yourselves brave under fire, but trustworthy beyond question. And that is perhaps the most important, as this mission is quite... sensitive. Less military, and more... sneaky, I shall say. It must remain top secret—you are to share nothing of what you learn today with anyone who is not in this room, or who doesn't accompany you on this mission, depending on if you feel you need additional personnel. I will leave those details to you." He looked at Torres. "What is they say in the spy movies?"

"Classified? Need to know?" the inspector answered.

"*Sí, eso es*, need to know," the president said. He looked at them seriously. "Utmost secrecy," he told them. "You'll see." He nodded at his attorney general, said, "I must go," then paused and looked at Kresge. "Colonel," he asked, "what does Raven think of the Cuban offer?"

"You mean the New Democratic People's Republic of Cuba offering asylum to any and all of their warrior brothers of *La Fraternidad Progresista para un México Nuevo*?" He chewed on the question.

"What is it with communists calling themselves democratic? I don't quite understand it," Seamus jumped in. "The old East Germany was the DDR—*Deutsche Demokratische Republik*." His pronunciation was perfect, but he wasn't nearly as fluent in German as he used to be. Not much call for it in Mexico. Argentina, on the other hand...

Kresge ignored Seamus' interruption. "Political posturing and rhetoric," he told the president, "but I don't know that anything substantive will ever come of it, or if they even mean it. It's been over a week, and I haven't seen any intelligence stating that it's had any effect on actions in the field. Then again, things are a bit chaotic, as *La Fuerza* is busy scattering to the four winds. Half their units seem to be dissolving rather than staying in the fight."

"They made the offer last week, but it only became public knowledge two days ago," the president said. "I have been asked by the press whether I will grant passage to *Fuerzan* fighters who wish to leave the country."

"How would they even get to Cuba?" Torres asked aloud.

"Do any even want to go?" Sergeant Alvarez asked.

The president was nodding his head. "These are all good questions, and partly why I have meetings all day. Thanks to men like you, *La Fuerza* seems to have no command structure left to make a decision." He looked at Kresge for confirmation.

Kresge nodded. "After the airstrike that took out the two generals, the highest ranking FRAP officer still alive and at large—we think—is Colonel Jose Ruiz Alameda Salamanca de Baptiste."

"Who?" Seamus said.

"Pepe," Alvarez told him.

"That's Pepe? That's his full name? I thought 'Pepe' sounded a bit of a muppet, but I understand now why he uses it, saddled with all that cabbage."

The president snorted. "Gentlemen," he said with a nod. And he was gone.

Kresge, Seamus, and Alvarez were left in the room with Torres and the attorney general, who had a full-size tablet under his arm. He placed it on the table.

"I've spent the last few months reviewing documents captured from *La Fuerza*," he told them, "including some dating back to the early days of the war. Reviewing their finances. Timotéo Sandoval was a thief."

"You mean in addition to being a murdering, raping, drug-dealing, genocidal communist? Color me shocked," Seamus said.

Arturo nodded. The man had a point. *La Fuerza* had grown out of a drug cartel, and Sandoval had been high up in that organization before moving into politics and war. "He was taking a percentage for himself. Stealing it."

"Seems… unsurprising," Kresge observed.

"True," the attorney general admitted, "but what got my attention was the amounts involved. Perhaps .5 to 1 percent of their drug and war profits a year, every year, which he claimed for himself. I'm still not sure whether the generals didn't know, or they knew and just didn't have the power to do anything about it. They were skimming as well, just not nearly as much."

"Didn't you seize all that?" Seamus asked him.

"We seized or froze all the accounts we could locate, but a substantial percentage of their income every year, and Timotéo's *propina*, seems to have been cash. American dollars, mostly, but some euros."

Sergeant Alvarez blinked at that and cocked his head to the side. Then he laughed, a loud, short bark. "How much?"

The attorney general sighed. "Enough to keep the war going, or fund a new one. Conservatively, all told… perhaps ten billion. Possibly ten times that."

Seamus opened and closed his mouth. "Wait. You said billion? With a B? Ten billion. Or perhaps a hundred. Hundred. Billion. Dollars. Hold up." He popped his neck loudly and took a deep breath. Then he walked slowly around the table, swinging his arms to stretch them. They might have heard him muttering to himself, then coughing out a laugh. He ended back in his same spot. "Right. Nothing to it. Just another Tuesday, a handshake from *el presidente*, and a few billion quid between friends." He cleared his throat and observed, feigning nonchalance, "Seems like a pile of dosh that large would be a bit dodgy to hide."

"Yes, well, it wasn't easy to find." Arturo thumbed the tablet to life. They saw a map. "For most of the past few years of his life, Timotéo was spending a lot of time at the *hacienda* in Zaragoza where he was killed. He traveled around frequently, making it harder to find him, but he seemed to return there at regular intervals. And when he did, I have records of trucks being rented, or filled up with petrol, repairs, receipts, tracing a trail from Zaragoza north, around the mountains to Xicotepec de Juarez, and then back." He traced the route on the interactive map. "The timing of this truck activity was often coincidental with large incoming payments, for drug shipments, mostly. I'm confident he was moving cash."

"Jicotewhat? What's that?"

"Xicotepec de Juarez. A town in the mountains. Smaller than it used to be due to the war, but aren't they all? Maybe ten thousand people, now. While isolated, it is right on Highway 132, which runs northwest from Mexico City, through the mountains, through Poza Rica, all the way to the coast and Tuxpam, and north from there to Tampico. Many quick and easy ways out of the town. Straight line, across the mountains, it is only ninety kilometers between Xicotepec and Zaragoza. By truck, it is far longer, a big loop west, as you see, but…"

"He had trucks *and* helicopters," Seamus said, peering at the map. "So what's in Xicotepec?"

"Not much," Torres said, speaking for the first time. "It is *una pequeña ciudad*, with small, mostly local industry. It never saw any real combat, and checking back, we never had reports of guerrilla activity in the area, even though *La Fuerza* controlled that region." He looked at the assembled men. "Maybe that was deliberate to avoid attracting attention." He shrugged.

Seamus laughed delightedly. "So it's a treasure hunt? Do we have a map with a big X on it? Will I need an eyepatch?" They didn't get the reference, and he assumed it was lost in translation, if not his accent. Kresge gave him a dirty look.

"I checked records and located several buildings in town owned by *La Fuerza* shell companies."

"Big enough for ten billion in cash?" Seamus honestly had no idea how big ten billion in cash would be. He imagined it would fill a truck, at least.

Torres said, "We flew a drone over to look, but that was a waste of time. So I went out there in person last week. One of the addresses was nothing but rubble. Another was a small office building that looked vacant. Another was a warehouse."

"Warehouse?" Seamus said. A more likely hiding spot than a truck.

Torres shook his head. "Got a look in a window, it appeared to be empty, but just nosing around and peeking in windows isn't going to be enough."

"What was your cover?" Seamus asked him. "Did you have one?"

"Pemex. I was in jeans and a work shirt, driving a plain car, but I never needed it; nobody seemed to care. I don't think the town ever saw any war. People left town to find work; they weren't killed. And they seemed to think the war was all but over. They were far more concerned about animal attacks than they were *La Fuerza*, although they still seem to have a presence in the area. Not in town, but in the mountains."

Alvarez was surprised by that. "Animal attacks?"

"Yes, apparently they're having an issue. They're in the Sierra Madre Orientals, and a bit isolated, and parts of the town are sparsely populated. They've had some residents attacked, children, dragged off by *fantasmas*, 'ghosts.'"

"Ghosts?"

"That's what they're calling them, because they almost never find the bodies, just blood. My guess is, it's a big cat or two, maybe a jaguar. The war emptied *el campo*, the countryside, of people, and in many places, it has grown wild again."

Kresge scratched his neck. "So, what, you're thinking another reconnoiter? With more bodies? Poking around town."

"If there was ever any money there, it is gone now," Alvarez said. "How would they keep it secret? That much cash. What, guarded by *La Fuerza* guerrillas, *campesinos*, peasants who likely grew up with dirt floors? Who'd never held enough pesos in their hands to buy more than a good meal? They would have run off with it as soon as they heard Timotéo was dead."

"That's as likely as anything else," the attorney general admitted, "but we have to look. That amount of cash is… destabilizing." They understood what he meant. After twenty years of war, the Mexican government and economy was on life support, and only oil revenue—administered through Pemex, the state-run petroleum company—had kept the economy from collapsing. Tens of billions of dollars was a lever big enough to topple it if applied in the right place.

"So what's the plan? Head into town, and…?" Kresge said, looking at the attorney general.

"The president wants this handled quietly. There may be nothing in town. If there is something, he doesn't want word of it getting out, not until it is in the right hands. But until we know what's there, he doesn't want an overt military presence, not Mexican Army, not Raven. No planes, no tanks, no men in armor in the streets. He's afraid that might spook them into doing something with the cash. As bad as that amount of money is, word of it getting out would be just as bad. It is only dangerous when it is in play."

Seamus was nodding. "So… civilian clothes. Non-military vehicles. Heavy hardware tucked away. If we spend any amount of time in town, we'll need a cover. Your Pemex tale seems solid. Searching for new oil fields now that the war's winding down or some such. That would explain my pale face. But I have to ask—why invite Raven at all?" He gestured at Alvarez. "The good sergeant here seems quite capable."

"An amount of money that large is no longer money. It is a political tool. So the president thought having men from both national forces and Raven would provide balance, calm our American friends and neighbors, who somehow have already heard whispers of my investigation. None of us really think you'll find anything. Or if you do, the cash will be a small amount, maybe a few million. But if you do find that mountain of riches… it would be very tempting to even the most honorable men. The president thought having both Raven and Mexican forces there would be a good mix. The two have historically been not so friendly, yes? Less likely to conspire on a…" He searched for a good descriptor. "Bank heist."

Seamus had to smile. "Betting on bad blood between the indigenous personnel and the *gringo* interlopers, so we can keep a keen eye on one another in the unlikely event we do find more than a few rusty coppers? Instead of mutually assured destruction, mutual enmity and distrust. Such cynicism." He looked at Kresge. "Colonel, were you planning to tag along on this snipe hunt?"

The corner of Kresge's mouth curled up. "I can't say I'm not intrigued at the thought of looking for that money," he admitted, "and I feel I could play the part of an oil executive well enough, but I just have too many things to do, and I wasn't called in to be part of the operation. I'm logistics, getting you anything you need."

"¿Señor Fiscalía General?" Alvarez asked the man.

Arturo waved off the squat Special Forces sergeant. "I too am intrigued," he admitted. "Any man who says otherwise is lying. A mountain of cash? Enough to buy your own island? But I belong behind a desk. Besides, my wife would kill me if she found out I was heading somewhere there could be guerrillas." He smiled. "If you find anything, I will show up afterward with news cameras and take all the credit." They all understood he wasn't joking.

"Yes, about that," Seamus said. "I'm no expert, Señor Attorney General, but I'm pretty sure billions of dollars is more than a few lads can carry, whether it's cash, diamonds, platinum, whatever. I don't know if it would be a mountain, but…" He looked at Alvarez. "How much cash did you blow up in that airstrike?"

"Thirty million? Fifty million? It was in two small trucks." Seamus and Alvarez looked at the attorney general.

"Yes. That much cash, it would likely be on pallets, based on other *La Fuerza* cash reserves we've seized—bricks of cash on pallets, wrapped in plastic." The mere thought of it took Seamus' breath away. Pallets of cash. *Pallets.* "If you find it, you'll need to secure it, then call for support and transport." He paused. "If there are any *La Fuerza* in Xicotepec, they were staying hidden when the inspector visited. The area around the town, in the mountains, there was no fighting, but there are no Army troops, and haven't been. *La Fuerza* controlled that whole region for most of the last decade. I think there may be many *Fuerzan* in the hills, living, hiding. You military types might call the area 'contested,' especially if the Army moves in."

Seamus nodded. "Hmm. So we'll need enough men to take out any guard force, then secure and defend truckloads of cash against an unknown number of guerrillas for an undetermined length of time." He looked at Alvarez. "That's more than me and you, especially if I'm going without my armor."

"I will be returning with you," Torres said.

Seamus nodded. He'd assumed as much. "Still, three isn't much better than two."

"Four? Five? Six?" Alvarez mused out loud.

"Can't be too many, if we're to be discreet." Seamus pointed. "So, Torres and the good sergeant here, myself, and then, what, one more? Four total? A group of four men isn't a remarkable number. We'd all fit into the same vehicle if we had to, although two vehicles would be better; something's always breaking down. And I don't want to presume, but another white face to balance the team out as *el presidente* suggested? And sell the idea of oil surveyors?"

"Yes, I think so," the attorney general agreed.

Seamus looked inquiringly at his colonel. Kresge told him, "It's your ass that's going to be out in the wind up there. In the mountains, with no armor or air support other than maybe a surveillance drone, and reinforcements hours away, at best. I'll let you make that call."

Seamus nodded. "I know just the man for the job. He'll be delighted."

The attorney general said, "We have men still looking into their finances, their holdings, and if anything else in the area shows a link to them, we'll learn of it and pass it on for you to investigate. I'll let you and the sergeant work up a plan, but we expect you to be in regular communication. It is a small city, but it is a city that has not seen combat, so you will have cell service, plus your satellite palms. Maybe, probably, you will find nothing. But perhaps you will find something. A mountain of cash. The stuff of legends. If you do… you may have a hard choice to make. If you can't arrange transport, as a last resort, you'll need to destroy it in place. Make sure it does not wind up back in the hands of *La Fuerza*. From what I know of both you men—" he looked from Alvarez to Seamus, "—I trust you to do this. You are soldiers who follow orders."

* * * * *

Chapter Six

Marie's door was open. Sadie plopped into the chair on the far side of the desk from her department head at École Pratique des Hautes Études, one of thirteen constituent schools in the Paris Sciences et Lettres Research University, known to everyone as PSL.

Marie Bernard set down her university-issued Sirion D12 datapalm and regarded Sadie over the rims of her reading glasses. Sadie's hair was wild, half of it having escaped from her ponytail. She looked exhausted, radiant, bewildered, amazed, triumphant, happy, her face was flushed… "Did you just have sex?" Marie demanded.

"What? No! Well, I mean…"

Marie laughed. "Your English soldier. When does he leave?"

"He left last night."

"Hmm." The older woman leaned forward. "I presume he said goodbye in proper fashion." In truth, she was quite jealous, but also happy for Sadie, who'd been through so much. "Stay seated as long as you need to. *Il y a un sac de glace dans le congélateur.*" Sadie snorted. "When will you see him again?"

Sadie shook her head. "I don't know."

One of Marie's eyebrows slid up. "Will you see him again?"

"I don't know. I'd like to. He is… a good man, and good for me. He loves Paris. Ten days with him seemed… short. But he is a professional soldier. He has gone back to Mexico."

"Ah, yes." Marie knew well Sadie's fresh distaste—*non*, hate—for the country that had killed her assistant and lover, and had almost killed her. It was unfair, and perfectly understandable. Perfectly human. "So, why are you here? Did you finally finish the gene sequencing on the butterfly and griffinfly samples you collected in Mexico?"

Sadie blinked in surprise. "What? No, I told you," Sadie said, "we finished the gene sequencing on those last month."

"You did?" Marie shook her head. She'd been so busy with an administrative reorganization she'd barely had any time for actual supervision of her subordinates.

Sadie had gone to Mexico specifically to research the giant butterflies that had been spotted there, undoubtedly relics of the Pangaea animal park that had offered herds of genetically engineered dinosaurs brought back to life—until communist guerrillas had attacked it twenty years earlier, killing a lot of people, some of the animals, and closing the park permanently. The official story had been that all the park's animals were killed in the attack, but it seemed the truth was, very few of the dinosaurs had perished, and the survivors had fled into the lush biosphere surrounding the park. They included some specimens of Coelophysis—two-legged, dog-sized carnivores—which had continued to breed in the wild. A pack of them had killed Karl and nearly killed Sadie, and while she'd been laid up in the hospital, recovering from her wounds, she'd researched dinosaur attacks in Mexico. Even if half the reports were hoaxes, the animals—perhaps two dozen species—had spread through half the country over the subsequent twenty years. Seamus himself had laid out a long list of animals he'd personally seen, and/or which had tried to kill him, including *un putain* Tyrannosaurus rex. She was never going back. Never.

That said, the butterflies she and Karl had found had been fascinating, as were the giant griffinflies she'd observed hunting them. She'd collected samples of those, as well—huge insects with wingspans the length of her arm that resembled and were closely related to dragonflies. Watching them zip through the air had been almost magical.

She'd done gene sequencing in part because she was trying to categorize them, see if they were related to any modern species. Officially, there was no record of anyone at the park having created any insects. No butterflies, no dragonflies—no animals at all smaller than a velociraptor, which were feathered and the size of turkeys, completely unlike the movie depictions. But the insects had to have come from the park, along with the numerous extinct and prehistoric plant species she'd found in the park during her visit, and which were spreading throughout the region. The insects could be seen in old promotional videos of Pangaea, flitting through the air above roaming Jurassic herds and park visitors.

"If the gene sequencing is done, what have you been doing?" Marie wasn't being accusatory; she knew Sadie's work ethic, but she was drawing a blank on what the talented young woman with a doctorate in entomology had been doing the last few weeks.

"I've been corresponding with geneticists, pulmonary specialists, xenobiologists, hematologists, and doctors who are the leading minds in their fields, regarding theoretical medicine. I honestly wasn't sure what I was looking at—my degree isn't in anything approaching this—but I reached out to *mon oncle* Claude, who just retired from Pitié-Salpêtrière, and he put me in touch with a couple of specialists. They put me in touch with a couple more, and so on. I made them sign non-disclosure agreements, and I didn't tell them where I got the data or tissue samples, but…"

"What data?" Marie said, lost.

Sadie came around the desk with her full-size tablet and laid it on Marie's desk. The screen was filled with graphs and scientific notations. Marie studied it all for a few minutes. She had two doctorates, but it had been quite some time since she'd needed to use any of that knowledge. "*Mon dieu, qu'est-ce que je regarde?*"

"Conservatively? A Nobel Prize in science, medicine, or both— or so I've been told. Not for me, but for whoever can unravel it. I just discovered it."

"Unravel what? Discovered what?" Marie said, exasperated. She pointed at some of the equations before her. "Are we sending a team to Mars?" The equations looked closer to astrophysics than whatever chemistry she remembered from her long-ago graduate classes. "*Ce sont des hiéroglyphes.*"

Sadie smiled and sat on the edge of her desk. "Remember, one of the reasons I wanted to study the butterflies was their size. Modern insects don't grow nearly as large as the Paleozoic ones; not even close. We're not sure why, but we suspect it has to do with the oxygen content of the air and how insects breathe."

Marie nodded, leaning back. Insects breathed using a network of tiny tubes called tracheae. Air entered the tubes through spiracles, holes in the insect's abdomen. Insects have no lungs, so it's the movement of their body that causes air to flow into the tracheae, and the oxygen, the gas, then diffuses directly into their tissues, as they have no circulatory system comparable to that found in humans, where blood, oxygenated in the lungs, carries the necessary element throughout the body. The bigger the insect, the farther the air has to travel, so there's a functional limit to how big insects can get before they're no longer able to oxygenate all their tissues.

If the oxygen content in the air was higher, that would enable insects to grow bigger. The oxygen content in the prehistoric era was significantly higher than modern levels.

Sadie flipped through the tablet a bit, to photos. "Physical examination and dissection of the specimens collected in Mexico show nothing unusual in the animals' physiology. Standard spiracles, standard tracheae distribution, but... they're huge. That one griffinfly, it would scare a dog, although I doubt it could lift more than half a kilo. So that led to an examination of their cells, their body chemistry, and finally genetic sequencing. I used our computer to make sense of some of it. And... it wasn't making sense. Honestly, most of it was far beyond me, so I called in a few experts, and they called in a few more. They looked at the data." Sadie laughed.

"At first, they assumed it was some sort of joke, but no. Then I provided tissue samples. After they studied the chemical and genetic analysis, the tissue samples, and did a few tests themselves—oh, you should have seen them. 'Near-orgasmic' is the best description I can come up with." She pointed at the screen. "There's a protein in there, a 'good' prion, of a type none of them have ever seen before. Engineered, man-made, that drastically increases the gas absorption ability of tissues."

"Ah. So the insects can grow larger without needing the same oxygen-rich Paleozoic atmosphere. Okay, I see. Fascinating."

Sadie laughed. "Whoever did this, he or she was a mad genius."

Marie cocked her head. "*D'accord, je comprends* the genius part, but why mad?"

"Because he did it with insects. For an amusement park," Sadie said in amazement, and with some small amount of disgust. "So he does this," she said, pointing at the data, "for all we know, in his spare time, while he was working on the park dinosaurs, completely changing the mechanics of tissue oxygenation as we know it in the natural world. Then he never publicizes it, never publishes a paper. *Jamais, rien, nulle part.* As near as I can tell, he never even told anyone about it, like they were secrets, even though they were flying around. I doubt park management did more than look at the butterflies and what they assumed were dragonflies and thought, 'Oh, that's nice, that's pretty, the tourists will love those.' We know they never patented or trademarked anything having to do with insects, no names, no genetic sequences, nothing."

"*D'accord, oui, et?*" Marie asked Sadie.

"And that had to be twenty-five years ago or more," Sadie said. "The park was shut down twenty years ago." She stuck her hands in the air. "So what's he been doing since? Busy? Where is he? In jail? *Est-il mort?* If he's not dead, what the hell else has he been doing?"

"A number of park staff were killed in the attack if I remember correctly. Not just tourists."

"Were they? Well. Hmm. Anyway, this protein, this good prion, this is gene therapy. If it translates across species—and there's no reason to think it wouldn't, the basics of oxygen transfer to cells is pretty universal, only the method of delivery varies based on the species—if it does transfer across species…" Sadie said, then faded off, shaking her head.

"What?" Marie said. "I guess I don't understand your excitement about this."

Sadie threw her hands up. "You wouldn't even need lungs to breathe," she said in disbelief. "That's how much it improves your ability to take in oxygen. You very likely would be able to absorb enough oxygen from the air through your pores. With this gene therapy, humans might not even need lungs to oxygenate their tissues. Might not even need *blood*. Could conceivably breathe underwater, like *putain* fish, Marie."

Marie blinked. "*Merde.*"

"*Oui.*"

Marie held up a hand. "Lepidoptera aren't exactly mammals," she reminded Sadie, "much less human."

"*Non, mais l'oxygène c'est de l'oxygène.*"

Her supervisor wasn't convinced. "Maybe the reason he never published or publicized his work, or expanded it beyond butterflies and griffinflies, is because he tried and failed. Realized it didn't…" She waved her hands as she searched for the words. "Scale up."

"Which is why I've been consulting with specialists," Sadie said. "And all of them, *all* of them, think this has promise for people; that it's transferable. Think of the possibilities. Lung cancer? *Pfft.* Cut out that lung; you don't need it. Cut them both out. Poor circulation due to diabetes, worried about amputation? *Pfft.* No more, your toes and fingers themselves absorb oxygen."

Marie leaned back, thinking. "Well," she finally said.

Sadie snorted, then pointed once again at the tablet. "There's no record of that prion anywhere. Not in the Pangaea records, not at any government office regarding trademarks or patents. Just as big a mystery as the insects."

"You should patent it," Marie told Sadie, "you found it. Or trademark it, or whatever you do with genetic technology. Biotech. According to your contract, the school would own half, but...."

Sadie smiled. "I think I've spent more time talking to Luc Dessín this past month than he has his wife." Luc was one of the school's lawyers, specializing in biotech issues. "He's been searching records for me, researching the corporation that owned the park. I already have the application in with the appropriate government office. Maybe nothing will come of it, but then again..."

"When you buy your own island, just promise you'll invite me," Marie said wistfully. "Does your soldier have a friend? I'm old, but I am French," she said, wiggling her eyebrows seductively. Sadie burst out laughing.

* * *

Sadie had been back in her office an hour when her phone rang. She recognized the number, but then half the calls she'd taken in the past week had come from the same number; she likely could have picked the phone up blindly and it would be Luc on the other end.

"*Bonjour*, Luc," she said.

"Because of you, my wife is going to divorce me," the lawyer said without preamble

"Normally when a man says that to a woman, they've been having sex," Sadie said. "I'm not sure I've ever seen you with your tie loosened." Luc was not a bad-looking man, especially in a suit, but he wasn't her type. Too old to start, at nearly fifty, plus he was happily married. But he was smart, and funny, especially for a lawyer. "Do you wear your tie when you're in bed with Renata? Flip it behind your back? Hold it between your teeth like a pirate with a knife?" She fought down a giggle at the mental image.

"*Très drôle. Hilarante. Non*, it is because I spend hours every night, after coming home from the office, working on your bugs. Without my tie," he felt obliged to add, which made her snort.

"They're the school's bugs," she corrected him. "*Insectes de PSL.*"

"Do not burden me with facts when I am trying to complain," he told her. The truth was, he was spending so many hours of his own time on the project because it fascinated him. Not just the possibilities of the prion, but the mystery of how it, and the butterflies and griffinflies, could have been created without any corporate paper trail. He didn't think such a thing was possible in the modern era. Biocorps like GenVen were heavily regulated, as was the entire industry of genetic engineering, but especially the process of "reestablishing" extinct species.

Pangaea had to have been crawling with government inspectors and regulators. Sure, everyone knew Mexico played the game a little loose, and maybe a few bribes had changed hands, but Pangaea was built with international money, and those investors would have demanded full and complete records of everything. Total transparency.

So he'd taken a deep dive into history; the history of the park, the lengthy period when Pangaea was in development, and the short few years it was open. Perhaps a ten-year stretch, from twenty to thirty years earlier. If that wasn't work enough, he'd also had to take a crash course in medical science just to understand the significance of the prion Sadie had discovered. He'd thought he was smart until he'd spent a few hours talking to the best hematologists, endocrinologists, and medical theorists in the country. Now he knew just enough to understand how ignorant he was.

"Do you want the good news or the bad news?" he asked Sadie.

"Why would I want bad news?"

He laughed. "Do you have a few minutes?"

"Pour toi? Tout à fait."

"I have been trying to educate myself on this prion, as well as on Pangaea, because I refuse to believe these insects could not only have been created in a vacuum, but flying around the park, with absolutely nothing in the official record about them."

"Flying around the park?"

He sighed long and theatrically. "I have watched endless hours of videos taken by visitors to the park and posted online. Some of it was posted on social media platforms that are little better than ghost towns now, but it's all still out there. There were butterflies every-where. They had feeders to keep them in sight of the tourists, to give them a show. Amateur photos and videos, in addition to the promo-tional films put out by the park, and documentaries... Wait, let me start at the beginning. Before I started watching home movies, I went to the documents. All the legal filings, from the first plans for the park, all the way through to the court transcripts."

"Transcripts?"

"From the lawsuits."

Sadie pursed her lips, and leaned back. *"Procès?* I never thought about it, but it makes sense."

"Yes," Luc told her, "there were a number of them, but the big-gest was the class-action lawsuit from family members of the victims who died in the attack—sixty-seven, I think, which doesn't include the staff members killed—claiming the park didn't sufficiently pro-vide for the safety of its guests. Ineffective or insufficient security measures, etcetera, etcetera. That was the lawsuit that bankrupted GenVen, Genetic Ventures Incorporated." He paused.

"I will say, after reviewing all the evidence, it was a miracle more people didn't die. *Une vraie merveille.* The park's security was top notch, mixed American and Mexican, with a few former military and police in the ranks. They were well-armed, due to worries about growing guerrilla activity in the country, and apparently well-trained, as they killed at least thirty guerrillas out of the hundred or so who attacked. The guerrillas were expecting a slaughter. Instead, they got a battle. The first real battle of the war."

Sadie shivered. She remembered seeing signs of violence in the park—spent cartridge casings, bullet holes in the faces of buildings, even some damage that had to have come from explosives.

Luc went on. "That unexpected resistance slowed the attack and saved the lives of hundreds, maybe thousands of tourists in the park that day, as the guerrillas had planned to round up the capitalist tourists and execute them. Instead, most of the park guests who died did so only because they got caught in the middle of the fierce fighting between the guerrillas and park security. The rest escaped."

"What?" That was the opposite of what she'd thought had happened.

"Not the story you've heard, *oui?* Well, the surviving family members in their lawsuits claimed the park was responsible and incompetent, and the guerrilla army—what is it, *La Fuerza?*—shouted about their 'great victory' to reporters, and denied they'd lost more than a few soldiers in the attack, but in truth, the attack nearly failed. The battle lasted into the second day, when the Mexican Army finally arrived.

"GenVen never paid out on those claims; they declared bankruptcy and dissolved, and between the outstanding amount hanging over the park like a dark cloud and the ever-present threat of attack by communist guerrillas in a country embroiled in a civil war, no one has ever touched the property. They sued Mexico, too, the country and the state of Tamaulipas, but those lawsuits went nowhere." He chuckled. "I'm getting distracted, but I've had a very interesting couple of weeks. Far more colorful than my traditional patent law work. Anyway, a lot of GenVen executives died that day, so when it came to getting answers during the lawsuits, many of the questions went unanswered."

"Executives?"

"There was a big meeting at the park, of board members as well as investors, timed to coincide with the Second Anniversary celebration. Lots of special events, including a concert. GenVen flew in a number of VIPs to show them around and ask for more money, as they planned an expansion to the park. You can never have too many dinosaurs, but designing and growing extinct prehistoric creatures doesn't come cheap. Executives and a few celebrities. That was when the guerrillas attacked, and there was some indication they knew about the meeting and specifically timed their attack to target the executives and not just the celebration. That part of the attack was somewhat successful. During the battle, a group of these investors and board members found themselves trapped between attacking terrorists and a pack of Utahraptors."

"Raptors?"

"Yes." Luc laughed. "The world was disappointed to learn they'd been lied to by Hollywood. Velociraptors are feathered and not much larger than chickens. So GenVen also created Utahraptors, which are much larger, the size of the velociraptors seen in the movies, if not bigger. Also feathered, which you would think might make them less scary and intimidating, but if you'd seen videos of them…"

"No. I know how scary they can be," Sadie said quietly.

There was a pause on the other end of the phone. "Yes, of course," Luc said. "*Je suis désolé.*"

He'd meant no offense, and she knew it. "I didn't know you knew so much about dinosaurs," Sadie said.

"I didn't, not before I started looking into this, but it's been amazing, I have to admit. And what boy doesn't love dinosaurs? Okay, I'm turned all around, where was I?"

"*Vidéos? Procès?*"

"Ah, yes. *Alors,* many of the people who could have answered questions about park operations died in the attack. A lot of the records and supporting documentation was only at the park, not stored off-site, and apparently the guerilla attack destroyed most of the Administrative offices."

He paused deliberately, waiting. Sadie didn't disappoint. "Mmmm, *non.* Karl and I went to that section of the property. Business offices." She tried to remember. There had been signs. "Administration was a small cluster of buildings. Production was a larger four-story building that seemed to be offices as well." She shook her head. "None of them were destroyed. I don't know that any of them were even damaged." She tried to replay the images in her head. She'd spent a lot of time trying *not* to think about the dinosaurs who'd attacked her and Karl, but they'd had no problems in the business section, only later, when they'd entered the park and set up camp.

"We went into the Production building, through it, and up to the roof. There was some graffiti, some vandalism, but no bullet holes, no destruction. The administration buildings were... across a parking lot and field. Maybe a hundred or two hundred meters away? We didn't go over there, but they weren't destroyed, either. They weren't blown up or burned. I don't remember seeing any damage." She'd looked at them from both ground level and up on the roof. Overgrown with vines, the landscaping gone wild, but the walls had been whole.

Luc gave a small laugh. "Yes, that's what I thought you said when we talked about this before. Which I find interesting, because the main testimony on behalf of park staff during this class action lawsuit came from the junior vice president of Operations, who was the senior-most employee there that day who survived. He insisted that all the records had been destroyed when their offices in the park were attacked by guerrillas using—" he looked at the digital document before him "—'machine guns, grenades, and Molotov cocktails.' He said the Administrative Office as well as the Production Facility were damaged beyond repair by the fire and explosions. All on-site records were lost. *Complètement détruit.*"

"But they weren't," Sadie said with some confusion. "Production? That's the building I was in. It was dusty. I saw no signs of fire. Only a few of the windows were even broken. *Je ne comprends pas.*"

"I do," Luc told her. "The man was covering himself, and covering for the company—and probably paid very handsomely for his testimony."

"You mean he was lying? In court? Under oath?" She was outraged. "*Quel bâtard.*"

Luc laughed. "I love that you are so naive and innocent; it gives me faith in the human race. Yes, and he figured it was safe enough that he could get away with it, because who could prove him wrong? The war in Mexico was raging hot at that time, and nobody was going to send personnel to the abandoned park to double-check his story in the midst of a civil war, especially since what he was saying seemed perfectly reasonable in light of the attack, which did destroy a lot of facilities, and killed dozens and injured hundreds of people.

"Have you forgotten that GenVen claimed the guerrillas killed all the park animals? There'd be more of an insurance payout that way, but they definitely weren't going to admit that after the attack there were triceratops and Tyrannosaurus rexes and velociraptors wandering around Mexico. I suspect Mexican authorities told them to keep that quiet, hoping the animals would die in the wild. Anyway, I've used the online satellite sites and looked at pictures of the facility, and the buildings looked whole, if a bit overgrown, but you can only tell so much from orbit."

"So the records he was talking about, claiming were destroyed, could be still sitting there? *Après tout ce temps?*"

"That's what I'm thinking," Luke told her. "That's exactly what I'm thinking. There may have been looters, but would they have been interested in that? *Improbable.* Which brings us to the prion, and the actual reason I called. This isn't coming from me; this is what I was told by our experts. I specialize in biotech law, but my actual science background is limited to an undergraduate natural sciences degree I received before deciding to go into law."

"*Oui, et...?*"

"The prion. We know what it is. We can see what it is. They've sent me pictures taken with... what, an electron microscope? Something like that. But we have no idea how the hell they created it. Not me, our medical specialist friends. They can guess, but without a starting point, you're looking at years of lab work to reproduce it. Three, five, maybe more. I'm sure they've told you much the same. Reverse engineering always takes longer, costs more money, and is less precise." He sighed. "There's absolutely nothing in the public record, court transcripts, GenVen's corporate filings, anything concerning this prion or the creation of these insects. Their laboratory protocols had to be provided to the government as part of the international genetic research and engineering requirements, in addition to all production records, which I've reviewed, and there's nothing in there. Nothing."

"Would there have been a legal exception because they were insects instead of theropods?"

"*Non, absolument pas.* So, let's talk about GenVen as a corporate entity. While they had some small biological production capacity at the Pangaea site, they had two main biolabs, one in the United States, and one in Mexico. The building in the United States was bulldozed ten years ago. If any equipment or data was removed from the building between them shutting down operations and it being destroyed, I can find no record.

"The facility in Mexico stood vacant for eight years, and then was bought by Agua Caliente, a joint Panamanian-Mexican conglomerate. Near as I can tell, it was turned into a food packaging plant, and again, no record of any documents being removed, put into storage, sent to their attorneys of record, nothing. I have reached out to the law firm that represented them, and they were no help whatsoever. If they do have the information we want, they've previously denied it in open court.

"I believe they are in possession of all the data removed from the GenVen corporate headquarters not otherwise seized by the courts, but they've denied my requests to review it, unless I arrive with a court order. Which I cannot get. Thus, that's a dead end. So, after all that, I've concluded the only place where we might possibly find records related to the creation of the prion, and the insects, is inside the administrative offices at Pangaea, which were supposed to have been destroyed, but in reality were not.

"Think back very carefully, specifically. Did you see facilities where they might have been doing any genetic research, or even biological production? Did you see offices where they might have kept records? What exactly did you see?"

Sadie leaned back in her chair and closed her eyes. "The employee section was off to the side, away from the park and the tourists. The road there was almost overgrown. It was a small complex, set up like a business park. Off to the right were a few small buildings that we could see as we drove up. There was a sign for Administration, with an arrow pointing to those buildings, all single story. There was another sign for…" She sat and thought. "Maintenance? Something like that. I think that was beyond the Administrative offices, but we didn't go there; we were tracking our butterfly swarm. We went the other direction, to a four-story building like an office building, with a glass exterior. There were a few windows broken on the ground floor, but that was it. The front door was open, some graffiti, some vandalism. Weeds and dirt had blown in. The ground floor was nothing but offices, cubicles, pens on desks, computer screens and keyboards, family photos, paper strewn everywhere."

"I imagine when you hear the rebel army is attacking next door and hear the gunfire, you don't wait to clean off your desk or shut off your computer before running out the door," Luc said. "Were there any signs indicating what offices or departments were there?"

Sadie shook her head. "Not that I remember seeing. Power was out, of course, so we had flashlights, but we didn't need them much with all the windows. Elevators didn't work, so we took the stairs. Second floor was some sort of laboratory. They had a cleanroom, a pass through to get to where the work was done, but all the equipment had been removed. You could see the marks on the floor where it had been. Gene sequencers, maybe 3D bioprinters.

"They claimed they never went back, right, but I can't imagine guerrillas even knowing what genetic sequencers are, much less how to disassemble and transport them without damaging them. Or the locals; peasants wouldn't know a gene sequencer from a generator. They're worth millions, tens of millions. I suspect agents of GenVen came back out at some point and took them. Seems... risky."

"My guess is, they hired specialists, third party contractors with technical expertise, perhaps employed through a shell company, and if they got caught, GenVen could disavow all knowledge. Maybe not even GenVen—they were imploding at that time—maybe just an executive who knew how much money was sitting there in those machines and wanted to salvage them, sell them to finance his forced retirement. That means the retrieval team likely wasn't interested in anything other than the pricey equipment."

"Like what?"

"Like the records we're interested in. No money in it. What else?"

"In the building? I don't think we really looked too much at the third and fourth floors." Had she peered in the windows from the lobby? They'd been pressed for time, wanting to get up on the roof and set up the drone before the butterflies arrived. "Maybe more offices. There had to have been signs for various departments, but I didn't pay any attention to them. We spent most of our time on the roof." She paused. "Do you really think there could be anything left there after twenty years? You expect to find top secret company documents just lying around? Memory sticks still stuck into computer hard drives? What did they use back then? CDs? No, flash drives. Flash drives?"

"Were the offices open to the elements?"

"Well, no. Most of the windows were intact, except for those on the bottom floor, but the air conditioning wasn't running. Twenty years of heat and humidity—it was like an oven in there. Maybe paper would be fine, but what would that do to a computer or a memory drive?"

He ignored the question and instead said, "You're by your computer, right? I just emailed you two attachments. Can you look at them?"

"What? Sure." She spent several moments clicking and found the email. She clicked on the first attachment as Luc told her, "The first is a map I found in the court filings of the entire property, not just the park, including the employee area we've been talking about. The other's a photo from satellite footage, downloaded from TerraTracker about six months before your visit."

"Checking my memory?" She zoomed in on the cluster of buildings south of the park itself. "I'm looking at the map first…" It was just as she'd remembered. The bigger Production building off to the left as you drove in, and Administration to the right. Administration was five small buildings in a rough H shape. Past Administration on the map was… "Facilities Maintenance, not Maintenance," she said.

"I knew it was something like that. We couldn't see it. When we drove in, we could only see two, maybe three of those Administration buildings, but the ones we saw weren't visibly damaged."

"Okay, look at the satellite photo," he told her.

She opened it on her computer. The first thing that struck her was the green. The buildings were islands in a green sea... and slowly being swallowed. "You honestly can't see much of the Administration buildings; the bushes and trees are climbing all over them." She zoomed in as much as she could and squinted. "I don't see any real damage. If you look at that big Production building, you see why we went to the roof. It's still clear, too high for vines to reach, and the surface gets so hot, it probably bakes any seeds that get blown up there; we had to stay in the shade." Memories cascaded over her, good and bad. She and Karl had stood on the roof and watched the swarm of giant butterflies come in from the south like a fluttering cloud of sunflowers.

"The employees ran out the door during the attack. You said it looked like everything was still sitting there as they left it. They sent someone back for the expensive equipment, but left all the documentation, right? It seems there is a good chance of finding something."

She suddenly realized what he was saying. "You want to go there?" she shouted, eyes bulging. She sat up so suddenly, she almost flipped her chair. "*Connard!*"

"I think I have to," he said, sounding almost apologetic. "I admit, I—we—have arguably done our due diligence in trying to establish the provenance of this biotech. However, that's not all, and it might be the least important aspect. Without a... I can't remember the technical term our doctor friends used, but let's call it a recipe. If we can't find the recipe they used to create this prion, or the insects, it will take years of expensive lab time to replicate their work and produce a viable sample. Years. And only then can you start exploring its possible benefits for humans, which you know will take additional years. *With* the recipe, it will take just a few months for a working prion. Maybe only a week or two, I'm told, with the right lab, but likely months instead of years."

"The chance of there being anything there, much less surviving uncorrupted all this time…"

"Is small, yes, but if no one goes, there is zero chance. Paper should have survived just fine, but there is likely less of that than digital information on computer drives. I reviewed a number of behind-the-scenes videos of the park put out by GenVen and Pangaea itself. Smiling employees in offices, maybe in the same building you visited. Behind them, on their desks, were computers… I had computer experts look at them. They tell me that it appears the park employees were running top-of-the-line—for that time—Sirion Quads. Fast, but known more for their nonvolatile storage capabilities. Nonmagnetic, and built so they don't require power to retain data. My tech experts tell me that even if they experienced temperature spikes, if they were indoors, even after all this time, likely most of their data would be uncorrupted and easy to retrieve. The Quads were, and I quote, 'tanks.' You saw computers there, right? In the cubicles? They weren't looted?"

Sadie was gnawing at her lip. "I think a few might have been taken from the ground floor, but many weren't. I don't think many people went into the park to steal. They were scared by the animals, or maybe the guerrillas returning, and the business site was hidden off to the side." She frowned. "There was nothing in the area but the park. That was why they located it there; nobody wants dinosaurs in their neighborhood. The biosphere was huge, and beyond it was more mountains, fields, jungle… There's only one town nearby, and it's tiny."

"So we agree, the fighting never reached the business section of the park, despite GenVen corporate testimony to the contrary. The attack targeted the public areas of the park, thick with tourists, and the executive meeting was at a building inside the park, located adjacent to one of the exhibits, for VIPs. They could watch dinosaurs out the conference room window or some such. Which means the buildings you saw, and went into, could be a goldmine of information, some of which could be valuable in ways completely unrelated to the prion and these insects. I think I *have* to go, to try to retrieve some of those hard drives."

"Luc, Karl *died* there." She found herself fighting back tears. She stared at the satellite photo on her computer screen. She and Karl had driven right up that road, parked there, stood on the roof right in that spot…

The lawyer made a few soft noises. "I understand what you're feeling," he told her, "but Karl did *not* die there, in those buildings. He died out in the park, in the jungle."

"Those buildings are surrounded by thousands of hectares of fields and jungle, and they're just a kilometer or two from where we were attacked."

"Sadie, I have no death wish. Mexico is a wild country, with wild men and wild animals. I will only go if I can assure myself it is safe. Safe as can be… I could get hit by a Peugeot tomorrow *traverser le boulevard*. I believe I will have no problems hiring locals for security. Maybe Raven. Do they do that? They have a presence in Mexico. If not them, another company. One man, two, as many as necessary to make the trip to an empty office building safe and boring. And I would like you to go with me," he said. She wasn't surprised by the request.

"Luc," she nearly moaned, shivering with a brief, intense flashback of the attack. The leaping, snarling animals, the bright pain, the fear... She'd hit one with a chair, and fought others, punching and kicking. Karl had shot one with the shotgun they'd brought—or maybe two, her memories were a bit fractured—and the noise had driven them away, but not before tearing a hole in Karl's neck, and he'd bled to death next to her in the truck. She'd nearly bled out as well. So much blood...

"I want to go," he told her. "It sounds like an exciting trip to a place I've only read about, or seen in old videos. Pangaea, a piece of history. I could never afford to go to one of the working dinosaur parks—it is ten thousand dollars just to walk in the front door—so this is as close as I will ever come. I understand your feelings, but you do know you were in the wrong place at the wrong time. The animals were there to feed on the insects, not you. I am not suicidal; I will take precautions. *We* will. I am the school's lawyer and the expert on this, so it makes sense for me to go, or so I've told the school, and Renata, who thinks I am foolish and acting like a child going to a fair, but she won't tell me no. And I've enlisted Michael Ferrand."

"Who?"

"That tech expert I told you about. Knows all there is about Sirion Quads, and how to strip out their drives. I don't want to bring back truckloads of useless hardware. Twenty or fifty drives will fit into a suitcase, and he has equipment he can use on-site to determine whether they're viable, if they're still holding data, or if the time or heat has fried them. Several buildings, several floors… he expects it will take at least a few hours to explore, even if we find nothing, but maybe it will be the work of several days.

"I understand you not wanting to go," he said, his voice soothing, "after what happened. *Parfaitement compréhensible*, but you've been there before. Not just Mexico, but at the park, inside those buildings. You know right where to look, and you can direct us exactly where to go, so we are quicker. Looking at maps and satellite photos is not the same thing. Better information means less time in the wild park, so safer, *non?* Maybe we find nothing. Likely we find nothing. But don't you have the responsibility to look? Not just for this project, but for Karl? Getting his name on those butterflies?"

"What?" she said, surprised by the unexpected turn in the conversation. The butterflies weren't on any official register anywhere, which meant officially, scientifically, she'd "discovered" them, and thus had naming rights. She'd wanted to name them after Karl. He would have liked that.

"There is a chance we might find information about the butterflies on the hard drives in Pangaea. We've done a lot of research and haven't been able to find any mention of the bugs, but you said yourself, they would have been created thirty years ago. Maybe we've been looking in the wrong place. I don't think you want to claim the butterflies, name them after Karl, and only then discover they'd previously been registered and named, do you? Wasn't Marie planning a big public announcement next month of the insect discovery and the naming? With a party afterward. It would be very embarrassing for the school if they were found in the wrong, claiming discovery of species already known…."

"Luc, you… you're just saying anything you can think of to get me to go."

He sighed into her ear. "Maybe, but after the time we've spent together on this, Sadie, I consider you a friend, and I think going back there, seeing the place again, might be good for you, help you put it in the past. You've still been having nightmares, haven't you? After six months?" She didn't answer. "Me, you, and Michael Ferrand," he said, "and guards, however many you want, with as many guns as you want. The war is over, so there is no worry about guerrillas. Four, five, six of us, the guards with guns, inside a building. It will be as safe as safe can be, and maybe you will get some sense of closure."

"Don't try to use psychology on me."

"You know someone in Raven, don't you?" Luc asked. "Can you check about hiring them for security? Even if you don't decide to go, we will need someone."

She blew out air in a hiss. "I can call and ask."

"Good, I appreciate it. Listen, Sadie, we are going, no matter what. I've already started making plans. But I really believe you should come. It will help us, and I think it might help you. Think about it. After what happened last time, I can get the school to authorize whatever number of guards you want so it's guaranteed that nothing bad can happen."

"Something bad can always happen." She'd learned that the hard way. "But I will call my Raven contact." She'd been attacked, and nearly died—her fear of returning was justified. Wasn't it? It had been a freak accident, an unlikely attack, bad luck, but it had still happened. Was she so out of line in thinking it could happen again if she returned? She needed to talk to Seamus. He, more than anyone else, knew what she had gone through.

* * * * *

Chapter Seven

Ruggerio, who was a supervisor with the city building department, and whose niece had been taken several months earlier, had organized the hunting party. He didn't know much, if anything, about hunting or tracking, but he felt he had to do something, especially since his complaints to the city had fallen on near-deaf ears. He'd announced his plans at the last city council meeting—not really to them, but rather the assembled citizens—and set a date and time. The mayor and many on the council weren't too pleased with him, but he didn't care.

They'd done nothing, and the police force in Xicotepec de Juarez was worthless—instead of being upset at the deaths, they were upset at him for pointing out how they'd done nothing of substance. Encouraging people to walk in pairs, fixing a few streetlights, telling people living on the edge of town to buy dogs for protection. Near-worthless suggestions. Actually going out after the murderous creatures? Apparently they were too scared or lazy to do that, and he'd said as much to their faces.

The only searches ever done by local police had been short and perfunctory. People were scared, and at least nine people had been taken by the ghosts in the past few years. Probably more, but nine for sure. If no blood or signs of violence were seen, the mayor insisted the missing people had just left town, as so many residents had. But there was often blood. They'd never found anything left behind but blood and, once, the finger of a little boy. No one had ever found any bodies.

The ghosts tended to take the small and weak—children and women, mostly, but a few seniors as well. Almost always alone, and usually early in the morning or in the evening, often when the fog rolled down from the mountains. Targets of opportunity. Everyone knew they weren't ghosts, but rather animals—but the type of animal was the source of much argument. Some said dogs, some said a pair of jaguars, a few even said dinosaurs, but they were mostly just laughed at. However, it was clear there had to be more than one. They hadn't just taken people—the farmers and coffee growers in the nearby hills had lost dogs, chickens, goats, cows, and even horses over the years—and the attacks seemed to be increasing. What few prints the attacking animals had left hadn't made much sense to the few men in town with hunting experience. The town doctor who acted as a coroner had examined the boy's severed finger, but other than observing that the animal had sported long, sharp teeth, he'd had no insights.

It was 4:00 am as they gathered in the vacant lot. Ruggerio hadn't known how many would come, and as expected, many who said they would didn't show, but there were eighteen, in six vehicles. The men were all half-asleep. Many of them had brought guns, for the most part old shotguns. Ruggerio had a large map of the Sierra Norte de Puebla spread out on the hood of his truck.

The northern section of the state of Puebla was rugged and mountainous, due to the intersection of the active Trans-Mexican Volcanic Belt with the Sierra Madre Oriental Mountains, and at the tip of the Sierra Norte de Puebla was the municipality of Xicotepec, which encompassed the city and spread north and east from it. Between the headlights of the vehicles and a few flashlights, they could see well enough. Above them, through breaks in clouds and fog, twinkling stars occasionally appeared.

"This will take a few mornings at least, I'm thinking," Ruggerio told them. "We have to find the area they live in, nest in, and then, like Jorge said, I think we set out meat to bait them."

"We know where they live. South of town," one of the men said, pointing. "That is where all the attacks have been."

"That is where *most* of the attacks have been," Ruggerio agreed, "but that is where most of the people are; maybe we just don't know when they're elsewhere." He shrugged. "Maybe they don't like crossing 132D." The highway ran east/west just north of Xicotepec, and north of it was the river. That area was in fact far less populated, not that there were many people anywhere in the region, outside the few small towns. The main crop in the area was coffee, which only required a heavy human presence during harvesting.

"We need to look for trails, footprints, piles of shit... the bones of the animals they've killed..." The larger animals, cows and horses, were often eaten where they were killed, stripped down to the bone, but the smaller ones were always taken away, and the thought of finding bodies, skeletons—of women, of children—chilled the men.

"Maybe they are hiding in the Army base," someone suggested.

It wasn't a bad thought. A kilometer or so south of the city limits sat the former home of El 70th Batallón de Infantería—Xicotepec de Juarez. The small Army base had been abandoned near the start of the war, as the Mexican military had consolidated its forces. The once neatly-trimmed parade grounds had nearly been swallowed up by the jungle. Many of the buildings had been built sturdy, and still stood. With so many people leaving the area, the base was rarely visited by the locals. There was nothing there, and no reason to go, making it a likely place for animals to make some sort of home.

"Why would they go there when the base is surrounded by jungle?" another man asked. "South, east, west of it is nothing but forested hills."

"Why are we going so early?" another complained. "We'll see nothing."

"The sun will be up shortly," Ruggerio told him. "We're looking for trails and footprints, but now is the time of day when we are likely to see them as well. Driving down the road, or yes, driving onto the Army base at dawn, you are likely to flush any animals in the area."

"It is a jaguar," one of the men insisted. "Maybe two."

"They do not come this far north," he was told.

"Apparently they do."

"Did you not see that track? Two toes."

"That was not a footprint. What animal has two toes? If anything, it was an old hoof print from a goat."

"You wouldn't know a goat if one bit you."

"Are you going to make this much noise when you are out hunting?" Ruggerio snapped at them. "You couldn't sneak up on a running dump truck with the noise you're making." He glared at them, then continued.

"How many vehicles do we have? Six. Seven with my truck. We should split up, try to cover as much area as possible, but don't be in a hurry; if you're racing along, you won't see anything. Who is going in which vehicle? I need the phone number of someone in each vehicle. Keep track of where you've searched, so we're not searching the same area twice, and I will mark it on the map. We'll meet back here at, what, noon?" He looked at them.

"Don't shoot just to shoot. The police and mayor don't want us doing this, so we don't need to cause any trouble. Don't knock down any fences or drive through coffee fields without permission, even if you think you see something. When you find farmers, ask them what they know of predators in the area—maybe they can help. Likely, they will be the ones who send us in the right direction. Keep your

guns out of sight if you can and don't shoot any cows or horses. Or
dogs, unless they're part of a wild pack and attacking you. We don't
want trouble."

* * *

H e worked up a rough plan for the teams. Five of the
vehicles would head out from the south side of the
city, going west, east, and south. Two, including Ruggerio, would head north, checking the area around the Rio San Marcos.

Running northeast between 132D and the river was a tall, heavily
forested range, but west of that, the land became a little more forgiv-
ing, with slopes that weren't quite so steep, and there were isolated
ranches and farms in the green hills and valleys. Ruggerio wanted to
search that area, and with him he had Raul Cruz, one of his neighbors. On the north end of town, he turned onto Calle General Lin-
doro Hernandez and took that west out of the city. The street turned
from cracked pavement to dirt and wound through the hills.

In the dark, and with the thick fog, Ruggerio drove slowly. After
the *calle* passed under Highway 132D, the dirt street became little
more than an overgrown two track, and brushes and trees scraped
the sides of his truck as he crawled forward slowly in four-wheel
drive. West and north of Xicotepec, there was nothing but tiny vil-
lages until you passed out of the mountains, with few roads. Fewer
of those were paved. The land was rough and rugged—beautiful, but
nearly empty of people.

Ruggerio and Raul bounced and swayed in their seats as the truck
rolled over the uneven dirt roads at walking speed, the suspension
creaking. The foliage grew in so close, it was like driving through a
dark, mist-filled tunnel. Their headlights seemed to do more harm

than good, reflecting off the fog before them and turning it into a pearl white curtain.

"Do you know these trails?" Raul asked nervously.

"No, but I have a GPS watch that links to my phone," Ruggerio said. His wife had given it to him when they were younger, before they had children, and when they still had money, as he'd liked to ride his mountain bike around Xicotepec. She hadn't wanted him to get lost. "I can pull up our route. We'll be able to retrace it if necessary." He swiped his phone to activate it and showed Raul.

Raul snorted. "It says there are no roads here."

"I'm not sure this counts," Ruggerio said, peering out the windshield. He kept having to run the wipers to clear off the water droplets. They climbed steadily for twenty minutes, then started descending. His phone rang—other teams checking in as they searched various areas and local landmarks. Ruggerio couldn't talk and drive, so he handed the phone off to Raul. Raul found some paper in the glove compartment and began making notes.

"Nothing, nothing, and nothing," he told Ruggerio.

Ruggerio was glad when the morning fog started to burn off. Visibility went from a few feet to a few dozen feet. The sun rose, and although they couldn't see it, the land around them went from charcoal to a light gray. The vegetation pulled back from the road, and the land opened up. The road grew wider, more like an actual road than the trail it had been. Then dark forms appeared in front of them.

"What are those?" Raul asked, squinting.

"Coffee trees," Ruggerio said. He pointed. "See, rows." They marched away from the road in orderly columns.

"They don't look like trees."

"Do you never leave the city? The growers trim them into bushes, so the berries are easier to reach." They crawled beside the orchard for a minute. The low shape of a house resolved in the morning fog, but it was dark. Ruggerio didn't want to wake the family inside so early, so he didn't stop.

Engine a low growl, the truck continued past the house. Several minutes later, the narrow dirt road forked. Left, west, or right. Ruggerio chose the right fork, and it curved back northeast, and began to rise once again.

The road leveled off, and they had the sense of a small field around them. The warm glow of a small fire appeared ahead, then dark shapes, which resolved into the blocky forms of vehicles.

"*Hijo de puta*," Raul spat, sitting up. "*La Fuerza*."

"*Cálmate*," Ruggerio hissed. He was already slowing down. The guerrillas had heard the low growl of the truck approaching. There was a man on the edge of the road before them, holding up a hand. In his other, he held a HK G3; the rifle seemed huge. More men appeared out of the fog, all carrying rifles. Ruggerio recognized AK-47s. Past them, Ruggerio saw a pickup with a big belt-fed rifle mounted in the back and a bulky armored Vaquero with knobby tires.

Ruggerio rolled down his window. One of the guerrillas sauntered up. In his hands he held a modern gray rifle that seemed mostly plastic, but it wasn't pointed at them. "*Buenos días*," Ruggerio said, trying to sound relaxed. They had a shotgun with them, but it was out of sight behind the seat.

"Are you lost?" the soldier asked. He looked them over. Two middle-aged men in a truck that wasn't new, but was still in good condition.

"No, we are searching for a lost cow," Ruggerio told him. "Have you seen one? It got out last night."

"Her name's Betty," Raul said helpfully.

The guerrilla squinted. "You named a cow?"

If you were from the country, you knew you didn't name the animals you would later be eating. Ruggerio quickly jumped in. "My daughter, Violeta, she named it. We'd only ever had chickens before, *y las gallinas son pendejas*, but the cow... we got it as a calf, and it had those big eyes..." He shook his head. "When it comes time to slaughter it, she will realize her mistake in giving it a name." Several other guerrilla soldiers had approached the truck and now surrounded it. Not overtly hostile, but not friendly, either.

The guerrilla snorted. Chickens were indeed assholes. He looked inside the cab and saw the paper on Raul's lap. Were they taking... notes? "What's that?"

"We have friends out, helping to look. They are checking in. Violeta loves that stupid cow." Ruggerio's phone, in Raul's hand, rang suddenly, and he almost dropped it. Ruggerio nodded toward it. "Friends."

The guerrilla wasn't quite convinced. "Answer it. Put it on speaker."

Ruggerio nodded at Raul. His hands only shook a bit as he answered it. "*Sí*," Ruggerio called out.

"This is Umberto. We checked the old Army base. There's no animal there."

Looking at the guerrilla, Ruggerio rolled his eyes and said, "How about instead of you calling me every time you *don't* find something, you wait to call me until you do find something? Just keep a log of where you check for the animal. That's what we've been doing." He reached over and disconnected the call. "My nephew," he said apologetically. "Nice boy, but not too smart."

"There's an Army base?" of the other guerrillas said nervously.

"Empty for twenty years," Ruggerio told him. "South and west of town."

The man beside his door relaxed and cradled his rifle. "Lost cow or not, we can't have just anybody driving up and down these roads like it's free." He gave Ruggerio a look.

A minute later they were driving on, relieved of all the cash in their wallets as a "travel fee." The two men stayed quiet for five minutes as the truck creaked and swayed, making its way back up into the mountains. Then, finally, after he guessed they'd traveled at least a mile from the encampment, Ruggerio slowed to a stop and turned to look at Raul.

"Fucking *Betty*?" he said in disbelief, and the two men burst into laughter. Ruggerio wiped tears from his eyes, then nodded at his phone. "Call Tony." They were the other team working the north side. "Let him know where those *cabrones* are so he avoids them."

"Do you think there are *mas Fuerzan* in the hills?"

Ruggerio shrugged. "I don't know. I wasn't expecting any."

"Were they hiding?"

"I don't think even they know what they were doing. What do you do when you're a soldier and your war ends?"

"And you're on the losing side."

"*Sí, y eso.* They didn't look like they'd been there for long. Hopefully they'll move on soon." Luckily he'd only had a few pesos in his wallet.

As the sun rose overhead, and they moved higher up into the mountains, the fog thinned, but smoky clouds filled the sky from one side of the world to the other. Ruggerio worked back and forth across the ridgelines, following trails and old roads, occasionally having to backtrack as the path he was following dead-ended or grew too steep for the truck to climb. They stared out at breaks in the trees, fields of dense green grass and the occasional wildflowers, looking for movement or animal trails. Nothing.

Shortly after 10:00 am, they were in a shallow, lush valley. The road, little more than a trail, wound across the valley floor, angling gently downward. Long grass, wet with dew, brushed against the sides of the truck. To their left were tall bushes and young trees, which hung over the truck and ran up the steep slope. To their right, the valley floor was covered in thick grass and bushes as tall as a man. The low, squeaky rumble of the truck was enough to flush several large birds, and they rose into the air, wings beating powerfully. Ruggerio stopped the truck. "¿Que?" Raul asked.

"I have to water the plants," Ruggerio admitted and climbed out. Raul snorted, but jumped out as well. Each man took a side. It wasn't hot, but the air was so humid, the sweat was dripping off them. As he was zipping up, Raul heard his friend swear, and walked around the rear of the truck. Ruggerio was staring at the rear tire on the driver's side. It was nearly flat.

"I felt it, but I thought it was just the muddy ground," Ruggerio admitted.

"Do you not have a spare?"

"Of course I have a spare. That doesn't mean I'm looking forward to changing a tire on a muddy road. All right, get out of the way and let me do this; it's not a two-man job."

Raul stood and watched him for a few minutes. A small flock of birds took to the air nearby, rising from the valley floor in loud, squawking protest. Neither man paid attention to them. Raul said, "I'll call the other men, see how they're doing. Where are we?"

"We went out west and north, and we're circling back in. Maybe ten kilometers northwest of town. *El Rio San Marcos* is a few kilometers in that direction." He pointed.

Raul grabbed Ruggerio's phone and his papers out of the cab and put them on the hood of the truck. He made calls, his voice loud in the quiet morning air. There was just the sound of insects, a few birds in the valley, and the random metal clanks as Ruggerio worked.

Raul talked to several of the teams, who had little to nothing to report, then put Ruggerio's phone on the hood, pulled out his own, and called his wife. "Have those idiots you're with shot any dogs yet?" was the first question out of her mouth.

"What? No."

"They will. The police should be doing this, not you. What do you know about hunting or animals?" It was far from the first time she'd said it to him.

"They should be, but they're *not*. Have they ever done more than spend half a day searching empty buildings, even when it was a missing child?" He wandered away from the truck as he talked, his voice rising.

"And what should they do, *Señor Experto?*"

"I don't know, hire a tracking dog, maybe. Maybe this." He threw his free hand up into the air. "They act like the children have run away, or the ladies were suddenly overcome with dementia and wandered off into the jungle to die, even when there is blood, or they were but forty. I honestly don't understand it." He turned and walked back toward the truck, pacing. Phone calls with his wife always got him pacing.

"What do you know about wild animals? Do you know more than the police?"

"From what they've said and done, I think *you* know more than the police," he said, his voice somewhere between a growl and a shout. "And you don't know *anything!*" he added, and immediately regretted it. There was silence on the other end. He leaned a hand on the truck's hood and opened his mouth, then the truck violently shuddered under his palm. Ruggerio's phone slid off the hood and landed in the grass.

He looked up. "Ruggerio?" he said worriedly. He thought the truck had slipped off the jack. Ruggerio could be pinned, or worse. Forgetting his wife was still on the phone, he scrambled around the side of the truck, only to skid to a stop in the wet grass.

Ruggerio was facedown beside the truck, unmoving. There was a spray of blood on the truck's quarter panel above the wheel well, where his head had impacted. An animal squatted beside the truck, one massive foot in the center of Ruggerio's back, claws dug in deep. It lifted its head, ripping out Ruggerio's throat and most of the meat of his neck, leaving little but vertebrae. It stared at Raul, huffing quietly.

The animal was *huge*. It squatted on its thick legs, tail shoved nearly straight out behind it for balance. *Utahraptor ostrommaysi* was the largest of the raptors, and this male was nearly full grown. Five feet tall at the hip, and twenty-one feet long including the lightly feathered tail, it weighed over three-quarters of a ton, and seemed nearly as large as the truck.

It wasn't as fast as many of the smaller raptors, but it could still run nearly thirty miles an hour over rough ground, faster than many of the large iguanodonts and therizinosaurs upon which it had preyed during the Cretaceous, but it was also, more importantly, far faster than a human being.

Its slower speed was balanced by strength and deadliness—unlike T. rex, the Utahraptor had large, powerful arms. Its arms were longer than a man's, and decorated with a spray of blue-gray feathers. Each hand boasted three broad, flattened, blade-like claws longer than a man's finger, capable of gripping and killing.

Its leg bones were thicker than that of the much-larger allosaurus, good for running or kicking. It stood and ran on two toes, but there was a third it held up off the ground, tipped with a curving talon ten inches long, excellent for gutting prey. Its jaws were nearly two feet long and contained dozens of teeth, each one two inches long and serrated.

Mouth open, Raul stared at the blood dripping off the animal's chin. He smelled the creature now, a bestial stench, somehow terrifying on a primal level. He turned to run just as the second animal, which had crept up behind him, darted in to bite. The second Utahraptor was nearly as big as the first, with gray-green feathers and glittering amber eyes.

Raul screamed as he lost a chunk of flesh from his shoulder, spinning away from the snapping maw, and he leapt past the animal in a stumbling run. He tripped and fell, rolling off the slightly raised road into the thick grass. The second raptor was after him instantly, running with its head low and tail straight out behind it, almost silent.

In the last few moments of his life, as the raptor's jaws closed on his head and neck, and blood sprayed, Raul realized they hadn't thought it through. The animals weren't just *killing* people, they were dragging, maybe even carrying them off. The animals never left any bodies to find. How big did an animal have to be to carry off a human being?

Big was the answer. Far larger than a jaguar.

The raptor shook him like a cat with a mouse, snapping his neck. It let go and nudged the lifeless body with its snout. Then it used its snout to roll the man onto his side, so it could get a better grip around his waist. With little effort, it lifted the body into the air and walked back up onto the road. Its mate was there, kill in her own mouth, and together they carried their prey into the underbrush, toward their nest and their hungry offspring.

* * * * *

Chapter Eight

Seamus leaned back in the chair and put his feet up. He couldn't keep the smile off his face, hearing her voice, even though it was a serious call.

"They're not monsters; they're animals," he told Sadie. The satellite connection was good, with just a tiny bit of hiss and pop. There was a seven-hour difference between Mexico City and Paris, which meant she'd be home from work and likely thinking about dinner. "Man-made, aye, and maybe a bit on the large side sometimes, but still part of Mother Nature. They're only interested in three things: fighting, food, and fu... uh, female companionship. Those seals you ran into were there after your big bugs, and they only attacked you because they thought you'd be tastier." He smiled. "I know for a fact that's true."

"Oh, you," she said then sighed.

"I don't mean to make light of it," he told her. "It was a terrifying experience for you and would be for anyone. You've handled it as well as anyone could have, but you've got scars from the ordeal, and only some of them are on your body. You lost a good friend. It's perfectly natural not to want to return there and to be scared at the thought. I like to fight—I do it for a living—and yet I still have nightmares here and there, and none of them are about these FRAP twats, not anymore. All my nightmares are red in tooth and claw, if you understand me."

"Yes." He'd had a few of them, sleeping beside her. As had she.

"So that's you. As for the mission, it sounds like they're doing everything they can to ensure nothing like *that* happens to anyone on the return trip. Hiring blokes with guns whose mere presence should keep the dinos away. They're not crazed serial killers, not like in those daft movies; the dinos are just looking for dinner, and if something doesn't look like an easy, pain-free meal, they'll go elsewhere.

"So you have to ask yourself—would going back, ultimately, be better for you than not? Do you need to prove anything to yourself? Get back on that bicycle, or whatever the French say? Or are you fine with never setting foot in this country again? I can't answer that; only you can. And I don't mean better for them, or better for the mission, but for you. I don't care about them or the mission."

"But…" she said slowly, "to some not-so-small degree, it *is* my mission. The butterflies, the prion… Luc and Michael are only going because of me, because of what I discovered. What if something bad happens to them?" The thought made her heart ache.

"Are they going to go whether you tag along or not?" he asked her.

"Yes."

"But you feel some responsibility." It wasn't a question.

"Yes," she answered again.

"You have none. They're grown lads. You're not their mum. They're responsible for themselves."

"Maybe, but I don't feel that."

"You Parisienne women and your hearts."

She groaned. "You're sure Raven couldn't send you…?"

"I'm in the middle of something, luv, that I simply can't bow out of. Likely a waste of time, but orders are orders. Raven does do some executive protection, but… you can't afford us. Maybe once you patent this prion—like as not, you can buy your own battalion then. I'd pay a right mint to be able to breathe underwater. Many a lady would appreciate a bloke what can breathe through his ears."

"I don't want them going if they don't have guards."

"Don't fret. There's no end to the local lads you could hire to stand by. However, they're more apt than not to have rusty shotguns with which they might blow off their own toes. The school is paying for security, are they not?"

"Yes. I don't know how much, but…"

"What an administrator of a Paris *université* thinks is a fair working man's wage will go a long way in war-torn Mexico, but before they go interviewing the local toughs, let me make a call. I know just the man, if he's available and interested. Knows as much as any man alive about dinosaurs, the flesh and bone kind, and no wilting daisy if it comes to a fight. Which it won't."

After the call, Seamus didn't move for a bit. The fuselage of the aircraft was warm against his back. Outside, the sun was piercingly bright, but inside the cargo bay of the Peregrine, it was dark and, by comparison, nearly cool. Chris Evers stepped out of the cockpit and leaned a shoulder against the door frame. She eyed Seamus, with his feet up. "I like your idea of mission prep," she told him.

"Even a hard-charging lad like meself has to take a break now and again," he said cheerfully.

"Was that hard-charging lad talking to a woman?" she asked. Men spoke and sounded far differently when on the phone with a girlfriend or wife.

Seamus smiled at her. "That's why I wanted you on this boon-doggle," he said, climbing to his feet. "Ace of a pilot, that one, I said to *el presidente*, but it's the feminine insights I value more."

She snorted. "When do you actually expect this mission to get off the ground?"

"Likely tomorrow morn. Just gathering a few odds and ends. Have you drop us off in the neighborhood, then we're to poke about, see if we find anything interesting."

"That's your plan of action?"

"A bit informal, this job, which is why you're not taking us all the way there."

"I'm surprised you trust me to take you anywhere after my last parking job," she said, eyeing the Peregrine. Her previous bird, named Lucille by Ted Billings, had ended up buried in the tenth floor of the Aquamarine Hotel in Cancún.

"Everyone has an off day." He gave her a sly look, a twinkle in his eye. "Even *La Bruja de Guerra*." He jumped down into the bright sun and took two steps, then turned.

"The last bird was Lucille. So what's this one?" The V-35 Peregrine was obviously brand new.

"We lost our crew chief on the Zaragoza mission. He killed General Aponte on that raid—the man was a wizard on a mini-gun, but still... so I thought I'd name it after him."

"Aren't ships and planes supposed to be named for birds? Women, that is."

"Yes, but pilots and captains were traditionally male."

"Fair enough."

She held a hand out toward the cockpit. "Still have to paint the name on the nose, but meet Mad Sweeney."

Seamus blinked. "Oh, lass," he said. He clasped a hand over his chest. "Be still my heart."

He walked off, and she stared after him. *La Bruja de Guerra*, The War Witch, was just one of the nicknames given to her by her brothers- and sisters-in-arms for her uncanny ability to sense when trouble was inbound. It hadn't been enough to keep her from planting Lucille in the beach side of a hotel tower, but it had, admittedly, saved a number of lives over the years, so much so that it was now the stuff of legend. If Chris Evers' hands started to shake, everyone assumed trouble was on the way. She'd never been wrong.

* * *

"Were you taking a nap in there?" John Corey asked Seamus. The younger contractor had joined Raven after two combat tours with the Marines and had seen quite a bit of action in Mexico, much of it alongside Seamus.

"No, your mum just wouldn't stop talking dirty long enough for me to end the call. Quite a mouth on that one."

"She always had a thing for older men." Corey had just turned 27 and made a point of eyeing the graying hair at Seamus' temples. They shared a smile.

"Oh, lad, let me tell you, I'm feeling it more every day."

"That's because soldiers your age are officers."

"Or more likely dead, and I'd rather die than become a bleedin' officer. They'd have to remove me brains and me bollocks, and I'm rather fond of both." The two men stood on a wide stretch of pavement between two landing pads for tilt-rotor aircraft. Seamus lifted a hand to his forehead to block the sun. "Where are Alvarez and Torres? They pop into town for a quick tryst with *las señoritas?*"

"I don't think Inspector Torres has ever broken a law or bent a rule in his life, which I didn't think was possible as a Mexican cop."

"Aye, you'd think he would have been shot by his coworkers for setting a bad example. I can't picture him taking a bribe. I think his head would explode."

"You trust him?"

"Echevarria does, father and daughter. So does Beni, although there's some bad blood there. And he dropped onto that roof of Timotéo's house and fought his way to the lass while you were napping in that field."

"I'd been shot in one leg, and my other knee was broken!" Corey'd been healed for a while, but it had taken quite a few more months for him to shed his subtle limp.

"Like I said, napping. So, people we trust trust him, and he's not a coward. He can keep his head when all about him are losing theirs. But he's not military, so keep that in mind if things get spicy. Which I doubt they will."

"His experience as a detective will likely be more useful on this op than any skills we bring." Corey crossed his arms. "Alvarez seems solid."

Seamus nodded. "Pure soldier, that one, but how pure will he stay if we find a few billion quid lying about?"

"How pure will any of us stay? Maybe I'm planning on stuffing my ruck with cash."

"The attorney general implied that he expected us all to do as much. I'd be offended if I wasn't over here worrying that he's right about my low morals and questionable character. But a few hundred thou, maybe a million between the four of us—"

"Not Torres."

"Right, not the good inspector, but a million or two stuffed into our greasy pockets and packs ain't but a rounding error on ten billion."

Corey shook his head. "I can't even wrap my head around that."

"And likely you won't have to. I'm sure this is just a waste of time, but we have to look. Ah, is this them? It is."

Seamus and Corey watched two vehicles roll across the tarmac and park near the staging area they'd claimed beside two steel shipping containers. Alvarez climbed out of a small green Nissan pickup. Torres had driven up in a tan Toyota Land Cruiser. Both were unmarked civilian vehicles—older, but well-maintained.

"The trick was finding vehicles that were unremarkable, but in better shape than they looked," Alvarez said. He flipped up the hood of the Nissan pickup and gestured at the engine. "I checked it and the Toyota out. Both have comprehensive maintenance logs and low mileage for their age. Recent oil changes. The truck is Mexican Army. The Land Cruiser we found in the Raven lot. They didn't want to hand it over to two Mexicans. We had to make a call. Colonel Kresge intervened. Then they were very polite." Smiling, he dropped the hood and locked it into place.

"These are good. They'll work," Corey said, walking around the vehicles. "Truck could use some new tires, though." He glanced at Seamus. The Irishman was frowning. "What, you don't like them? They look perfect."

"Aye," Seamus said. Then he stomped off, back toward the Peregrine. He returned shortly, carrying a five-foot crowbar. He hefted it in his hands and spun it leisurely. Alvarez and Torres watched him silently.

Seamus did one circuit around the two vehicles. "A little too perfect," he announced, and swung the crowbar in a low, lazy arc as if it were a cricket bat. The curved end of it thumped into the quarter panel of the truck, leaving a large dent. He walked around to the passenger side of the truck and kicked a door, then again. Seamus rested the bar on his shoulder and cocked his head, evaluating his work. Apparently satisfied, he moved to the Toyota. One overhead swing left an irregular line across the hood. One jab left a fresh, shiny gash in the tailgate. "Better," he said. "Now they look like what they're supposed to be, and they'll get appropriately covered in dirt on the way in. Now, weapons—hold on," he interrupted himself. He trotted to the Peregrine and returned the pry bar, then came back.

"Okay, Corey and I raided the armory while you were searching for transpo," Seamus said. Corey opened the big door of the shipping container with a loud metal screech, and the men peered inside. "If Corey and I are to be the daft oil corp explorers, and you our trusty local guides, we can't come in too heavy—but we'd also have something, dodging about a country at war." He gestured. The rifle closest to the door was an AK-47, old and a bit worn on the outside, but in excellent condition. Even though the design was over a century old, it was perhaps the most common rifle in Mexico. "AK near to hand, just in case, not hidden but not out of sight, if you catch my drift, and perhaps a pistol on our persons. Between my beard and Torres' pale skin from hobnobbing with *el presidente*, we should be able to sell our story as businessmen." The inspector looked far more like a harried, mid-level office manager than a soldier or *federale*, providing he wasn't scowling. "Corey as a junior assistant, and Alvarez as local muscle to keep us safe."

"In with our gear, between the two vehicles, we've got enough room for whatever we want if things go sideways, and we have to go to guns. So I grabbed a handful of grenades, because, well…" He shrugged. He was a big fan of grenades. "Sergeant, you bringing your Fire Snake?" Alvarez nodded. The "Fire Snake" was the issued rifle of the Mexican military, officially the FX-05 *Xiuhcoatl*, which meant "fire snake," but literally translated into "turquoise serpent" in tribal Nahuatl.

"Inspector, you said you were familiar with the Bren 805, so I snagged one of those."

Torres nodded, then looked pointedly at Seamus. "If we are to play the role, you need to call me Ramon."

"Right you are, Ramon," he said, then nodded to Alvarez, "Miguel, Johnny Corey here, and I'm Finn."

Torres blinked. "Fin?"

"Aye, with two Ns. Seamus O'Malley still has a price on his head. I don't know how recognizable my gob is with this ruddy blanket I've got growing across it, but there can't be but one or two Seamuses in the whole country. Best not tempt our luck by shouting it out. So I'm Finn Murray of Gaelic Unlimited Petroleum, here to do surveys of the region for oil deposits. As I can't bloody rid myself of the accent, and don't exactly sound like a Pablo Diego Jose Francisco de Rodriguez."

"Finn?" Alvarez said dubiously. "*¿Este es un nombre real?*"

"Yes, it's a real name," Seamus said, sounding offended. "Always wanted to be a Finn. Good name, that. Sounds like a fun lad. Always up for a pint and a sparker with the ladies. We grabbed another AK for Corey, as he can run that as well as he can anything, but for me, I thought…" He shrugged. "I can't believe we'll find anything, can you?" They shook their heads. "Right. But if anything is there, there's a good chance it's guarded. In which case, we might want to be quiet." He gestured at the last weapon in the container. "Blackbird. Integrally suppressed, and with subsonic ammo, as quiet as quiet gets. Great for popping a sentry or six. With supersonic ammo, it's near the power of an AK. You don't find them much outside of Raven—they're meant for aircrew who go down in hostile territory—but if we're pulling out the big guns, likely the time for playing make-believe is over."

Seamus worked his neck. "Okay, you should give the keys to the crew chief, and he'll pull the vehicles into the Peregrine and strap them down." He looked at the faces of the three men with him. "If we call for an extraction or need overwatch, it'll be at least fifteen minutes before the bird can be on station overhead, likely more, which is practically forever if people are shooting at you, so bring however many magazines for your rifles you need to feel comfortable. On that note… today, we should verify zero on our rifles and check the comm equipment. Plan is to lift off tomorrow at 0700. Do we have spare cans of petrol for the vehicles?"

Alvarez shook his head. "No."

"Well, that's one. We're on our own on this one, not quite spies out in the cold, but definitely not with the kind of support structure I'm used to. Let's start a list. I was hoping to head out tomorrow morning, but we'll go when we're ready. That cash, if it's there, has been sitting there for years. It can wait another day."

* * *

Colonel Jose Ruiz Alameda Salamanca de Baptiste stared out the window of the safehouse. As safehouses went, it was just fine—comfortable, even—on the outskirts of Morelia, in Michoacán, territory once firmly under the control of *Fraternidad Progresista para un México Nuevo*. But he was under no illusions about the current state of affairs. He was a hunted man, and the forces he now commanded kept shrinking, seemingly by the day. The *escaras* were capturing or killing a few here or there, sure, but mostly he was losing the men to the thought of peace. They were laying down their arms, taking off their shoulder flashes and armbands, and disappearing, heading back home, or finding new homes, which was easy to do in a war-torn country filled with refugees displaced from their cities, and even more empty homes.

His biggest secret? He yearned to do the same. After eight years of fighting, they'd lost, and everyone knew it. He was tired, but he couldn't go home. Even if there was a home to go to, his face, bland as it was, was too well known, more so now than ever. At the height of its power, there were a dozen men between him and Timotéo. Now, he might be the highest-ranking officer left in *La Fuerza*. The fact that he wasn't sure was even more telling.

Now he had a decision to make.

They'd first gotten the email nearly a week earlier. It had taken them a few days to verify it was genuine, but it was real, an invitation from the Cuban president himself. An offer to welcome, house, and treat like heroes the valiant fighters of *La Fuerza*, with a brief explanation of their plans to maneuver the Mexican government into a ceasefire and/or guarantee of safe passage. A few days after that, word had come in that the Mexican government had been made aware of the offer.

If it hadn't been clear—to everyone—that the war was lost, he never would have even appeared to consider the offer, but he was, to a large extent, a realist. Continuing to fight would be futile and result in a quick death with little or nothing to show for it.

His assistant walked into the room, talking on an ancient satellite phone. "*Si. Claro. Gracias, y tu.*" He disconnected the call and looked at the colonel with an unreadable expression.

"Yes, Major?" the man known as Pepe asked.

"That was our source inside Congress. *El presidente* has already had several meetings about the Cuban offer. He is being pressured on many fronts to allow those *Fuerzan* who wish to leave the country. While he has yet to make a decision, our man is confident that he will, ultimately, grant at least a temporary ceasefire. Especially when he discovers what the Cubans plan to do to get us all there. *El presidente* will be outmaneuvered by the situation, overcome by events."

Pepe grunted. "And your opinion?"

The major shrugged. "We have all fought. Some will never stop fighting until they are killed, but others, like us, see the reality of the situation and perhaps would prefer not to live in fear of the secret police showing up at their house one night, years from now, and shooting them in the head in front of their wife and children because they dared to fight for what they believed in."

Pepe stared out the window, not seeing what was in front of him as he thought. Finally, he said, "It's a long way from here to Tampico."

The major shrugged. "We have time, and while the men can, for the most part, make their own way, we have safe houses all over the country, properties where we can hide for a day or a week."

Pepe continued staring out the window, lost in thought. Finally, he turned and nodded. "Spread the word."

* * * * *

Chapter Nine

The Peregrine gradually slowed and lost altitude as the rotors tilted up and their RPMs dropped. Just as the nacelles reached vertical, the landing gear touched down in the center of the helipad, so gently Seamus barely felt it in his boots. He hid a smile. It was as textbook perfect a landing as was physically possible. Exactly as expected.

"So you can still land these things without needin' the side of a hotel," he said into his microphone on the crew channel. "Brilliant." He undid his seatbelt and stood up. The two vehicles were secured to the Peregrine's floor before him, and all their gear was inside or strapped onto the vehicles. The flight over had been short and uneventful.

Hatch gave him a grin, then the crew chief unhooked his harness from the cable mount hanging from the ceiling behind the big minigun. "Nobody touch shit," he said, jabbing at finger at Corey, then Alvarez. From the look of the man, he didn't think he'd have a problem with Torres. "*I'll* unhook the vehicles."

Corey knew better than to touch the cargo. Crew chiefs were very particular.

"You and this guy have history?" Chris Evers' copilot asked her, cupping his hand over his helmet mic. Blake was in his mid-thirties. He'd been flying for Raven for five years, after doing eight with the Air Force. They'd been flying together for a few months now, and while he was a competent pilot... that was about it. He was very tightly wrapped and kept to himself. She didn't like him, didn't hate him, he was just... there. She'd really liked her last copilot, Varga, but he'd died when they'd crashed in Cancún, and even though she'd done nothing wrong... she still carried that guilt. Maybe this was better.

Chris laughed out loud. "He pulled me and Hatch out of Lucille after I planted her in that hotel. You might have seen him before, naked and holding a machete."

Blake blinked and looked over his shoulder, through the doorway into the cargo area. "That was him? That was real?"

"Yes, and yes. Lucille's gun camera took that shot."

"You're shitting me, really? I thought that photo was a hoax."

Hatch stuck his head into the cockpit. "We lost our crew chief on that run, and I burned through the entire five-thousand-round belt on my mini while Billings and this crazy fucking *bruja* here were slow-rolling above that T. rex as two hundred assholes shot at us, so no, not a goddamn hoax."

Blake blinked. "Wow. I'm surprised you didn't shoot the T. rex. *Did* you shoot it?"

Hatch shook his head. "He was eating FRAP. The more he ate, the fewer guys there were to shoot at us." Then he was gone, crawling underneath the Nissan pickup to undo the ratchet straps.

Blake made a face. "Jesus."

Chris smiled. "Well, he does think he's God's greatest gift."

"Who, Hatch or O'Malley?"

"Yes." She unbuckled herself and stood up. "Run the checklist while I go talk to O'Malley, see how long we're going to be here." She gave him a look. "It might be a while."

"What's 'a while?'"

"Days was the impression I got." Blake sighed and made a face.

Seamus was standing before the open side door, one hand on the gleaming mini-gun beside him. Terry Lister, the fourth member of their crew, was helping Hatch with the vehicles. Seamus was looking out at the small airbase and refueling depot. Miller Station was southwest of Poza Rica, roughly fifty kilometers northeast of Xicotepec de Juarez. There were four helipads, and a short runway just two kilometers long. There was one medium-sized building, which housed what little staff was stationed there.

"What do you need from us?" Chris asked Seamus. She knew he and his team were heading into Xicotepec, but not why. She didn't need to know, and she was okay with that; it was part of the job.

"Perhaps overwatch, air support, or extraction, but likely nothing. We're just nosing around a bit, hence the civilian kit. However, if we need your help, we'll need it right away, so you'll need to remain on Alert Standby." The term had very specific meaning inside Raven.

Chris nodded. "In the air in five minutes, so likely we can be overhead in fifteen, twenty minutes at the outside, pushing it hard. For how long?"

"That's the question, isn't it? At least a day, maybe as much as a week. We'll be checking in with you twice a day, 8:00 am and pm, but we'll also likely be talking to the person running this hooley just as often, and it'll be up to him how long we keep poking our beaks in." He turned and watched as Hatch backed the Toyota Land Cruiser out of the Peregrine and down the ramp. The aircraft had a surprising amount of cargo space inside the fuselage. "What's your payload capacity?" he asked.

"Listed, or actual?" she asked with a smile. "With a four-man crew onboard at this altitude? Fifteen thousand pounds, easy. Twenty thousand if you don't care about speed or range. Or do you need that in kilos?"

"I can do the math in my head; I've been dealing with you daft Americans and your shite measurements for a decade." But, he realized, he had no idea how much a pallet of cash might weigh. A thousand pounds? Two? How many pallets could fit inside the Peregrine? He was about to ask her, then shook his head. He was getting way ahead of himself, counting the cartel billions before he even proved they existed.

"The Imperial system of weights and measurements came from England," Chris protested.

"And we got rid of it just like we did you colonials," Seamus said with a smile.

Hatch heard him as he walked back up the ramp. "Yeah, Britain just walked away from her colonies; she didn't get her arse kicked out of every single one of them by the podgy natives," he said, using a hideous English accent.

"Podgy?" Seamus repeated.

"It sounds stupid enough to be an English swear word," Hatch said with a shrug.

Corey heard the exchange and laughed. "He's got your number," he told Seamus. "Did you bring any spotted dick to snack on?" he asked innocently.

"Just for you," Seamus told him. Chris Evers burst out laughing. "Podgy actually means chubby," Seamus told Corey.

"I knew it sounded British," Hatch said triumphantly, then set to work unhooking the green pickup from the floor of the Peregrine.

Seamus was looking across the fuselage at a large cabinet that protruded into the cargo space. There was another on his side. "What's this?" he asked Chris. "Onboard fuel bladders?"

"No, WarDogs, just when the war's ending and we don't need them. One on each side, to keep the weight even. We can drop them right out the bottom, we don't have to cycle down the ramp."

"Oh?" Seamus perked right up at that. He stepped to the closer cabinet and was trying to figure out how to open the door when Chris did it for him. The WarDog squatted inside, folded into a rough cube, its stainless-steel chassis painted a mottled matte grayish-brown. The four-legged robot was six feet long, five feet wide, and three feet high, not including the big automatic rifle on its back, which deployed when it was armed. Seamus couldn't remember the official military designation for the tech, but everyone called them WarDogs.

They could run twenty miles an hour over rough ground, flip themselves over if they landed on their backs, and were powered by an armored battery that would last four hours at maximum activity. They had daytime, night vision, and thermal sensors, and weighed five hundred pounds—not including whatever armament was mounted on their backs, which was usually a single-barreled 7.62x51mm belt-fed machine gun. They could be remotely controlled or put on autopilot, and programmed to engage any heat sources, man-shaped objects, or simply patrol a certain area. Seamus had seen a few of them over the years, but usually they were too pricey to waste on a Third World civil war. Or so he'd been told when he'd asked.

"Could have used a few hundred of these over the years," Seamus observed.

"Nobody cared about Mexico when it looked like the Caliphate was going to start World War III, and all the high-tech gear was going over there," Chris said.

"And never made it back here. Truth be told, these beasties scare the pudding out of me."

Chris cocked her head. "Really?"

"When they're on autopilot and patrolling next to you? All that's between you and getting minced is a few ones and zeros in their programming. We wear IFF tags, but still... they stare at you with those lifeless blue eyes." He shook his head. "I'm glad we've got them; I'd just rather not be in the area when they're out and about."

* * *

The drive from the small air base to Xicotepec de Juarez took less than an hour and was unremarkable. Highway 132D was a little further north, with limited access and a higher speed limit, but Seamus wanted to get a feel for the area. Mexico Highway 130 was two lanes of blacktop running southwest that roughly paralleled the Rio San Marcos. Every five kilometers or so, it passed through what, on their maps, was a named town, but they seemed little more than a collection of crumbling homes and maybe a sagging market surrounded by thickly forested hills and higher slopes in the distance, away from the river.

Mexico 130 curved due south and began to descend. As they rounded a curve, the northern limits of Xicotepec appeared in the valley before them. There were single story homes, but also two and three-story buildings, stretching across the valley southward and up the slope to either side of the angling highway.

"Bollocks," Seamus said. He was in the passenger seat of the Nissan pickup, with Torres driving. Corey and Alvarez were in the Land Cruiser behind them. "I thought this was a small village."

"Xicotepec stretches along the valley for almost five kilometers," Torres told him. "It is a small city." He pointed out the windshield. "A third of those buildings are empty, maybe more."

"Still, mate, I thought we'd have half a dozen flats to poke our noses into, looking for our pot o' gold, then call it a day."

Torres made a sound. "Soldiers. If you can't shoot it or blow it up, *si no puedes joderlo*, you don't care about it." He gestured at the town spread out before them. "We have addresses. We check them. Maybe we find nothing, maybe we find documents that lead us somewhere. We go there, but that is a dead end. So we talk to people—neighbors, the man who delivers the mail, the old woman who lives nearby and watches everything. She says something that sends us in a different direction. More clues, threads to pull on, people to talk to. Some tell the truth, some lie. Maybe they lie for a reason. There might be records to look for. We sniff and poke until, maybe, we find something." He gave Seamus a dirty look. "That is police work."

"That sounds like absolute shite," Seamus told him. "A lot of work to find something that never existed or is long gone." He flashed a bright smile at the inspector. "But maybe I can find something to shoot or blow up before we leave. I've got a lass, so the other's off the table for me, I'm afraid."

Once in town, Mexico 130 expanded to two lanes in each direction, separated by a narrow, grassy median, and its name changed to Boulevard Benito Juarez. There were one- and two-story buildings to either side, cafés, auto repair shops, small apartment buildings, and private residences, everything from nicely maintained, free-standing houses with landscaping, to tarpaper shacks, many of them with brightly painted trim.

There were cars and pedestrians moving up and down the road, young men on scooters being chased by stray dogs, a high-walled wire trailer filled with plastic for a recycling center, a dump truck trundling by filled with chunks of old concrete. Seamus saw signage for hand-rolled tortillas, beer, used tires, and bottled water. A small town, somewhat poor, but... "You were right," he told Torres. "Not much sign of the war here."

"Other than the poverty."

"There is that." Seamus eyed a low, peach-colored building as they passed. It wasn't clear whether it was apartments or a small motel. "We staying in a hootch like that?"

"You are a rich, foreign oil executive, and I am your corrupt Pemex liaison," Torres told him. "We are staying in the nicest hotel in Xicotepec. Downtown, right across from the main square." He looked at Seamus out of the corner of his eye. "Anything less would seem suspicious."

"Well, it is what I rightly deserve, after all," Seamus agreed. "Nothing but the best for Mum O'Malley's boy."

"Murray," Torres corrected him. "Finn Murray."

"Bugger me. Right you are."

Torres shot him a look. "I still don't believe that's a real name."

* * *

Driving through downtown to get to the hotel, Seamus had seen narrow streets lined with two-story buildings, most of them brightly colored. There were many people about—more walking than driving, which wasn't unexpected, given the price of petrol. The town might have been suffering through the nationwide depression caused by a two-decades-long civil war, but it was still alive.

"The nicest hotel in Xicotepec" could have described any number of atrocities, but Seamus was pleasantly surprised as they pulled up in front. Hotel San Martín Plaza was a three-story building overlooking a large plaza with a fountain and a large metal sculpture of what, at first glance, looked like praying hands.

The hotel seemed well maintained, painted a dark orange with white trim. Some of the rooms had balconies with wrought iron railings overlooking the plaza. As they climbed out and stretched, they got a few looks from the locals, but none of them were openly hostile, just curious. European faces were likely rare.

"I'll stay with the vehicles while you check in," Alvarez said. They'd decided he'd play the role of manual laborer/security while in town.

Seamus looked at the plaza and the buildings surrounding it. There were several children playing in the fountain, their mothers nearby, chatting. A large yellow lab was sprawled in the sparse shade, sleeping. On the far side of the plaza, he spotted a restaurant. It had tables with umbrellas spread out into the plaza, and several of them were occupied. "I don't think we'll have much of a problem here," he observed. "Nicest hotel in town, indeed." Of course, the issue wasn't the vehicles themselves, but the gear sitting in the back of the pickup, much of it irreplaceable.

Torres had made the reservation under Gaelic Petroleum, which made Seamus smile, as did the clerk's butchered pronunciation.

"Four rooms?" the clerk said in rapid-fire Spanish to Torres. "Would you like the second or third floor; you've got your choice."

"If they give us a choice," Seamus spoke up in English, looking at Torres, "can we get rooms on the second floor? I always prefer the second." He smiled cluelessly at the clerk. Torres passed on the request in Spanish. Seamus didn't want anyone peering into their windows, and in the event of an emergency, the second floor wasn't so high they'd be guaranteed injuries if they had to leap out the windows.

"And how long will you be staying with us?"

"The reservation was for a week. Can we extend that if we need to?"

"Of course, *Señor*. And how would you like to pay?"

Torres pulled out a corporate credit card provided to him by the attorney general. A search of the company name would reveal it was located in Mexico City and engaged in 'market research,' a description so vague it could mean anything.

It took them several trips to bring all their gear up, then they gathered in Torres' room. "Okay, now what?" Corey asked. He was wearing a casual button-down shirt, white with vertical multicolored pinstripes, untucked to hide the pistol at his waist. The other men were dressed similarly, all carrying concealed pistols. "Re-check those addresses?"

Seamus shook his head and pointed out the window. "Now we get a nice meal at that restaurant, sit for an hour or three drinking some cervezas, lazy gringos on a fat expense account, faff about right out on that patio in the open. Look around, ask the waitress about the town, standard tourist questions. Eye a shapely *señorita* or two. See what there is to see, hear what there is to hear. Maybe someone interesting will come by and want to take a look at the strangers, at the *pinche gringos*. We can't hide, so we might as well stand out, see who comes to us. If there's any FRAP stationed in this posh burg, they'll stroll by."

Torres gave him a measured look. "You're not as dumb as you pretend."

Seamus shot him a big grin. "Isn't that sweet. Me mum used to say the same thing."

Ten minutes after sitting down, they had their first round of drinks in front of them—bottles of beer all around—and the waitress brought over the appetizer Torres had ordered. She set a big plate of tiny fish down in the center of the table.

Seamus stared at it. "Are you having me on?" he said in disbelief. He leaned forward and picked up one of the deep-fried fish. "We're eating minnows now? What's next, cockroaches?" The waitress waited a few feet away, a smile on her face.

"This is *charales*," Torres told him, "a traditional appetizer from Jalisco." He pointed. "Deep-fried, sprinkled with salt and dried chiles." He grabbed the cut half of a lime and squeezed it over the plate of tiny fish. "Try it, you'll see." He grabbed one of the small fish by the tail and popped it into his mouth. He chewed with relish.

The fish were the size of French fries. Frowning and still not sure he wasn't being pranked, Seamus grabbed one, stuck it in his mouth, and chewed. He cocked his head. "Okay," he said, slowly nodding. He finished chewing and swallowed. Sour, salty, spicy, crunchy, and chewy. "Not quite to my taste, but I can see how a bloke could favor them." He turned and nodded toward the waitress. "*Gracias, Señora*," he said with a deliberately horrible accent.

She smiled and looked at Torres. In Spanish, she said, "You will enjoy Xicotepec. It is very beautiful. We are named one of the 121 *pueblos mágicos* in the country because of our culture and natural beauty." She headed back to work.

Torres saw Seamus eating another fish. "You will see. They will, I think you say, grow on you."

"Whole deep-fried fish served with their heads and tails on sounds gross enough to be a traditional English dish," Corey observed, chewing one of them, "except they have too much flavor. You'd find a way to boil them or something. Serve them with intestines and lard on stale bread."

"That sounds more like a Scottish dish," Seamus said, grabbing another fish by its tail.

The bright blue sky was clotted with thick, fluffy clouds. When the sun was out, the restaurant patio was pleasant. When the sun ducked behind one of the clouds, it was... perfect.

"I could get used to this," Corey said. He lifted his bottle up to peer through the glass. Empty. Was it his second, or third? The fact that he couldn't remember meant he needed to slow down. "*Una mas, y una agua, por favor,*" he called out to the waitress, who was hovering close to the table containing the wealthy foreigners. She smiled and nodded. She was back in a few seconds with a cold bottle of beer and a glass of water with a few ice cubes.

"I don't know if you should be drinking the water," Torres said quietly.

"Are you kidding me? After torching my guts with local tap water for the past few years, mostly unintentionally, it doesn't do anything to me anymore. Seam—Finn, here, he could probably drink out of ditches and be fine."

"The boy's not wrong," Seamus admitted.

Roughly half the tables on the patio were occupied by what appeared to be the wealthier citizens in town, if Seamus had to guess by their dress. Which made sense. The poor weren't eating out, especially not for lunch in the middle of the week. Church bells began to ring, loudly and close. Seamus checked his watch. It seemed an odd time for a church service. He could see the narrow roof peak of the church on the next block over, topped with a cross. After the bells stopped tolling, the conversation around them rose significantly in volume. Seamus didn't look around, but his expression got thoughtful as he listened. He traded a look with Torres, who gave him a slight nod. Then the inspector turned in his chair.

"Excuse me, I couldn't help but hear you talking," he said in rapid Spanish to the middle-aged couple sitting behind him. "What did you say about *La Fuerza*? They killed two men in town?" The tolling church bells were for the funeral.

The wife said, "Yes," just as the husband said, "No," and they scowled at each other. "Of course it was *La Fuerza*," the wife said. "They walked right into them."

"They were nowhere near them," the husband insisted. "They called Dario after they left the area. It wasn't them. It was the ghosts." The wife made a rude noise.

"I'm sorry, ghosts?" Torres said.

"We've been having some animal attacks," the man explained. He looked past Torres, an unfamiliar face, and saw two white men at the table with him, and realized they might be tourists. He quickly held up a hand. "At the edge of town. Infrequent, but... there have been some deaths. Some men went out to hunt down the animals in several vehicles. One of them ran into soldiers from *La Fuerza* in the mountains."

"And they killed them," the wife pronounced with a sharp, definitive nod.

"Then how did he get on his radio and tell Dario to avoid the area with the soldiers?" the husband demanded to know.

"So, what, you think they were killed by ghosts?" She scowled.

"Not ghosts. They call them ghosts. Animals. The mayor said jaguars."

"The mayor wouldn't know a jaguar from a chihuahua," she said with a dismissive wave of her hand. Seamus fought down a smile. He was watching the heated exchange, but still pretending he couldn't speak Spanish.

"There was blood, but no bodies. Why would *La Fuerza* hide the bodies and leave the truck? Why would they even kill them? It was animals," he insisted.

"Who knows why soldiers do what they do? Maybe the men said something stupid and rude." She gave her husband a look. "Ruggerio had a GPS watch, but the signal stopped, so no one could find his body. Animals don't care about watches. *La Fuerza* destroyed it to hide evidence of their crime."

The husband shook his head. "You don't think a tiger that can chew through bone could chew through a watch?"

"How many soldiers?" Torres interrupted them

"I think he said a couple of vehicles. They are sometimes in the mountains around here, but rarely come into town. Now, maybe they are hiding, since the war seems to be over."

"Do you know where in the mountains?" Torres asked. He smiled apologetically. "I'm with Pemex, and we have to go up there. I'd like to avoid any trouble."

* * * * *

Chapter Ten

"K resge."

"Ah, those dulcet tones always make me heart skip a beat," Seamus said with a smile. He had the scrambled satpalm on speaker. They were in his hotel room, the door locked. Outside the open window, the sun was heading toward the horizon, and the air was starting to cool.

"That's my line," Kresge said. "Every time you call, it's more trouble. What's your status?"

"Slightly inebriated, to be honest," Seamus told him. "We spent a beautiful afternoon drinking out on a restaurant patio and flirting with the local girls. Tried some interesting dishes. Have you ever heard of *charales*?"

"Sergeant," Kresge growled.

"Right. Save the pleasantries for later. Anyway, as we're sitting there, some nearby church—La Parroquia San Juan Batista, a bit famous, that—"

"O'Malley!"

"Sorry, sir, the excitement of the mission has me distracted. Anyway, the church bells start a right din. Funeral. Double funeral, actually, for a couple local blokes who ran into some FRAP north of town. I'm hoping you can get an eye in the sky for us to spy them out. I don't much care if it's an American or Mexican satellite, or a drone out of Miller station, but location and strength would be good to know if they're still in the area. Don't know if their presence is related to the reason for us being here, but…"

Torres jumped into the conversation. "There seems to be some disagreement among the locals as to whether the deaths were due to a misunderstanding with the guerrillas or simply an animal attack, but there's no doubt *La Fuerza* forces were spotted in the area."

"Animal attack? Didn't you say something about that previously?"

"*Sí, Colonel.* Apparently they're having a problem with some kind of meat eater. Most people seem to think it is a jaguar or two. The men were out looking when they ran into *los guerrilleros.*"

"Maybe," Seamus felt obliged to point out, "probably, but they never found the bodies. Just a lot of blood, or so they say. Empty caskets for the weeping widows."

"Roger that. Give me the coordinates."

"No coordinates, but I can tell you the general area," Seamus said. "We did several satellite sweeps of the area before we flew out, with negative result, so they probably just moved in and likely already moved on, whether or not they were involved. This was three or four days ago. But color me curious." He gave Kresge what information they had on the enemy troop location, and he put them on hold for a minute before he was back.

"It might be a couple hours. I presume you want visible light imagery, not thermographic, infrared, or the like. I should be able to swing it before dusk, but if not, it'll be first thing tomorrow."

After Seamus ended the call, he turned and looked at the three other men in the room. "I didn't notice anyone coming by to spy on us as we made merry. What say we all pile into the Land Cruiser and take a scenic drive? Reconnoiter a bit before the sun disappears?"

Torres was the oldest man in the room, but this was closer to a military mission than the traditional law enforcement he was accustomed to. He was willing to let the veteran *escara* take the reins until it came time to do police work and gave a polite nod.

Seamus brought his backpack with the Blackbird inside it, and Alvarez carried a blanket in which he wrapped his Fire Snake and an AK for Corey. It wasn't pretty or professional, but it was the quickest way to get the rifles in and out of the hotel without causing a scene. He set them on the back seat between them. They weren't expecting trouble, but that was no reason to get sloppy.

Torres drove. Seamus had a hardcopy printout of the city. Nothing was marked on it, just in case, but they all knew where they were going, as they'd studied maps of the area for hours. First stop was the small office building distantly connected to La Fuerza, located about a kilometer from the hotel. Torres wound his way through the narrow downtown streets, in no hurry, trying to get a feel for the area. There were as many pedestrians as vehicles. "That's it, on the left," he said.

The office building was two stories tall, off white with apricot trim. It was small, not much more than twenty-five meters long and half that wide. The adjacent parking lot was only big enough for six cars, and was empty of everything but a bit of wind-blown litter. Torres drove slowly past it, then pulled to the curb halfway down the next block. He turned in his seat. "There's a little *mercado* back there," he said to Alvarez. "Our *gringo empresarios* are thirsty."

Alvarez nodded. "*Sí, claro.*" He climbed out.

"I'll come with," Corey said. He left the rifles in the back seat, under the blanket. The two men walked slowly down the sidewalk, in no hurry, looking around.

Seamus leaned back in his seat, adjusting the Toyota's side mirror so he could see the address in question. "We can sit out here all you want, but eventually we're going to have to go in," he said, drumming his fingers on the windowsill of the door. Torres nodded, studying his mirrors and the foot traffic around them without being obvious about it. He left the Toyota running. Seamus had his backpack between his knees, the top unzipped just enough to accommodate a hand. He had a concealed pistol, of course, but pistols were for when you didn't have anything larger. So far he'd seen absolutely nothing worrisome.

"It's mostly businesses around here," Torres said. "It will be quite empty at night."

Seamus feigned a stretch, looking around. "FRAP could be set up in any one of these businesses overlooking that address," he said. He thought about it for a bit, then shrugged. "Nothing to it but to do it." In his mirror he could see Corey and Alvarez. They'd exited the small grocery store and were standing on the sidewalk, bottles in their hands, talking to a local, a short, dark man in an apron, who was gesturing animatedly. They were almost directly across from the vacant apartment building that was, at least on paper, connected to *La Fuerza*. Three minutes later, the men came ambling back up the sidewalk to the Toyota, bottles of orange soda in their hands.

Cory handed a bottle to Seamus and leaned against his closed door. "It's nice not being in a combat zone," he said. "People see a white face here, and they just assume I'm a dirty capitalist, not a dirty *escara*."

Beads of condensation were collecting on the bottle in his grasp. Seamus took a sip, then nodded. "That chap seemed to be chatting you up."

Corey eyed the surrounding buildings. They were almost entirely commercial, and at least half of them were vacant. "Lots of investment opportunities in town," Corey said. The owner of the small grocery had said that to him numerous times, Alvarez posing as his translator. "Everyone's full of hope that money will show up now the war's over."

"Everyone keeps saying the war's over," Seamus mused, "but I've yet to hear anything official from our friends on the other side."

Corey jerked his head back toward the grocery and the target address. "For example, that building has been vacant for a number of years now, three or four."

"You asked him about it?" Torres said, the disapproval plain in his voice.

Corey smiled and shook his head. "Not at all. He volunteered it. Didn't you see him pointing? He gave us the history of every building on the block."

"Very friendly," Alvarez agreed. "Very helpful."

Half the street was in shadow as the sun sank in the sky. "Where next?" Seamus said, looking down at the map. "The vacant lot is close, isn't it?"

Torres nodded. Corey and Alvarez climbed into the back seat. "He recommended we visit the... what was it?" Corey said, looking to Alvarez.

"*La Majestuosa Cruz Celestial de Xicotepec.*"

Seamus frowned. "The majestic heavenly cross? What's that?"

Alvarez leaned forward between the front seats, squinted, and pointed out the windshield. Seamus leaned forward and followed his finger, which was slanted up at a significant angle. "Ah," Seamus said. "That would be a majestic heavenly cross. Is it... blue?"

Alvarez nodded. "Blue and crystal, thirty meters tall, and lit up at night. Set in the middle of a big glass and concrete platform at the top of Cojolico, a local peak. One of the biggest tourist attractions in the area, not that they've seen many *turistas* these past few years. School children still go, though. Night or day, the view is said to be *muy bueno*; you can see all of Xicotepec." He shared a smile with Corey. "He noticed we appeared to be in shape and said we might like to jog up to the cross and back; it's the local…" He searched for the word as Torres put the Toyota in motion.

"Crucible," Corey said helpfully. "The access path is a kilometer and a half long, and somewhat steep. Lots of stairs." The cross was northeast of town, just outside the city limits, perhaps a mile from where they sat. "'Two young men in such fine shape,'" he said, repeating what the shop owner had said, while looking intently at the two of them. "He might have thought we were a couple."

"No might, definitely," Alvarez observed.

"Aye, you'd make a fine wife for Sergeant Alvarez, but before we start on the wedding plans, p'raps we can finish this mission?" Seamus drawled.

"Why am I the wife?" Corey wanted to know.

"Because you're the pretty one," Torres said as if it was obvious, which got all four of them laughing.

* * *

Colonel Jose Ruiz Alameda Salamanca de Baptiste took hold of the bar above the door as the pickup bounced over yet another huge pothole in the narrow, muddy road. All four men in the big truck swayed back and forth. His *culo* was both numb and sore, which he didn't think was possible, but he didn't complain. He was far past complaining. Plus, if he complained, the men would think it acceptable to complain themselves, and he didn't wish to hear it.

"We are close?" Sandoval asked, leaning over the steering wheel to peer out at the mountainous jungle around them.

"Are you late for an appointment?" Pepe asked him casually.

The young guerrilla flicked his eyes over at this commanding officer. "No, Colonel, I…"

Pepe pointed. "There, you see that road going off to the right? Take that." He looked at his man, who was just as tired from the endless hours in the car as he was. "We are close." He hadn't been to this location in years, but during his last visit, while recovering from a minor injury, he'd been there over a week, coming and going, so he remembered the route in well. Provided there were no issues, the site was large enough for a lot of men. He glanced over his shoulder. The two other vehicles were still right behind them. Three vehicles was pushing their luck, enough to draw the eye of *escara* satellites, but he hoped they were in such a remote area it wouldn't matter.

Sandoval made the tight turn onto the narrow track in the big truck, and the transmission shifted down as he started up yet another incline. The road worked its way back and forth up the ridgeline. Once they reached the top and started down, they were almost immediately in thick brush. Pepe stared out at the trees. The valley was thick with growth, but because of the altitude, it was halfway between jungle and evergreen forest, with both vines and pines. The air was heavy with moisture.

They bounced along the shallow valley floor for several minutes until they broke out of the tree line. There was a large open area before them, and past that, a coffee tree orchard Pepe was surprised to see was clearly abandoned. The formerly closely-trimmed dark green coffee trees were growing wild, and they were full of unpicked fruit.

"Are those cherries?" one of the men in the back seat asked.

"Coffee cherries," Pepe told him.

"Are those cherries that taste like coffee?"

Pepe fought the urge to roll his eyes. "No, coffee beans are the pits in fruits that are like cherries. Those fruits." He nodded at the passing coffee trees. "You can eat the fruit, but there's not much meat on them compared to a regular cherry. The animals love them."

"I could go for some fresh fruit," Sandoval said. "Do the cherries have caffeine?"

Pepe shook his head. "*Yo no se.*" He pointed. "Follow that drive there."

At the far end of the orchard, a two-track split off from the road. It ran between the overgrown orchard on the left and another dense patch of jungle forest on their right. The men were looking instead at the two buildings ahead of them, tucked under the trees. "Stop here," he told Sandoval.

The truck rolled to a stop thirty meters from the closest building, built of low stone and concrete, the size of a modest house. Past it was a large wooden barn with a steel roof. "Check to make sure we're alone," Pepe told his men.

They climbed out of the truck, glad to be stretching their legs, and approached the buildings with rifles in their hands. Pepe opened his door, got out, and stretched. He looked around. The valley was quiet and peaceful. The only thing they'd seen driving in were a number of large birds eating coffee cherries, and they'd taken off at the sight of the trucks.

Sandoval came jogging back to him. "They are clear, Colonel. It has been some time since anyone has been here, it seems."

Pepe nodded. "Okay. I'll call the other vehicles and tell them how to get here."

He walked along the overgrown driveway, the long grass getting his pantlegs wet, as he pulled out his satpalm. His men had opened the large doors at the front of the big barn, and Pepe stepped inside and looked around. The large, two-story barn was mostly empty. There were a few farm implements rusting along the back wall, hung on pegs. A pile of something that might have been straw, but which had rotted down into a lump of near-dirt. There was a loft accessed via a ladder, and above that the steel roof. Pepe looked around and nodded. This would do nicely while they waited. He gestured at one of the men. "Pull the vehicles in here, out of sight, and the others, when they get here, around back under the trees."

* * *

The vacant lot owned by a FRAP shell company was just that. It was in a mixed residential and commercial area, and there was no way to tell exactly what had been in the lot, just that something had once, years past. There were chunks of concrete scattered about the mid-size, nearly square space now filled with little but weeds. It was bordered on one side by an auto repair shop getting swallowed by listing stacks of used tires, and a mid-sized, dilapidated house on the other.

Lights were blinking on all over as the sun dropped below the ridgelines to the west of town. "Let's pop by the warehouse before it gets too dark to see," Seamus said.

The warehouse was on the south end of town in an industrial area. It was somewhat isolated, which was both good and bad. There were few people in the area to notice anything, but conversely, any activity would be likely to stand out. Torres passed by on the access road, which was cracked and heaved, and in dire need of repair, giving them a reason to drive slowly. Most everything in the industrial area was in poor condition, including the warehouse in question. It was a low metal building with windows up near the eaves.

"I went walking by last time," Torres told them as he pulled over a kilometer past the target building. "Late morning. Didn't see anyone but one car driving by. Climbed up on top of some pallets in back to peer into a window. I could see most of the inside, and it was empty, but for a little garbage."

"Pallets?" Seamus repeated.

"Yes, they are all over." Torres pointed. Fifty feet from them was a broken pallet sitting half in the gutter.

"Hmm. Okay, well, we'll need to stick our noses in, just for due diligence. Should we plan for that office building tonight? A few hours after midnight, when the locals are most apt to be gettin' some shuteye? Two in to poke about while two keep watch seems the best plan to me, but I defer to the inspector," Seamus said, gesturing at Torres.

The wide, open streets on the outskirts of the city grew narrower and more choked with parked and abandoned vehicles the closer they got to downtown. As they neared the hotel, they realized just how many pedestrians were on the street, and over 90 percent of them were headed in the same direction.

"Something's going on," Seamus said, leaning forward.

Torres had noticed the concerned looks on passing faces three blocks back, and had deliberately started following the crowd. "We will make a detective out of you yet," he said to Seamus.

As they neared an intersection that abutted a small square, the brisk foot traffic around them flowed into an agitated crowd of several hundred people, all facing an official-looking building.

"Local government," Torres said, nodding at the building. "City hall, police."

There were several men on the wide steps of the building, and one of the men, in a suit, was talking and waving his hands. He was a hundred yards from the Toyota, and his words were lost over the loud, unhappy murmur of the crowd. "Lads," Seamus said casually, glancing over his shoulder at Alvarez and Corey, "want to see what this is about?"

Without a word, the two younger men climbed out of the vehicle and moved into the crowd. Most of the faces seemed to be closer to unhappy than angry, and it seemed a far cry from a violent mob, but it paid to be on top of such things. Torres inched the big SUV forward through the people standing in the street, deliberately not using the horn to keep from drawing attention, and eventually found a spot off to the side, mostly out of the way. He and Seamus had their windows down, enjoying the cool night air, and they listened intently, trying to make out the words of the speaker. He was just too far away, but they could sense that the crowd was unhappy and dissatisfied with whatever he was saying.

Ten minutes later, Corey and Alvarez came wading back through the crowd, which continued to grow. "That is the mayor and the chief of police on the steps," Alvarez said, gesturing back over his shoulder. He and Corey stood outside Torres' door.

"I can certainly tell which is which," Seamus said. The mayor was the one in the suit doing all the talking. He looked like a politician, slick and completely insincere. The police chief was in some sort of informal uniform, wearing a button-down shirt with fancy epaulettes, an even fancier pistol in a flap holster on his belt. The mayor was thick, the police chief downright fat.

"It's the two dead guys," Corey said. He nodded at the crowd, many of whom were holding candles aloft. "You've got angry friends and family at the front, and they're demanding that the police do something."

Seamus sat up. "Against man-eating tigers or FRAP?"

"Either. Both. They don't care, I think," Corey said. "They just want somebody to do something. Before the men, there was a young girl who went missing. That's her picture you see them holding up."

Seamus traded a look with Torres. "That's a bit of two different things," Seamus observed. He squinted. "Our police chief doesn't seem quite the type to know much about man-eaters."

"Or *La Fuerza*," Alvarez commented. "*Churros, flan, tres leches, dulce de leche*... those he seems to know." He scowled as he stared back toward the city hall. There were a dozen uniformed police officers lined up to either side of the steps, but they didn't seem especially concerned by the crowd.

"Are they thinking of going after the guerrillas?" Torres asked. "I think that would be... unwise," he finally finished.

"Lots of ways for it to go wrong," Seamus agreed.

"I don't see how it could go right. Do they have supporters in town?" Corey asked.

"*¿La Fuerza?*" Torres shrugged. "Probably a few; there are always a few sympathizers. *¿La Fuerza lucha por el pueblo, sabes?*" La Fuerza fights for the people. It was one of their many slogans.

"Especially the stupid ones," Seamus muttered. He glanced around the square once more. "All right, this doesn't look like it's going to turn into a riot. Let's head back to the hotel, do a little planning, then maybe we can catch some shuteye before heading out tonight."

"Shuteye?" Corey said. "The hotel has a bar, and we've got an expense account!" Alvarez nodded vigorously, and he and Corey got back into the Toyota.

Torres turned to Seamus and tilted his head toward the two men in the backseat. "Newlyweds," he said, deadpan, with a tiny shake of his head. Seamus laughed so hard, he had tears streaming down his cheeks.

* * * * *

Chapter Eleven

"*Mon dieu*," Sadie breathed. She stared at Michael Ferrand. "How old are you?" she demanded. He looked fifteen. Pale, short, and a little pudgy, with a baby face. "*Tu n'es qu'un bébé.*"

"Twenty-one," he said, looking and sounding guilty. He could barely look her in the eye.

"Since when have the experts in computers looked like me?" Luc asked her. "They are all teenagers working out of their garages."

"Or their parents' home. Do you live with your parents?" she demanded of him.

"Leave him alone," Luc said as Michael sputtered, "*J'ai mon propre appartement.*"

"Sadie," Luc said, softly but firmly, "you agreed to come. Don't take it out on Michael."

Sadie frowned and nearly growled, but she knew he was right; that was what she was doing. She huffed. "*D'accord.*" She was standing at the end of a row of seats in the airport concourse, staying on her feet as long as possible. She'd be sitting for ten hours or so, and that was just the length of the flight to Atlanta. There were no direct flights to General Pedro Jose Mendez International Airport in Ciudad Victoria, their final destination, so they had to fly past it to Mexico City, then take a regional shuttle. With the layovers, it would take them nearly 24 hours to get to Ciudad Victoria, crammed into a tiny seat, because there was no way the school was going to pay for three first-class tickets from Paris to anywhere, much less the United States. "A nightmare," she muttered.

The aircraft was a Boeing 777 with two aisles, three seats to either side of the aisles, and four between them. Luc had paid a tiny bit extra for two aisle seats, and he sat across from her. Michael was to her left in one of the center seats. He didn't mind—this wasn't just his first international flight, it was his first time on a plane, period. Sadie tried not to roll her eyes as he stared at everything like a wide-eyed boy. Luc saw her and tried not to laugh. Luckily, Michael wasn't much larger than she was, so she wasn't crowded in her seat.

The young man listened intently to the pre-flight briefing by the flight attendants as only someone who's never heard one before could, then sat with his mouth slightly open in wonder as the big plane taxied, then accelerated, and took to the air. It was clear he wanted to be peering out a window. After a while, he relaxed, pulled out his top-of-the-line laptop covered with bright stickers, and put buds in his ears. Sadie pulled out her tablet and keyboard, and tried to do some work. After several minutes, she realized Michael was staring at her. No, not at her, but at the shiny pink scars on her arms. She looked at them herself, then up at him.

He blushed but didn't look away. "Luc told me what happened," he said quietly. "I can't..." He took a breath. "I understand you not wanting to come back. You're incredibly brave."

"I'm not brave for coming back; I'm stupid."

"No, not for coming back, for fighting the velociraptors. Luc said you punched and kicked them, attacked them with a chair, while your friend went for the shotgun. Then you drove yourself to the hospital with those." He nodded at her scars, wide-eyed. "*Je veux dire, putain de putain de merde.* You're a badass. I feel better that you're here."

Sadie wasn't sure how to respond to that. She'd never considered herself tough. She'd been fighting for her life. "Have you ever even been with a woman?" she asked, the question sounding mean.

But Michael didn't recoil. He pressed his lips together, colored a bit, and shyly said, "Is that an invitation? I like older women." At which point Luc, who'd been eavesdropping, barked out a laugh. Sadie glared at him, but he didn't care; he was laughing silently, squeezing out tears.

Sadie growled and sighed loudly. "They weren't velociraptors," she felt obliged to correct him, "they were Coelophysis. Not as big as the movie velociraptors… but there were a dozen of them, black and red. So fast…." She shivered, and the hair on her arms stood up. She clenched her fists.

Michael saw it all. "*Putain* badass," he repeated.

They had to clear Customs in Mexico City before boarding the smaller jet bound for Ciudad Victoria. The flight was only a few hours, but by that time, Sadie was exhausted, and she dozed fitfully sitting up in the narrow, cramped seat. The sleep barely seemed to help, and they were all dragging as they retrieved their luggage and made their way through the concourse of General Pedro Jose Mendez International Airport.

"He's waiting outside," Sadie said. She'd gotten a text as she'd turned her palm back on after they'd landed. She led the trio outside, blinking in the bright sunlight. The air was intensely humid and smelled of vegetation. The airport was eight kilometers east of the city and surrounded by fields and low tropical forests.

"Do you know what he looks like?" Luc asked, then stopped short as he hit the sidewalk where the vehicles were waiting. "Oh, my," he said.

There, squatting amongst the taxis, compact cars, and old, mud-splattered pickups, was a huge tank of a vehicle, all flat steel panels and sharp angles, with giant, knobby tires. It was twice as tall as the sedans and hatchbacks around it. A middle-aged European man with a dark tan was leaning against the front fender, and upon seeing Sadie, he stood up and walked over.

"*Mademoiselle* Simon? Peter Hein." He held a hand out.

Sadie shook it automatically. "Did Seamus send you my photo?" she asked him as he was shaking the hands of her companions. He was in his forties, balding, tall, slender, and deeply tanned, in a button-down shirt and khaki shorts.

Hein's mouth twitched. "He said you looked very French, and you do. He meant it—"

"As a compliment. Oh, I know."

"This is Emiliano, Leo, my assistant," Hein said, gesturing to the man with him. He was a native, about thirty, with a thick head of hair and a very intense smile.

"Good afternoon," Leo said. His English was good, with only a bit of an accent. He grabbed their baggage and began loading it into the rear of the big vehicle.

"What is that?" Michael asked, staring in wonder at the vehicle before them.

"A Vaquero. Far more than what we usually need, but many of my regular clients are wealthy and appreciate a bit of... spectacle. It's an armored personnel carrier."

"How much did that cost?" The young man was eyeing the huge tires, the roof rack for cargo, and the angular, armored bulk of the body.

Hein laughed. "Much less, I imagine, than you would expect. With the war winding down, both Raven and the Mexican military are selling off materiel. Before long, you'll be able to purchase tanks and planes. Don't think I'm joking. This is brand new, or new for me. My last one suffered an… accident." Hein looked the three of them over. "I imagine you're exhausted just getting here. Most of a day on planes, plus the time change? I was thinking I'd take you to the hotel. You could shower, maybe get a meal, and sleep, try to get your bodies adjusted to the local time. Then we could start fresh in the morning, after a civilized breakfast. From the hotel to the park, it's maybe an easy forty-five minute drive."

Sadie blinked. "Is the city that close? Last time we came up from the south." Where there hadn't been much more than the occasional cluster of huts beside the road.

"There's not much south of the park, but yes, from *La Ciudad Victoria* to the front gate of Pangaea is maybe only fifty kilometers, straight down Highway 85." He smiled at them. "You don't want dinosaurs in your back yard, but rich people also don't want to have to bounce over rutted roads for hours to get there. Ciudad Victoria was to Pangaea what I hear Orlando is to Disney World, although I've never been to Disney.

"There was a helipad at the rear of the park, and most guests flew into Victoria. Most of the employees lived in a large apartment complex here in town, owned by the park, and rode shuttle buses in to work." He glanced at Leo. "Everything loaded? Okay, get in. You'll need to use the steps and the handgrips; it's a bit of a climb. Accord-

ing to my rich hunter clients, it puts hair on their chest." Sadie snorted. She immediately liked the man, as Seamus had said she would.
He had a confident air about him; she could plainly see he could
handle himself. And Leo looked competent as well, like a soldier.

"I don't understand how the park has been left alone by people,
then," Sadie said after everyone was in their seats. The rear of the
Vaquero was huge, with two seats on either side facing the center,
and enough cargo room past them to fit several couches. The diesel
engine of the Vaquero was loud, and the military vehicle groaned and
rattled as Hein pulled away from the curb, but Sadie really liked the
feeling of security, being surrounded by so much steel. No dinosaur
would be able to get to her inside such a vehicle. It was a literal tank,
armored steel and tempered glass. "A famous park, less than an hour
away from a city?"

Hein shrugged. "It is young people who are the explorers, who
like to vandalize. Young men, usually, and with the military draft and
the war, there are far fewer of those about. But how famous is it?
The park's been closed for over twenty years. Most of them don't
even know it's there. The city's less than half the size it once was. It
was the support base for the park, and when the park closed, all the
industries in town supporting it disappeared, and all those people
had to leave to find work. The war drove many others out of the
country."

He pulled to a stop in front of a red light. The drivers of the cars
around them stared at the Vaquero, which towered over their cars.
Most of the military vehicles kept to Joint Base Victoria, which was
on the opposite side of the city. Hein turned around and gave her a
wry smile. "Besides, either you believe all the dinosaurs were killed,

in which case there's nothing to look at, or you don't, in which case you might fear walking around the park."

"What does a professional hunter even do?" Michael asked him. He honestly had no clue.

"I'm more of a guide than a hunter," Hein admitted. "Our clients pay to hunt the theropods, dinosaurs, which officially didn't exist for so many years. Keeping track of their movements is a big part of what I do, so I can get my clients in position to take the shot. They escaped from the park, but honestly, I spend very little time in this area. They avoid the city, like you might expect. They're up in the mountains, or loitering around farmers' fields, looking to eat the crops."

He looked to either side and pointed. "These all used to be farmer's fields, but you see, a lot of them are uncultivated, and have been for some time. That's happened all over the country. Farmers have fled, died, or simply stopped being farmers because they couldn't get seed, or afford the petrol to run their tractors. Mexico has a serious agriculture problem because of their twenty-year war, but overgrown vegetable fields are exactly what you want if you're looking to support and grow an animal population. So what's bad for the country has been good for the dinosaurs, and PaleoSafari."

"What dinosaurs have you seen?" Michael asked, as excited as a child on Christmas morning.

"When it was operating, Pangaea had twenty-two species on display. I've seen maybe twelve of those in the wild, and the few I haven't seen, I know people who have. But it takes a bit of work. They're no different than any other animals; they avoid people." He caught Sadie's reflection in the windshield. "Generally," he added.

"Have you ever been inside the park?" Sadie asked.

Hein nodded. "Once, years ago, not too long after I started doing this. Started doing this *here*," he corrected myself. "I was a PH in Africa before this, which was where I met Aarne Anders, who founded PSI. He said Mexico would be a land of opportunity, and he was right."

"Did you start doing this here right after the park was attacked?" Luc asked him, curious.

"Oh, no. The park was attacked, what, twenty-one, twenty-two years ago? I came to Mexico eight years ago. At first, remember, the story was that all the animals had been killed in the attack. They weren't, of course, but there still weren't that many. Had to give them time to get their numbers up."

He gestured out the window at the passing scenery. "This was a perfect spot for that to happen. The park is in a natural biosphere, mountains and forests, fields, and even some jungle, and apart from Ciudad Victoria, there isn't much more than small towns within two hundred kilometers in any direction. Go west from the park, and you're in the mountains. Past them are arid plains, the plateau stretching across the middle of the country that includes the Chihuahuan Desert.

"It's always been sparsely populated, and I don't think there are much more than fifty million people left in the country, after two decades of war. A tenth of those are in Mexico City, and maybe half of the rest are in the other big cities, which means animals can wander for days without seeing people."

He stuck a thumb over his shoulder. "East from here, the land goes down toward the ocean, and you've got real jungle. Forests and fields like these, and the mountains, stretch from here south for hundreds and hundreds of kilometers. Desert, jungle, forests, and fields… just about every environment you'd need if you wanted a variety of species to breed in the wild—and they've done just that. Aarne brought me in when their numbers were getting to be such that you could track them and provide clients a right good chance of getting an animal. Since then, they've spread quite a bit. I've tracked some big game up near the border with the US, and all the way down near the isthmus—the narrowest part between the Gulf and the Pacific. The only problem when following reports of a big animal…"

"They're fake?" Luc said.

Hein shook his head. "Getting there before one of the locals shoots it with his grandfather's rifle, or hits it with his truck. We had a beautiful two-day stalk on a juvenile stegosaurus east of San Luis Potosí, had to be five meters tip to tail, and lost it to a *campesino* and his *pokkelijer* Mitsubishi tractor."

Five minutes later, Hein pulled off the road and into a large parking lot. He drove right up to the front of a large building. Sadie looked out the window, and her mouth opened in surprise. "Hampton Inn?" she exclaimed.

"It's the nicest in town, or so I've been told," Hein said apologetically. "I reserved separate rooms for everyone. Probably not up to your standards, but…"

"Last time I was at the park, I slept in a tent!" When she'd been injured, they'd transported her to Ciudad Victoria before flying her to Mexico City, but she'd been in and out of consciousness, and had been under the impression the city was hours away from the park.

"Oh. Well. Then yes, this might be an improvement, although you should only drink bottled water. The hotel restaurant is sub-par, according to online reviews, but that steakhouse over there—" he pointed across the parking lot, "—is supposed to be quite good.

They've got a continental breakfast in the lobby every morning, starting at six. How about we meet up at eight tomorrow morning in the
lobby?"

"You're staying here?" Michael asked him.

Hein smiled. "I've spent enough time sleeping on the ground and
in a vehicle. When I've got a bed and air conditioning, I take it." Luc
was giving Sadie a bemused look, thinking that perhaps he'd wasted a
lot of money on Hein. After all, everything had been very civilized so
far. Then Hein added, "There are bomb scanners and metal detec-
tors in the lobby, thanks to *La Fuerza*, so if you've got any weapons,
leave them in the Vaquero. We lock it up. Nobody's getting into this
thing."

* * * * *

Chapter Twelve

Sadie had nightmares. She'd been expecting to; in fact, she would have been surprised if her sleep had been untroubled. This close to Pangaea, where the attack had occurred? Where Karl had bled to death next to her? Where *she'd* almost died? The place that had given her so many scars, inside and out?

But at this point, the nightmares were old acquaintances. They held no surprises. Horror, yes, as well as fear, sadness, and a feeling she'd learned was called 'survivor's guilt,' but no surprise.

Her body clock was completely destroyed by the time change and spending the better part of 24 hours in planes and airports, but being so exhausted helped her sleep when she otherwise would have been awake. Still, she was out of bed by 4:00 am local time.

She showered and dressed for a day in the field, then caught up on emails on her laptop until six, when breakfast was put out downstairs. The pastries had obviously been frozen and reheated, and the coffee was weak, but it was still a long way from what she was expecting—sleeping inside a vehicle or one of the abandoned Pangaea buildings while on this expedition. Not a tent like she and Karl had set up—a tent wouldn't stop claws—but deep inside one of the buildings behind a closed door, or maybe up on the roof of the Production building; that would be safe. Get smelly and dirty and go days without bathing. Instead, she was sitting in an air-conditioned lobby, an awful instrumental version of *The Girl From Ipanema* playing softly in the background, and they'd likely be back every night. Still, her heart hammered in her chest at the thought of returning to the park.

"Sadie. Sadie? *Como ça va? Est-ce que ça va?*"

She shook her head to clear it. "Fine, I'm fine," she told Luc. He gave her a look that said he knew she was lying, but he didn't challenge her. He eyed the pastry on her plate. "Is the food any good?"

Michael Ferrand walked up, his mouth stuffed with an entire pastry. "Good, it's good," he said, spraying a few crumbs.

Sadie gave a little shake of her head as she maintained eye contact with Luc. "The eggs are reconstituted, the pastries are tasteless and still half-frozen, the sausages are greasy and rather disgusting, and we shouldn't eat any fruit they have to wash with water, which is everything but the bananas."

"So…?" Luc said, one eyebrow raised.

"I'm trying to distract myself from the thought that in a few minutes we're heading to the park, and all I have to complain about is packaged pastries while I sit in an air-conditioned lobby sipping *café horrible*."

Luc nodded knowingly. "Hein seems competent," he said, "and Leo is former military."

"I'm sure we'll be safe as sitting in a café in Paris, but that doesn't mean I won't be *irrité et méchant* and just generally unpleasant to be around the whole time we're here."

Luc nodded. "Duly noted." He gave Michael a pointed look, hoping the young man understood.

The lobby door opened, and Hein strolled in. He passed through the metal detector, saw them, and walked over. "We're ready to go whenever you are. Leo's outside with the Vaquero."

Tears sprang into Sadie's eyes, and she fought back a loud sob that drew Hein's eyes. She spit out a very unladylike word, wiped angrily at her face, and stood up. "I am ready," she said. She wasn't, but she'd realized she never would be. If she didn't force herself to go, to fight her fears, they'd be with her forever, controlling her, and that was unacceptable.

The drive there was quiet. Sadie was alone with her own thoughts. Luc could sense her mood and stayed quiet. Michael was visibly excited, but kept his mouth shut.

"I drove by the entrance yesterday off 85," Hein said. "It looked unchanged from when you visited, the way you described it," he told Sadie, "but I didn't go inside. I didn't want to draw any more attention than necessary."

"GenVen went bankrupt a decade ago," Luc told him. "It's not private property anymore, at least not that anyone would claim."

"The local *policía* still might not like anyone poking their nose in there. Vandals, looters, and such."

"Do we look like looters?" Luc said. He threw up his arms at the vehicle enclosing them. "We're in a tank. I'm a forty-year-old French lawyer."

"Forty?" Sadie said, one eyebrow climbing up her forehead.

"If you round down."

"From fifty-three?"

Hein was smiling. "We look rich, or likely would to them." He looked at his clients. "I've secured hunting permits for the three of you."

"What?"

"Hunting permits?"

Hein held up a hand. "For feral hogs, which are quite common in this area. If we're confronted by local authorities, we can say we tracked them into the park, which will give us a legal reason to be there. We'll still probably have to pay a bribe, but that's the cost of doing business in this country. *La mordida* is an old friend." He traded a knowing look with Leo.

Highway 85 was two lanes of blacktop, winding leisurely southward. Off to their right, to the west, were the Sierra Madre Orientals. Not far from the road, the land rose in foothills, then to the first rolling slopes of the mountains, which were covered in green. Beyond them were the peaks and ridges, more brown than green. The land to either side of the road was mostly low scrub, tall grasses waving in the light breeze, and mesquite bushes.

Traffic was light, most of the vehicles heading south passing the Vaquero, which was doing the speed limit. "Do people leave you alone because they think you're military?" Luc asked, looking around at the inside of the armored personnel carrier.

"Sometimes," Hein admitted, "but sometimes it's more trouble than it's worth." He didn't want to say that the armor of his previous Vaquero had saved his life. You didn't want to scare the clients. Most of his wealthy clients were more than impressed by the armored personnel carrier, which was the point.

"How do you hunt them?" Michael asked Hein suddenly.

"What?"

"You're a professional hunter of dinosaurs. So how do you hunt them?"

"I'm not sure what you're asking," Hein said.

"I mean, do you crawl through a forest looking for their tracks?"

Hein shook his head. "Most of them are herbivores, and most of the time, herbivores travel in herds for protection, even the very large ones. And most dinosaurs, as you probably know, aren't cold-blooded." He let that statement hang in the air.

"Satellites?" the young computer expert guessed.

Hein nodded. "Exactly. While we do occasionally use drones on a short-range basis, we rent time on imaging satellites—some of them military or Raven—that have infrared and thermal capabilities. We spot the herds that way. It helps to know what areas to search in, to know what size animals you're looking for, and from an overhead shot, to be able to tell the difference between a cow, a horse, and a Massospondylus. Between a velociraptor, Coelophysis, and Deinonychus.

"That's where the experience comes in. I've been tracking and hunting these animals in this country for the better part of a decade. We locate a herd using airborne tech of one sort or another and verify the species before we ever start a stalk. Our clients are paying a lot of money, and it's not to hike through the Mexican countryside. It's very rare that I can't get a client on an animal. After that, it's up to him, although I'm usually there with my rifle to back him up in case of a botched shot. It sounds like cheating, but it's not nearly as easy as it sounds. You always end up having to do a stalk, even if you're talking about a stationary herd of long-necks. You have to get in close enough without spooking them. That's not so simple; they're hard-wired to react to predators."

"What about the meat-eaters?" Michael asked him

"What?"

"You said *most* were herbivores. What about carnivores?"

Hein nodded. "Those are often tougher," he agreed. "Many of the smaller carnivores also travel in packs, like Coelophysis and Syntarsus. The larger ones often travel alone or in a bonded pair. That's not nearly as easy. Their numbers are smaller, and always will be—it takes a population of hundreds of herbivores to sustain one meat-eater if they keep to a territory, and if they haven't claimed a specific territory, they have to travel great distances to keep themselves fed. When it comes to finding them, tracking them; that's where I earn my money. Once we know their territory or hunting grounds, it's often simply a matter of getting them to come to you."

"How do you do that?"

"You put out bait," Hein said simply.

"Bait? What kind of bait?"

"Goat or sheep," he said. "Raw meat or staked out alive, depending on what the animal prefers, although sometimes the client isn't content to simply hunt over bait, not even when the game is as exotic as a raptor or Carnotaurus." He stared out the windshield, not seeing the road before them. "Whether you're after a lion or a raptor, following their trail through the brush, trying to stay downwind, wondering whether they've sensed you and have circled around, and are now stalking you…"

Michael's eyes were wide. "They do that?"

Hein laughed at his innocence. "Predators stalk prey. That's what they do. And if you're out in the field with them…"

"Just how smart are they?" Sadie asked him, curious.

Hein cocked his head. "Well, carnivores are always smarter than herbivores," he started by saying.

"Why is that?" Luc asked.

"It's natural selection, evolution, what have you," Hein explained. "It doesn't take any intelligence at all to sneak up on a leaf."

Luc blinked in surprise at the simplicity of the explanation. He'd never thought of it in those terms. "Oh. *Oui, d'accord.*"

Hein went on. "Dogs, wolves, and hyenas are relatively smart and work in packs to take down animals much bigger than themselves. They'll work a herd using various techniques until they succeed in separating an animal. That takes some intelligence, but you don't need to be as smart as you think if you've got a team and a good plan."

Leo laughed. They all looked at him. "You have just described every military," he said with a smile.

Hein smiled and nodded, then continued. "Lions and tigers and other solo hunters have very involved stalks and display a lot of patience, which can make up for a lot. As for pure intelligence, monkeys and apes are often said to be as smart as human toddlers, but they've discovered that gray parrots are at least as smart as chimpanzees."

Luc was surprised to hear that. "Really?"

"Yes," Hein said with a nod, "and many birds are descended from dinosaurs. Are raptors and the other pack hunters as smart as dogs? They seem to be, but to some extent, I find their intelligence to be irrelevant."

"Really?" Sadie said. "Why?"

"If you were being stalked through the veldt by a tiger or a pack of hyenas, would it really matter how objectively intelligent they were? I'd say they've proven themselves intelligent enough to get the job done, and after twenty years of living in the wild, any carnivore dinosaur species still in existence has proven the same thing."

"What's the most dangerous game you've ever pursued?" Michael asked him excitedly.

"Utahraptor," Hein said without hesitation.

"Really?" That wasn't the answer he was expecting. He was expecting, perhaps, to hear Tyrannosaurus rex, or Triceratops, because of the horns.

Hein nodded. "At least as smart as dogs, maybe as smart as monkeys; they can run thirty kilometers an hour while hardly making a sound, sprint fifty, they can kill with their teeth, claws, or feet, and they weigh well over five hundred kilos—over a thousand pounds—when mature. They're big enough that they usually don't travel in packs, but singly or in breeding pairs. A client was stalking one south of here. I was backing him up as we followed its path through a field thick with bushes and grass up to our shoulders. But like lions and tigers sometimes do, it had circled around and was stalking us."

He cocked his head. "I don't know if we heard it, smelled it, or just sensed it, and I don't know which one of us hit it as it charged." He laughed. "Client definitely got his money's worth on that safari. With the tail—they're feathered—it was nearly five meters long, and perhaps four hundred and fifty kilos. A male. They're smaller."

Sadie was close enough to see the hair on the man's arm standing up. She understood exactly what he was feeling, and yet he still did this for a living. She swallowed. "Do these dinosaur species behave the same in the wild as... as other species?" The image of beady eyes in the dark came to her, the Coelophysis making small sounds as they circled her. Not threatening sounds; they were talking to each other. Communicating.

"From what I've seen? Yes. There will always be some argument because of their patchwork DNA that they aren't real dinosaurs.

Hybrids. That there's no way to know if how they look and act is anything like the original animals millions of years ago. But didn't they use programs in their gene machines to plug the holes in the dinosaur DNA with what they thought was identical, or at least similar, DNA from living organisms?"

"Yes, predictive algorithms. Once they mapped the human genome, they started mapping other species, and figuring out what part of the sequence did what. Some sequences seemed to be pretty common across species." The mere fact that the dinosaurs weren't just living but apparently thriving in the wild showed that the theoretical bio-engineers seemed to have been successful in their educated guesses.

They slowed down as they drove through Llera de Canales. The small town was nearly abandoned, and not much more than an intersection around which clustered half-collapsed buildings slowly getting eaten by foliage and a long-abandoned, once fancy gas station where visitors to the park likely stopped for snacks and fuel. Just a few minutes past that, Hein slowed and pointed past the windshield.

"You don't see the turn off the highway so much as you see the entrance road running up," he observed. He slowed the Vaquero, then pulled onto the shoulder.

Whatever signage had existed had long since been removed. The tall chain link gates topped with razor wire that had stretched across the entranceway had fallen down—or been knocked down—years earlier and were half buried under grass and blown, decaying leaves, but the four-lane entrance road stretched straight as a razor due west, up into the forested hills, the Sierra Madre Orientals filling the horizon beyond. Overgrown, cluttered with rotting vegetation, barely recognizable as the road it once was, it was still a wide, straight line running through the brush-choked fields, and straight lines didn't exist in nature. The chain link fence that stretched along the property line against 85 had mostly collapsed, and what still stood was sagging and rusty.

"This is it?" Michael said dubiously.

"This was it," Hein said. He waited until there were no vehicles visible in either direction on 85, then turned onto the entrance road. The blacktop was cracked and heaved, with grass and even small bushes breaking through, but it was still in surprisingly good shape after twenty years.

Hein pointed before them. They could see tire tracks through the fallen leaves. "The place still gets visitors, but those look at least a week old, maybe more. I'm not sure what the weather's been like over here."

For over a mile, the four-lane entrance drive ran straight as a runway due west, gently climbing. The land to either side was fields and scrub, then the trees started and gradually pressed in around the road, leaning over it. Evergreens, palms, banyans, and mesquite bushes abounded, with vines crawling up everything and draped across the road like curtains and thick tufts of knee-high grass that Hein learned he needed to drive around if he didn't want the Vaquero bouncing wildly.

Sadie found herself panting, nearly hyperventilating, and clenched her hands. "Are you okay?" Luc asked her.

"Stop asking me that," she said, biting down on the words, then she physically forced herself to relax. She worked her neck, shook her hands out, and wiped her sweaty palms on her shorts. Then she shot a guilty look at Luc, but he hadn't taken it personally.

"This is the entrance drive? How long is it?" Michael asked in wonder. It kept going, and going…

"Ten kilometers," Luc said confidently. He'd studied the maps at length.

Everyone was staring out the windshield as the jungle grew thicker and leaned in, the road growing dark, and then suddenly the world brightened, and the entrance road fed into a massive parking lot.

"Ah, I remember this," Hein said. He stopped the Vaquero and looked at Sadie. "Where are we going?"

"Can we drive by the front of the park?" Luc asked. "I'd like to see it." He was squinting. The park gates were at least half a mile away across a sea of buckled asphalt slowly being consumed by nature, just out of focus, as a thin fog had drifted down from the mountains.

"So would I," Michael said, looking and sounding like a child on Christmas.

Hein raised his eyebrows and looked at her. "Don't treat me—" she started to say, then stopped and took a breath. "I'll be fine," she told them firmly, "or I won't, but back off."

"*Oui, madame,*" Luc said, with a smile.

Hein gave her a small nod and started slowly through the parking lot, the Vaquero bouncing over the heaved pavement. "It is beautiful," Hein admitted, staring out at the mountain slopes in the distance. Wisps of clouds scudded across their slopes.

La Reserva de la Biosfera el Cielo had been created to protect the northernmost extension of tropical and cloud (rain) forest in Mexico. It was nearly a hundred and fifty thousand hectares in size, more than five hundred and fifty square miles, over half of that steep mountain slopes.

Pangaea itself was far smaller, taking up less than eight square miles, leased for 99 years from the struggling state of Tamaulipas for a sizable sum. It was located at the northeastern corner of the natural reserve on land that, while not flat, was much more conducive to the construction of a combination theme park and zoo, as many of the nearby mountain ranges were over two thousand meters in height.

The property was bordered to the north by the Guayalego River, and to the west by the slopes of the Sierra Madre Orientals. The far western edge of the park had contained steep cliffs and waterfalls, with botanical gardens for the adults and zip-lines for the children running over a few of the—non-carnivorous—animal exhibits. The pricey hotel located inside the park was on the shore of the Guayalego on the northwest corner of park property.

Most of the leased land was outside the park itself and not open to visitors. The corporation had left themselves room to expand the park, but some of that additional land had been used for infrastructure and support, including the buildings their group intended to visit.

The sawgrass in the parking lot was as tall as the Vaquero's tires. The lines on the asphalt had been faded by the unrelenting sun, although it was a dim morning as fog drifted down out of the mountains. Sadie shivered. "It's like a ghost town," she said, remembering the feeling she'd had the last time, when she and Karl had driven up in their borrowed truck.

Hein didn't pull up to the curb; he drove over it and between the ticket booths, the bump of the curb almost unnoticed under the vehicle's huge tires. Hein stopped in the middle of a larger circular area, where groups once gathered before entering the park, beside a large, now-dry fountain filled with cartoonish concrete dinosaur statues. There was a small building marked Guest Services facing them, and another building to the side that appeared to have been a gift shop. All the glass was gone from its windows, and Sadie saw what looked like bullet holes. She didn't point them out.

"Wow," Michael said. He peered out the windows. "Can we get out and look around for a little bit?"

"How long is it going to take to do what we need to do?" Luc asked him.

"I don't... how would I know? There's no way to know until we look in those buildings."

Luc controlled the urge to look at Sadie and fought back a smile. "Exactly." He paused as long as he dared, then added, "But a few minutes couldn't hurt." There was no way he wasn't going to get out and look at the famous Pangaea.

They all climbed out and stretched. Hein made no attempt to conceal the big rifle he pulled out of the Vaquero and held casually by his side. Leo had a rifle as well, something that looked military, with a huge box magazine. The sight of them comforted Sadie, as did Hein's familiarity with the weapon.

Michael's eyes went wide at the sight of the rifles, then wider as he beheld the faded glory that had once been the entrance to one of the few dinosaur parks in the world. "*Merde*," he whispered. He walked around the ticket booths to get a better view of the magnificent display that had once greeted visitors.

A thirty-foot wall styled to look like something out of King Kong, with oversize coils of fake razor wire atop it, stretched far left and right across the front of the park. Across the front of it was the

Pangaea name in two-meter-tall, multi-colored letters, the famous—infamous?—Pangaea globe logo beside it showing the single super-continental mass of the Mesozoic era, which was the original Pangaea. And of course, the life-sized rendering of a roaring T. rex was front and center, with other dinosaurs running to either side, their silhouettes instantly recognizable—triceratops, brachiosaur, stego-saur, and a raptor of some sort—without feathers, unlike the actual animals found inside the park. While the colors had faded over time to a shadow of their former brilliance, the vines and wild grass, and the silence of the park somehow made it far more eerie and impressive.

"It's like visiting the grave of the Titanic," Luc observed. He'd spotted the bullet holes in the one building. Parks and zoos were supposed to be full of people talking and laughing, not silent and filled with the memory of death. It was akin to attending a funeral in a playground.

"How big is the park?" Michael asked, peering past the entrance gates and down the long promenade.

"Michael, didn't you look at the map?" Sadie said.

"*Oui*, but I wasn't paying attention to the scale. It's bigger than I thought."

"Zoos are bigger than amusement parks; the animals need room to live," Hein told him. "They had their own train, which made a big circle around the exhibits."

"The challenge is designing their habitats so the animals aren't cramped, yet the visitors can still see them," Sadie said. "They did a good job here with large enclosures. That's why the guerrillas didn't kill many of the animals. They were too spread out. I imagine the zoologists, the animal caretakers, left some of the access gates open so the animals could escape." She shrugged. "Or maybe not. They couldn't have known they weren't coming back, that no one was coming back."

"Once the shooting started, the animals would have run in the other direction," Hein added, "same as the people."

"They also had hidden viewing areas and walkways over the enclosures," Sadie added. She'd done far more research on the park prior to this trip than the last, when she hadn't known where she was going to end up.

Sadie leaned against the Vaquero and waited while Michael and Luc wandered down the wide concourse running down the center of the front section of the park, looking into the darkened buildings. Hein stayed with her, while Leo accompanied the two Frenchmen, his HK G3 rifle slung over his shoulder.

Sadie and Hein watched the trio moving deeper into the property. "Where were you attacked?" Hein asked after several minutes of silence.

Sadie frowned reflexively, but said, "At the back of the park. We drove in. There's a botanical garden with extinct species of plants, some very pretty cliffs, and a small waterfall. The butterflies we were tracking seemed to be nesting on the vines and bushes on the cliff. They attracted the animals."

"Coelophysis, you said?" Sadie nodded. Hein made a non-committal grunt. Coelophysis were carnivores that ran on two legs, and were quite quick—graceful, even. Pack hunters, long and slender, and with the tail up to three meters long, but they rarely weighed more than twenty kilograms. Hein assumed the park operators had brought them back because Coelophysis fossils were so common, but the animals themselves were... boring, pedestrian, at least for dinosaurs. Narrow heads, a light coating of feathers on their bodies… they looked as much like flightless birds as they did dinosaurs and weren't big enough to be scary.

He'd read that to generate interest in them, the zookeepers had put live rabbits in their habitats, so the park visitors could watch them hunt. He imagined they made short work of the hares; he'd seen what they could do to goats. A dozen darting bites, and the animals bled out, bleating. He fought the urge to glance at Sadie's scars; she seemed self-conscious enough about them.

"Did you have a firearm?"

"A shotgun in the truck. Karl shot one or two, but it was the noise that drove them off. If we'd had it with us…" She eyed the rifle in his hand.

He heard the tone in her voice and knew what it meant. "Life is full of what-ifs," he said simply. He glanced down at the rifle. He'd spent so much of his life with a rifle in his hand, it was second nature to him now. In this case, it was a bolt-action Winchester chambered in .300 Winchester Magnum, the ammunition loaded with partition bullets designed for penetration and expansion. The wood stock was dented and scratched. Simple iron sights adorned the rifle, and the leather sling was permanently discolored with sweat.

He'd used it a few times to back up a client, or to help put down a wounded animal. It was a simple rifle, built for hunting medium- to large-sized game at close range, capable of taking animals up to the size of a mature Utahraptor with proper bullet placement.

The Heckler & Koch G3 over Leo's shoulder, on the other hand, was a big-bore battle rifle, fed by blocky twenty-round magazines, meant for the wars of men, and Leo had a spare magazine on his belt. There were twenty more loaded magazines for it in the

Vaquero, and a shotgun, and a pistol. After his experience in Cancún, Hein had decided there was no such thing as being too heavily armed.

Fifteen minutes later, the men were back. Michael's excitement appeared to have doubled. Luc had a glow on his face. Sure, it was abandoned and empty of dinosaurs, but it was still *Pangaea*, the infamous dinosaur park in the middle of the Mexican jungle with mist-shrouded mountain peaks in the background. At that thought, Luc took out his palm and took photos to show Renata. There might not have been any dinosaurs left in the park, but they were still in the area. Sadie's scars were proof of that.

At that thought, he glanced over at them, and the lawyer felt a brief tinge of guilt for pressuring her into coming. But it would be good for her. He was pretty sure of that. He took a deep breath. It smelled exactly like he'd thought jungle would smell like—wet earth, pungent, living greens, and a faint hint of rotting vegetation. There was a faint breeze. The air was humid, but the sun was hidden behind clouds, so it was quite comfortable. He could hear bugs and birds occasionally, but half the time he wasn't sure which was which. "*Exotique,*" he breathed.

He hoped to see dinosaurs—of course he did—and it didn't take a genius to guess Michael had similar hopes. He hadn't said that to anyone, especially not Sadie, but his wife had guessed as much. Not meat-eaters, necessarily, but he wasn't terrified at the thought. He didn't actually want the two security men to be anything but a wasted expense, and assumed if they did see any carnivores, the animals would keep their distance and/or likely run off. Sadie's unlucky experience had been just that. He would have been happy seeing just a plain, boring herbivore—Massospondylus, for instance, one of the skinny leaf-eaters—even if it just ate leaves, it was still a dinosaur. A living, breathing, previously extinct piece of the planet's history.

"I wish we had time to look around the animal exhibits," Michael said. He'd been taking photos the whole time, including several selfies right at the front of the park, with the larger-than-life Pangaea bas relief supercontinent and name towering above him. He couldn't keep the smile off his face.

"There aren't any animals," Luc said, frowning. *Not in the pens, at least*, he almost added, then remembered Sadie.

"No, I know, but maybe there are skeletons. I'd love to bring home a dinosaur bone. Not a fossil, an actual *bone*." Would customs let it through? He had no idea. He could claim it was a bone from his dog, maybe, a good luck charm, although it might be hard to convince them if it was a skull. From a baby triceratops, maybe. They'd had a few of those in the park. He could claim it was fake. Plastic. A novelty gift. At that thought, he headed off again, his eyes searching the cracked concrete for the off-white shine of bone.

"This would have been packed with people, *sí?*" Leo said to Hein, pointing down the wide thoroughfare. There were stores and gift shops and restaurants lining both sides, all the way down to the start of the animal exhibits.

"When they were open? Yes. This would have been the most crowded part of the park. Thousands of people."

Leo shook his head. "That attack would have been bad. Very bad." He gestured off to either side. "There is nowhere to run to. *Es un embudo.*" He snapped his fingers, trying to think of the English word. "Funnel." Nowhere to run except inside the buildings, where they would have been trapped. He'd seen evidence of it, bullet holes in the front of buildings and obvious explosive damage.

"Michael!" Luc called to the computer expert. He looked up. "We've got three days before our flight back. If we finish our work, you can come back here and look for souvenirs, but we can't finish our work until we actually start it." He jerked his head toward the Vaquero.

The young man sighed. "Fine." He glanced back down the concourse into the park before heading to the vehicle.

"Over there?" Hein asked Sadie, pointing across the parking lot once they were all back in the Vaquero.

She nodded. "Yes, south side. I'm pretty sure there had to be a separate employee entrance off 85 for the business park, but we never saw it. Maybe it's completely overgrown, or they tore it out close to the highway to discourage, well… this."

Hein wove the big vehicle leisurely around medians that were overgrown islands of grass. In a normal-sized vehicle, the grass would have blocked their view, but in the big APC, they sat as high as a commercial truck. "It's right over there somewhere," Sadie said, gesturing. The south side of the seemingly endless interconnected parking lots was bordered by thick foliage. Hein drove slowly until he saw the mouth of a narrow access road. "That?" Sadie nodded. He swung the nose of the Vaquero away from it, as the angle was too tight, then turned back.

"Will we fit?" Luc wondered. The road didn't look much wider than a walking path, and the bushes to either side had grown nearly together in the center.

"Our truck did," Sadie told him.

"This was marked 'Employees Only' on the maps I looked at, but I don't see any signs."

"See the post?" Michael said, pointing. "There was a gate there forever ago. Twenty years is a long time."

Hein nosed the big vehicle between the bushes and let it roll slowly forward at an idle. The bushes and young trees scraped down the sides of the Vaquero. After less than fifty feet, the thick undergrowth opened onto a large, shallow valley filled with tall grass and scrub. The road curved right, toward the mountains, and before them they saw a cluster of buildings.

"Ah ha!" Luc exclaimed.

Hein drove the Vaquero a short distance forward before pausing where the entrance drive forked. There was a badly faded metal sign before them, indicating Production was off to the left, Administration was to the right, and Facilities Maintenance was past Administration.

Luc moved forward and peered out the windshield. The Production building was four stories, and like Sadie had said, few of the windows were damaged, and most of those were on the ground floor. Off to the right, the smaller Administration buildings were half-concealed behind giant bushes and decorative trees growing wild. "Where to first?" Hein asked. He looked at Sadie, who looked at Luc.

"Administration," Luc said decisively. Hein nodded, turned the steering wheel, and accelerated slowly toward the cluster of buildings. The drive was blacktop, but nearly hidden under twenty years of leaves and grass.

"Can you do a circuit of them?" Luc asked. He pulled out his palm. "I want to document this just in case, and GenVen's position has always been that their records were lost when these buildings were attacked and destroyed."

The Vaquero's knobby tires were so big they barely felt the bump as Hein drove over the curb and commenced a slow circle around the cluster of admin buildings. They were small, square, single-story buildings, each about the size of a house, and had been painted in festive, tropical colors—yellow, orange, and pink, but after twenty years, the paint had faded where it wasn't obscured by the landscaping growing unchecked for two decades. The decorative bushes in some cases reached nearly to the eaves, and the diminutive trees, which had been regularly trimmed by the grounds crew, now, in many places, had limbs that were rubbing on the building walls. Many of the windows were cracked and missing, but... "I don't see any damage," Luc said, "not from bombs or Molotov cocktails."

"If there is any, it's not obvious," Hein agreed.

They completed a slow loop around the five buildings, and Hein parked half in the shade of a large banyan tree beside one of the low offices.

"All right," Hein announced. "Leo and I will check the buildings for any animals that might have made a home, and then it's all you."

He and Leo climbed down and sauntered into the closest building, rifles in hand, but appearing unconcerned. They were out thirty seconds later and walked to the adjacent building. In less than five minutes, they'd checked the five small buildings, and Hein looked up at them, peering through the windshield, and made a grand sweeping gesture.

Sadie felt a little sheepish as she climbed down, but then she got angry at herself. The chance of an animal attack might be low, but it wasn't zero. She had the scars to prove it. She looked around, then exclaimed and pointed. "*Vois! Est-ce que tu vois?*"

They followed her finger and saw in the distance a few flutters of yellow, dancing above the field grasses. "Are those...?" Luc asked.

Sadie nodded. The same giant butterflies she and Karl had followed into the park. The distance was deceptive—they didn't look especially large, but they were fifty meters away. Their wingspans were as wide as a man's shoulders.

Sadie watched them for a bit, then noticed something in the field near the insects dancing in the air. She looked at the field, past it to the tree line, then turned and examined the flora around the administration buildings.

"Do you see something?" Luc asked her. Hein was nearby, paying close attention.

Sadie pointed at the field. "Benettites," she said. Past them, to the tree line. "Ginkgoes." She gestured at the closest building. "Cycads. Extinct, or not native to this area. Plus horsetails and ferns, which either aren't native to this region, or are rare." She'd noticed a few extinct plant species during her previous visit to the park, but hadn't realized just how widespread they were. The greenery was positively primordial. She looked at Luc. "In your research, did you find any documentation about them bringing back plants?"

He shook his head. "No butterflies, no griffinflies, and no plants."

"Those are all over," Hein observed. "I've seen them in many different locales. They've spread at least a few hundred kilometers from here. I thought they were just native Mexican plants."

"They're native *Pangaea* plants," she said, "and I don't mean the park." She chewed at her lip, deep in thought. "You have to wonder what the long-term consequences are of the introduction of so many foreign species, flora and fauna. It's only been twenty years, which isn't very long, but once they reach maximum natural density, I wonder if they'll push out native species, and how far they'll spread."

"They've already seen small raptors in the United States," Hein said. "Texas or Arizona, one of the border states. The Texas border is two hundred kilometers from here."

"They'll continue to spread to the limits of the climate and human population density they can survive. Plants and animals."

"Isn't the center of the United States sparsely populated?" Michael asked.

"*Oui*," Sadie said, "but not as sparse as Mexico." She gestured at the building closest to them. She was behind Luc as they stepped through the door that Hein had forced open. The interior of the small building was dim, and they waited a few seconds for their eyes to adjust.

"They all have similar layouts," Hein told them. He'd followed them in. The interior smelled dusty, moldy, and damp. There was a desk near the front, presumably for a secretary, and half a dozen cubicles in the open space behind it. Along the back of the building were several offices.

"*Merde.*" Luc sighed. Sadie snorted. He'd been doubtful they'd find hardcopies of anything, but instead, the floor and desks were covered with paper. Apparently the occupants had left in a hurry. "Michael, why don't you look for computers, and Sadie and I will look through this paper."

"There's one right here," Michael said, pointing underneath the front desk. "It's not a Sirion Quad, though."

"What?"

Michael squatted down. "It's a Sirion Quint."

"Is that going to be a problem?"

"No, not at all."

"Then why are you... never mind, just get to work."

* * *

"Okay, I'm starving," Michael announced four hours later as he walked up. He looked around. Both Sadie and Luc had blackened their knees and were grimy to their elbows from sifting through the voluminous papers left behind in the offices. Luckily most of them were in English. For the documents in Spanish, they'd enlisted Leo's help.

Hein had already provided them with beverages before they'd thought to ask. He said, "I've got a cooler in the back of the Vaquero with sandwiches. We can go to Llera de Canales, or even Ciudad Victoria, but I figured this might be better, since you're limited on time."

"That's perfect," Luc said. Sadie and Karl had brought along a cooler during their visit, but she'd had so much on her mind, she hadn't thought about food.

They sat on the desks, as the chairs were moldy. Luc and Sadie were on the third of the five Administration buildings. There'd been a surprising amount of paperwork left behind, and it was taking a lot of time to sort through it. Most of it dealt with the day-to-day physical operation of the park—supplies, maintenance, personnel schedules. Michael was having a much easier time of it. There were only a handful of computers in each building, and it didn't take him long to pull their hard drives and plug them into the scanning equipment he'd brought. He'd cleaned out all five of the Administration buildings, with Hein tagging along. Leo had stayed with Luc and Sadie, scanning whatever documents they'd found in Spanish.

"Three-quarters of the hard drives I've pulled have recoverable data," Michael told them around a mouthful of sandwich.

"What kind of data?" Luc asked.

The young man shrugged. "I don't know; I'm not looking at it. The smallest had ten gigs on it, which could take days to actually look through, and I've got twelve drives already. I'm just scanning them for uncorrupted files. Maybe back at the hotel tonight, I can start looking through them, but it's going to be a very time-consuming process." He shrugged. "You'll likely have to do most of it; you know what you're looking for better than I do."

"I'm happy to finish looking, but I don't think we're going to find what we want here," Sadie told Luc. "This—" she waved at the paper-strewn desks around them, "—is payroll and how many Lem-on Squeezies each SnackShack was selling. The average number of toilet paper rolls consumed in each of the public bathrooms. How many towels and robes were stolen every week from the hotel. Tabu-lated sick days by park employees. Work schedules. Shuttle bus repair logs. How many metric tons of trash were removed every week. Likely we'll find the same on the drives Michael pulled. The infor-mation we want is going to be over in Production if it's anywhere."

"So do you want me to just wait until you're ready to go over there, or…?" Michael inquired.

Luc frowned. "No, if you've done all you can with the computers here, you can help us pick through the papers. Another set of eyes and hands will make it go faster."

Michael made a face, but didn't say anything. Hein had eaten his sandwich and was drinking a bottle of water as he nudged something on the floor near a wall with the toe of his boot. "What's that?" Michael asked.

"Scat," Hein told them. "Something got in through the windows and spent some time here maybe a month or two ago."

"Dinosaur?" Sadie asked, hating the fear in her voice.

"Family of raccoons, looks like." He turned. "I haven't found any serious damage in any of the buildings other than the bullet holes in the next one over, which likely occurred after everyone fled."

"*Oui,*" Luc said. "*C'est ce que je pensais.*" He was unsurprised. He'd been documenting the interiors of the Administration buildings. He had no idea what he was going to do with the footage, but you could never have too much supporting evidence.

"This is really the only thing I've found that seems interesting," Sadie said, lifting a sheet of paper.

"What is it?" Luc asked.

"A summary of utilities consumption—water, electricity—for the 'non-public' section of the property. Administration, Production, Facilities Maintenance, and R&D."

"Research and Development? That must be a part of Production."

She wiggled the sheet. "This seems to indicate it was a separate operation."

"There were no signs for it." Luc shrugged. "Stick it in the pile."

Sadie set the paper down in the stack of interesting items they'd found that merited a closer look. Over a hundred sheets of paper, so far. Suddenly, Michael jumped and stared toward the open door. He wasn't the only one surprised. "*Connard! Ca c'était quoi?*" It had sounded like a woman's scream, loud, and very close.

Hein moved slowly toward the open door. The professional hunter appeared unperturbed. "A cat."

"*Connerie. Ce n'était pas un chat.*" The young man's eyes were wide.

Hein fought back a smile. "Not a housecat, a jungle cat. There's wild, undeveloped land all about the park, and the park itself is more nature than not. The area is full of wild cats—mountain lions, bobcats, even jaguars. There might be bears, in addition to deer and wild pigs. All native. Even before you add in whatever dinosaurs might have remained in the area. You're from Paris, you said?" Michael nodded. Hein pointed at the world around them. "They call this nature," he told the pale young man. Sadie snorted.

Hein stood before the doorway, in shadow, and peered outside for some time. "Come here," he said softly. "Move slow, and stay in the shadow. Take a look." Sadie, Luc, and Michael moved in close behind him. Hein nodded out the door. "The second building. In the shadows, on the right side, under the tree. Do you see it?"

"I don't see anything," Michael said, squinting.

"*Non,*" Sadie said, shaking her head.

"Look for the silhouette of its head," Hein suggested, but as he did, the cat decided to leave. It sprang lightly out of the undergrowth, and prowled into the tall grasses, disappearing in just a few seconds.

"A jaguar," Hein said, impressed. He traded a look with Leo. "You don't see many of those."

"Should we be worried?" Luc asked.

Hein shook his head. "We're just in his territory, and he was investigating. He might have a mate around, but even with two of them, we shouldn't have a problem, not with so many of us. But don't anybody wander off alone." He looked over his shoulder at Sadie. "His presence should make you happy."

"Why?"

"Predators are very territorial. If there's a jaguar out there—and he was a big one—there aren't any carnivorous dinosaurs. They'd fight, or one would displace the other."

"Forget the dinosaurs, what about the jaguar?" Michael said. "That thing was huge."

"We'll be fine," Hein assured him.

Michael gestured at the Vaquero, parked nearby. "We'll be safe in there, right? If anything happens."

"Absolutely. From cats, from dinosaurs, from anyone who's got less than a rocket launcher."

"What about, you know, big dinosaurs? Aren't there big ones out there?"

Hein nodded. "Absolutely, but they're not going to attack the Vaquero. And even if they did… the biggest animal I ever saw was a mature brachiosaur. Huge. Incredible. It *might* be able to tip the Vaquero over, put a dent in the side, but that's it. The Vaquero isn't like a regular car, built with areas designed to crush in an accident. It's a rigid steel box. Nothing we don't want to is getting in." He neglected to mention that the brachiosaur, and his mate, had been in a berserker killing rage at the time, protecting their offspring by stomping guerrillas into puddles and kicking vehicles around like they were soup cans, silhouetted by smoke and fire. He'd been half-conscious at the time from a near-miss by an RPG, but still, it was a scene he'd never forget.

* * * * *

Chapter Thirteen

Pepe was a good combat commander, leading men in a fight, but he wasn't much of an organizer, Sandoval had discovered. Almost no one had thought to bring blankets, so the first night, most of the men slept in the vehicles, in the seats. After that, Pepe had sent men to the nearby town to buy blankets and food. And of course they'd come back with beer.

More and more men had arrived over the next few days, but before the end of the first day, it was obvious that they needed something more than pillows; they needed a place to relieve themselves, which meant another trip to town to buy shovels. Pepe sent several men into the trees beyond the large barn to dig a trench, and they'd laid boards over it.

No one seemed to know exactly how long they'd have to hide out there before moving on, so it was a good thing there was a town nearby where they could buy supplies. Pepe made sure they took off any unit designations before heading in, which made a few of the men grumble, but so far there'd been no problems. They were running a bit low on cash for supplies, though.

At night it got chilly, if not cold, but it was so wet, raining at least once a day, it was almost impossible to find dry wood for a fire. What little loose wood they'd found inside the buildings had already been consumed, and Pepe made it clear he didn't want them dismantling the buildings and throwing planks on a fire just to keep themselves warm. So the most recent fire at the back of the barn was a smoky, sputtering, weak mess, but the men made the most of it, wrapped in blankets, singing songs, drinking beer, and trying not to think about past glory and shattered dreams. Trying to look ahead at what might await them in Cuba if they could just reach it safely.

Ballasco came stumbling back into the barn, face pale even in the orange firelight. Everyone laughed at him. "How many of the coffee cherries did you eat?" Sandoval asked him. He was sitting on the bumper of one of the trucks pulled into the barn. Most of the vehicles were parked outside under the trees, as their numbers had grown.

"Too many," the man groaned, which prompted more laughs. In truth, he wasn't alone; several of the men had wandered among the coffee trees at length, eating much of the ripe fruit, only to later suffer from diarrhea. And with that thought...

Sandoval climbed to his feet. "My turn," he announced. He shrugged off the thin blanket he had around his shoulders and headed outside.

Under the trees, the light, steady rain was irregular heavy drips, and they seemed to have an unerring ability to find his bare neck under his collar. It was also shockingly dark, as even when it wasn't cloudy and raining; the leaves were too thick overhead to let even the moonlight through. He pulled out his palm, turned it on, and used the light from the screen to navigate between the vehicles.

Men were sleeping in the seats, the windows fogged on both sides with moisture. A few of the vehicles were running, not specifically to use the heaters (although that was happening) but to charge the men's palms without draining the batteries. Pepe didn't want them running the engines all night and burning up their petrol, so he'd been strict about it—and with reason, as without his scolding, the men would have used up half their fuel the first night, keeping warm and listening to music.

Past the dozen or so vehicles parked under the trees, the undergrowth pressed in, and it grew black as a mine. Sandoval used the light from his palm to find the narrow path they'd trudged through the ferns and vines. Their commander had wanted the ditch dug far enough away from the buildings that the smell wouldn't carry back, so by the time Sandoval reached the spot along the winding trail, it felt like he was alone in the jungle.

He smelled the ditch before he saw it in the feeble light of his phone. The coffee cherries had disagreed with a number of the men's guts; that was clear from the stench. Sandoval bent down and used the light to make sure nobody had made a mess outside the trench, then dropped his trousers and sat down on the narrow plank, hanging his backside off the back side.

He checked his palm. He still had no service, but he had several games on the device, and his battery was at 26 percent. More than enough. As he tapped the icon for the game, he looked around.

Beyond the warm glow of the screen, the night was black around him. The jungle wasn't completely silent—while the rain kept the bugs and birds quiet, the rain seeping through the leaves and falling to the ground in large drops kept up a constant patter.

Even if it hadn't, he was so distracted by the game, it was unlikely he would have heard the animal moving behind him. The forest floor was covered with damp leaves, which muffled all sound. Alerted by the strange noises, then drawn by the smell, the animals had come to investigate and discovered the valley was filled with creatures that seemed to be completely oblivious to the danger around them.

The Utahraptor pounced on Sandoval, knocking him to the ground, and with one darting move, ripped most of his throat out with its serrated teeth. It kept him pinned with one foot while Sandoval flopped and flailed senselessly, the blood pouring from his neck making wet sounds indistinguishable from the falling rain. Thirty seconds later, he was dead and still, and the animal crouched atop its kill, sniffing the air and listening.

The Utahraptor was a juvenile, barely five hundred pounds, and was still learning about these strange creatures. They were loud and walked on two legs like predators, but they were weak and not wary at all—and they were delicious. The stalk had been silent, the kill nearly so, and none of the other prey in the area seemed to have been alerted, but the raptor could hear, and smell, other raptors close by, drawn in like him by the promise of meat.

Utahraptors were much like wolves, in that they worked both alone and in packs, depending on the prey. When working in groups, the alliance was often uneasy. The raptor who'd made the kill swung its head back and forth warningly, as it had learned to do, to defend its kill. It was a reflex, part instinct and part learned behavior, but this circumstance was different.

With a snuffling grunt, the young Utahraptor picked the body up in its teeth and trotted away into the underbrush, the noise of its passing masked by the heavy raindrops falling all around, which slowly washed away the blood. It carried the body a hundred meters through the thick foliage, past other animals half-hidden in the undergrowth, to an open spot beneath several large banyans. It set the body down beside the stripped carcass of a previous kill, then looked up and around.

A dozen Utahs emerged from the shadows, most of them not much larger than the juvenile, many of them members of the same brood. They approached slowly and sniffed the fresh body. Their vocalizations—grunts, hoots, and hisses—were quiet, not confrontation, but communication. The scientists and zoologists who'd brought the species back to life and raised them had observed that even the animals raised in captivity were at least as smart as dogs.

There was a pause, then all at once they began to eat, ripping at the clothes and meat. Far behind them, back at the slit trench, a different young raptor got into position, taking its turn, waiting for another unsuspecting animal to wander by.

Inside the barn, Pepe was wrapped in a thick blanket and leaning against one wall, checking for messages and news on his palm, which was sat-linked and very difficult to track or trace—or so he'd been told. Still, once he was done, he pulled the battery out and put the unit away, then stood up to stretch his legs.

"Have you seen Sandoval?" he asked one of the men standing near the fire.

The man shook his head. "No, jefe."

Pepe looked around but didn't see the young man, who'd become a sort of assistant to him during the trek east. He had a list of things for him to shop for in town tomorrow, and he'd have to do another head count. Several of the men who'd shown up at the safehouse had apparently decided to leave on foot without telling anyone, but the secrecy wasn't unexpected. Even though they themselves were planning on leaving, they were doing it proudly, head high, as fighters. Sneaking off into the woods because you were afraid the offer of amnesty was a trap—well, it was no wonder they were ashamed and told no one. He wasn't sure where Sandoval was, but the man would turn up. He wasn't the type to sneak off.

* * *

There were streetlights, but they were widely spaced, and not very bright. It was just before 2:00 am, and the streets were quiet. The dark-skinned Mexican man ambled down the sidewalk, doing his best not to weave, humming lightly. He wore a faded green work shirt and worn blue jeans, both of which appeared black under the orange streetlights. He spooked a cat, which ran across the street, silent as a shadow. He looked after it, mumbling something, then continued on.

Half a block further on, he stopped, rested a hand against the brick wall of an abandoned business, and urinated into a recess. He leaned forward, pressing his forehead against the brick, and stayed there for almost a minute before rousing himself. He found the sidewalk again, almost headed back the way he'd come, then noticed his mistake, and continued in the right direction.

Thirty meters further on, there was a narrow gap between two buildings, and without a sound, he slipped into it. The gap was a meter wide and black as tar, and standing just an arm's length back from the mouth of it, he was invisible. He stood still, not moving for five minutes, his eyes scanning the street and listening. Then, finally, he lifted his hand to his mouth.

"Delta in position. Clear," Sergeant Miguel Alvarez whispered into the radio. The long-deserted office building was located on one corner of a T-intersection, almost directly across from him. He could see two sides of the building from where he stood, and several hundred meters down the street past it, before the street made a jagged turn to the left.

He waited. He saw nothing, but ten minutes later, his radio came to life. "*Charlie in position*," Corey whispered. "*No activity*."

Alvarez nodded. Corey was somewhere in front of him, opposite the far end of the target building. They now had it under surveillance from two different angles. He raised his radio. "Alpha and Bravo, clear to proceed."

"*Roger*," he heard, so quietly he almost missed it.

The night air was cool, and he was glad he was wearing a t-shirt underneath the canvas work shirt, the sleeves rolled down and buttoned. The shirt itself was untucked to conceal his pistol, three spare magazines, and the short fixed-blade knife on his belt. The night was quiet. In the distance, he could hear vehicles and one faint voice. The narrow pass-through smelled of fresh garbage and stale urine. He was glad he couldn't see the ground he was standing on.

Two minutes later, he saw movement at the far end of the street. Shadows. Two men strode quickly down the sidewalk toward him. As they drew abreast of the office building, they crossed the street and disappeared behind it. A short time later the radio hissed. "*We're in.*" Alvarez raised his arm and checked out the tritium-illuminated dial of his watch. It was 2:02 am.

* * *

Seamus and Torres stood just inside the rear entrance of the office building. It was coal black. They took out flashlights. Even clicked to their lowest setting and pointed at the floor, they seemed bright as daylight.

Seamus had his pistol in his hand, and Torres drew his. Without a word, they checked the ground floor together, then the second floor. No people or any sign that anyone had been inside the building for months, if not longer.

"*Entry team.*" It was Alvarez' voice.

Seamus looked at Torres and lifted his radio. "Go for Alpha and Bravo."

"*The flashlights are visible in the windows. Very. People passing by will likely see.*"

"Call them out, and we'll shut the lights off," Torres said into his radio.

"Sí, entendido."

Torres looked at Seamus and pointed at the opposite end of the second floor. Seamus nodded and headed that direction. Each floor had four small offices, they discovered. Three of the second-floor offices were empty of everything but dust and clutter. The fourth was filled with office debris—loose papers, outdated office equipment, and several metal cabinets, two of them locked. Seamus and Torres ended up in there together, working through the debris, quietly breaking into the filing cabinets, looking for any intelligence related to the guerrillas. Several times Alvarez or Corey alerted them on the radio, and they shut off their flashlights as pedestrians walked by outside.

After an hour, they finished with the office, finding nothing, and headed downstairs. The first office was empty of everything. The next three were stuffed with filing cabinets, their floors covered with thousands of sheets of paper. Seamus leaned against an open doorframe and sighed. "Oh, you bloody wankers," he growled. He lifted his radio to his lips. "We've got a bank vault of documents in here. It's going to be a while. Better get comfortable." He traded a look with Torres, and they got to work.

* * *

As dawn approached, the street turned from black to gray. The orange streetlights seemed to lose their strength, then blinked out as the city began to wake up. The few people who lived in the area, above or behind businesses, moved about. Vehicle traffic increased, and pedestrians appeared. The small grocery was the first to open, catering to the locals who passed by on their way to work.

The narrow pass-through alley remained comparatively dark, but as the sky grew bright, Alvarez sank down, sitting against the wall next to a seeping pile of garbage. As long as he didn't move, he was virtually invisible, and he still had a good view up the street. People passed by the mouth of the alley from time to time but never looked in.

The air slowly grew warmer. It had never gotten cold, but standing and then sitting without moving for hours had him chilled to the bone, and he kept working his hands to keep them from getting stiff.

The sun rose in the sky, and soon it was shining bright and orange on one side of the office building. Morning grew old, and the city was fully awake. And still he waited. Finally, his radio came quietly to life. *"Clear to exit?"*

"Charlie is clear," Alvarez heard.

With a grunt, he climbed to his feet, his knees popping, and moved to the mouth of the alley. He looked left and right, then studied the area around the building. Nobody was paying it any attention. "Delta is clear," he said into his radio.

He watched, and fifteen seconds later, Torres and Seamus walked into view. They turned away from him and headed up the street, out of sight. Alvarez looked around; nobody seemed to take any notice of them. He waited another thirty seconds, then checked his watch for the first time in hours. Just before 11:00 am. No wonder he was so stiff. He clipped the small radio to his belt under his shirt, stepped out of the alley, and walked away. He'd take a completely different route back to the hotel. The few people he passed on the sidewalk paid him little mind. Yes, his clothes were a bit soiled, and he smelled faintly of garbage, but in Xicotepec's struggling economy, it was not, unfortunately, uncommon.

They assembled in one of the two hotel rooms. Seamus and Torres were begrimed from elbows to fingertips from digging through dusty paperwork for the better part of eight hours.

"Any luck?" Corey asked.

Seamus was working his neck, trying to get the stiffness out of it. Torres shook his head. After the sun had come up, they hadn't needed to use their flashlights, and that had helped the work go a little more quickly, but still, it had been a grueling task, sorting through thousands of sheets of paper left at the site.

"Lots of paper, none of it cash," Seamus said. He nodded at a thin sheaf of papers on the nearby bed. "We've got a few names, business and people, to send upstairs to check out, but this seems to have been a bust." He looked at Torres. "You do this kind of thing often?"

"More often than you'd expect." Especially now that he was the liaison with CNI; he often spent hours reading through intelligence reports. It was a far cry from when he'd started with the *federales* and rode through the streets like a cowboy, kicking down doors and putting rough hands on *pendejos*.

"I think I'd rather gouge my eyes out. How about we all grab showers, pop into the restaurant across the way for lunch, and make a plan for tonight?"

They got the same waitress, and she gave them a big smile that was sincere, as the *gringos* had been big tippers. She brought chips and salsa and took their orders. Seamus watched her leave, then took a long drink of his cold beer. "I could use a nap," he announced. He traded a look with Torres, who nodded. The inspector was no longer a young man, and working through the night and nearly until noon the next day had tired him out.

"Any reason not to do the warehouse tonight?" Corey asked.

"Seems wrong to rush what feels like a vacation, but the air crew sitting on pins and needles, waiting for our call likely wouldn't agree," Seamus observed. He'd checked in with Chris Evers several times.

Torres waved the waitress over. "Excuse me, *señorita*," he said in Spanish, "but last night we saw a large crowd near what I think is the city hall. They were upset over the deaths?"

She nodded. "Yes, several people have died. They want the police to go into the mountains."

"The police chief didn't seem to like that idea. Is it because he is afraid it wasn't animals but *La Fuerza*?"

"Yes." She quickly added, "We have occasionally seen *Las Fuerzan* up in the mountains, and there has never been any trouble before, but two men, and before that children… many people over the last year or more. I think he has to do something. People are angry."

"Has he made a decision yet?"

She shook her head. "The mayor will make the decision. Later today, I think, there will be an announcement."

"Hmm. I'm interested to hear what that might be. Thank you." He watched her leave, then looked at the other men at the table.

"Satellite flyby didn't show any obvious FRAP presence," Seamus pointed out. "Likely the group the two men ran into went on their way." Kresge had sent them voluminous information, both raw data and images processed by military AI using algorithms, looking for vehicles with military silhouettes, men carrying guns, and the like. There were enough farms and residences in the area around the city that roads and fields were dotted with random vehicles. They'd scanned the images of the mountains north of the city, looking for any clusters of vehicles, military or civilian, without any luck. If there were FRAP hiding out in the hills, they were either being very careful, or their numbers were small.

"Negative sat or drone feed doesn't mean anything," Corey said. "They use a lot of civilian vehicles, and they know we own the skies, so they've gotten very good at concealing their numbers from airborne surveillance, travelling singly, or in groups so loose they don't appear together. Parking inside buildings and under cover. Mixing in with the local traffic." He gestured around them. "This town's big enough that they could hide a whole battalion here, and it wouldn't look like anything from the air."

"The residents would notice, though," Alvarez pointed out.

"But would they say anything?" Seamus asked. "*La Fuerza* has always enjoyed help, even in communities otherwise hostile to them. They're the bloody underdogs, after all. Everyone loves the underdog, even if he is a murderous wanker."

"Especially if ratting them out to the *gringos* will get your throat cut," Corey observed.

"If you were going to hide such a big, valuable... package," Alvarez said, taking a sip of his beer, "would you put it in town, where it was anonymous, just in another building, maybe where you could station men to guard it or keep an eye on it, or would you put it out there?" He gestured at the mountains beyond the city. "Away from the eyes of men, where it couldn't be accidentally discovered."

"The intelligence said Xicotepec," Torres reminded him.

Alvarez nodded. "Yes, and the truck came here. This is the biggest city in the area, where they have petrol stations, hotels, grocery stores. All places you might stop before heading up into the hills, or heading back to Zaragoza. But this is Xicotepec de Juarez," he reminded them, waving a hand at the city around them. "A city located inside the Xicotepec Municipio, inside the state of Puebla. And Xicotepec the municipality is roughly three hundred square kilometers of almost nothing but mountains and jungle. How many vacant farmhouses and buildings are there out there?"

"The only property we found connected to FRAP was inside the city," Seamus reminded him.

Alvarez took another sip of his beer and shrugged, but he'd made his point. The men turned and looked over the low roof to the east, where one of the surrounding mountain ranges, clad in a thin layer of mist, was visible.

* * *

Just past midnight, Torres drove into the industrial area. There were few lights, lonely beacons among the large, isolated buildings, although the waning moon did provide some illumination. He stopped the Toyota at a stop sign and heard the rear door open and close. The ceiling light had been disabled, and the interior of the vehicle remained dark. He drove slowly past the warehouse they were interested in.

"I don't see anything," Corey observed, peering out the open window.

Torres drove to the end of the street, then shut off his lights and pulled in beside one of the other buildings, turning around so the vehicle nosed out. Corey and Alvarez quietly exited the vehicle. "I'm in position; they're moving," Torres said into his radio.

"*Copy that, nothing here,*" Seamus said from his position on the other end of the street. He'd exited the rear of the vehicle and found a nice spot in front of a machine shop, hidden by several bushes. Torres was maybe a kilometer away, with the warehouse halfway between them.

Corey and Alvarez moved quickly through several parking lots, climbing over walls and jogging over cracked concrete festooned with tall weeds. They reached the back of the warehouse in less than a minute.

Torres had told them that the rear door appeared sturdy. Alvarez had a pry-bar, and he went at the door, but the door was steel set into a steel frame. After thirty seconds, he looked at Corey and shook his head.

The pallets Torres had moved up against the back wall were still in place. Corey climbed atop the stack, which got him high enough to see through one of the grimy windows. The interior of the building was dark, but he couldn't see much else, and he didn't want to use his flashlight outside. He examined the window for a short time, then squatted and held out his hand for the pry bar.

It didn't take much work to get the window open, although the metal frame flexed enough that one of the thick panes cracked in the process. It sounded loud as a shot, and Corey paused to listen. Both men tilted their heads and looked left and right, but all they heard was the soft breeze rustling through the weeds and trash littering the lot. Someone was playing music, but it was in the distance, outside the industrial park, the melody carried by the wind.

Corey climbed through the window, dropped down, then used his flashlight to look around. Thirty seconds later he pushed open the back door, and Alvarez stepped inside.

"Alarm?" the stocky sergeant asked.

Corey shook his head. "Not that I saw." They played their flashlights around the inside of the warehouse. It was perhaps fifteen by thirty meters and nearly empty. A few ragged pieces of paper were taped on the walls, remnants of the previous business. Concrete floors were stained with oil and other fluids. Empty bolt holes and faint, shadowed outlines indicated where pieces of large equipment had sat. There was a small office in one corner.

The two men spread out, playing the beams of their flashlights across the floor, nudging piles of trash with the toes of their boots. They worked their way to the walls, then across the building to the office. Inside it was a small wooden desk and an olive green filing cabinet that looked to be a hundred years old. Both were empty.

* * * * *

Chapter Fourteen

"Paper. I hate paper," Michael said. "There are no shortcuts with paper, just papercuts." He smiled at his witticism.

"Are you going somewhere with this?" Sadie asked him. She was tired from the activities of the previous day, and hadn't slept well. Once again, they were meeting in the hotel lobby before heading out. Was she frustrated at how little they'd found? She honestly didn't know. She hadn't known what to expect. A part of her thought they wouldn't find anything, but one day of exploration had proven that wrong. Reams of documents and dozens of computer hard drives.

"You only care about your prion—which is a kind of protein; I looked it up—and the butterflies. And the giant dragonflies that aren't dragonflies."

"Griffinflies," Sadie said.

"*Oui*. So instead of looking at every file in each hard drive, which could take months or years, I ran a search program last night, searching for any of those terms—prion, protein, butterfly, griffinfly, insect, even dragonfly and bug, in both English and Spanish." Luc nodded appreciatively. Michael had been his chosen computer expert, after all. "It doesn't work with images, but I figure those are secondary to your purposes."

"And?" Sadie asked.

"The only data I found concerned setting up butterfly feeders inside the park to keep the bugs near where the visitors were. Purchase orders for the feeders, internal memoranda back and forth as to where they should be located, how to make the nectar to fill them with, and two complaints by female guests about butterflies getting in their hair. I put everything I found into a separate folder, but I fell asleep in my chair before I could do anything else. I'll email what I have to both of you today."

"Nothing on where the butterflies came from?" Sadie asked in disbelief.

Michael shook his head. "I was falling asleep, but chronologically, the first thing I saw seemed to be a memorandum from a junior executive inquiring about the viability of installing butterfly feeders along the Promenade, which is what they called the wide street running from the entrance straight down the center of the park to the front of the animal habitats with shops and restaurants to either side. There was quite a lengthy correspondence between him and one of the staff biologists about it. Whether nets might be a necessity to keep the butterflies from bothering guests, etcetera. They wanted them close, but not too close. I got the impression that the butterflies were already around the park; they just wanted them where the guests could see them."

"I'll have to look those over; there might be something in there," Sadie said. They'd left the park after searching the five buildings. It had still been light out, but they were tired, and had they more than enough material through which they'd needed to sift. She and Luc had split the stack of papers they'd recovered from the Administrative offices which, at first glance, looked like they might contain pertinent information. They'd had a nice dinner together at the nearby steakhouse, then headed to their rooms to resume working. "Did you find anything? I went through what I had, and other than a few references to the R&D Department, I didn't see anything relating to what we're interested in." It had taken her a few hours.

Luc shook his head. "Not specifically, no."

Michael looked at the lawyer. "You didn't think you'd find much paper at all. If I'd known it was going to be like this, I could have brought a handheld scanner. Uploads and turns every page into a searchable digital document."

They glanced over as Hein appeared at the front entrance and waved to them across the lobby to let them know he was ready, then headed back out to the Vaquero.

"That Production building today?" Michael asked.

"Yes. It won't be so dark—it has a lot more windows—and it won't be nearly so dirty," Sadie told them. Assuming her recollection was accurate.

The drive to the park on the second day seemed faster. It was sunny and warm, and Sadie wondered how hot it might get inside the large building. The windows of the four-story office building that was the home of Pangaea's "Production" gleamed in the morning sun as they broke through the underbrush in the big Vaquero.

"Wonder what the story is there," Michael said, pointing at the lone vehicle left in the parking lot in front of the building as they rolled up the access drive. The Administrative buildings had been served by one medium-sized lot that had been empty of everything but vegetation. The lot for the Production building was larger, but in one corner of it sat a vehicle, faded by twenty years of sun, rusted nearly through, not a speck of glass remaining in the frames, sitting on flattened tires, and starting to get consumed by weeds and vines.

The very make and model of the car seemed impossible to determine. It had been a small sedan, but beyond that…

"Were they too scared to come back for it? If it was that scary, why aren't there more cars in the lot?" Michael mused aloud.

"Everyone drove them away when the shooting started," Luc said.

"Then why not this one?" the young man asked, pointing. "Did it refuse to start? Did they get a ride with someone else? Did the sound of gunfire give them a heart attack, and they never made it out here? We'll never know. I just find it interesting."

"We never saw any bodies," Sadie said, "here or in the park." She cocked her head, thought for a bit, then said, "I assume they were recovered. The Mexican Army did show up to fight the rebels, didn't they?"

"After the fight was pretty much over, and they were gone," Luc said. "It's not clear whether there was a communication problem, they didn't believe *La Fuerza* was so far north, or it just took them that long to get organized and get here. There are, as they say, conflicting reports. Surviving family members tried suing the Mexican military and Mexican government."

"I imagine that went nowhere," Hein said with a laugh.

"You would be correct."

The four-story building was rectangular, the glass exterior more suited to a middle-America office park than the Mexican jungle with picturesque mountains in the background. The sliding front doors were missing from their tracks, and maybe a third of the ground floor windows were fractured or missing altogether, but other than that, the building showed very little damage for having been abandoned for over twenty years.

"Looks like it did when we were here," Sadie commented, peering through the Vaquero's side window into the dim lobby. Hein and his assistant climbed out and walked into the building. They were back a few seconds later.

"There's no way you checked the whole building," Michael said through the open vehicle door.

"Any animal larger than a squirrel heard our diesel engine as we drove in and headed the other direction. They don't like people, and they don't like loud noises." He shouted, "Yah yah hah!" and banged the butt of his rifle on the door frame with a smile on his face.

Michael gave him a dirty look. "Yeah? Then why are you even here?"

"You remember that jaguar yesterday? We'd been there for a few hours. Quiet. That's when they might get a little curious, wander in, and investigate the smells."

"Then you shoot them."

"If we need to." Hein swung an arm and pointed inside. "Looks like you've got a little more work for you today."

The small lobby was at one end of the building. With the doors gone, a lot of leaves and grass had blown in over the years, and there was evidence of some animal visitors. Someone, years past, had vandalized one of the walls with spray paint—likely a boy named Carlos, as that was what had been painted in stylized, angular letters.

All the doors sported electronic locks with keypads, but with the power off, they hung open. Sadie gestured at Hein and followed him through a door into a large office space that took up most of the ground floor. While the windows were grimy, they still let in light, and where the glass was missing, the brightness increased dramatically. There was more than enough light for them to see.

There were dozens of cubicles in the center, with small private offices running down one wall. Sadie hadn't been able to remember many details about the computers or if there'd been any paper documents visible, probably because she'd had no interest, but staring at the scene before her, she saw that the employees in the Production building had relied quite heavily on hardcopies. There were loose papers on many of the desks, stacked in plastic trays, and strewn across the floor.

"*Putain de merde*," Luc swore. He'd followed her in. He sighed, then pointed. "We start with the offices. More likely to find something we want there." He turned to Michael and gestured at the cubicles before them. "These should be the Sirion Quads you were expecting."

"This building is huge," Michael said. "You think you're going to get through it all in two days?"

"The second floor was completely cleared out," Sadie told him. "It might be less work than you think."

"If I have to, I can change the flights," Luc said, "although I'll never hear the end of it from Marie; it'll nearly double the price."

* * *

Sadie and Luc leapfrogged through the offices. She finished her third and was moving on when she saw Luc sitting on the desk in the next office, looking at a plastic-coated three-ring binder, with several packets of papers resting on his thigh. He seemed very interested in what he was reading. Michael was nearby, on all fours underneath a desk in one of the cubicles, struggling with a computer tower. Hein walked in holding bottles of cold water, and everyone decided to take a break together.

"I think it's more humid today," Michael said. He had sweat dripping off his nose and wiped it away with a sleeve.

"At least you're out of the sun," Hein observed. Leo was bored, and after standing in the shade by the front door, he'd decided to do a slow circuit around the building, rifle in one hand, and water bottle in the other. The grass reached nearly to his waist.

"What do you have?" Sadie asked Luc, gesturing at the binder.

After a few seconds, he looked up. "I think this was intended for investors. I found supporting documents as well," he said, gesturing at stacks of papers covered with dense lines of type. "They were planning a huge expansion to the park, doubling the size. Private cabanas around a lagoon. More dinosaurs, of course, but also a water exhibit, and an area for extinct animals that weren't dinosaurs, like saber-tooth tigers, mammoths, and those giant sloths."

"That would be interesting," Hein said. "Doesn't the park in Japan have mammoths?"

"And saber-tooths," Sadie said. "When the geneticists first figured out how to bring back extinct species, they started with recent ones, where we still had tissue samples from mummified corpses and the like. Saber-tooths, mammoths, the dodo."

"Is it saber-tooths, or saber-teeth?" Michael asked.

"A lot of places had those," Luc observed, ignoring the question, "but they'd be an interesting addition, and far less expensive to buy or produce."

"Expensive?" Hein repeated.

"Sometimes zoos get animals for free, but often they have to buy them, whether that's crocodiles or antelope. A park like this operates differently. It's owned and operated by the same biotech firm that creates the dinosaurs, and it's creating them in a lab. But which ones? How many?" He waved the binder in his hand.

"This was the final product to be shown to investors, but these—" he indicated the paper packets, "—were various proposals that went back and forth between management for over a year. To a certain extent, which species they can bring back depends on available biologic material. Wooly mammoths lived during the Ice Age, and their remains aren't just fossilized, some were simply frozen. There are samples of hair, skin, blood, and bone. Complete DNA.

"With blood and DNA, it's just a simple cloning job, unlike with true dinosaurs that have been extinct for millions of years. Some dinosaur species they only know from a portion of a skull and a leg bone. The trilobite—" he pointed at the binder in his hands, "—they've found fifteen thousand specimens."

"Is that like a triceratops?" Michael asked.

"No, it's a… giant water bug," Luc said. "It has a round shell. Here, look, they have pictures for the investors." He turned the binder so the computer expert could see the slightly faded photo.

Michael made a face. "How big is that?"

"There were some small ones. I doubt they were interested in those; when it comes to animal exhibits, bigger is better. So, half a meter. Weird, which is good if you're looking for something to keep the attention of the tourists, and as cheap to produce as any of the extinct species. Many of the water animals got just as large as the land dinosaurs. Here, look at his initial list, when they were trying to figure out which species they wanted for their Phase Two expansion." He spread the papers out on the desk.

"You've got iguanodon. That was a very successful dinosaur—and there are a lot of specimens out there—but it's boring. Not much to look at, and the park already had a number of herbivores. Struthiomimus. That's like the dinosaur version of an ostrich. Lots of specimens in the fossil record, so common and not expensive, but unimpressive. Another one they were looking at was Argentino-saurus, because it might be the largest dinosaur ever, but between the fact that it might take twenty years to grow to full size, and there were only a few fossils in evidence, they cut it from the subsequent list of possibles."

"You've been doing your research," Sadie said with a smile.

Luc shrugged. "Boys and dinosaurs. But still, even I haven't heard of some of these species. Not surprising; I think they've found over five hundred different dinosaur species." He read from the binder. "Megalosaurus, sure. That's the first dinosaur to ever be de-scribed or given a scientific name. They found it before anyone came up with the word dinosaur. Smaller than a T. rex and more like a lizard. Like, um…" He snapped his fingers, searching for the memory. "Godzilla. But I have no idea what a Muttaburrasaurus is, or a Minmi."

Michael snorted. "That sounds like a character from Japanese anime. Actually, I think it is…" He cocked his head. "Third season of *My Ghost Vampire Girlfriend Apocalypse*?" He pulled his digisat palm out and typed rapidly. "No, fourth season. And this minmi, it's an ankylosaurus," he announced, reading. "Small, only a meter tall and three long."

"Most dinosaurs were that size or smaller," Luc told him, "and from a business perspective, I wouldn't be surprised if the park wanted more of them, as they would grow to maturity more quickly. Larger dinosaurs would have taken ten or more years to grow to an impressive size. The smaller ones would have been nearly full grown in a year or two. But if they're going to be small, they'd need to look interesting to keep the tourists entertained."

"Minmi has some small spikes and bony armor, but no tail club," Michael said, sounding a bit disappointed. Sadie couldn't help but smile. "What other dinosaurs did they want to introduce?" He walked around to stand next to Luc, and they flipped through the documentation together. "Brachylophosaurus?" Michael said, pointing and stumbling over the pronunciation.

"They've got information packets on each species," Luc told him. "It's a hadrosaur, a duck-billed dinosaur. See?" He turned the page and showed Michael an image of what the geneticists thought a live animal would look like. "It doesn't look like much, but it was on the list because of how many specimens there were out there. Genetic material was plentiful, which means cheap."

"I thought fossils were just stone," Hein said. That was one of the things that had always confused him about the dinosaurs. He knew how to track them in the field, knew their behaviors as well as anyone, but as for how the scientists had brought them back from extinction, he hadn't a clue.

Luc shook his head. "*Non.* They've been recovering genetic and biologic material from fossils since the 1990s. Genetic material has been extracted from Egyptian mummies, from mammoths, and other animals they've found frozen in glaciers. They were interested in this species because of how many near-complete skeletons they'd found, including a mummy."

"How can you have a mummy when something's a hundred million years old?"

"It's not a true mummy, it's more of a cast, but there was biologic material in it. And I realized that I'd heard of it. That Brachylophosaurus mummy—which was named Leonardo—was the best preserved dinosaur in the world, at least until the living ones came around. They were able to examine its last meal—plants and bark—and even see parasites in its stomach. Some kind of worms, which I assume is why it made the first list, but it didn't make the final cut. The ones they decided to go with are all quite something."

Sadie told Hein, "Originally it was thought that fossilization eliminated all DNA, but they discovered that fragments, proteins, did exist, and if you grind up enough bones and recover enough fragments, eventually you're able to put together a puzzle with just a few missing pieces. In some cases almost no missing pieces at all, once they refined their extraction techniques. Dinosaur DNA is easier to extract than mammalian DNA. To clone a mammal, you need nuclei, which means you need to find a white blood cell, which are rarer than red cells.

Dinosaurs have nucleated red cells, as do modern birds, so you find DNA in their red blood cells. Like you mentioned before, you don't have to recreate the entire DNA molecule; you only have to look at the sections of the strand that differ from animal to animal, or from contemporary DNA, and that's only a small percent. It's still a hugely time consuming and expensive process, which is why you only saw huge biocorps bringing back dinosaurs and financing parks like this; they were big enough to have the investment capital required." She frowned. "I hate that they're picking and choosing which species to bring back using such… superficial reasons."

"Like profit?" Luc asked, the corner of his mouth curling in a smile. "Profit is the only reason anyone brought back any of these extinct species once the first lab showed it could be done."

"Museums brought back a few," Sadie insisted.

"Yes, museums, with the aid of huge corporate donations, because that was the only way they could afford it. The corporations got a giant tax write-off and laid the path to bring back additional animals."

"For parks like this. What else is there?" Michael asked Luc, peering down at the folder.

"Euoplocephalus. It's an ankylosaur with a lot of spikes and plates, and a big bony tail club." He showed them all the image in the binder. "Smaller than some of the others, so it would grow to full size faster." He flipped to the next page. "Leptoceratops. Not nearly as amazing as Triceratops, but it had a beak and a small head frill, and only grew to two meters including the tail, which means they would have been nearly full grown within a year." He flipped the page again and pointed. "Microceratus. Frill, beak, but they barely got more than half a meter long. This one is interesting. Therizinosaurus." He showed them the image. "It had the largest claws of any animal in the history of the world."

"It doesn't look like much," Sadie said. She cocked her head. "Looks like an ostrich."

"A bit, but the biggest ostrich is maybe two and a half meters tall. This was eleven meters tall. *Eleven.* Its claws were a meter long. See, there's a human silhouette for comparison; it's like you next to a dachshund standing on its back legs. The claws were straight. They think it used them to strip foliage from branches, not killing."

"It's an herbivore?"

"Omnivore, they think. No one had ever grown one, and between that and its size, and the price of its genetic material, it was nearly dropped from the final cut. Full grown, they estimated it was three tons, but for big dinosaurs, that's not very heavy, and they suspected it would get to be that 'impressive' size within a few years."

Hein was in the doorway of the office, leaning his shoulder against the door frame. He crossed his arms. "So were they growing these species? Or just planning to? Pangaea opened with twenty-two species on the roster."

Luc lifted the binder. "It looks like they settled on an additional twenty species for the Phase Two expansion, but these binders were part of a presentation for investors to raise the money to do it. All the large, famous dinosaurs, Triceratops, Stegosaurus, T. rex, Brachiosaur—the ones with names everyone knew—they had when they opened the park.

"They seemed very concerned with shortening the 'production cycle,' namely how long it took to get a nearly full grown, viable specimen, so the land-dwelling dinosaurs in Phase Two were mostly smaller, so they'd have mature specimens more quickly, and species you likely haven't heard of, but that looked intriguing. Stygimoloch made the final cut." He reversed the binder and showed them the image. "Pachycephalosaur, four to five meters long, with horny spikes on the back of its head, and bony ridges running down the center. But the water exhibit was new. The animals they planned for that..." He turned a page and showed all of them an image.

"*Merde*," Sadie said, shivering.

"Dunkleosteus," Michael said, reading. "Stupid name, but *nom de dieu*."

"*Oui*," Luc agreed. "It makes a shark look like a friendly stuffed animal. That's the stuff of nightmares."

The fish had an armored face with the semblance of a beak, and the scales seemed to flow down to form massive teeth closer to the jaws of a vise than something that should be in the mouth of a living creature. "Dunkleosteus has the most powerful bite of any animal ever," Luc read, "four times as strong as a T. rex."

"It looks like a piranha mixed with a chainsaw," Michael said. "How big did it get?"

"Eight meters. Four tons."

"*Non. Putain non,*" Michael spat, vigorously shaking his head.

Luc laughed. "That's exactly the reaction they wanted. The other swimming dinosaurs don't look quite as evil, but they get bigger. The Mosasaur was as big as a whale with a head like a raptor. Megalodon got to nearly twenty meters, but it didn't make the cut because they thought it looked too much like a regular shark, and estimated that it might take twenty years to get to full size. Maybe more."

He looked at Hein and said, "Genetically engineered and cloned creatures are very tightly regulated and controlled, but the methods the various biotech corporations used to create them are often shrouded in secrecy, as they wanted to stay ahead of the competition. Some of the processes were trademarked, and most of their product was patented. This isn't much of an issue when cloning an extant animal such as a goat or sheep. It's much more important when you are trying to recreate an animal that's been extinct for tens of millions of years, and you're dealing with partially corrupted DNA. The less corrupted, the better.

"You want species that will bring in the rich tourists, and that you you have plenty of genetic material of with which to create your animals." Luc smiled. "But there are always surprises. Many of the scientists' initial theories about dinosaurs were disproven even before they started bringing them back to life, but much more so when they had live animals to observe."

Luc had done hours and hours of research. "For instance, many of the large herbivores had nostrils on top of their heads instead of at the front of their noses, which made many scientists think they spent a lot of time in the water. They just couldn't believe animals that size could exist on land. They've since realized that almost all those were land animals, and the position of their nostrils allowed them to breathe while they ate, because they would need to eat almost constantly to maintain their bulk. Sometimes the animals that grew from the samples were unlike what the paleontologists predicted. Colors, frills that were never preserved in the fossil record, that kind of thing.

"By the time they started bringing them back, they realized many of the dinosaurs, especially the two-legged carnivores, had fluff or full-grown feathers. Unlike the small lizards running around on two legs as depicted by Michael Crichton in his books, and then later in the movies, Compsognathus was covered in fine, downy feathers. It and many of the raptors are basically just flightless birds. But you can't blame Crichton for not getting it right; new discoveries are being made almost every day, forcing scientists to reevaluate their theories."

"Were," Sadie pointed out.

"What?"

"*Were* being made. Not anymore. Interest in, and grant money to support, expensive and lengthy fossil digs dropped to near zero once geneticists brought back actual live animals, even if they weren't genetically identical. It's like paying to dig up cow skeletons."

"How long does it take to get a species up and running?" Michael asked.

Everyone looked to Sadie. "What do you mean?" she asked.

"From the time they decided on a species, to the geneticist whipping up a fetus or an egg or however they did it—how long from the beginning until they had a living creature? I imagine there were always problems filling out the DNA, because most of them, didn't they have gaps in the genome?"

She'd done more than a little research as part of her involvement in the butterfly/griffinfly project, but about the actual cloning/biological production process, she knew little. "I don't know. I imagine it all took some time."

Luc gestured at the papers. "It took them over a year just to narrow down their selection of which species they wanted in the Phase Two expansion. Once they secured funding for that, I imagine it would be at least another couple of years before they would have animals ready for public display, which is why they would want smaller animals that could grow to near full size in the shortest amount of time possible.

"Oh, I almost forgot," he said, looking at Sadie. He pointed at the papers again. "Absolutely no mention of insects anywhere, but as part of the selection process of these twenty new species, there was a lot of correspondence with the R&D Department. They provided estimates on costs of production of various species, and likely viability of live specimens. That's a second mention of R&D. They seemed to have been important, but did all their work behind the scenes. Maybe it's in one of the floors above us. I'm beginning to think that's the only place we'll find any information on your bugs."

Sadie nodded. "Okay, break time's over," she announced.

* * *

They took a short lunch, as there was still so much to do. When they finally finished with the first floor, it was mid-afternoon, and they took another quick break together. They were all sweaty and dirty from picking through the detritus. For whatever reason, a larger percentage of the Sirion Quad hard drives were unreadable. Michael suspected it was because the office building, due to the windows, had gotten hotter than the small, dark Administrative buildings, but he couldn't say for sure. He removed and scanned nearly forty drives, but only found eight with uncorrupted data.

Together they trudged up to the second-floor lobby. There, Sadie pointed out the keypad and the retinal scanner on the wall beside the door, then pushed through and showed them the former cleanroom. "Hermetically sealed doors, UV lights, and those pegs are for the suits they would have worn," she said, pointing. "I think this was the heart of Production. Maybe this was where R&D was, too. But past here…" She pushed through the doors and showed them the vast, empty room. Dust motes glinted golden in the sunlight slanting in through the grimy windows. Her voice echoed in the bare space.

"You can see the outlines on the floor of large machines. There's a freight elevator in back; that's how they were brought in and out. I can guess what they did here, but we might never know."

Luc had his palm out, filming, and did a slow pan of the giant space. Once again, there was no sign of any damage due to combat.

"You said gene sequencers?" Michael said.

"That's just a guess. I did a little research into how they went from fossils to live specimens. Gene sequencers, 3D bioprinters, CRISPR, CRAKR, advanced biochem labs, incubators…"

"Incubators?"

"For the eggs. Dinosaurs pretty much come from eggs, and this is Production."

"I'm confused as to why this is here at all," Luc said. "GenVen had two biolabs. That's where they grew and raised the dinosaur specimens, according to their court filings. There was one in the US, but it was smaller, and subject to more stringent regulations. The big one was in Mexico, outside Chihuahua, which is a thousand kilometers from here. I don't see why they would have needed production facilities like this at all here, adjacent to the park."

"Maybe this is R&D," Michael said.

"It said Production on the door," Hein said, pointing with a thumb over his shoulder.

"R&D is likely a division of Production." Michael gestured at the space around them. "What is this, a couple thousand square feet? This seems the size of a research operation." He looked at Luc. "How big was that biolab in Chihuahua?"

Luc had looked into it, including photos of the facility. "As big as this entire section of the park, including the admin buildings. Bigger. They weren't just working on dinosaurs; that was only a small part of their business. Remember, they were in biotech, a multi-billion-dollar company. Vaccines, bio-synthetic implants, lab-grown meats, gene therapy. Pangaea was a small side project. It just got the most attention." He shrugged. "And it ended up being their ruin."

Sadie was frowning. This might have been where the butterflies and griffinflies were made, but they were designed somewhere else on a medical computer. The prion had been created on a computer somewhere, but it appeared increasingly likely that she'd never find those records.

Luc checked the time on his palm. "Okay, let's see what's upstairs; we've got two more floors."

The third floor seemed to be mixed-use. A few offices, a few cubicles, two conference rooms, and several small- to medium-size storage rooms stuffed with boxes, the sight of which deflated Sadie.

"I don't see any computers here at all," Michael said. "Before we start on those boxes, let's check the fourth floor. Maybe I can work up there while you work here."

Beyond the small lobby, with its marble floor and the still-glossy doors of the elevators, the fourth floor was unfinished. Only half the walls were up, and some of those were unfinished, and showed bare wiring. "This looks like it was going to be more office space," Luc said, wandering through the space. "Larger, private offices. That is a conference room," he said, pointing. "Executives would want to be on the top floor."

"I don't know if we looked in here at all, we just went up onto the roof," Sadie said.

"Hmm." Luc wandered over to the windows and looked out. This high, they seemed to be cleaner, kept free of grime by wind and rain. He looked south, across the big field that stretched away from the building across the shallow valley. There were random bushes, and a hundred meters away was a thick tree line. The sawgrass in the field grew in thick, meter-high tufts and looked like it would be tough to walk through. He—

Luc's eyes bulged in his skull. "*Sa mère la pute*," he swore. "Come here! Get over here," he shouted, pressing his forehead against the window glass. He heard them running up behind him. He didn't need to point. It was impossible to miss the animal slowly making its way across the field. The astonished profanity from the group was colorful.

The double row of kite-like plates running down the back of the Stegosaurus as it ambled through the tall grass somehow reminded Luc of the fin of a shark cutting through the water, but the Stegosaur towered over the grass, and moved slowly, almost majestically, more like a whale than a shark. The Stegosaurus was mostly brown, with a gray belly and green stripes along its back, neck, and tail. The pointed plates jutting from its back were covered in a thin layer of brown skin.

Its wedge-shaped head was narrow and small compared to the bulk of its body. The small head was at the end of a relatively short neck mated to a large body, with a high, towering back made to seem even taller by the giant, pointed plates running along its spine from its neck to its tail. The plates were largest—over half a meter in length—across its back, and grew smaller fore and aft. They swayed gently back and forth as the animal walked along. The meter-high grass brushed its belly.

"It's not eating the grass. I thought they were herbivores," Michael said. The dinosaur was moving at the speed of a walking man and intent on the distant tree line.

"Not every herbivore eats every kind of plant. Stegs prefer tree leaves," Hein told them, "preferably saplings. Its neck isn't that long, so it can't reach too high, although I've seen them put their front legs on the trunk of a tree and stand on their hind legs to reach higher. Those plates on the back are for thermoregulation. It can tighten and loosen the skin, making it thick or thin, and turn so the plates have just their edges to the sun, or completely sideways so they can soak up the heat. I think I read that they can enlarge the blood vessels as well." He looked at Sadie. "Paleontologists are mostly out of a job, but there's a whole new career in studying these creatures, seeing how they actually work compared to how they guessed based on the fossils. They've developed a number of amazing new drugs because of them."

Luc couldn't tear his eyes away from the dinosaur, which stretched twenty-five feet from nose to tail. It moved slowly and gracefully through the grass. "Is there just one? I thought they traveled in herds."

"Animals travel in herds for protection. Stegs have mates, and the males and females travel and stay with their children until they're large enough to go off on their own, but you see those tail spikes?" Hein nodded out the window. "They could protect themselves against anyone." At the tip of the Stegosaurus' tail were four spikes, nearly two feet in length. They jutted upward at 45-degree angles, two to the left, two to the right. "They can whip those around hard enough to bury them in an attacker and kill anything up to the size of a T. rex. I read they found fossils that showed a Steg had punched one of those right through the tailbone of an Allosaurus." He laughed. "The Thagomizer."

He got a lot of puzzled looks. "The what?" "What's that?"

"Scientists didn't have a name for those four tail spikes on the Stegosaur, but a cartoonist joked about it once, calling it the Thagomizer, after writing that it killed a caveman named Thag. The name caught on among scientists and paleontologists, and gradually became the official name."

"Really?" Sadie said. That didn't sound appropriate. "What cartoon?"

"*The Far Side*, an American cartoon series in newspapers. Before you were born."

Sadie shook her head. "Americans," she said with a disapproving frown. She continued to watch the big dinosaur as it moved away from them. She'd thought if she ever saw a dinosaur again, she'd faint or have a panic attack, but the sight of the Stegosaur had only filled her with excitement, as if she was a small girl once again. Of course, it helped that the Stegosaur was an herbivore and she was safe up on the fourth floor of an office building, while the animal moved by below…

They stood and watched as the Stegosaur made its way across the field and then disappeared into the thick underbrush. Sadie sighed, feeling the smile on her face. Then she looked at Michael. "Looks like all we've got is the third floor. Double-check that there are no computers, then you can help us go through the boxes."

He nodded, feeling like a little kid after seeing the dinosaur. "*Oui, professeure.*"

* * * * *

Chapter Fifteen

They had breakfast in the hotel restaurant. The restaurant across the plaza didn't open until ten, and the hotel restaurant was noted for its breakfast.

"I could get used to this," Corey said, surveying the table laid out with fresh fruit, juices, sausage, oatmeal, scrambled eggs, and coffee.

"I could get fat like this," Seamus said.

"Aren't you getting old for this?" Torres asked him. It wasn't meant to be insulting. He gestured at his temples. "You have more gray than me."

"And I earned every one of those little bastards," Seamus assured him, "but you're not wrong; it's a young man's game. At some point I'll have to think about retiring. I have a bit saved up."

"I hope it's more than a bit; you've been doing this forever," Corey told him, then frowned. "What have you been spending money on? Do you even take any time off?"

Seamus nodded. "At the end of every contract I spend a bit on travel." Their contracts were six months. "I've gone back to Ireland, toured the States, Italy, France…" At that thought, a small smile twitched his lips. He sipped at his coffee, set the cup down, then slapped the thick wooden table. "So. Plans? Ideas?"

"I scanned and transmitted all the documents you found to Kresge, as instructed," Corey said. "He was going to get some eyes on them, analysts or investigators. Am I right in thinking it's not just

217

him, he's still working closely on this project with the, ah, locals?" He glanced around. Nobody was close to them or overtly paying attention to their conversation, but it always paid to be careful.

Torres nodded. "*El pr...* the company president is in receipt of the same documents we obtained and has specialists reviewing them. Maybe it will lead somewhere." He flashed them a quick smile. "I check in, too. They want to make sure my information is as full and complete as yours."

Seamus fought a smile. "Bastards don't trust any of us. Not that I can blame them, with the reported size of these oil deposits."

Alvarez caught his eye and nodded. "I can't decide which I want more—to find it, or not to find it. Finding it would be..." He searched for the right description. "A big problem. For everyone."

Torres sipped at his black coffee and looked around. The restaurant was small, and most of the tables were occupied, but after a few initial curious glances at the white faces at their table, they'd mostly been ignored. Still, he leaned forward before he spoke. "Before you came down, I was talking to the desk clerk and one of the other employees. It seems the chief of police will be heading up into the mountains to search for the killers of those two men."

"Backed into a corner on that one," Seamus observed. "It will be a right dog and pony show, no doubt. That pudgy muppet doesn't look like he could find arse in an outhouse. What's the plan, to drive up hill and dale, making so much noise that neither animal nor FRAP will be anywhere to find?"

"Likely," Alvarez said with a smile. "Because then he'd have to do something."

Torres shook his head. "If he was going on his own, maybe. On his own, I suspect he would drive up to scenic spot and take a long nap before coming down to report he had no success. But the citizen pressure on the mayor was strong, so a group of concerned citizens will be accompanying the chief and many of his deputies, and everyone will be armed. Their blood is hot, from the deaths and the city fathers doing nothing for so long, insisting there was no problem."

Seamus didn't know whether to frown or laugh. "Those dull-eyed deputies we saw, with a dozen or two angry farmers and mechanics with guns, led by a man who looks like he could roll everywhere faster than he could walk? That's likely to be a right comic bloody circus. I can only hope none of them end up dead of misadventure—that they don't run into anything they're looking for, because both FRAP and tigers alike are apt to take a bite."

Torres gave Seamus a look, the corner of his mouth crooked into a smile. "Do you... want to go along?"

Seamus leaned back, both eyes and mouth wide. "Are ye shite mad?" he said a little too loudly. Corey snorted. Seamus took a drink of orange juice and rubbed at one eye, then lowered his voice. "It wouldn't fit with our cover, but even if it did, I can't think of a more likely way to die a fool's death than to shag after a rabble of amateurs waving their guns around and nosing after man-eating tigers, FRAP, or both." Alvarez nodded in agreement.

Torres gave him a measured look and spoke quietly. "If there's a *Fuerzan* presence in town, we haven't spotted it," he pointed out. "If there's even any cash to find, or someone guarding it, we could spend six months knocking on doors and peering in windows, bring an army of accountants and investigators into town to talk to everyone, read every scrap of paper, and still, as you say, come up empty. Until we hear back on the information we found and submitted, we have no leads, except for word of *Las Fuerzan* up on the hills north of town. If there *are* guerrillas up in the hills… maybe they're guarding something. There's only one way to know for sure."

Seamus chewed on that for a bit. "Bollocks," he finally cursed. He nodded. "You're not all wet. Still, tagging along on this cock-up is not something blokes the likes of us would do. But… being out in the field, checking mineral deposits or whatever oil company scout men do, accidentally in the same general vicinity, might be a play. We might keep a wary eye on the festivities from afar. It wouldn't hurt to be seen doing something other than eating and drinking. When are they scheduled to head out?"

"Tomorrow morning, I think. I heard early, but I doubt what Capitán Ibarra considers early is actually early."

"Is that the chief's name? Right. Well, you keep tabs on their expedition, and tonight we'll plan our shadow mission. Likely as not, we'll be stumbling all over each other; there's only so much real estate out there, but who's to say. We won't try to hide. I'll contact our fearless leader and see if I can get a high altitude drone or some satellite flybys for support."

"What do you have for us?" Corey asked, nodding his head at Alvarez to include the man.

"For all of us," Seamus said. "Seems like we've got most of the day to kill. There might be something hidden in this town. Wandering around like the tourists we appear to be might be the just the ticket for spotting something that looks out of place. There's a big farmer's market in the center of town, an abandoned Army post to the south, and then, of course, there's the big, majestic, blue cross."

"I hear it's a very romantic destination," Torres said to the two young men. It was the complete lack of humor in his voice that made it so funny.

* * *

The office had been soundproofed, but there was a difference between soundproof and soundproofed, and it shook slightly with the muted roar of a Hydra jumpjet taking off. Colonel Richard Kresge didn't even notice the noise of aircraft at the nearby airfield anymore. He was typing up yet another status report, occasionally pausing to take sips of coffee, even though he was already jittery from too much caffeine. Not that, objectively, he believed in such a concept as "too much caffeine."

His communications console beeped, and he hit the intercom button. "Yes, Jerry?"

"Sir, I've got a call from the president of Mexico. Are you available?"

Kresge laughed. He loved that his aide didn't make any assumptions. "Yes, put him through."

A few seconds later, one of his lines lit up. Kresge grabbed the handset, hit the button to enable the encryption, and connected. "Colonel Richard Kresge."

"Colonel," a warm female voice said in his ear, only slightly distorted by the encryption, "please hold for *el presidente de los Estados Unidos Mexicanos.*"

"*Sí, por supuesto.*"

He waited on hold less than a minute, then the man's loud voice filled his ear. "Colonel, *buenos tardes*, thank you for taking my call."

"Of course, Mister President. How can I help?"

"Well, I am calling for two reasons." He paused. "You are encrypted on your end? I wish to discuss sensitive manners."

"Yes, sir."

"*Bueno.* Well, first, I am checking in on the status of our... operation. You know the one to which I am referring?" For all the talk of encryption, neither man completely trusted it.

"Yes, of course. I have nothing substantive to report yet. They've searched the few buildings connected to FRAP that we were aware of, and found nothing but a few documents they forwarded this morning, which my people and yours are reviewing, but on the surface, they seem to hold no value. Nothing else was found."

"Hmmpf. Well, I am not surprised. Disappointed, perhaps, but... perhaps not. One less headache, as they say. So, are they heading back?"

"Not yet. They are going to look around for another day or two. There are reports of *La Fuerza* in the area. Likely unrelated, but they will investigate."

"Yes. Well, that is the other reason I have called. We have talked, *sí*, about the Cubans offering asylum?"

"Yes, but you hadn't decided how to respond."

The president chuckled. "I was not sure I needed to. It seemed more a stunt for the media than anything real. But the Cuban government has announced this past hour they are sending ships across the Gulf of Mexico to pick up any *Fuerzan* who want to leave. In fact, I believe they made this fact known to various units of *La Fuerza* days ago, but just now made it public, alerted the media. Worldwide."

"Ships?"

"To pick up and transport back to Cuba any and all fighters of *La Fuerza* who wish to come join their glorious revolutionary republic, or whatever lie is in the name. It is not just the announcement; our satellites have picked up evidence of this convoy. It just left port,

Havana, heading west across the Gulf. Nineteen ships, including two very large ones our analysts have determined were former cruise liners seized by the government. I will very shortly be in discussions with our Congress about this, and likely we will all be hounded by the media, asking questions for which I do not yet have answers."

"Isn't the Mexican government's official position that *La Fuerza* is a terrorist organization born from a drug cartel, not a legitimate political entity, correct?"

"Technically, yes. So the question is whether we should let any of them leave, or grant them amnesty or free passage, when we do not consider them soldiers but criminals…"

"From our intelligence, it seems most of those who've left the fight are simply taking off their uniforms and heading back home."

"Yes, but many others have not. Perhaps they are afraid of later retribution by government forces." Kresge didn't respond, but he knew that was very likely. Instead of lengthy trials for "war crimes," the Mexican military was far more likely to drag former *La Fuerza* soldiers out of their homes and shoot them in the middle of the street in front of friends and family, when they weren't making them disappear in the middle of the night. Death squads might have originated in Europe, but they were perfected in Central and South America.

"So you're weighing the political repercussions of amnesty. Well, not amnesty, a… suspension of hostilities. Ceasefire. Perhaps free passage to the coast?"

"What do you think about that?" the president asked him.

Kresge blew out a long breath. "From a military perspective… a temporary ceasefire could immediately end the war for good, stop almost all the fighting, as even those who don't want to leave the country will take advantage of the situation, depending on how it's arranged. A temporary ceasefire that may not be so temporary, depending? With the current situation, with their morale, once I see them laying down their arms, I see hardly any of them picking those guns back up when the ceasefire is over. They'll use the opportunity to disappear."

"And amnesty?"

"As in forgiveness for all acts committed during the conflict so they don't have to look over their shoulder? That would surely knock the wind out of their sails, but… there are a lot of points to consider. I don't need to tell you how ravaged your country has been by this war. As I'm sure you know, politically, it could be a very risky move. Your supporters have always liked your aggressive stance toward *La Fuerza*. Switching from zero tolerance to free passage to a country not friendly to Mexico, much less amnesty for deeds done, could have serious negative political consequences for you and your administration. As I'm sure you're aware."

"I am aware."

"It has to be a tough decision for you. These people have been waging war on your country for two decades. To just let them go, even if it ultimately saves lives…"

The president sighed. "Yes, and no. Many of the *soldados* now fighting were barely born when the war started, and can barely remember the glory days of *El Fraternidad Progresista para un México Nuevo*. Timotéo and his generals, who were behind the war, are dead. Our intelligence seems to indicate many of their units are taking this offer seriously, already heading east. In, how do you say it, anticipation, deliberately avoiding fights, it seems. And at the end of wars, armies have always surrendered. It is the civilized way, no matter how much I would love to personally slit the throat of every *pinche Fuerzan*."

Kresge smiled, then sat and thought. "This convoy, heading across the gulf. Military, naval ships?" he asked. "Or commercial?" That detail was important.

"Both," the president answered. "There are several large passenger liners, several small commercial ships, and they are being escorted by smaller Cuban Navy vessels, not a giant armada. Or is it flotilla, with ships? Fleet? Either way, half a dozen navy ships, most small; the largest is what they tell me is a very small destroyer. Not overtly provocative. However, that many civilian vessels could be stuffed full of Cuban soldiers."

"Do you think that's likely?" Kresge asked him.

"Do you?" the president responded.

Kresge thought about it for only a few seconds. "No," he said. "If their intentions aren't obvious, if they're not filling the Gulf with military ships and passenger liners, that means they don't have room aboard to bring enough soldiers to make a difference in the fighting. At this point in the war, FRAP would need an influx of tens of thousands of troops to turn it around, so Cuba wouldn't do it, wouldn't send troops meant to fight here; there is no upside for them. And it's not like they could sneak them off the boats onto a beach; they know everyone will be watching them. Sending purely humanitarian aid, however, empty civilian ships to evacuate oppressed fellow soldiers… it's great publicity for them, especially if you attack any of those unarmed civilian vessels and the news media gets video of bodies floating in the surf."

He thought. "There is no downside for Cuba in this. If you turn the rescue fleet away, you're the bad guy, and they're the victims. If you attack the soldiers en route or on the beach, that just looks horrible for you. The media will make it look like you were kicking puppies. And if you let FRAP soldiers board the boats and get transported to Cuba, their state media will spend weeks if not months publicizing their heroic struggles against what they already call your puppet government."

"That was my thought, but I wished to get your impression of the situation. An American perspective."

"I hate politics, although I understand them. As for the military perspective, if you allowed them to enter Mexican waters, to land, you would have complete air coverage, and could sink them in a heartbeat if there was a problem. FRAP has never had air assets in any numbers—drones, sure, a number of small civilian planes, and a few stolen helicopters, but that's it—and we've ground down their inventory to nothing. Each one of our drones can be outfitted with a penetrating bomb that could take out any of the ships in that convoy. Well, the military ships; those cruise liners are massive." Provided such an attack was authorized. Engaging forces of a third party nation was an action that would need to be greenlit, not just by the Mexican government, but the convoluted American chain of command that ostensibly was just the State Department, but in fact involved military generals and a Congressional oversight committee that, thankfully, he rarely had to interact with.

"Agreed, but personally, I hate the idea of letting communist Cubans step foot on Mexican soil, or sail to within sight of it. The Cubans might want to draw us into something, force our hand, for some gain we haven't discerned. They would have no problems even blowing up one of those ships, a commercial passenger liner most likely, killing the crew and blaming it on us. I'm not sure I want another international incident on my record."

"They're communists. They can't be trusted about anything. Ever."

The president laughed. "*Sí, claro, tú entiendes.* You are a soldier, not a politician, which is why I trust your judgement. Hmm." The president hummed to himself a bit, then said distractedly, "They want to land at Tampico. They are sailing slowly across the Gulf at a speed of twenty knots or so. That would put them at Tampico in forty-eight hours, so I have a limited amount of time to make a decision before they are sitting on the edge of international waters, just over the horizon."

"You're sending your own naval vessels out to meet them?" Kresge asked.

"Yes, but as you know, what we have is a Navy in name only. A handful of old ships in poor condition, most left over from the days of chasing drug smugglers. If there is to be a fight, it will be carried by our aircraft, Mexican and Raven. I have talked to your president, the American president, and he does not wish to get involved in this, so other than a few of your Coast Guard vessels monitoring the situation from a distance, and the Raven aircraft already in Mexico, we will likely have no more assets available to us. Meanwhile, I have *Fuerzan* sympathizers in my Congress and yours, urging me to call a ceasefire and grant them free passage to those ships. In truth, I see no good choice here, only bad and worse options."

"Whatever you decide, Mister President, Raven will support you in any and every way possible." *Unless the US government, which was paying most of their costs, decided otherwise,* but Kresge didn't see that happening. Cuba was a wild card nobody trusted. They were only entering the conflict at this late date because they saw some gain to the move. "Have our rules of engagement changed?"

The president of Mexico let out a long breath. "Not officially, not yet, no."

"Would you like me to move some of my air assets to the Gulf Coast, just in case?"

The president didn't answer for a few seconds. "That would be wise," he said finally.

After the call, Kresge pulled up a map on his computer of military airfields in the country. For simplicity's sake, they were color-coded to indicate if they were Raven, Mexican military, or a joint facility. He studied the map for a minute, then clicked one of the digital buttons. Information about the airfield spooled out at him, including the callsign of any aircraft currently located there. He frowned and clicked on Viking-23. "I thought so," he muttered. Kresge looked up a phone number, enabled encryption, and dialed.

* * *

Chris Evers was standing beside Mad Sweeney's left tilt rotor. Her crew chief had an access panel off and was looking at her expectantly. "No," she told him.

Hatch frowned. "But I just checked the log. The motor's almost due for a full—"

She cut him off. "Can you get it done, beginning to end, in five minutes?"

"Five minutes? Evers, you know it's a full two-hour job at a minimum. And that's if, after the tear down, we don't have to flush anything, or replace any parts."

"Did you forget we're on emergency standby? In the air five minutes after we get a call."

"Aw, come on, you know that's bullshit. The brass—"

"If I thought it was bullshit," she cut him off again, "I'd march in there right now and take a real goddamn shower, use up all the hot water, wash my hair properly—wash *everything* properly. Then I'd send you in there after me, you dirty grease monkey; you look and smell like those hairballs I pull out of my drain."

Hatch shook his head slowly, looking at her sadly. "I thought you were pulling the pin at the end of the month. Shouldn't you be more laidback than this?" She could see him trying to hide a grin.

Her Raven satpalm in her breast pocket vibrated, and she held up a finger at him. She dug it out and looked at the display, then gave Hatch a look.

"What?" he said.

"Evers," she answered the call. She recognized the number as coming from Raven HQ, but didn't recognize the last two digits.

"Evers, Colonel Kresge."

"Yes, Colonel, how can I help?" she asked, glaring at Hatch. He threw his hands up with a *What did I do?* look.

"You're currently at Miller Station?"

"Yes, sir."

"I've got a description here in my database, but I don't trust it. Describe it for me."

"Yes, sir. Small airfield. Four helipads, my bird on one, the other three currently empty. One two-kilometer runway that has yet to see any traffic since we've been here. One small hangar for maintenance, and that's where they park the refueling trucks. One building for staff that contains living quarters and the radio room. Property surrounded by a ten-foot chain-link fence topped with razor wire, seems to be in good shape. Nothing much outside the wire but fields and the occasional passing car; we're a few kilometers outside of town."

"I'm thinking of cycling some air assets east, and Miller Station and Victoria Base seem to be the only airfields we've got east of the Orientals between Veracruz and Monterrey." Tampico was nearly equidistant between the two, but in fact Miller Station was about forty kilometers closer to the coast city. "Apart from the helipads, inside the fence, how much space is there to park additional aircraft?"

* * *

Corey walked to the railing and looked out. Xicotepec was spread out before him. The city below was a riot of color, buildings, and vehicles, surrounded by bright green hills. The ridgelines were fuzzy with the mist that seemed common to the area, and that descended on the small city every evening and withdrew every morning—when it wasn't just flat-out raining, which it seemed to do at least once a day.

"They were right, it is a hell of a view," he said.

Alvarez was standing beside him, also looking out. "Very romantic," he agreed, which made Corey snort. They turned around and looked. Towering above them was *La Majestuosa Cruz Celestial de Xicotepec*, perhaps the prettiest and most modern cross Corey had ever seen. Constructed of blue and clear glass, it was probably quite a sight at night, all lit up. It was definitely the largest cross he'd ever seen in person.

The top of the hill had been leveled and paved with bricks for a *plazuela*—small square—for the cross, which was situated near one end of a rectangle that was as large as a football field. The west end of the rectangle was extended five meters out into the air, the bricks giving way to meter-square glass sections so visitors could look down the steep slope below them. *El Mirador*—the lookout—*de la Cruz Celestial.* At the opposite end of *la plazuela* was a small white building—bathrooms, as it wasn't a quick or easy trip up or down Cojolico. There was a narrow trail at the rear of the property meant for maintenance vehicles, but tourists had to walk the ascent.

"They weren't wrong; it was a bit of a climb," Corey said. Fourteen hundred and sixty meters of stairs, according to the large sign at the bottom of the hill for *Al Sendero de la Cruz Celestial*—the path to the celestial cross. It was a beautiful staircase, constructed of local stone. "I guess sometimes the clouds roll in, and they're underneath this, or at the same level. Looks like you're inside them."

Alvarez grunted and lifted the binoculars to his eyes. In any other situation, they'd seem out of place or suspicious, but they were exactly what tourists would bring to such a spot. In fact, Corey had spotted a retired couple trading a small pair of binoculars back and forth. There were no schoolchildren atop the mountain visiting the cross, and what few visitors there were mostly seemed to be older couples, wealthy couples, as most *Mexicanos* lucky enough to have a job were working it on a Tuesday afternoon. Corey's white face had garnered a few surprised looks, but mostly just polite nods. One young mother had made it to the top with a child too young for school, but old enough to walk.

There was a wooden A-frame sign nearby, posted with instructions and warnings, including one expected for a site that saw a lot of schoolchildren—*Prohibido brincar, correr o empujarse sobre el cristal*—Jumping, running, or pushing on the glass is prohibited, in addition

232 | JAMES TARR

to the standard "no drugs or alcohol," "no fireworks," and a 300-kilogram maximum for each glass panel, which were one meter square and tinted blue.

Corey felt strange, looking around, and couldn't place the feeling. Then he figured it out. He felt happy to be in a place inside Mexico that had seemingly remained untouched by the war. At the base of the cross was a fancy brass plaque, indicating the cross and its *plazue-la* had been constructed in October 2018. All that time, including twenty years of war, and it was still untouched and beautiful. It made him hopeful for the whole country now that the war, seemingly, was grinding to a halt.

"See anything?"

"*Una ciudad siendo una ciudad*," Alvarez said. He handed the binoculars over and pointed. "Up here, you can see the vacant areas a little better, how many empty lots there are. How few cars there are compared to how many there likely were before the war." He looked around, but none of the other visitors were close enough to overhear. "But nothing that looks like *La Fuerza*. No Vaqueros or gun trucks, no men on roofs with rifles, although we can see only so much, and the fog is rolling in." The cross was located on the northeast corner of the city, which stretched over two miles southward. The binoculars were a high-end military model with 30X digital zoom, image stabilizer, and a laser range finder, but even at maximum magnification, the far end of the city was fuzzy and indistinct.

Corey was scanning the city through the expensive binoculars. "Everything always looks peaceful at altitude," he observed. "No smells, no sounds. Where are the search parties going to go?"

"North of the city. Northwest of here." Alvarez pointed. Corey scanned the mountains and rugged ranges that bordered the small city. They were rapidly being swallowed by mist and maybe rain, but for the most part seemed free of the works of man, covered with bright green foliage.

"Is our truck four-wheel drive?" he asked. They'd taken the Nissan pickup.

"Yes, but..." The sergeant shrugged. "Not much tread on the tires, and no weight in the back. *¿Por que?*"

"It might get a little nasty out there. Rains a little every day, seems like, which means the roads will be muddy, and steep. The Toyota has good off-road tires and better weight distribution."

Alvarez shrugged. "I don't think it will much matter. We will drive around, not seeing anything, and trying not to get stuck, which is exactly what the citizen search parties will be doing. Most likely we'll be pulling each other out of the mud."

* * *

La Xochipila was thought of as the center or heart of Xicotepec de Juarez. The giant rock was at the intersection of two streams. There were crevices and small caverns in and around the rock, which was eleven meters in diameter. Early residents of the area, using stones and mortar, had built a platform atop the giant rock, with half a dozen stairs and some low walls. It had been used for religious rites. Locals would still light candles, stick them in the holes and crevices in the rock, and come to the location to pray. It was now more of a local tourist attraction than anything, though, located in a small park right in the center of downtown.

Seamus and Torres stood on the grass of the park and stared up at La Xochipila. A beautiful stone bridge passed by it on one side, leading to a narrow pathway. Colorful apartment buildings on the steep slope above overlooked the park. Seamus examined La Xochipila, looked around the park, then back at the cultural centerpiece of the city.

"Aye, it's a big rock," he said, bored.

Torres fought down a laugh. "Have you no appreciation for local culture? It was dedicated to the Zapotec god Xochipilli. He's the sun god, with a mouth like a butterfly. Xochipila means flower that springs from the water."

"It's a big fooking rock," Seamus said, "that some daft, long-dead twats built a little stone altar atop. That's not culture, it's… well, I'm not sure what it is, but it's not culture."

Torres was smiling as he eyed the local touchstone. "My wife would love this. This is exactly the kind of place she loves to visit. Small, quaint town, with interesting landmarks. I wonder what that cross is like…" Torres looked off to the east, but couldn't see the giant cross positioned at the top of the nearby mountain.

"You're married?"

"*Sí*, over twenty years."

"You're a tight-lipped bastard, aren't ya?"

The inspector shrugged. "I don't bring work home, or home to work. I have a wife and children, but I try to keep them insulated. *Federales* have often been targeted by *La Fuerza*."

"Smart, that." Seamus looked from Torres to La Xochipila and back. "Should I go find a shady spot to lie down in while you caress it with your eyes? Or can we head to the market?"

The local farmer's market was close, just a few blocks away, on the edge of what the locals considered "downtown." *El Mercado de Agricultores* was an informal collection of stalls and tables filling most of a small square and spilling out into the adjacent narrow streets. The local farmers sold their wares, everything from fruits and vegetables to locally grown and roasted coffee. You could even buy chickens, rabbits, and piglets, but not full-grown pigs—the town assembly had forbidden any animals over twenty kilos due to the noise and smell.

Seamus and Torres wandered around, looking over the wares. Seamus got a lot of attention from the vendors, who seemed to assume from his face that he had money to spend. He bought a couple of ripe bananas, and they ate them as they wandered.

"*Señor. Señor!* You like coffee?" The seller had a thick accent and a wide smile. "I have fresh roasted beans. You'll never have a finer cup of coffee than with beans just roasted. These come from my son's farm, just over the mountain. Arabica, a medium roast with hints of nut and caramel."

Seamus stopped. Some of the beans were loose, others professionally packed in colorful bags. "No doubt it's the finest coffee in all Xicotepec, but I'm a long way from a grinder."

The vendor, an old, slender man, blinked in surprise at Seamus' accent, but was undeterred. "You can take a kilo or two home with you. For you. For your wife?" Seamus smiled and shook his head. "No? How about a fresh cup of coffee? I grind. I have hot water right here." He gestured at a battered kettle on a hot plate.

"I appreciate your determination. One cup of coffee it is; you've sold me."

"Excellent." The man got to work, putting a handful of beans into a hand grinder, and spinning the crank.

"You spent all morning drinking coffee," Torres said.

"I spent all morning breathing, too, but that doesn't mean I want to stop."

The inspector snorted, and the two men stood and waited patiently, looking out across the square, while the vendor prepared the cup of coffee. One stall was stuffed with brightly colored flowers, cut and growing in small pots. Beside it, an old, wizened woman had baskets of herbs set out, fresh and dried. A chicken somehow got loose from its small wooden cage, and a young boy chased it. Much to everyone's surprise, he caught it quickly. There was laughter and applause. "That lad's quick on his feet," Seamus observed. "Chickens are a right bastard to catch."

"You've chased chickens?" Torres said dubiously.

Seamus gave him a look. "Sometimes you get tired of eating out of a can or a bag, and you don't want to have to worry if the locals are friendly to the FRAP and poisoned your food." He shook his head. "You know what's a bigger pain in the arse than catching a chicken? Plucking it."

Off to the side of the chicken-chaser and his newfound admirers was the mouth of one of the streets that fed into the square. Seamus saw a large pickup driving down the narrow, crowded street. The driver apparently realized he wasn't going to make any further progress and pulled to the curb. After a few seconds, all four doors opened, and five men climbed out. They stretched as if they'd been in the vehicle for a long time, then, laughing and joking, walked out into the square and looked over the foodstuffs. They seemed hungry, and immediately started dickering over tamale prices.

"Torres," Seamus said quietly.

"*Sí, los veo,*" Torres said. He moved around in front of Seamus, putting his back to the square, and in the process, concealing Seamus' face, and his interest. Seamus continued to watch the men over the inspector's shoulder. Five military-age men in a dirty pickup, not in uniform, but in the bland, utilitarian clothing that would have been perfect for day laborers, or FRAP guerrillas looking to blend in. Seamus might have assumed they were working men taking a lunch, but he'd seen the pistol casually stuffed in one man's waistband. And while his eyes weren't as sharp as they used to be, the front license plate showed the vehicle was out of Oaxaca, known for many things, including a lot of FRAP strongholds.

"*Señor, su café*," he heard. Seamus took the steaming cup and overpaid the man, who watched him with interest. Seamus blew on it, then took a healthy sip. He gave the man a nod.

"'Tis the best cuppa I've had in a long while, and that's no lie," Seamus told the man, who beamed. He and Torres moved on and found a small alcove, putting most of a fruit stall between them and the guerrillas shopping in the square.

Seamus felt his satpalm vibrating in his pocket, and he lifted it to his ear without taking his eyes off the men across the square. "Aye?"

"You been paying attention to the news?" Corey asked him.

"Not so much."

"Heard some people talking and went online. Apparently Cuba's offered to take in all the FRAP fighters still yearning for a communist utopia. They're steaming a flotilla of empty cruise ships, plus a few Cuban Navy cutters, across the Gulf of Mexico. To Tampico, which is what, a hundred miles from here? Mexican Congress is currently debating whether to call a ceasefire and give them free passage."

"Interesting," Seamus said, staring past Torres. He looked at the inspector. "Cuba's offering amnesty, sailing a lot of ships across the

Gulf to Tampico." The news made the man frown. Seamus spoke into the phone. "That might explain why I've got one—no, now *two* truckloads of the blokes stopping by the local market, picking up some food. Tamales, tortillas, fruit…" Torres turned slightly to better eye the second vehicle. It was an ancient Ford pickup that appeared to have been rolled down a mountain from the collection of dents it sported. Three men had exited it and were shopping for food as well. They seemed to know the first truckload of men well enough to exchange nods. "Maybe they're planning a seaside picnic."

"You need backup?" Corey said tensely.

"More eyes would definitely be helpful, seeing as we've finally got something interesting to look at. They're trying to blend in," Seamus said, "no long guns, no uniforms, no problems, but I know what I'm looking at. I'd like to know if they're staying in town or moving on, so if you could wander down here…"

"On the move." Seamus disconnected the call.

"If they are not here to guard what we are after, they are not our mission," Torres said softly.

"Well, we don't know why they're here, do we? Perhaps it's that lovely rock you made googly eyes at all morning. Perhaps they're on the way to sunbathe beneath the majestic cross. Perhaps I could go ask them. Nicely." He patted at his shirt over his concealed pistol.

Torres looked pained. "Please, don't." Eight to two weren't odds he favored.

Smiling, Seamus placed another call. "Reaching out to my betters," he told Torres. He hummed to himself as he listened to it ring.

"Kresge."

"What's this I hear about Cuba?" Seamus asked quietly, without preamble.

"Sergeant. The situation, as they say, is in flux."

"Aren't they always. Been badly fluxed more than once, I have. Well, I've got two truckloads of new faces here belonging to the opposition, playing nice, dressed and acting like civilians. I don't know whether they've been here and this is the first we're noticing them, if they just moved in, or if they're moving through, perhaps as a result of current events."

Kresge pondered that for a few seconds. "You're right on a major highway heading to the coast, and not too damn far from Tampico."

"Exactly my thought. Has a ceasefire been declared?"

"No, not officially, but there are… discussions, I guess you could say. Factors in play. As combat's not your mission, simply observe. Assume a defensive role. Only fire if fired upon. I'll keep you apprised of any political developments."

"Well, I'd like to thank you, sir."

"For what?" Kresge said warily.

"Because I was hoping this assignment could get even more vague, confused, complicated, and cocked-up, and you've delivered. Fluxed us good and hard. Bravo, sir."

* * *

"No, no, no. We can't follow them up there," Seamus said. "They'll spot us in two seconds. Pull over." He pointed, then glanced in the side mirror at Corey and Alvarez in the Nissan pickup right on their tail. Corey and Alvarez had raced into downtown as fast as they could, maintaining radio contact with Seamus and Torres in the Toyota, then they'd all followed the two truckloads of FRAP guerrillas out of Xicotepec. The FRAP vehicles had continued north into the hills, the paved road they were travelling turning to dirt and narrowing as it wound into the mountains. Seamus leaned out the passenger window and looked back. Corey leaned out his open window as well.

"What are we doing? Do we chance it?" Corey called out, but before Seamus could answer, Corey was out of the Nissan and jogging up to them.

"What?" Seamus asked.

"We've got a goddamn drone," Corey said.

"Bugger, I forgot all about that," Seamus said as Corey opened the back of the Land Cruiser and frantically dug for the hard case. "That's on you; I haven't piloted one of those in a year, I'd have it eating dirt in a heartbeat."

Corey found the case and jogged around the side of the SUV. He opened the rear door, set the case inside, and opened it. The case itself was a secondary controller with a view screen. Corey pulled the drone out, checked its battery, and set it on the grassy shoulder. Then he pulled out the controller and tugged the headset and goggles over his eyes as Alvarez walked up.

Seamus leaned into the backseat and snagged the case, setting it in his lap. The viewscreen lit up with what Corey was seeing in his VR goggles. It was a small reconnaissance drone less than six inches long that could be piloted directly or programmed using GPS waypoints. It wasn't a military drone, but a common, inexpensive commercial model that had proven very useful over the years, and Raven had purchased thousands of them.

The drone started with a low, buzzing hum and lifted straight up. Seamus turned the screen so Torres and Alvarez could see. The

Toyota quickly shrank to toy size as Corey brought the drone up to five hundred feet and sent it north into the hills along the twisting dirt road, which was half hidden beneath the trees. It only took him a few minutes to spot the two vehicles as they made their way along the narrow road, which was in poor shape.

"Try not to lose them," Torres said.

"Really? Thanks," Corey said from the back seat of the Toyota, grinding his teeth in concentration. "Great advice."

In the front passenger seat, Seamus bit back a smile. Torres and Alvarez were leaned in, watching the video feed from the drone. Corey kept it above and a bit behind the two vehicles as they headed into the mountains. Their progress was slow—the narrow road was in rough shape and mostly mud.

The drone tracked their progress over one ridgeline and down into a valley, then the road wound back and forth up another steep incline. "How long does the battery last?" Torres asked. The drone had been following the trucks for almost ten minutes, but it seemed longer.

"It's got 70 percent of its battery left," Seamus said, pointing at the readout, "which means it's probably fighting some wind." He peered more closely at the screen. "Corey, are you gaining altitude?"

"No, but they are, and I've got clouds and rain coming in. I'm going to have to drop down so I don't lose visual."

"Are we keeping track of the coordinates somehow?" Alvarez asked, pointing at the latitude and longitude displayed in the corner of the screen.

"The whole flight's being recorded, video and all the data," Corey said distractedly. "No audio."

The trucks reached the next summit, and headed down a short slope before entering a shallow, picturesque valley. The floor of the valley was filled with a riot of green, either thick forest or thin jungle. The road, now barely wider than the vehicles, snaked in and out of view beneath the canopy, the trucks slowly bouncing along. At the far end of the valley was a large, square field, and the trucks popped into view as they followed the rutted road along the edge of the field. Several buildings were evident at the far side of the field, underneath another dense patch of forest.

"Is that a farm?" Torres wondered aloud, leaning forward and squinting at the image. He pointed at the field. There seemed to be large bushes planted in rows underneath thin tree cover.

"Maybe," Seamus said. He peered at the buildings beyond. "That looks like a barn. Two barns. I don't see a house. Maybe there's one nearby.

"I don't want to get too close," Corey said. "Don't want them to see or hear the drone." It wasn't big or loud, but there was always a chance.

"Can you put it on station there and zoom in?" Seamus asked as the two trucks approached the larger of the two barns.

"Sure, hold on."

The camera on the drone had 15X magnification capability, and Corey zoomed in to the vehicles most of a kilometer distant. Several men appeared and opened the big barn doors. The spectators saw several other vehicles inside.

"Can you adjust the gain? Make it brighter?" Seamus asked.

"I think. Hold on." It took several seconds, but then the image brightened. The vehicles inside the dark barn came into sharper focus, and the men saw additional vehicles parked in the shadows under the trees. They all leaned forward, squinting at the image.

"Eight… nine vehicles," Seamus said, counting, "at least."

"How many men?" Torres said. The men exited the two vehicles, and many others appeared in and around the tall barn. "Two dozen? More?" The new arrivals were clearly handing out the food they'd purchased at the market.

"Are they FRAP? They look like FRAP," Corey said.

"*Sí, ellos son Fuerzan*," Alvarez said. He pointed. "Rifles."

"That explains why they bought so much food at the market," Seamus said. Corey kept the drone on station, and they stared at the display. The men were talking and eating lunch, some of them sitting on the vehicles. Others had gone back inside the barn.

"This doesn't feel like a base. A headquarters," Torres said finally.

"They look more like they're hiding out," Corey agreed.

"Two barns," Seamus said, chewing at his lip. "Corey, can you pull back on that? I want to see that end of the valley." The camera's view widened. The two barns, large and small, were set inside a dense patch of forest at one end of a valley over a kilometer long. Two ridgelines came together in a wide vee to form that end of the valley. The larger barn seemed almost built up against the sheer granite cliff that formed the north ridge. The ridge opposite it, on the far side of the patch of jungle, was a much gentler slope, with a low spot that dropped nearly to the tops of the trees.

"Is there any other way in or out of the valley than the road they drove in on?" Seamus asked.

"You could likely drive over the low spot in the ridge, there," Alvarez said, pointing at the low saddle. He leaned forward and squinted. "The road they drove in on might keep going past the buildings. The drone's too far away to see."

"And the foliage is bloody thick everywhere but that field. There could be a hundred vehicles and a thousand men under the trees. If they're not just passing through or hiding out here, the question is whether there's anything else in those buildings besides men and vehicles," Seamus said.

"You mean like pallets of cash?" Corey said, smiling under the goggles.

"Something like that. How far away from us is that?"

"Straight line? Maybe ten kilometers. But you saw how long it took to drive."

"Aye. A heli'd be the best way to get in and out, but it wouldn't be able to carry much cash. Well, not what a cartel would consider a lot."

"Is this where the locals reported running into *La Fuerza*?" Alvarez asked.

Seamus thought for a second, then shook his head. "No, that was at least another five klicks west. Corey, keep that drone on station as long as you can, but bring it back before the battery dies; we may need it before this is through." Seamus pulled out his satpalm and made a call.

"Sergeant. What's your status?" Kresge asked.

"We followed two truckloads of FRAP up into the mountains to some sort of base camp and are currently keeping an eye on them with our drone. We've got at least nine vehicles hidden in and around two buildings that look like barns in an otherwise unpopulated valley. There's a close spot, now a bit overgrown, that could have accommodated a helicopter. Enemy numbers are unknown, but at least two dozen, if I had to guess."

"Do you think they're guarding our high-value target?"

"Unknown, which is why I haven't yet called in our Peregrine to do strafing runs. Don't want to damage the merchandise if it's there. God knows the aircrew is like to appreciate doing something other than sitting on their arses. Do you think you could swing a satellite or high-altitude drone? They're partially hidden under cover. It's not quite triple canopy, so a non-visible-spectrum scan, thermal or LIDAR or whatnot, might reveal some details we're not seeing up here."

"Send me the coordinates. And Sergeant, tread very carefully. While nothing has officially been declared, unofficially, the Mexican government seems likely to honor a temporary ceasefire with FRAP, giving those who wish time and opportunity to leave on those Cuban ships."

"Hold on, Colonel, let me put you on speaker. Pretty sure I'm having a stroke based on what I thought I just heard. Could you repeat that?"

Kresge sighed. "I just spoke with the attorney general of Mexico, who's been in close contact with their president, who's been in meetings about this all day. It seems likely that by the end of the day, some sort of temporary ceasefire with FRAP will be declared. Whether it'll be a few days or a week, I don't know, but long enough for them to make their way to Tampico and board the incoming Cuban ships.

"*Valió verga*," Torres spat, and Alvarez growled, "*Anda a cagar.*" Seamus snorted at the vulgarities.

"Yes, well," Kresge said drily, "nothing's official yet, but if and when, I may not be able to authorize those airstrikes you mentioned. You'll have to handle things on your end as best you see fit." He paused to think. "If at any point you confirm the presence of that high-value target, I need to know immediately, especially if it looks like they're planning on taking it with them to Cuba. That's on the short list of things we absolutely *can't* allow to happen. Better destroyed than in unfriendly hands."

"Aye, sir."

"I'll get those eyes in the sky ASAP."

"Roger, out," Seamus said. He looked at the men with him. "We need to post a man up there to get eyes on. The drone's not going to last much longer, and we can't assume they'll be able to put something better on station."

* * * * *

Chapter Sixteen

Peter Hein walked in the front door of the hotel, paused before the security station, and waved to his three clients. Then waved again. They were deep in conversation and didn't see him. He signaled to Leo, behind the wheel of the Vaquero, that it might be a minute and navigated the scanner so he could make his way between the tables to the trio.

"You already know—not suspect, but know—that they created not just insects but plants completely off the books," Luc was saying to Sadie. "I know it sounds crazy, but it looks like they must have done the same with dinosaurs."

Hein was startled at that revelation. "What are you talking about?"

They looked up, surprised to see him. Michael was sitting at one of the small, round tables, a plate of pastries in front of him, and crumbs around his mouth. Both Sadie and Luc were sipping cups of coffee.

"I've done a lot of research on this in the past few months," the lawyer told Hein, "and I stayed up far too late last night doing even more research because of what I saw in there." He pointed at the table, where the binder from the day before was sitting. The proposed expansion plans for the park. "Do you know how much work it took to bring *one* of these species back to life? It's incredible.

247

"A year or more effort just to collect enough genetic material to get a near-complete DNA strand, then the work to fill in the gaps. And then, once they have that, they have to try to bring them back, inserting the DNA into artificial eggs. Incubating and hatching them in specialized labs with what they figured out, through trial and error, were the right temperatures and humidity. Seeing if they plugged those holes in the double-helix with functioning code, or if the fetus would be stillborn.

"In the early days, the survivability rate was only something like one in five thousand. Five thousand eggs before you get one dinosaur who hatches and survives beyond infancy. By the time Pangea was up and running, they'd drastically improved that, but still, they fertilized something like five hundred eggs for every dinosaur that was healthy and lived more than six months.

"These days, the technology is vastly improved. The company that owns the park in Japan apparently has an embryo-to-adult survivability rate of 4 percent, but still, today, it takes them two to three years from when they start trying to breed a new species of dinosaurs to when they have animals worthy of exhibit."

"Okay," Hein said, "and?"

"And I was up all last night reading and rereading the prospectus on their planned expansion," Luc told him, looking around the group, including all of them in the discussion. "Their proposal stated that once they got full funding for the new species and the construction of the new habitats, they would have functioning exhibits—with animals—open to the public within eighteen months."

"How is that possible?" Hein said with a frown.

Sadie nodded. "Exactly. It's not."

"It is not… if they waited to start on the project until they had the new funding," Luc said. "An eighteen-month timeline is simply not feasible. It is barely enough time now, and for their technology at the time, it is frankly impossible. To go from fossils to viable juvenile or adult creatures would have taken them three to five years." He looked at them. "So unless they were planning on lying to shareholders and VIPs… they had already started the process of bringing back additional dinosaur species."

"The production facility outside Chihuahua, I think you said?" Hein wondered.

"Anything is possible, but it seems like they had quite a lock on their secrets. I am thinking they wanted this closer to home."

"The R&D Department?" Michael said.

Luc shrugged. "If I had to guess."

"The biotech companies that were behind all these dinosaur parks. Did it surprise you—would it surprise you to learn they were doing things in secret? Off the books, off their own books?" Sadie asked.

Luc frowned. "I admit, it continues to surprise me."

Sadie snorted. "That's because you're a lawyer. You live on documents, rules, and records."

"Corporations like to have records, as governments like to have records," he pointed out.

"So you're saying governments have never done anything in secret? Kept their records hidden, or never kept any records of certain heinous activities?"

"Well…"

"Not every government is like Nazi Germany, documenting in detail every atrocity they commit. Most aren't. And corporations have even less of an obligation to humanity and the truth. They're only interested in profit. Is there any law that says they can't?"

Luc tilted his head. "Can't what?"

"Create new species of dinosaurs whenever and wherever they want."

That was a good question. "Well," Luc said slowly, thinking, "that depends on a number of issues."

Sadie snorted. "And to a lawyer, what does 'that depends' mean? If you're a corporation."

He thought about it, then smiled at her. "It means you do it, and then if they find out and don't like it, you argue about it in court for years, and eventually end up paying a small fine." Hein laughed.

"Exactly. And what kind of strict enforcement and supervision do you think there was in a country known for government corruption and bribes?" They didn't answer. "*Exactement*," she said. "They likely could do whatever they wanted without fear of government intervention. And between the insects and plants, it appears they did." She sighed. "We still haven't found any information on the insects, or the prion. Unless…?" She looked at Michael.

He shook his head. "I did the same search on the hard drives we recovered yesterday. There's nothing you'd be interested in. Of course, that's just a superficial scan of keywords, but I can't imagine a detailed dive would recover anything more. It's always possible, though, I suppose."

"Maybe today will be the day," Hein said.

"We're supposed to go back home tomorrow," Luc pointed out. They'd worked late and finished going through the papers they'd found in the Production building storage closets and offices, with no success.

"What's left?" Michael asked around a final mouthful of pastry. "Facilities Maintenance?"

"Yes," Luc told him. "From the satellite photos, it's a small collection of buildings, and I can't imagine we'll find much in the way of offices, computers, or paper. Plumbing and electrical infrastructure, most likely, if we can even get into the buildings."

"I'll get you in," Hein assured them.

Michael looked at him. "Do you know how to pick locks?" he asked, curious.

The older man smiled. "Something like that."

* * *

"There were actually quite a few buildings outside the perimeter of the park," Luc was saying as Hein piloted the big Vaquero across the uneven parking lot. He'd spent more time studying satellite images of the area than the rest of them put together, quite annoying his wife. "One here, one there. I presume they're all infrastructure or support, but almost none have been labeled on the site maps that I've seen."

"Undoubtedly there were buildings like that inside the park as well, hidden or disguised to go unnoticed by the guests," Sadie said. "Wasn't it Disney World that had a whole series of underground tunnels beneath the park for employees to move around out of sight? Garbage collection? They didn't want the guests to have the illusion ruined."

"*Oui*, although Disney World was built on a swamp. There's not much in Florida more than a few feet above sea level, which is why that tsunami a decade ago reached so far inland. Dozens of kilometers. So those Disney tunnels were actually built on ground level, and the park was built on top of them. Pangaea didn't have anything like that, no tunnels, at least not on any plans I've seen, but there are a lot of unnamed buildings on the public maps of the place, and many of the corporate maps simply have them listed as Support or Maintenance, with no further details. So I'm curious what we'll find at Facilities Maintenance."

Hein drove up the narrow access road into the valley south of the park. As they broke through the brush line, a flock of small, light brown birds was startled and took to the air right in front of them, and they caught a glimpse of several unusual animals bounding through the grass.

"What are those?" Michael asked. "They were fast."

"Compsognathus," Hein told him, "the smallest dinosaur in the park. Two-legged carnivores. Sometimes they work in packs, sometimes they don't. Fine, downy feathers—green, brown, gray, even blue. They remind me of birds, to be honest. Sometimes you see them alone, and sometimes they're in… well, 'flocks' seems a more accurate term than 'packs.' Not quite a meter in length, with the tail, and about a kilo; they're lighter than they look. When the grass is that tall and thick, they tend to bound like kangaroos rather than run. It helps them see over it. They were probably stalking the birds. They eat lizards, voles, bugs, small birds…"

Sadie was frowning. "How common are they?" she asked.

"They're everywhere. Everywhere," Hein repeated. "They're like squirrels, except they can't climb trees. I don't think." He saw the expression on her face. "What?"

"A single invasive or non-native species can have a huge impact on an ecosystem. Zebra mussels in the Great Lakes. Rabbits in Australia. They can cause multiple extinctions, or completely change the natural ecology, whether you're talking an animal or a plant—and we've got both here. Half a dozen plants for sure, two insects, and as many as twenty-two new species of vertebrate animals. That's how many were at Pangaea, right? How many survived the attack and escaped into the wild?"

"And lived and bred?" Hein shrugged. "There's no way to know for certain. Aarne Anders, who runs PaleoSafari, likely has the most comprehensive database of sightings, and I think he's confirmed the existence of fifteen of those species outside the park. Sixteen with the T. rex, although I don't know if he's still alive, and I believe he's a single specimen."

"There's a T. rex?" Michael said in surprise.

"There was one last year," Hein told him. "A juvenile, not yet fully grown, offspring of the pair that escaped Pangaea. I took a client on a hunt, and we tracked him down to the isthmus, but we... lost him in the jungle."

"How do you lose a T. rex?"

"There were, as they say, extenuating circumstances." Hein stopped the Vaquero before the sign listing Production, Administration, and Facilities Maintenance. The Production building stood tall and proud, and only slightly grimy in the morning sun. The low Administration buildings squatted under the bushes and trees that were slowly consuming them. Beyond them, the ground sloped down, and the foothills of the Sierra Madre Orientals appeared in the hazy distance. "We're done here? On to... whatever's in back?"

"Yes," Luc told him. On the map and the satellite photos, they were multiple buildings of various sizes, spread over several hectares. There were large aboveground pipes leading in and out of several buildings.

With a grunt, Hein turned the wheel and gently accelerated the Vaquero. They passed between the Administration and Production buildings. The access road followed a gentle slope down, and they passed through a thicket. Beyond it, the road curved across a field of tall, pale grass and thick, dark bushes, then disappeared over a slight rise.

"Where are they?" Sadie asked, meaning the maintenance buildings.

"Probably over this rise," Luc told her. "They were closer to the mountains." They both looked up at his comment and saw the mountain range towering above them. They drove in sunlight, but the ridgelines were hazy with fog, and behind that, thick clouds filling the sky.

"It looks like there's a front coming in," Hein said. "If it makes it over the mountains, we'll get some rain. Did anybody bring rain gear?" He looked over his shoulder.

"I have some… back in my hotel room," Sadie admitted. She'd never unpacked it; she'd been too distracted.

Hein chuckled. "Well, we've got the Vaquero to keep you dry, or the inside of a building."

Diesel engine rumbling, the Vaquero crested the rise. There in the distance, slightly below them in a narrow, shallow canyon paralleling the mountains, they saw what had to be the Facilities Maintenance buildings. While the paint had faded over the years, most of them were white, although a few small buildings had been red. The red had faded to an odd pinkish-brown.

"I think the red indicated electrical," Hein said. He drove a kilometer, and then stopped the vehicle on a small rise above the first of the buildings. There was a small parking lot that was overgrown.

Most of the buildings weren't much larger than garages. The group peered out the windshield.

"We're looking for papers or computers that would contain information on breeding those insects," Luc said, as much to himself as anything.

"I don't think you're going to find much of that here," Hein observed. Several of the fifteen or so buildings were smaller than the Vaquero. Many of them had large-gauge pipes exiting their sides that disappeared into the nearby earth. "Do you see that symbol with the diagonal orange stripe? That means water pipes under pressure. Water, electrical, maybe gas, but…"

"I think you're right, but due diligence."

They exited the vehicle. The closest building was one of the largest, metal in construction, and maybe ten by twenty meters, with a tall roof. There was large roll-up door one side, and around the corner another pedestrian door, metal in a metal frame, closed with a very large, very rusty padlock. Luc tugged on it with no success.

"It's not that rusty," Hein said, smiling.

"Can you pick it?" Michael asked.

"I do believe I can," Hein said. He walked around the Vaquero and opened the back. He rummaged around for a few seconds, then withdrew a sizable pair of bolt cutters. As he walked by, he winked at Michael, who gave him a dirty look.

"Occasionally we need to get through fences," he explained to Sadie and Luc.

The new bolt cutters went through the old lock with ease. Hein tossed the heavy lock to the side, set the bolt cutters down, and with Leo's help, wrestled the door open, fighting against rust and the grass that had grown up against it. Unlike her rain gear, Sadie had remembered her flashlight, and she stepped through the open doorway behind Hein, playing the flashlight around.

"Tractors?" she said.

"For lawn mowing," Hein said, pointing at the attachments. The air inside the closed building was hot, dusty, and stale. "Likely for just this office park area; the ones for inside the park would be parked in there, in one of those unmarked buildings you were talking about."

Sadie moved between the large, wheeled vehicles. She'd spotted a small cubicle against the far wall, perhaps an office. A small animal skittered off at her approach, but it was too quick for her to catch it in the beam of her light, so she didn't know whether it was one of the compys or just a mouse or possum.

"You can tell they evacuated in a hurry," Hein said from behind her, his voice echoing off the bare walls. "They're old and outdated now, but tractors like these would have been worth a good amount of money at the time. If this building had been closer to the entrance, likely it would have been looted." Luc had joined him and was peering at the heavy equipment. Most of the tires were long flat, the rubber cracked.

Sadie found a small desk with one drawer. A few notes had been tacked to the wall beside it, as well as a calendar that was browning and curling. "Anything?" Luc called out.

"*Non*," she said. It was hot inside the stuffy building, and she wiped sweat from her face as she walked out.

The next closest building was small, not three meters to a side, and painted red. They ignored it, as well as the adjacent building, which was maybe five meters square and had pipes as thick as a man's thigh running out of the walls and into the ground.

"Plumbing, obviously," Hein said. "I'd guess there was some sort of pump or filter in there." He stepped back and looked around, peering east. The very top of the Production building was visible. "Likely just servicing this area; it's too far removed from the park itself to have done anything there. I can open the door if you want…"

"Not necessary," Luc said. He walked through the thick grass, eyeing the various buildings. Hein watched him. "I think only these three are likely to have anything," he finally said, pointing. They were larger buildings, with no exterior signs indicating their purpose.

Michael walked over to the nearest one. Once again, a metal door in a metal frame, set into a cinderblock wall. Above the knob was a metal pushbutton keypad. He tried the knob and found it was locked. He tried the buttons, but they made no sound, and the keypad itself was so corroded, one of the buttons remained depressed, stuck. He turned and looked at Hein. "How are you going to pick this?" he asked. There was nothing to use the bolt cutters on.

Hein smiled. "One of two ways," he said and traded a smile with Leo. Leo jogged off and returned in the Vaquero, pulling it to within ten feet of the door. He grabbed the cable hooked to the front bumper of the Vaquero. "Twenty-thousand-pound winch," Hein told them as Leo pulled the cable out, looped the end around the knob, and tightened it. "Better stand back."

Leo climbed back into the Vaquero as the spectators moved back. He shifted it into reverse, inched it backward until there was no slack left in the cable, and then lightly touched the accelerator. The metal doorknob snapped off the door and bounced off the grille of the Vaquero with a loud *Spang!* before falling to the grass.

Michael had been hoping the door would fly off the hinges and was a little disappointed. "What's the other way? You said two ways."

"See if we can push down a wall with the front bumper. It weighs eight thousand kilos, empty."

"No wonder you've got so much petrol," Luc said, looking up at the jerrycans strapped to the roof rack. "Your mileage must be horrible."

Hein nodded. "And fueling stations are often few and far between." The twenty-five emergency gallons of diesel on the roof—which they cycled through to keep it fresh—would get them nearly three hundred kilometers.

Hein retrieved a short pry bar from his toolbox and approached the door. He attacked the damaged collar of the knob, and with a little effort was able to retract the bolt from the door frame. Luc and Sadie followed him in and clicked on their flashlights.

"What is this?" Sadie asked. Most of the space was taken up by large industrial shelving. There were scan codes on the front of the shelves.

Luc and Hein stepped in and looked closer. "Spare parts, I think," Luc said. "Plumbing and electrical."

"There are light bulbs over here," Hein said, agreeing with the man's assessment. He looked around what appeared to be a small warehouse. "I have to say, breaking and entering is a nice change of pace."

Sadie shot him a dirty look. "See if any of it has to do with computers or breeding animals."

* * *

It took them just over an hour to check the remaining buildings. They'd only found one computer, and it had been sitting in a puddle of water. Michael just frowned at it and shook his head.

"All right, how about we take a little break and figure out what we want to do next," Luc said.

"I vote for heading back into the park," Michael said.

"Yes, we know, you want souvenirs," Luc said, trying not to smile.

Sadie turned to Hein. "Can you pull the Vaquero up here, alongside this building?"

"Sure," he said. He didn't bother asking why. His clients often had strange requests. When they were wealthy clients, you got into the habit of not questioning them unless they were doing something stupid or dangerous.

He maneuvered the big vehicle alongside the low, white building, which had housed some giant electrical junction boxes and smaller industrial machinery of indeterminate purpose. Sadie grabbed a bottle of water and a sandwich from the cooler in the back of the Vaquero and stuck them in the satchel she tended to carry slung over her shoulder when she was working in the field. Hein watched her as she climbed up the front bumper of the Vaquero onto the hood, then onto the cluttered roof rack, then hopped across onto the roof of the building.

"What are you doing?" Michael asked, shielding his eyes from the sun as he looked up at her.

The roof of the building was a faded gray material. She felt it with her palm to make sure it wasn't too hot, but the sun was mostly hidden behind the clouds that were moving in. She lowered herself cross-legged and leaned to look over the edge of the roof. "Having a picnic," she told him.

Michael blinked twice, then laughed.

Everyone decided to join her, grabbing snacks from the Vaquero before climbing up. Sadie found herself sitting with Michael and Leo, while Hein and Luc sat together on the far side of the roof, looking out across the field to the south and talking quietly.

"How did you find yourself doing this?" Sadie asked Leo, curious. Both he and Hein had brought their rifles up onto the roof, which soothed her. Leo's rifle was shockingly ugly, which she presumed meant it was very effective.

The man was short, somewhat thick, and very dark-skinned. He wasn't bad looking, just not her type, although he had a great smile. "I was in the Army, but I got injured and had to find something else to do."

"You couldn't go back into the Army?" Michael asked him. The Mexican didn't seem to have any visible infirmities.

Leo smiled and pulled up the sleeve on his left arm. His upper arm was disfigured, half his bicep gone. The scar was pale, ugly, and thick. "The bullet went in here, and came out here," he said, pointing. "It is healed, and I can move it around freely, but it will never be as strong as it was."

He looked at Sadie and nodded at her arms, and the shiny pink scars visible there. "We match," he said. He stared at her, and it looked like he wanted to say more, but was struggling to find the words. Finally he said, "Do you have a man? A boyfriend? I see no ring."

Michael's eyes opened wide at the question, and he looked back and forth between the two of them. Sadie smiled. She was flattered by the interest and appreciated his directness. She pondered the question. Did she have a man? Was the thing with Seamus serious, or just a fling? "Yes," she said finally.

"Is he a French man?"

She shook her head. "I think you would call him a *pinche escara*," she said with a smile.

Leo nodded and smiled ruefully. He was unsurprised that she had attracted a strong man. Strong women often did. And she was pretty, with an exotic accent.

"What do you do when you're not doing this?" she asked him.

"I have a small house that I tend. I live there with my sister. It was our parents' house. They were killed when we were young."

"The war?" Michael asked. Leo nodded.

"I'm sorry," Sadie said.

Leo shrugged. "Everyone in Mexico has lost someone."

Sadie was enjoying the view from the top of the building. They were surrounded by nature, fields and forest, and farther to the north and west, actual jungle. The park had been situated in a biosphere for a reason; the area was beautiful and had many natural attractions even before they'd added dinosaurs. Luc had his palm out again and was taking photos of the buildings, the fields beyond them, and the low mountain range in the distance.

She spotted a line in the fields west of the cluster of buildings, and her eyes followed it. The grass in the valley had almost completely overgrown it, but as it wound its way up into the foothills, she saw it was a Jeep trail, a two-track. She squinted and traced it up further. It seemed to be heading toward a distant saddle, a low pass between two higher peaks in the mountain range, now gray and indistinct.

"We've got rain coming," Hein remarked loud enough for everyone to hear. He was staring up at the mountains as well. The front had pushed over, and dark clouds were heading their way. "Maybe half an hour," he guessed.

Sadie looked at the rain inbound, then studied the mountains. The steep slopes were nearly bare of trees to the south, but to the north, the foliage was thick, even on the steep slopes. One long, sharply-angled face to the northwest bristled with green, bushes and trees. It seemed to drop almost straight down into a thick patch of near-jungle spreading out from the cliff face more than a kilometer away. Sadie stared at it and frowned. She shielded her eyes with a hand, and squinted. "Do you have binoculars?" she asked Leo.

"*Sí, un momento*," he said, jumping up. He stepped over to the Vaquero and climbed down. He was back in just a few seconds and handed her a well-worn pair of Steiner 10x42 binoculars.

Sadie stood, raised the binoculars to her eyes, and fiddled with the knob until everything was in sharp focus. Then she peered to the northwest at the dense patch of jungle.

"There's a building there," she announced. It was hidden beneath the trees, its lines and corners disguised by the dense shadows and the vines climbing it, but with the binoculars, it was unmistakable. And it wasn't small.

* * *

"It wasn't on any of the maps," Luc said as the Vaquero bounced across the field toward the distant edifice.

"It could be newer, and they just didn't update the maps," Hein said with a shrug. "Is it outside the park?"

"Yes, southwest of the park boundary, but on Pangaea property, at least half a kilometer from the nearest animal habitat." Luc peered out the windshield. The sky was growing dim as the rain clouds approached. "I see why I didn't spot it on the satellite photos; the trees have grown up all around it."

"On top of it," Michael said. "Vines. There might even be bushes growing on the roof," he said, squinting. Twenty years was such a long time.

"There's the access road," Leo said, pointing off to their right. Everyone looked. They couldn't see a road, just a somewhat regular line across the field, a gap between the wild tufts of grass. "It looks like it must come this way from the back side of the Administration complex."

Hein grunted and turned the wheel. He cut away from the building toward the half-glimpsed road, the Vaquero bouncing up and down. When he reached the road, they saw patches of pavement between long, thick grass that had grown around and through the asphalt. He turned the big vehicle, and once on the ghost of a road, their journey smoothed out. A few trees sprang up to either side of them, palms and pines and banyans, and then the road plunged into deep jungle, almost as if nature itself had thrown a switch. The trees were so thick overhead they nearly blocked the sight of the sky, wrapped with vines that draped across their path, and thick, glossy bushes reaching to the windows of the Vaquero.

Sadie had spotted the narrow south end of the building through the trees. The parking lot for the mystery building was on the north side of it, big enough for twenty vehicles. Where it wasn't covered with dead leaves, it was ruptured and jagged, and grass and bushes had burst through. "It doesn't look like anyone's driven through here in years, if ever," Hein said, leaning over the steering wheel to study the ground. Vines scraped across the windshield as the vehicle slowly rolled forward.

"This area, running north along the mountain range at the back of the park, looked close to jungle on the satellite photos. Is this rainforest?" Luc asked, peering out of the window.

"Close enough," Sadie told him. "It's in a valley, and at the base of a steep, east-facing slope, moist and sheltered. It's a bit of a microclimate. There are a number of them throughout the biosphere." Farther north, the microclimate extended into the park, and it was there her butterflies had nested on dewy vines.

Hein drove across the lot until his front tires bumped against the curb directly before the entrance doors. The front door was glass, and set back under a small overhang. The frosted glass in the doors wasn't even cracked. Everyone squinted to read the lettering on the wall beside the doors, some ten meters away.

"Research and Development," Michael announced, his young eyes still sharp. "*Putain de merde*, you found it."

* * * * *

Chapter Seventeen

They climbed out of the Vaquero. Luc pulled out his palm and took photos of the building. It was long and low, a single-story edifice with a high roof, halfway between industrial and an office building in design, brick and glass. Small, decorative, flowering shrubs had been planted along the front of the structure, and after twenty years, some had died and been replaced by weeds and grass, and others had thrived and now reached nearly to the roof fifteen feet overhead.

"Different architecture," Luc observed.

"Very mid-century America," Sadie agreed. Brown brick and frosted glass. There was no way to tell what might be inside the building from the exterior.

The entrance was three concrete steps up from the parking lot. Michael nearly ran up them, he was so excited. The sign was textured steel letters set into the bricks beside the glass front door, and Michael reached out a hand and ran his fingers along them.

PANGAEA S.A.
RESEARCH & DEVELOPMENT

The steel of the letters was black, but it was impossible to tell if that had been their original color. Michael couldn't keep the smile off his face. He turned and looked over his shoulder as everyone else approached. "Do you have your lockpicks?" he asked.

Hein stepped up to the door, rifle in one hand, and tried the handle. When he pulled, it swung open with a long, moaning creak. Michael stared past the open door into the dark exterior and shivered, taking half a step back.

"That's like a haunted house sound," he said. "*Un film d'horreur. S'il vous plait*," he said in a sinister voice, raising his hands and waving them around, "come on in, absolutely no murderous spirits in here. *Pas de spectres, pas de monstres.*" He turned and gave everyone an exaggerated smile and two thumbs up.

"Have you noticed that in those horror movies none of the people have rifles?" Hein asked, and he stepped through the doorway into the gloom, rifle casually held in both hands. Sadie and Luc followed right after him. After a guilty glance at Leo, Michael followed them in. Leo found a broken branch nearby and used it to wedge the door open to give them more light.

They found themselves in a small, square lobby with two moldy chairs and one sagging loveseat. In the middle of the left wall was a sliding window above a counter, and beside that was a door. The wall facing the front door was festooned with photos and documents in frames. Sadie moved close, pulling out her flashlight and looking everything over. "Opening day in the park," she observed. There were two men in suits cutting a giant ribbon with a giant pair of scissors, dozens of beaming people standing behind them. "Patents and trademarks on some of the dinosaurs. Miniature map of the park."

Luc moved to the interior sliding window, which was cracked open. He opened it the rest of the way and peered in. "Secretary," he said. "She probably buzzed visitors in." He pointed at the keypad beside the door.

Sadie tried the handle, and it turned easily. She pulled, and the door swung open, revealing an even darker interior. Then they all looked up.

"Rain's here," Hein announced. They heard it approaching, a rush drawing closer, and then big, heavy drops began falling outside.

"It's rainforest now," Michael said to Luc with a smile. They stood and looked out the open front door as the isolated drops increased to a steady beat, and then grew to a downpour, hitting so hard they were bouncing off the Vaquero's hood in secondary spray. The overgrown space underneath the trees went from dim to dark, and the beam from Sadie's flashlight seemed to double in brightness. Everyone else pulled out their flashlights and turned them on.

Through the door, the secretary's desk was on the left, and to the right were several small executive offices. There was a pink laptop sitting open on the secretary's desk. "That's a Jadony," Michael said dismissively. "It was garbage when it was new." He opened the first office door and swung his flashlight beam around. "Computer," he announced. It was sitting atop the desk against the side wall. He strode into the room, bent down, and peered at it. "Hakkari," he read. "I think it's a Hakkari 23. I've never seen one in person." He turned and looked at the rest of the group clustered beyond the open doorway, watching him. "It's a specialized medical computer. Genetic engineering. Bio-CAD-CAM, I think the term was. We're in the right place." The wall facing him sported a small bookcase, and there were several dozen books there. What few titles he could read were very technical. There were also many binders and folders. He pointed them out.

The office had a row of windows. They'd darkened with age and grime, and were now streaked with running water as the rain came pounding down. Michael peered out the window. It seemed dark as night outside. The jungle started just a few feet from the building.

"Will that hard drive be any good?" Luc asked him.

Michael shrugged. "Only one way to know for sure."

"Let's check the rest of the building out first."

There were two more small offices, both desks sporting Hakkari medical computers. Between the computers and the books on display in every office, they seemed to belong to people with serious science backgrounds. There were names on all the doors, and Sadie made a note of them—two men and one woman. Their names weren't familiar to her or, surprisingly, Luc.

"Didn't you review all the corporate records?" she asked him.

"Yes, but I didn't memorize the employee roster. The park had hundreds of employees, maybe close to a thousand. They were divided by department, but as I said, there was never any listing of Research and Development. All this—" he waved a hand at the building around them, "—must have been included in another department."

"I wonder if one of them is the scientist who designed the insects," she wondered.

"Maybe they all did," Luc said.

She shook her head. "*Je ne pense pas*. If it was a group project, there would have been records, communication back and forth, progress reports. This feels like someone told management they could do it, design prehistoric insects and plants, and they were told to proceed on what was, in effect, a side project. I can't think of any other reason there'd be so little documentation."

"You'd think there would have been progress reports even with just one person working on it," Luc observed, "between him or her and whoever gave approval for the project."

"They left in a hurry," Hein observed. He gestured at the desk. There was a cup of coffee sitting out. Perhaps there'd been coffee in it when it had been abandoned, but after twenty years, there was just a dark stain on the inside of the cup. But, somehow both sad and alarming, beside the cup there was a pair of reading glasses.

"There might be interesting stuff in those desks," Sadie said to Luc.

Past the last office, the short hallway ended in a door. Hein opened it, and they found themselves in a larger area. They stood in a group and shone their flashlights around. To the left were some closed doors, including marked bathrooms. To the right was a break room, with two small, round tables, a refrigerator, and a microwave atop the counter.

"I dare you to open up that refrigerator," Michael said to Sadie with a twisted grin.

"After twenty years, the food's likely rotted and turned to dust," Hein told him. The man strode across the open space to another door. Both the door and the walls to either side of it were covered with warnings, notices, and admonishments. Sadie joined him.

"Proper protective equipment must be worn in all live breeding areas," Sadie read. Her eyes quickly scanned the other notices, and her heartrate increased, especially upon seeing the word Hatchery.

"Live breeding areas? Sounds like we're in the right place," Luc said.

Hein pushed through, and they found themselves in another open space, although it was smaller. There were lockers along the walls. Sadie walked up and opened one. "Clean suits," she announced. There was a diagram on the wall nearby, and she studied it. "Fertilization," she read. "Hatchery." According to the map, the departments were separate but connected, stretching southward through the building ahead of her like a string of pearls.

"If they did leave in a hurry," Sadie said to Luc, "I'm curious to see what they left behind."

Originally, the door before her had been secured with a keypad. It was glass and steel. She pushed it open to find herself in a small, bare room. "The decontam pass through," she said. She shone her flashlight up at the ceiling. "UV lights and I bet the nozzles are for a spray, something for decontamination and sterilization."

"Bleach?" Michael asked.

"Likely not that strong." She pushed open the door at the far end, and they found themselves in the section of the building where the work had been done. Stretching before them was a bare white hallway with a dirty tile floor, with doors on the left. The first door was marked Fertilization. Sadie entered it and found herself in a large laboratory. The rest of the group followed behind her.

"That's a microscope, I recognize that," Michael said, pointing.

They wandered between the countertops, looking at the room. Everything seemed to have been left out, as if the employees had run out in the middle of their workday. Trays of pipettes, test tubes filled with black gunk, digital tools strewn about the countertops, their batteries long dead. There were several refrigerators for samples. Sadie recognized a small centrifuge, two different brands of gene sequencers, and a 3D bioprinter that seemed capable of work on a sub-cellular level, but there were half a dozen other pieces of medical electronics that were a mystery to her.

"This is a big enough space for six people, easy," Sadie said, looking around. "Maybe as many as a dozen before they might get in each other's way. They spared no expense," she observed. She pointed. "The current model of that sequencer costs half a million euros. I have no idea what the other ones cost."

"And they just left them and ran out," Hein said, shaking his head.

"A hundred men with guns were shooting up the park a kilometer away," Michael reminded him.

Hein shrugged. "Still."

Michael looked from the older, calm, professional hunter to Leo, Mexican military veteran, both of them carrying rifles. "I think maybe your reaction to gunfire might be different than many people's," he pointed out.

Hein was looking up at the ceiling. "I don't think they would have heard anything in here. It's got a separate air filtration system. Everything seals up tight."

"They would have had phones, or palms," Sadie pointed out.

"They had an alarm system," Luc said, pointing at a unit on the wall. "Wonder if that's just for in here, or park-wide."

"Just in here," Sadie said, "this building, for a contaminant breach. Some of the chemicals they used would have been toxic," she said to their questioning faces.

"This is too small a facility for mass production, isn't it?" Luc said, looking around the room.

Sadie agreed. "I think they tested the viability of various species here—short runs, small batches, or however the geneticists refer to them—before giving the go-ahead to the main facility in Chihuahua."

"Why here? Why didn't they just build an addition to the plant in Chihuahua?" Leo asked.

Sadie shrugged. "Because the climate conditions here are the same as the park, eliminating one variable? Of course, that's just a guess. We'll probably never know."

"Aha!" Luc shouted and pointed. He'd spotted a binder on the counter next to one of the machines, and there right behind it, dozens of other binders stood neatly on a shelf. He shone his flashlight on the pages of the open binder and flipped back and forth, squinting. He really needed reading glasses, but was too vain to wear them outside his office. "Therizinosaurus," he said. "They were sequencing Therizinosaurus."

"Isn't that one of the new species for the park expansion?" Michael asked. He walked over and stood next to Sadie, who was examining the other binders.

Luc nodded excitedly. "Yes, the giant ostrich. Twice as tall as this building. What do you have there?" he asked Sadie.

"Most if not all of the other species they planned for the expansion." She rapidly flipped through the binder for Microceratus, frowning. She grabbed the next closest one and opened that, seeing it was for Dunkleosteus, the nightmarish fish. She scanned back and forth. "This isn't all their data," she announced. "This was just..." She waved a hand, looking for the right term. "Progress notes between the technicians involved, informal observations."

"They wouldn't waste paper printing out the whole genome anyway, would they?"

She shook her head. "It would take a whole tree, or ten. Most of the information has to be on computer." She looked around the room. Six feet away, a screen was mounted on the wall, and below it was a keyboard. She followed the wires from both into the cabinet below, where she found a computer tower. "Michael?"

Michael squatted next to her. "I think it's some sort of biomedical computer." He'd never seen anything like it.

"'MacLeod-Weiss 510e,'" Sadie read off the front of the machine. "Is that a brand and model number?"

"Maybe. I've never heard of it." He pulled out his palm and tried to look it up, only to find he had no satellite service. He looked up at the ceiling. "I've got no signal. I don't know whether it's the building or the storm."

"Likely both," Hein said. "Anything there on your insects?"

"Not that I saw." She ran her eyes over the spines of the binders again just to be sure. "Luc?"

"I haven't seen anything."

"So," Michael asked, "did they make them? Were they just thinking about making them?"

"What?"

He gestured at the binders. "The twenty new dinosaurs."

"This is where they finished work on each species' genome, near as I can tell, and fertilized the eggs," Sadie told him.

"So they fertilized eggs?"

"Umm…" She flipped back and forth through the binder, then grabbed another, and another. "They've got some abbreviations here, but I think this H," she pointed, "means they were successful and the new species, the fertilized ova, were sent over to the Hatchery."

"How many have the H?"

"Most of them."

"So let's go look at the Hatchery. Is that next door?"

"I think so."

"Can you open that MacMurray computer or whatever it is?" She asked him.

"What? *Oui, d'accord*, the case unscrews like any other, it just might take me a few extra seconds to locate the hard drive and extract it. Let's go look at the eggs."

There was a door on the south wall that led into a decontamination chamber, and likely connected directly to the Hatchery, but the sliding door was jammed and wouldn't open. "Is there another entrance through the corridor outside?" Luc asked. There were large windows in the doors, and he pressed his nose against the near one, but he couldn't see through to the Hatchery. The decontamination chamber was empty.

"Likely," Hein responded.

He pushed back out into the corridor and noticed two things. Just how dirty the floor was, and how much more humid it was outside the laboratory. Frowning, he walked further down the corridor. Near the end of the corridor on the left, a door hung open, and through it was a large, dark room. He shone his flashlight through the opening and only caught a vague glimpse of large blocky shapes further into the gloom.

The floor was dirtiest right before that open door, and on the right side, something was jutting into the corridor. As he drew closer, he saw it was a glass accordion door, halfway open. Past it was a large space, another decontamination room perhaps, as on the far side was an identical glass accordion door, also open. But past the second glass door was a metal roll-up door that led directly outside. The roll-up door was half open, and there was a meter-wide gap between the bottom of it and the floor. Beyond it was a cement loading dock getting hammered with rain. Dark green grass had sprung up through cracks in the concrete, and vines were growing up the sides of the loading dock. A small puddle had formed just inside the roll-up door.

"Why is the floor so dirty?" Michael said, looking down as he walked up behind the hunter.

A lot of it was old and long dried, but they both spotted it at the same time—a fresh, wet, three-toed footprint just inside the metal rolling door. Then another further into the building. And a third in the corridor at their feet, heading into the open dark room before them. Michael froze, his eyes going wide.

"You're okay, you're fine, everything's fine," Hein said, talking in a normal conversational tone. With his free hand he took hold of Michael's shirt and pulled him backward. "Everyone back into the lab," he announced, trying to sound relaxed and cheerful. He continued backing up, keeping his rifle trained one-handed on the open door before them.

"What is it? What's going on?" Sadie asked.

"Back in the lab," Hein said calmly. He could sense their bodies close behind him, but he didn't stop, he kept moving, and in just a few seconds they were all back inside the Fertilization lab. Hein took another glance out the glass door, closed it, then turned toward the concerned faces. Michael's young face had gone very pale.

"Looks like we've got some visitors," Hein announced with a smile, calm as could be. "Looks like they wanted to get in out of the weather, too."

"Coelophysis?" Sadie asked, trying to control the terror that had suddenly gripped her.

Hein shook his head decisively. "No," he told her, looking her in the eye. She gulped and nodded. It wasn't a lie, they weren't

Coelophysis tracks... they were too big. She didn't need to know that, however. He looked to Leo. "You stay here with them while I head back to the Vaquero to get something more... appropriate," he said, hoisting his rifle. A bolt-action rifle you had to manually work the action of after each shot wasn't the best weapon for close-in work. Leo nodded. Hein smiled comfortingly at the rest of them, then slipped out the door and headed up the corridor, back the way they'd come.

Leo leaned against the wall beside the door, his HK G3 in his hands, looking completely unconcerned. Michael was staring at the man. "Aren't you scared?"

"They're not monsters," Leo told him. "They're just animals. I'm sure they heard us, and they might be sneaking back out the door right now, which is why I'm not peeking out into the corridor. I don't want to spook them back into that room." He'd flipped off the safety on his rifle and wasn't holding it quite so casually, but he was nearly as relaxed as he was pretending to be.

"And if they don't leave?" Luc asked.

"Whether they do or not, we've got to finish searching the building, but we'll make a lot of noise, shine our lights around, and they'll run away. They're not looking for a fight." Which was true, as far as it went, but if there were a lot of them, or they were hungry, they might not be as easy to scare off as he made it sound. He didn't let any of those details interfere with his warm smile and his relaxed body language. This was why he and Hein were being paid, after all. Time to earn their money.

* * *

Hein jogged down the hallway, through the first door, past the break room, through the second door, past the offices and the secretary's desk, and into the lobby. The front door was still wedged open, and he peered out at the Vaquero sitting there, fifteen feet away, in the heavy rain. He sighed, slung the rifle over his shoulder, then jogged out into the downpour.

He shut the door behind him as he climbed up and into the Vaquero. The arms locker was directly behind the front seats, and he opened it. The firearm he was looking for was right where it was supposed to be—a worn Benelli M1014. The semi-auto shotgun had been military issue for over forty years in the United States and many other countries. This specimen had been a used, refurbished model purchased from Raven if he remembered correctly.

Shotguns were powerful weapons, throwing an ever-expanding cloud of pellets downrange with every pull of the trigger. They were the wrong choice for hunting massive dinos of the type many of his clients were after, and near-useless at long range, but were a good choice for backing up a client during a stalk through thick brush, and the perfect choice for clearing a building of carnivores the size of large dogs.

Aarne Anders spared no expense—he'd better not, for the outrageous sums he charged their wealthy clients—so the shells Hein grabbed out of the box and stuffed into the Benelli's magazine tube were the finest money could buy. Each shell was loaded with 35 tungsten pellets the size of BBs. Tungsten was almost twice as dense and heavy as lead, so the pellets would penetrate that much deeper. Hein knew he could kill something at least the size of a horse with one shot, provided it was within 30 or so meters. That got him thinking about what might be waiting for him back in the building.

The three-toed prints had come from a prehistoric predator, that much was clear—a carnivore that walked and ran on two feet. Too large to be Coelophysis. That meant it was either Syntarsus or Deinonychus. Not Utahraptor; the foot was too small, unless it was a juvenile.

Syntarsus—Syntax, as they were sometimes called—grew to over two meters long including the tail, and were very effective pack hunters who could run nearly 30 kilometers an hour. They were mottled brown in color, with purple-black crests on the backs of their heads. They were also smart, with larger-than-average brains.

Except for the showy crest on their heads, the fine downy feathers on Syntarsus lay flat along their bodies and went mostly unnoticed. Deinonychus, on the other hand, was fully feathered but for their face, hands, and feet. The feathers had orange and gray stripes which, if you only saw in shades of gray, provided very effective camouflage. They were slightly larger than Syntarsus, just over three meters long, and supposedly reaching seventy kilos in weight, although he'd never seen an animal much over fifty kilos. Hein had stalked both species, with and without clients, over the years. While he knew he needed to be careful, he wasn't worried. It wasn't anything he hadn't done before.

He loaded the underbarrel magazine tube with seven shells, chambered one, then topped off the magazine. A small flashlight was mounted on the side of magazine tube, and he tried the button to test the batteries. The bright beam inside the dark vehicle nearly blinded him. As he waited for the spots in his vision to fade, he eyed the sidesaddle shell carrier on the side of the receiver, thought a second, and then loaded it with six more shells. Then he threw a few more into his pockets. He wouldn't need them, but he thought the shiny brass rims of the shells on display there would put on a good show for the Frenchmen and woman.

He was finally getting to do something other than stand around or break into storage sheds. At that thought, he grabbed two spare loaded magazines for Leo's rifle and stuck them in his pockets. He wasn't sure if Leo had any spares on him, and the magazines were impressively large.

Hein climbed down from the cab carefully, now burdened with a near-comical amount of ammunition. He walked quickly to the front door and, once out of the rain, shook his head, spraying droplets from his nose.

"What took you so long?" Michael asked when Hein finally reappeared. Then his eyes grew wide at the sight of the big black shotgun in his hands. The Benelli was impressive, Hein had to admit, especially with the spare shells astride the receiver, bright red plastic and gleaming brass.

"I wanted to give them time to leave if they were going to," the professional hunter told the computer expert. He handed Leo the two spare magazines, then unslung the Winchester .300 WinMag from his shoulder and leaned it against the wall just inside the door. He wouldn't need it.

"Okay," he told the nervous faces, "this is going to take a few minutes. Just wait here, and we'll come get you when we've finished checking the building."

Sadie was in an active battle with her fear, but the professional hunter's soft-spoken competency helped her, at least outwardly, remain calm.

"You're leaving us?" Michael said, his voice almost squeaking.

Leo hid a smile. Hein said, "In a room with a door. It won't lock with the electronics out, but if you're worried, if it will make you feel better, pull one of those benches in front of it. They look heavy." He paused as a thought occurred to him, and the calming smile on his face disappeared. He stabbed a finger at the rifle he'd leaned against the wall. "Don't touch the gun." Then he and Leo were gone, out the door and moving down the corridor. Their flashlights were on and waving, and they were speaking loudly. Then they moved out of sight.

"They'll be fine. We'll be fine," Luc said. Michael gave him a dubious look.

"Take that computer apart while we're waiting, get the hard drive," Sadie told the young man, pointing at the MacLeod-Weiss 510e. "If any computer has the information we need, it's that one, or one of the three Hakkaris at the front." She crossed her arms and stared at him until he got to work. Then she casually turned around, looked down the corridor, and glanced at the rifle Hein had left. She was comforted by its presence. She knew how to work a bolt-action rifle.

* * *

"I was beginning to think that Stegosaurus was going to be the only dinosaur we saw," Leo admitted as they walked down the corridor. The loaded magazines in the cargo pockets of his pants bounced against his thighs. Completely unnecessary, but he understood the bit of theater Hein was putting on.

"That was a fabulous specimen, and you'll likely go years without seeing anything finer," Hein told him. They stopped near the end of the corridor, where the floor was dirty from dozens of footprints going in and out of the building. Lots of animals recently, or one or two animals over a significant period of time. The fresh, wet footprints were starting to dry, but still clearly visible.

"Syntarsus?" Leo asked. He squatted, reached out, and spread his hand above the print. It stretched from the heel of his hand to the tip of his middle finger.

"No, see how wide that track is?" Hein told him, pointing, but keeping one eye on the open doorway before them. "It's too wide for Syntarsus. They have narrow feet, shorter, too. Deinonychus, probably."

Leo stood back up. "So how do you want to do this?" They stared toward the open door. Past it were the vague shapes of machinery. The room seemed large.

"This is likely the only way in or out," Hein theorized, nodding at the open door. "Let's go in and keep to the wall. Flashlights, make a lot of noise once we get away from the door, work our way all around the room. That should flush anything hiding in there out the door." He hefted the shotgun. "I'll take lead, this is better for indoor work."

Hein clicked on the light attached to the Benelli, aimed it through the doorway, and played it around. He saw cabinets and tables, and some larger equipment. The floor between the machinery was grimy from so many footprints the individual prints didn't stand out. Apparently the animals had been coming into the building through the open door for some time.

Hein moved through the door and turned left, hugging the wall, swinging the flashlight beam in front of him and all around. It smelled wet and swampy in the room. He saw cabinets with glass doors, big metal tables, large, clear enclosures whose purpose he didn't quite understand, metal armatures possibly belonging to robots, desks and chairs, but he just let his gaze wash over all of it without seeing it; he was only concerned with spotting something alive, moving. The room was large, the largest he'd seen in the building, perhaps thirty meters long.

He pointed the flashlight beam under and around the tables and desks. Leo had a flashlight in his support hand, clamped around his rifle's forend, and was shining it all around as well. "Should we be making noise?" Leo asked.

"They hear us. They see the lights, too, but let's wait until we get a little farther away from the door before we get loud. You see any other way out?"

Leo aimed his bright LED flashlight deeper into the room. Windows lined two of the walls, but it was so dark outside, he couldn't see much of anything, and the standard windows seemed to be behind a protective clear layer. He swung his flashlight up and checked out the ceiling. It looked like it contained specialized venting. "I think this was another cleanroom or whatever they call it," Leo observed, "for germs. You can see out the windows, but you can't get to them; there's a clear glass wall. We're in a room inside the room. Probably only one way in and out."

"All right. Moving again."

In no hurry, being thorough, Hein worked his way across the room from the door to the far corner, where the floor showed barely any grime. They were fifteen meters from the open door, with a number of pieces of blocky machinery blocking their view of it. "Okay, now we can get loud," Hein said. "Hey hey hey!" he shouted.

He tried stomping his feet, but the floor was solid, and the thumping of his boots was somewhat quiet.

"Yai yai!" Leo shouted and banged the barrel of his rifle against the metal cabinet before them. The loud clanking echoed dully through the room.

"Oh, that's good," Hein said. He banged the magazine tube of the Benelli on the steel as well. "Go on!" he shouted. "Get out of here!" He banged the tube once more… and his flashlight died.

"Son of a bitch," he swore. With one less flashlight, the space seemed much larger, and more ominous.

"Did you break the bulb?"

"It's LED, there's no bulb to break."

"Well, you broke something."

"Yes, thank you." He tapped the flashlight against the cabinet in hopes it would turn back on, but… nothing. "All right, well, let's keep working our way along the room."

Staying side by side, they moved down a corridor that ran parallel to the back wall, between desks and cabinets to the left, and large cluttered tables to the right, shouting regularly. It wasn't clear what was on the tables, and Hein was too occupied to do much sightseeing. Ten meters on, he noticed the floor was much grimier, covered with so much dirt that he could feel it under his boots. Then he saw movement.

"There you are," he said. "Did you see it?" he asked Leo and pointed. It had been dark and muted in color, but it had definitely been alive, darting behind machinery, moving to their right. Likely heading toward the door. "Hey! Hey! Hey! Get out of here!" Hein shouted. Leo swung his flashlight around but didn't see anything. He realized he might have heard the clicking sound of claws on tile.

They waited a few seconds. "All right, that one's gone; let's check the rest of the room," Hein said. He walked half a dozen steps along the wall, came around a table, and there in the aisle between two rows of machines stood a full-grown Deinonychus. It stretched to full height, opened its mouth, and hissed at them. It was nearly eye-to-eye with Hein, feathers fluffed to make it appear even larger than it was, but it wasn't advancing. It also wasn't retreating.

"Shit. Go! Go!" Hein shouted, waving the shotgun at the animal. He banged the shotgun on a post in front of him, half hoping the flashlight would turn back on, and to his surprise, it did. Both he and the predator blinked in the sudden blinding light. Hein pointed the muzzle of the shotgun right toward the Deinonychus, and he saw the pupils of its eyes contract suddenly—but it stood its ground. "Go!" Hein shouted. He was seriously confused. The animal wasn't acting normally, hissing and dancing back and forth on its feet, claws tapping on the floor. Agitated, but refusing to give up any ground.

It was the oddest thing; in the dark room, its feathered body soaked up the light of the flashlight. It screeched at him angrily, stretching its neck out toward him, taking half a step—and Hein pulled the trigger, taking no chances. Half the animal's head disappeared, and it fell to the floor, dead.

Ears ringing from the shot, Hein shook his head and turned to Leo. "I don't know what the hell that was," he began to say, then he saw more movement down another aisle. He started to shout Leo's name, but Leo saw the look on Hein's face and spun. The second Deinonychus charged them, its feathered body soaking up the light. The animal was invisible in the dark room, but its eyes reflected the flashlight beams, glittering in the dark. With a shout, Leo let loose a burst from his rifle, the noise deafening, and the dinosaur slid to a stop at their feet, dead, glassy eyes open and unblinking.

"*¡Puta madre!*" Leo swore. Both men had their weapons up and swung them back and forth, playing their flashlights over everything they could see. The two Deinonychus seemed to be the only animals.

"I've never seen them act so aggressive," Hein said, "so territorial. I don't understand it. Did you see that? How it was puffed up, standing as tall as it could?"

"Hey, you're the expert, I just work here," Leo said. "*Mierda, eso fue jodidamenta emocionante.*" He stuck the tip of his pinkie into his ear and wiggled it around. His ears were ringing. Then he poked the animal with the muzzle of his rifle. It didn't move. One of his bullets had hit it in the center of its chest, traveled through its body, and exited the middle of its back, taking a section of spine with it. It's one eye stared unblinkingly up at him. "It's a feathered raptor."

"Basically. Let's check the rest of the room. I can't imagine anything's left in here with us after that noise, but…"

* * *

Michael had his small tool kit laid out on the floor, taking the tower of the medical computer apart, but kept nervously glancing over at the door. Sadie was standing beside it. "Can you see or hear anything?" he asked.

"Just relax," Luc told him. He glanced at Sadie. She wasn't saying anything, but her body language was easy to read, as was the sweat on her face. "That's why we brought them along, *non*? Hard men with guns, just in case. To be honest, I expected them to be a complete waste of money, to keep you calm." She shot him a murderous look, saw him smiling, and realized he was trying to distract her. He shrugged. "Turns out I was wrong."

Even after twenty years, the doors sealed tightly when closed, and she couldn't hear any of the noise the two men were making until the *boom* of the shotgun made her jump. Michael squawked and spilled his tools across the floor. Then, even louder, a burst of fully-automatic rifle file. Distant, deeper into the building, but unmistakable. Sadie and Luc traded wide-eyed looks.

Michael scrambled to his feet and hurried to Sadie's side, clenching his hands. Luc drifted over, trying to appear unworried. The three of them stood together nervously, staring out into the corridor for what seemed like forever, but was perhaps five minutes. Sadie was just about to open the door and call out when Hein and Leo appeared, striding down the hallway toward them. Sadie let out the breath she hadn't realized she'd been holding.

Michael grabbed the door and yanked it open. "Are you okay? What was that shooting?"

"A couple of Deinonychus," Hein said. His tone and expression were hard to read. He looked at Sadie. "You're going to want to take a look at this."

* * * * *

Chapter Eighteen

Sadie was a little hesitant, a little scared, but it helped that she wasn't the only one unnerved by the experience. It also helped that Luc and Michael were right there, as were Leo and Hein with their big guns, and everyone had their flashlights out, making the big, echoey room not seem so... spooky.

"It looks like they had the room subdivided into a number of cells," Hein said, standing just inside the door. He shone his flashlight around, and soon there were five bright beams dancing all about the big room. "Some of these tables are empty, but some of them have eggs on them," Hein said, leading the way down an aisle and pointing. "Or *did* have eggs, I think. I guess. The decades have not been kind."

"It's mush and goo," Michael observed.

"Not quite," Luc said as he peered at the contents of one wide, low table, "but I can't tell what it was." He looked at the next table over. "It looks like animals picked through whatever was there."

"These, I'm pretty sure, are incubation chambers," Hein said, pointing one out. Insulated cubes two meters square, with one or two small windows, and narrow tubes and pipes leading in and out.

"Yes," Sadie said with a nod. "Temperature and humidity controlled." There was a window in the door, but it was too dark to see anything inside. She opened the door and found it was empty. She wondered how long it had taken the first scientists trying to bring

287

back extinct species to figure out the proper temperature and humidity for successfully incubating dinosaur eggs. How many hundreds or likely thousands of eggs had never hatched. She wondered if the eggs had to be regularly turned, like chicken eggs.

"Most of them aren't empty," Hein said. "You'll see. I planned to ask you about them. But that's not what I wanted to show you first. Come on."

They followed him to the back of the large room, wending their way between steel tables and medical equipment. Hein was using the flashlight on the end of his shotgun and pointed it downward.

"Oh. Oh, my," Sadie said. The sight of the feathered dinosaur took her breath away, and she had to fight the urge to take a step back. It was clearly dead, but still... Hein pointed out the second animal about twenty feet away, lying in a puddle of blood. "These are bigger than Coelophysis," she said.

"Yes."

"I thought you... never mind."

"What are they?" Michael asked.

"Deinonychus, isn't that what you said?" Luc said.

Hein nodded. "Yes, and they should have run off with our yelling and banging. This is why they didn't." He moved down a short aisle running between a desk and a table and pointed.

The trio moved around the desk to see. "*Mon Dieu*," Sadie breathed. It was a nest constructed of mud and twigs and grass, perhaps two feet in diameter. Nestled in the middle of it, cushioned by greens and more mud, were... Sadie counted them. "Eleven," she said. "Eleven eggs." Each one the size of a big man's fist and off-white in color. She'd seen photos of their nests, of course, but it was different seeing it in person, and they weren't fossils, but fresh eggs, each one containing a living dinosaur.

"There are other, older nests in back," Hein told her, jerking a thumb over his shoulder. "Lots of eggshells, animals previously hatched. They've been using this room for their nests for quite some time. This is the only one with fresh eggs."

"So they were territorial, protecting the nest?"

"It seems so. A male and a female."

"It's a shame you had to shoot them."

"Trust me, we did everything we could not to. Too much, actually; that one was trying to circle around and ambush Leo while the first one challenged us." He pointed at the corpse further away.

Michael blinked in surprise. "Really?"

"Predators learn how to stalk, or they starve to death. They literally kill for a living. They use stealth, speed, distraction…"

Sadie went back to the animal and squatted down. It was missing most of its head, but she ran her hand down its neck and along its back. "It's not as soft as it looks," she remarked, "the feathers. There's a kind of down, underneath, but the large ones on top are thick and tough." Gray with orange stripes, but there was a sheen to them as well, showing hints of green and blue in the beam of her flashlight. Beautiful and terrifying.

Underneath the feathers, the animal was all muscle. She ran her hand down its body to its forelimbs. They were heavily feathered, enough to appear like short wings, but under the feathers, the animal's arms were thicker than she was expecting, and seemed strong. Each hand was tipped with three claws. The Deinonychus had three toes, two with standard claws, and one with the big, curving, sickle-shaped claw common to many prehistoric predators, most famously the raptors.

"The other one was hoping to gut Leo with that foot claw. It leapt at him, and Leo shot him right out of the air." Michael's eyes kept getting wider and wider as he listened, staring at the feathered bodies.

Eventually Sadie was able to tear her eyes away from the animal and look around. "Unlike Production, they didn't pull the machinery out of here. Maybe it was more specialized, so they didn't have a use for it."

"Maybe whoever was doing the salvage didn't even know it was here," Michael said. "*We* only found it by accident."

"I want to show you something," Hein said. "The thing I most wanted you to see, actually." He waved Sadie over to an incubation chamber. "The door was cracked, like you see here."

She opened the door and shone her light inside. While the contents of the chamber had degraded after two decades, it was clear that the Pangaea reproductive specialists had tried to replicate a nest on the floor of the chamber with some sort of artificial material that had held up well over the years. There were dozens of eggs inside it, only one species, it seemed, the eggs slightly larger than those she'd seen in the Deinonychus nest. Interestingly, while a few of the eggs seemed to have collapsed in on themselves, many of the eggs appeared to have cracked open from the inside.

"I wonder if they ran out of here in such a hurry that they left the power on, the incubation chambers kept incubating, and the eggs hatched, or at least some of them did. Door was open," he reminded them. "And this isn't the only chamber that looked like this."

It took them a few seconds to realize what he was saying. Sadie shook her head vigorously. "You know the chances against that happening?" she asked. She ticked them off on her fingers. "First, you'd have to have at least one of each species not just make it out of the incubation chamber, but the room and the building. This room was probably littered with their little newborn bodies, which were then eaten by animals, Deinonychus or whatever came before them. The sounds or smell of those infants was probably what drew the predators in here originally, but if any did live and make it out into the wild, they'd have to survive until they were mature enough to breed if you wanted the species to continue. They'd have to find each other and breed."

"Unlikely… but not impossible," Hein pointed out with a shrug. Overall, he was very pleased with how things had come out. Their presence had definitely been required. To his surprise, there had been dinosaurs, and they'd been territorial in a way he'd never seen before, and hadn't been expecting. They wouldn't have left the nest, and if he and Leo hadn't been there, it was very likely the researchers would have been injured or killed. A happy ending all around, except for the two Deinos.

Michael bent down and put his flashlight close to a display card in a plastic slot on the door. "Nodosaur," he said. He looked at Luc.

"Knobs all over its back like an ankylosaur," Luc told him, "but smaller. It was on the final list."

"So there could be Nodosaurs out there?" He looked at Sadie.

"I seriously doubt it, but…" She shrugged. It wasn't impossible, considering what they knew.

"What's this?" Michael asked. Sadie had just noticed the large piece of machinery as well. She walked over. It almost resembled a giant metal bathtub with a lid, and lots of piping and tubing running in and out.

"Para…something. It's hard to read. Para—something—thanium," Michael said, squinting at a piece of paper stuck in a slot on the side.

"Paraceratherium," Luc said. "It was on the final list."

"Which one was it?" Michael asked.

"It's like a giant, hornless rhino, shaped a bit like a horse. Makes elephants look small."

Sadie straightened up and turned to look at Luc. "It was a mammal." She looked back at what looked like a big bathtub, and that description wasn't so inaccurate. "It's a vat," she said, searching for the words. "An artificial womb for breeding mammals. They use them in cloning, but so many dinosaurs are reptiles, I didn't think… From the size of it, there might be multiple cells in here to grow several fetuses at a time."

"Lid's still on," Michael said. "You want to try to figure out how to take it off?"

"No," she said quickly. "If there's anything still in there, you don't want to smell it, even if the gases aren't toxic."

"You're probably right. So, no rhino horses out in the wild?"

Sadie opened and closed her mouth, thinking—and there was a lot to think about; this building was full of surprises. "Well… there's no way to know if what's inside is the first batch, or the thirtieth. If, or rather when, they were successful and had live animals born, they would have taken them somewhere, right? A nursery." She thought. "It would have been in a building, so they could control the temperature. With the species separated, fed individual diets. I imagine it would have been nearby."

"Another hidden building?" Michael said. "We barely found this one."

"Little frail infants?" Hein said. "They don't travel well. It would have had to be on the property." He chewed at his lip. "Maybe further north, along the valley, inside the same patch of forest, as it really didn't look like there was anything further south. Maybe there's a connecting road that's so overgrown we missed it."

"For every answer we get, we find three more questions," Sadie said. She blew hair out of her eye and moved off through the big room, checking it out. It appeared that each cell was meant for a different species. Some of the cells were standing bare and unused, but many of the incubation chambers were stuffed with man-made nests and dozens of eggs in various stages of disintegration.

Eventually she made her way to the far end of the room. The tinted windows before her looked out the south end of the building, the side she'd spotted during their "picnic." Her flashlight was reflecting off the glass brightly enough to blind her, and she shut it off. She peered out through the rain-spotted glass, but the fields stretching away from her were a murky green. She turned and called out to Michael. "See any computers?"

He looked over. She was a black silhouette against the gray windows. "All these things are computer-controlled, but no."

"Hmm. Okay. How about everyone spread out. Check the incubation chambers and the fetal vats, see if you see anything relating to our insects. Although they wouldn't have used either of those for breeding insects."

"What would they have used?" Luc asked.

Well, that was the question. "In nature, butterflies grow from caterpillars, but did the animals they resurrected grow straight into butterflies? Is that even possible? I don't know the mechanics of cloning sheep or cows, much less dinosaurs or insects. They were, to some extent, creating new DNA. I have so many questions. Hmm. So for caterpillars, you'd want a large container, filled with greens for them to eat, with holes for airflow, small enough they couldn't escape. In the wild, dragonflies and griffinflies lay their eggs in standing water, but..."

"We're not in the wild."

"I guess... look for anything unusual," she said, waving her hand at the whole room, "that's not an incubation chamber or mechanical womb. Then I guess we go back to the offices and pull the hard drives."

"You're thinking they did plants, too, right?" Hein said. "I haven't seen anything in or around the building that looks like a garden. Would it *be* a garden?"

Sadie shook her head. "I don't know. I'm getting a headache."

Hein was a dozen feet from her, his flashlight pointed down at the floor. He shut it off and strode up to Sadie, but he wasn't looking at her, he was looking past her, out the windows.

"Shut off your flashlights," he said over his shoulder.

"What?"

"Shut off your flashlights," he repeated, almost growling. They did as he moved close to the glass.

"Were you getting glare off the windows?" Michael asked, walking over. He looked out past Hein to see two lights in the distance. They appeared and disappeared, and moved up and down. A few seconds later, he realized they were headlights on a vehicle—heading their way. Behind it, the headlights of a second vehicle appeared. Then a third.

"Is it the police? Did they hear the shooting?" Michael asked in confusion.

Hein shook his head. "You could walk out the door and fire a whole magazine into the air, and no one would hear it."

"Are you going to get in trouble for killing the dinosaurs without a hunting license?" Luc asked him, moving toward them.

"It was self-defense," Michael insisted.

"They don't care about that," Hein told him. "It shouldn't be a problem," he said distractedly, watching the vehicles approach, "and if it is, a few dollars in the right pocket will smooth things over." He cocked his head. Something about the approaching vehicles seemed... odd. "I think they're coming down out of the mountains."

"On the road?" Sadie asked.

"What road?"

The headlights bounced wildly as the vehicles made their way across the uneven ground. Behind the lead vehicle's lights, he could just make out the shape of a pickup. There were five—no six, six vehicles in a column making their way north across the valley, churning across the tall grass.

"There's a road, not much more than a trail, that I saw. It went over a pass and ran through the fields past the maintenance buildings."

"Do you think they saw the building?" Luc asked.

"They do now," Hein said. The south end of the R&D building was hidden under the trees, but the windows were likely reflecting the headlights.

Leo had been wandering through the large room, examining the strange equipment, and finally walked over to join the group. They could just hear the engines of the lead vehicles over the steady rush of rain.

"Refugees?" Luc wondered.

"From what?" Michael said.

The lawyer shrugged. "Maybe there's fighting on the other side of the mountains. The war's not officially over, right? Or they're heading somewhere. Ciudad Victoria?"

"There are much faster routes," Hein said.

The vehicles weren't travelling much faster than a walking man as they bounced over the grassy hillocks, weaving back and forth, but as they drew close to the patch of jungle around the building, the grass thinned. The lead truck found the smoother ground, sped up, then slowed down, waiting for the other vehicles to draw close. Then it led them toward the low building and the gap on the east side as the trees grew too close on the mountain side.

The vehicles drew close and moved alongside the building, driving deeper under the trees. They were less than fifty feet away, and in a column, headlights from the vehicles behind illuminating the ones in front. The group could finally get a good look at their visitors.

"*¡Puta madre!*" Leo swore. "*¡Es La Fuerza!* Down, down," he hissed, grabbing at Luc and Michael to pull them below the windows. Sadie dropped to her hands and knees. Hein didn't have to ask if Leo was sure; he'd seen the rifles as well.

"Maybe they'll leave us alone or keep going," Luc said, panting in fear.

Leo watched the convoy for a second. "They're stopping, just pulling deeper under the trees. They're always worried about Raven satellites and drones." He looked at Luc, Michael, and Sadie. "They'll see the Vaquero. They'll come in here and find us. At best, they'll steal all our gear, but if they find us here, they'll do whatever they want." He looked at Hein. "We need to go."

"We can't outrun them in the Vaquero."

"On foot, out the door, into the jungle. We need to go now." He popped his head up and looked out. "We've got a minute, maybe two."

"The jungle?" Michael said. "In the rain?"

"Yes," Hein said. He knew Leo was right. At best, they'd be robbed, but likely things would go much worse than that. Sadie was very pretty, with an exotic accent. He wasn't about to gamble with his life or the lives of his clients. He grabbed the computer expert by the shoulder and shoved him toward the door. "Let's go. Everyone." He didn't wait to see if they'd follow him. He knew they would. Leo jogged ahead.

"We're just running? Leaving the Vaquero?" Luc said. "It's got armor."

"They're driving down to where it is. We'd never make it inside. Look, I'm no longer a young man, I've never been a soldier, and two against twenty aren't odds any sane man would take if he had a choice. Putting you in their hands and hoping for mercy is not something I'm willing to do. Hope is not a strategy."

They reached the hallway. Leo squatted and stuck his head out the open door. It was clear. He waved for them to follow him, then moved out onto the loading dock, jumped down, and ran into the jungle, which grew close to the building. He reached the first tree and hid behind it, gesturing again at them to follow. Hein covered the corridor with the shotgun as Luc and Michael, wide-eyed and panting with fear, scrambled under the door.

Sadie was about to follow them, then paused. After a second's hesitation, she ran down the corridor in front of Hein.

"What are you doing?" he hissed.

She ran nearly the length of the corridor, terrified that the door at the end of it would open at any second, spilling terrorists into the decontam chamber, but she reached the door without incident. She darted in and was back a second later, Hein's bolt-action rifle in her hands.

"Come on, come on!" he hissed, waving her on. She was past him a moment later, stooping to get under the door, then he backed around the corner after her and crab-walked out onto the loading dock. The rain immediately soaked his shirt. He and Sadie ran into the jungle together.

* * * * *

Chapter Nineteen

Seamus wasn't miserable, not exactly. The last time he could remember being truly miserable was while sorting through the piles of paperwork with Torres in the abandoned office building. By comparison, he was currently outside, armed, and with eyes on enemy combatants—exactly the kind of thing he'd signed up for when he'd joined the Paras, and then Raven PMC. There were only a couple things ruining what would otherwise be a lovely time. First, he wasn't allowed to shoot any of the FRAP bastards he currently had under surveillance. Second, it was raining and had been for hours.

He was tucked behind a large bush on the far side of the valley from the FRAP encampment, just below the crest of the steep north ridge, not quite twelve hundred meters from the large barn, according to the range finder on his binoculars. If he'd had Leonidas, his favorite rifle—a short-barreled 7.62x51 topped with a low-power variable optic—he'd have been able to cause some trouble. But Leonidas was safely tucked away in his locker. The Blackbird he currently had beside him wasn't much use past three hundred meters, although it was quiet as a whisper.

However, his armament was inconsequential. Currently, his mission was surveillance, and he was finding it less… romantic than he had in his youth.

He'd wrapped himself in a thermal blanket, which should serve to conceal his heat signature from any thermal imagers the guerrillas might have, and over that he'd wrapped himself in a dirty brown wool blanket that blended nicely with the hillside. He wasn't too worried; they didn't seem especially wary or observant. Once the rain started, an hour after dawn, they'd retreated into the buildings and vehicles. Those who were awake, anyway. Many of them dozed well into late morning. Occasionally one or two vehicles would leave, only to return an hour or three later. Corey and Alvarez would pick them up as they came into town, but so far, the guerrillas hadn't done much other than shop for food, clothes, and alcohol.

He'd pulled the two blankets over his head to keep the rain off and sat on the ground behind the big thorny bush, wet but not cold. Through a gap in the branches, he had a wonderful view of the two barns and the field before them. Near as Torres could discern, after eyeing the bushes closely and doing some research, it was a former coffee farm—or orchard, he wasn't sure of the proper term. The jungle had been heavily thinned around the coffee trees, but not completely eliminated, as they needed at least some shade. The coffee trees had apparently been trimmed into bushes to make the fruits easier to pick, but they seemed overgrown and likely had been abandoned for years. Seamus wondered what had happened to the farmer who'd planted and tended them.

His radio beeped in his ear, and he reached down to connect the call. He grunted loud enough for his earpiece to pick it up.

"*Alpha, enjoying the weather?*" Corey asked. Seamus could hear the smile in his voice. They had Raven-issued, digitally-encrypted, satellite-linked radios, but thought they might be a bad choice to use in this situation. The guerrillas might have a scanner, and while they wouldn't be able to understand the scrambled transmission, they'd be aware of it and see it was on a military frequency. So they'd brought along commercial radios, also digitally encrypted and voice-activated, but they used commercial frequencies. Exactly the kind of thing actual oil company employees might use in the field and much less suspicious. Their only negative was, because they weren't sat-linked, they had a much shorter range, likely ten kilometers or less in the mountains. Plus, though the radio signal was encrypted, that didn't mean they fully trusted it.

"I haven't washed away, which was my only concern," Seamus said, his voice a low mumble barely louder than the hush of rain around him. The slope was a bit steep, although he'd picked this bush to hide behind in large part because there was a nearly level spot behind it.

"*I'm here with Bravo at Site Two,*" Corey said, which meant he was with Torres at a half-hidden spot, just off the narrow road leading to the FRAP compound, and about two kilometers south. That was the closest they could position a vehicle to back Seamus up without being immediately spotted by passing cars, at least in daylight.

"*Delta is following the last truck that came down from there,*" Torres said. "*Some shopping, food, beer of course, but mostly they seem bored. Just driving around town.*"

Seamus lifted the binoculars and brought the large barn into focus. The big doors were open, and he could see a number of men looking out at the falling rain. "Aye, I've got much the same up here. No sense of urgency. They never put out any sentries on the roads or the ridges. No one on watch at all."

"*I talked to the colonel. He said the Cuban fleet is still en route and could make port as early as this time tomorrow. It's all over the news.*"

"I'm aware. He has me checking in with him every two hours, so if that's where these bastards are going, they know they've got a wait. Better here than sitting on the beach. They likely don't trust this ceasefire, even with *el presidente* announcing it on the news."

"*Would you?*" Torres asked. "*The attorney general just called. They were curious and researched the property you're watching. It was a farm owned by a collective. They looked into the collective, and it seems to be nothing but, how do you say, smoke and mirrors. They found a few names and looked into them. There is a connection to* La Fuerza; *they seem to have bought the land through many cutouts over fifteen years ago.*"

"Really. Interesting. So it's not just a random spot where they've chosen to hide." Seamus chewed on his lip. "Remember in our mission briefing when they mentioned Timotéo might have been moving cash here in helicopters? Straight shot north along the mountains?"

"*Yeah?*"

"There's a spot in the field, away from the buildings, that's been cleared of coffee and shade trees. Just grass there in a rough circle. Not a big spot, but it seems large enough for a heli to set down. While it's a bit overgrown now, it surely looks like an LZ."

"*I want to know what's in those goddamn barns before they decide to leave,*" Corey said, "*because if there's anything in there, you know they'll be taking it with.*"

"*Nothing showed up on the thermal,*" Torres reminded them. Kresge had cycled a high-altitude surveillance drone overhead, and its infrared camera had been able to see quite clearly under the trees, and even inside the buildings. There were thirteen vehicles, all civilian, and over forty guerrillas. While the image inside the barns had been fuzzy, there'd been nothing in the heat signatures that looked like pallets of cash.

The big barn backed all the way up to the granite cliff face, and Seamus—very briefly—had thought about climbing down the near-vertical rocky face and onto the roof. He'd soon realized that was likely a suicidal move for anyone other than an accomplished mountain climber with the proper gear.

"We don't have the manpower to knock on the front door unless we bring in a few drones or Mad Sweeney for air support," Seamus said, "but the brush is thick enough... I think I could creep down for a peek without being spotted. In fact, I think I will; we need a closer look. I'd prefer to have me armor—that reactive camouflage would keep me nigh invisible—but such is life. I can smear myself with mud and go old-school. They seem to be drinking as much as eating—they're buying beer by the case—likely I could just walk right up and peek through the boards without them noticing, but perhaps it might be smart to wait until the sun goes down before I try to make my way through that field for the final approach; it looks a bit open."

"*You were supposed to let me relieve you eight hours ago. You've been up for thirty-six hours,*" Corey pointed out.

"And I currently can't feel my legs, sitting on this hard, ruddy ground, but the blood'll start flowing once I shake them out." In truth, his body felt like it was made of cold, aching clay. He was definitely feeling his age, and the rain was bothering him far more than it would have in his younger days. "Unless you've got an objection to the recon apart from my advanced age?" He waited. "Right. Okay, put your drone in the air somewhere above me to keep an eye on them while I'm on the move; we don't want them slipping out. I'll be putting away my comm gear until I'm in position at the edge of the field. That'll be but a hundred meters from that big barn, so I should be able to catch a lot more detail. I might even be able to hear them, *la cerveza* has been flowing pretty freely." He was a little jealous, in fact.

"*Copy. I'll let you know when the drone is in position.*" Corey paused. "*Should we radio Viking-23 and have them on station nearby?*"

"Well, that's the question, isn't it? I'm sure they'd like to be doing something other than sitting on their arses."

"*If anything happens—if you get jammed up,*" Corey told him, "*we're at least five minutes away, and there's just the two of us against… what was the last count?*"

"I think with the two new blokes who showed up just after sunrise, that brings the enemy strength up to forty-five or -six," Seamus said.

"*I mean, I know you appreciate a good challenge, but that seems a bit optimistic, even for you,*" Corey said.

Seamus stared through the bush at the barn in the distance. With the rain falling, he couldn't see any of the men without using the binoculars, and even then, it was like looking through a gray haze. "The problem is, for it to be of any use, we need the Peregrine orbiting nearby, and we don't know if there are any more FRAP in the area who might spot it and get spooked."

"*So what if they get scared and leave?*" Torres said. "*There is a ceasefire. As long as they are not driving off with giant trucks that could be full of cash, do we care?*"

"Well, what if we spook them, and when they drive off, they in fact do have a large lorry that didn't show up on the scan?" Seamus asked. "What then? Considering we have a ceasefire in place. I hate daft intelligence missions like these, I much prefer straight-up military ops: I see them, I shoot them, I drink beer, repeat as necessary."

Corey thought for a few seconds, then said, "*Let me check back in upstairs, see if I can get any clarification on our rules of engagement.*"

"*I will pull Delta back here,*" Torres said. "*They are doing nothing in town other than shopping. If the package is here, it is* here."

"Aye, I agree," Seamus said. "Let's wait to call in the Peregrine until after the sun goes down. Then it can orbit nearby, blacked out, and none of them should be the wiser. I doubt they've got much night vision capability, and even if they do, the valley walls block their sightlines rather well."

Their mission was intelligence gathering under pretense, so Seamus hadn't even brought any camouflage clothing, much less his armored uniform. But there was more to camouflage, and hiding in plain sight, than a fancy pattern that blended in with the background. Before heading to his elevated observation post, he'd put on a pair of dark brown work pants over his tan boots, and above that a long-sleeved, button-down work shirt in a nice medium green.

Moving slowly, he dug his fingers into the wet ground before him, coming up with thick handfuls of rich brown soil. Using both hands, he rubbed it into his trousers, then his sleeves, then the front of his chest rig. He rubbed the dirt across the backs of his pale hands, and all over his face and neck, making sure to get his ears. It wasn't nearly as good as real grease-based camouflage face paint, but it would have to do. When he was done, he looked down at himself. He was a mess of mud and brown and green, with wet spots adding depth and complexity.

"*Drone's on station,*" he heard in his ear.

"Copy that," Seamus replied. He raised the binoculars and scanned the enemy encampment, but nothing seemed to have changed. "Be moving out in one mike." He dug up a few more handfuls of mud and scattered them across the wet ground beside him. Then, moving slowly, he shrugged the blankets off. He tilted over until he was on his back on the ground, and he wriggled back and forth for a few seconds to smear the small black backpack he wore with the mud. He laid there, looking down at himself, and had to chuckle. No armor, no air support, with smeared mud over civilian clothes for camouflage. He had a basic kit, a chest rig that held spare magazines, one of his two radios—the military one in his backpack—a tourniquet, and a fixed-blade knife, plus a pistol on his hip. It wasn't just old-school; it was like going back in time. No tech, just him versus the men below.

While he appreciated an unfair advantage as much as the next bloke, the pureness of it spoke to him. The blade was a particular bit of whimsy—a Goodman Special Operations combat knife from Abraham & Moses, a true classic that sported a beefy six-inch blade and hung upside down over the left side of his chest in its aluminum sheath. He'd been carrying it for a decade, and had yet to use it for anything other than cutting rope or prying at boxes.

The slope was steep and wet enough that he was worried about losing his footing and sliding, or falling, all the way to the valley floor. So he was very careful as slipped the slung Blackbird across his back, stuffed the binoculars back in his pack, and worked his way down the slope on hands and knees, sometimes moving on his belly. Slowly, very slowly, so the movement wouldn't be spotted by any of the guerillas, because the human eye picked up movement far more easily than it did color variations, and often at incredible distances.

His elbows and knees were soaked through in no time, and as he carefully made his way down the slope at an angle, the light, steady rain soaked through his clothes. It took him nearly half an hour to reach the thick shrubs near the base of the slope, and once he did, he took a two minute breather inside them, hidden from view. He rubbed his aching knees and elbows, listening more than looking for any sign of enemy nearby, as the brush was so thick. He dug a bottle of water out his pack and quickly chugged it down. He stuffed the empty bottle back in his pack, climbed to his feet, and in a crouch, made it the rest of the way down the slope. As he entered the dense forest filling the valley floor, the sound of the rain changed from a steady rush all around to a hiss above, accompanied by loud drips.

Seamus was pretty sure all the guerrillas were loitering in and around the barns at the opposite end of the valley a kilometer away, but "pretty sure" wasn't an acceptable metric in a combat zone, not if you wanted to live for any length of time. He crept forward, Blackbird up, eyes darting left, right, and center as he took one careful step after another. He wasn't worried about making noise; even if the rain hadn't been drowning out any of the sounds he was making, the ground was covered in a thick layer of damp, rotting vegetation that completely absorbed the sounds of his passage. It was like walking on wet carpet.

He moved through waist-high ferns dripping with water, weaving his way between hanging vines and the twisted trunks of trees. The canopy overhead was dark green, with gaps here and there between the treetops showing him sky the color of stone. The forest was a mix of temperate and tropical plants, cypress, pines, oak, and mesquite, interspersed with palms, banyans, and copal trees, everything draped with vines, and growing out of a tall layer of bright green ferns and long, thick grass. Seamus had fought in the Middle East desert and all over Mexico, but he'd never done a stalk through a dripping jungle before. He was soaked through, muddy, and only the physical exertion kept him from being chilled to the bone.

He loved it.

Of course, he realized, if he'd been stuck in the jungle for days and months on end, like the soldiers who'd fought in Vietnam, combined with insufferable heat, he probably wouldn't think it was so romantic—trench foot and crotch rot tended to dampen the ardor— but in the short-term, he was having the time of his life. Creeping through thick jungle toward an outpost of enemy soldiers? He had to fight to keep the smile off his face.

He paused behind the thick trunk of an *ahuehuete*, a Montezuma cypress, the national tree of Mexico. He slicked his hair back with his left hand, moving slowly, and turned his head left and right, water dripping from his nose. The wet forest was shades of glossy greens and mottled browns, with the occasional splash of yellow and orange. The shadows under the leaves were bluish black.

He raised the Blackbird and peered through the square window of the small optic to verify that it was working. The triangle reticle was illuminated by a fiber optic collector atop the body, old-fashioned, but designed to be impervious to EMP attacks. Even in the dim light under the forest eaves, the amber triangle glowed warmly, with backup illumination in very low light provided by radio-active tritium. It was in a quick-detach mount, so if it broke, he could quickly discard it and default to the iron sights.

Water was beading on the carbine's receiver and stubby suppressor, and dripping off. Water was dripping off everything, in fact, and running down the tree trunk before him in thin streams. His eyes followed the streams down to the roots of the tree—and he froze.

The magazine in the Blackbird was stuffed with subsonic ammunition, as were the five spare magazines in the rig across his chest. With that ammunition, the integrally-suppressed carbine was very quiet, each pull of the trigger not much louder than a cough. At distance, or muffled by a steady rain, he could pick off half a dozen of the guerrillas if he needed to before they even knew they were under attack. The sounds of the bullets impacting their bodies would be louder than the sound of his Blackbird.

However, to keep the bullets under the speed of sound and avoid that supersonic crack, the bullet weight wasn't just increased, the velocity was cut in half. Subsonic Blackbird ammunition was quiet, but was rifle ammunition in name only—in power, it was little more than a pistol. A pertinent fact that suddenly popped into his mind at the sight of the big nest of dinosaur eggs at his feet.

The nest was nearly a meter in diameter, vines and grass twisted into a rough circle, and padded with mud, grass, and ferns. All the eggs were cracked open or in pieces, long ago hatched or eaten by a predator, but what made him pause—and his heart beat a little faster—was the size of the eggs. Each one was half the size of his head.

So how big would that make the dinosaurs? Larger than a man, he knew that much. Had they hatched leaf-eaters, or predators? There was no way for him to know. Suddenly he didn't feel so alone under the trees, so invulnerable. For the first time, he looked over his shoulder, checking to see if there was anyone, or anything, behind him. He listened intently for thirty seconds before stepping out from behind the tree and moving on, Blackbird up and ready.

* * *

Colonel Richard Kresge, Raven PMC, was on yet another encrypted video call, this time with both the president and attorney general of Mexico. He didn't enjoy such political calls; his stomach was in knots at the thought of saying something that might be taken the wrong way by people who could, with a phone call, end his career. But that was part of the job.

"This property, what do we know about it?" the president asked.

"*La Fuerza* bought it through one of their shell companies more than fifteen years ago," the attorney general said.

"My men on the ground tell me it was a small coffee farm, but appears to have been abandoned for a few years," Kresge volunteered.

The president was in a shiny silver suit that seemed to reflect hints of pink when he shifted his body. It was far too flashy for Kresge's taste, but such outfits had become the man's trademark. He was in fact driving several men's business fashion trends in Latin America, although the expensive suits were a target for his opponents who said he was out of touch with the struggling, poor population of his country. "And how many men are there now?"

"Forty-five or so at last count," Kresge told him. "We've scanned the area with satellites and drones. No sign of anything that could be large amounts of cash." His inventory of military drones was as low as it had ever been. Raven corporate had sent more than half of them overseas to other brushfire wars, now that the Mexican conflict was finally cooling off. The one he'd tasked to surveil the site north of Xicotepec had needed to head back to Victoria Base for refueling, and then he'd been told to use it and all the other drones in the region, armed and otherwise, to cover Tampico and the Cuban flotilla making its way across the Gulf. He understood the command decision, even if he wasn't happy about leaving O'Malley and his team 'orphaned,' the current Raven slang for a team in the field without airborne support overhead. "They don't have any vehicles bigger than a large pickup, at least that we've seen so far. So if they're there for the cash, there's no outward indication. They could just be using a location they're familiar with on their way to the Cuban fleet at Tampico. Per your request, we've got so many drones and aircraft over there that you could walk across the sky."

He thought about how to say what needed to be said. "If none of us cared whether any money there was recovered or destroyed, I could order airstrikes right now, sidetrack a few drones armed with missiles, followed up by Ospreys and Peregrines with missiles and chainguns, and fill the air with confetti. I believe you'd prefer to have the cash recovered, for a number of reasons, which complicates things, but not as much as the temporary ceasefire has."

The president's face creased in a frown. "*Sí*. Authorizing that ceasefire was a political move, and I would be lying if I said I was happy about it, but I believe we are all aware of the realities involved?" The president looked at their faces. "Arturo, you are a man of law. Colonel, you are a military man. Neither of you are ignorant of the politics of this. Money in this amount is no longer money, it is a hammer, a political sledgehammer. Letting these *cabrones* simply show off to the world they have this money would be very bad. Having them transfer that amount of money to Cuba would be as bad, or worse, of a political development, and not just for Mexico, but our allies," he said, giving Kresge a pointed look.

He leaned back, scratched his chin, and looked around his empty office, then gave an expressive shrug. "So who's to say what happens in the mountains? The area is remote, no? Perhaps these guerrillas are unaware of the ceasefire, or perhaps they simply do not care, and might open fire on your men, who would have no choice but to defend themselves. That is perfectly acceptable under the terms of the ceasefire as I laid them out before Congress and the media. After everything that has happened, *La Fuerza* has very little political influence or voice in the media. If at some point they claim we violated the ceasefire, there are many who will refuse to believe them and just as many won't care," he said pointedly.

* * *

The area around him brightened perceptibly, and after another slow ten steps, Seamus found himself at the western edge of the coffee field. Most of the jungle had been hacked back, leaving just a few taller trees to provide shade for the coffee trees, which were planted in rows running east to west and trimmed to bushes.

Seamus peered out across the field. He suspected the coffee plants originally hadn't been much more than five or six feet tall, the rows the same distance apart, but after being so long untended, they'd grown both up and out, and now the branches of the rows were nearly touching. The coffee branches hung low, heavy with ripe fruit, clusters of small yellow and red cherries half-hidden behind oval, bright green leaves. Underneath their branches, around their trunks, the ground was nearly bare, but between the rows, the grass had grown wild, thick, and nearly waist high.

He'd thought, from this position on the edge of the tree line, he'd have a clear view of the buildings and the guerrillas, but that wasn't the case. Between the rows of overgrown trees curving gently back and forth, he could only see the top half of the big barn, and then only if he was standing upright. Frowning, Seamus took a knee behind a thick bush with dark, glossy leaves and stuck his earpiece back in. The rain had thinned to a light drizzle but was still coming down.

"Alpha is back. Did I miss anything?" he murmured. It had taken him half an hour to traverse the kilometer of valley floor. He could have left the earpiece in, but he'd wanted both ears available, considering how poor his hearing was after so many firefights, and especially after spotting the nest.

"*Drone's still on station. No arrivals or departures,*" Corey said in his ear. "*Delta is back in the area at Site Three, in the second vehicle.*" Which put Alvarez about five kilometers in the opposite direction from Corey and Torres on a small two-track.

"I'm at the west end of the field, but I can't see shite; it's too bloody overgrown. But… I think I can sneak in close to the bastards without them being any the wiser."

"*It's your call, I'm not there,*" Corey said after a brief pause. "*Be advised, we just spoke with the colonel. You want the good news or the bad news?*"

"There's good news? Color me shocked."

Corey snorted. "*Well, he doesn't have any more drones for us, armed or otherwise. Sounds like they're tasking all of them for the Cuban navy.*"

"Mmm. Is that the good news or the bad news?"

"*You tell me. He also said that our rules of engagement have changed, but I'm not sure to what.*"

"Excuse me?"

"*The colonel said about the new ROE, and I quote, 'Do whatever you can to not damage the package, but tell that Irish prick he finally got what he wanted. He's a double…' What did he say?*"

"*Double oh seven,*" Torres said helpfully. He didn't know what it meant either.

Seamus smiled and couldn't help but chuckle.

"*What does that mean?*" Corey asked.

"Now that's just not right," Seamus said, his eyebrows coming together. "The inspector can be excused, he's Mexican, but such a lack of culture on your part is inexcusable."

"*Is it from an old movie?*" Corey said.

"You're killing me, you baby-faced twat," Seamus said. "Death of a thousand cuts. I'm not that bloody old, am I?" He sighed as theatrically as possible while staying quiet as a whisper. "James Bond. They've made over thirty bleedin' movies about the man, haven't they?" The last one had come out over fifteen years earlier. There had been some talk about Randy Max, when he was younger, taking up the role, but that hadn't happened.

"*Oh, yeah, that guy, but what's 'double oh seven' mean?*"

"That's his code number, isn't it? He's a double-oh agent, which was a real thing for a time. Best of the best, left alone in the field, and trusted to do whatever needed to be done without having to ask permission or get approval from the boss. Which means he's got a license to kill." He smiled. "Complete personal discretion on pulling the trigger."

"*Isn't that pretty much how you operate anyway?*"

"Well, aye, but now I won't have to beg forgiveness, will I? Right. How much battery life left on the drone?"

"*At least an hour.*"

"Okay, I'm going to keep the earpiece in while I sneak into this field. Call out if it looks like any of them clue to me. I'll click twice when I'm in position."

"*Copy.*"

Seamus rubbed fresh mud on his face and hands. When he was done, he peered out into the field again. The tall grass was light brown and pale green, and dry, it was probably waist high, but the rain had weighed it down so it lay in sheaves angling left and right. The rain had stopped, but the air was so thick with moisture, he could see it, like a faint mist.

Cradling the Blackbird atop his forearms, Seamus got down on his belly and crawled out of the tree line. Even bent over under the weight of water, the grass reached above his head, which was the point. However, the grass was so thick he couldn't crawl through it, he had to crawl over it, pushing it down with his body. He made for the closest coffee plant.

Its heavily-laden branches reached nearly to the ground, but beneath it, the grass was sparse and short. The branches enclosed him much like an umbrella, the thick layer of leaves completely concealing him. The coffee cherries grew in small bunches along the branches. He got up onto his knees and plucked one of the dark red, nearly purple cherries. It was the size of a small grape, and firm. He popped it into his mouth and chewed, only to discover the pit was most of the cherry, but what meat there was was sweet and tasty.

Outside the reach of the cherry-laden branches, the grass formed a tall, thick hedge around the plant. In contrast, the area underneath the tree was practically bare. Rather than fight the tall grass between the rows, Seamus crawled from one tree to the next. There was very little grass to deal with, and it was like a dark tunnel heading in the exact direction he wanted to go.

"*Be advised, I'm trying to spot you, and I can't,*" he heard Corey say in his ear as he crawled past his eighth or ninth coffee plant. "*No change with our friends, they're in and out of the buildings and their vehicles. I'll shut up now.*" The radio went silent, and Seamus smiled as he kept to a slow but steady pace. His elbows and knees were smeared with mud and the meat of rotten coffee cherries dotting the ground beneath the trees.

Then his radio came to life again. "*Prepare to copy. Click when ready.*" Seamus paused and gave them one click on the radio. "*Okay. Two vehicles just passed us heading your direction. One truck full of men, and a police SUV.*"

"*The search parties,*" he heard Torres say. "*I thought that fat police chief would have called it off due to the rain. If they make the turn ahead of them, they will go right into your valley. Double-click to acknowledge.*" Seamus clicked his transmitter twice and stared out past the branches at the gray sky, the distant ridge just visible. A vehicle full of armed civilians, and another with local cops, heading right toward the more than forty armed men he knew were at the far end of the valley, potentially guarding a few billion in cash.

Several minutes later, the radio came alive again. "*Delta has multiple vehicles inbound to your location,*" they heard. "*Three, six… stand by.*" They waited for thirty seconds. Seamus kept crawling, elbow, knee, elbow, knee. Finally, Alvarez came back on the radio. "*Eight, total eight vehicles passing Site Three, southbound.*"

"*Delta, are they civilian search parties?*" Corey asked.

There was only a short pause before they got a response. "*Negative, negative, ellos son Fuerzan. At least twenty men. Pickups, SUVs, one van, and a truck with a big box on the back.*"

"Shite," Seamus swore soundlessly and resumed crawling, trying to go faster without making any more noise.

* * * * *

Chapter Twenty

The rain had been off and on for most of the day, but now seemed to have stopped, though the sky was completely overcast, the clouds in the elevated valley low enough to touch. Pepe was standing just inside the open barn door, talking to Cristobal, a sergeant he'd known for a few years, on his satpalm.

"*Sí*, and if you follow that for just over twelve kilometers—pay attention to your odometer—you will cross over a ridge and come down into a valley. There will be a narrow road off to your left. Look close, or you will miss it. Turn there, and we are at the end of the valley."

"*Sí, Jefe*, see you soon."

Pepe put his palm away, crossed his arms, and stared out at the long valley, scowling at nothing in particular. He was unhappy. Was he leading his men into a trap? There was no way to know if *el presidente's* announcement of a ceasefire was genuine or a ruse to draw them out. He was gambling with not just his life and freedom, but that of his men. He didn't like it, and apparently neither did some of them, as he'd lost a good number of men since they'd arrived. Six at last count had simply disappeared, walking off into the mountains, including Sandoval, which both surprised and angered him. He'd thought the young man had more faith in his leadership. That had put him in a foul mood. *Mas Fuerzan* were still coming, putting their faith in the offer, and in him. They had eighteen hours before the fleet was scheduled to reach port. And then… they would see.

"I've never been on a boat," one of the men standing nearby said.

"If we get on one of those huge cruise ships I saw on the news, it won't be like a real boat," another man told him. "They're like mountains on the water, you don't even feel the waves."

"How long does it take to sail to Cuba?" They couldn't stop talking about it. It was all they could talk about. Really, all they wanted to talk about. It kept their minds off losing the fight, off the fact that they were, in fact, running away. That was one reason they were drinking so heavily. Normally he wouldn't have allowed it, but this wasn't a normal situation.

"A few days, maybe?"

"I hear Cuban girls are incredible."

"I wonder if we'll be able to spend any time on the beach."

"Under the drones of the *escaras*? No, thank you."

"No, not Tampico, *estúpido*, Cuba. Havana or wherever."

"Cuba is supposed to have beautiful beaches."

Pepe walked away from the incessant, droning, inane conversation that had been going on for hours as the rain fell and he'd been trapped inside the barn with the men. He stepped out into the middle of the overgrown two-track that served as a driveway and looked around. All the vehicles were tucked between the trees behind the buildings, so they weren't obvious, but still, he didn't think they'd be hard to spot if the *escaras* or the Mexican military had drones or satellites scanning the area. They'd been there for two days already with no problems, and less than a day to go…

"Cristobal's here," someone called out.

Pepe frowned and checked his watch. The convoy shouldn't have arrived that quickly, unless they'd been racing at near-suicidal speeds down the curving, muddy roads, but he heard it as well, the sound of engines.

Men came out of the big barn and the trees, looking west. The sound of the engines grew in volume, then he caught a glimpse of a truck past the coffee trees. Then one of his men cursed, and he saw that in front of the truck was a police vehicle, an SUV painted black and tan, with a gold shield on the door.

"*¡Relajar!*" he called out loudly to his men. "*Nadie hace nada estúpido.*" Many of them had rifles in their hands, but pointed down at the ground.

"It's not military or *federales*, it's local police," one of the men with good eyes loudly announced, reading the logo on the door. It was the pickup behind the police SUV that concerned Pepe. He saw three men in it, one of whom had a rifle or shotgun in his hands.

A few seconds after Pepe spotted the police vehicle at the edge of the coffee field, it abruptly jerked to a stop as if the driver wasn't expecting to see men in this area. Then it turned off the road, which ran along the base of the south ridge until it crossed over the low saddle at the east end of the valley, onto the track that led to the barns.

Pepe had a pistol stuck in his waistband, and there were twenty men around him, most of them armed with rifles, when the two vehicles came to a stop before him. The police officer climbed out of the marked vehicle, and several of Pepe's men laughed quietly at how comically fat he was. He also didn't seem very confident as he walked around the front of his vehicle. Which was understandable, given that he was so outnumbered. One fat, uniformed police officer, and three men who looked like farmers or mechanics climbing out of the pickup, armed with shotguns and bolt-action rifles.

"*Hombres,*" the police officer said politely, nodding his head at them. He picked up by the position of the men around him that Pepe was in charge. "I am *Capitán* Ibarra, chief of police of Xicotepec de Juarez. And you are?" Chief of police, that would explain his age, and why he was so fat.

"Call me Pepe," he said, and several of his men snickered.

Ibarra looked at all the men behind Pepe. He knew they were *La Fuerza,* and Pepe knew he knew. The fat man chose his words carefully. "May I ask what you're doing here?"

"Weary travelers, just taking a rest before moving on," Pepe said.

The chief of police frowned and glanced at the three men with him, whom Pepe had to admit did not seem too friendly toward the cop. "I'm investigating the deaths of two men. Missing and presumed murdered not too far from here."

"We had nothing to do with that," Pepe said with an easy smile. In truth, he had no idea if any of his men had had run-ins with the locals, but until they got on those ships, they were still soldiers of *El Fraternidad Progresista para un México Nuevo,* his men, and they didn't answer to some fat local *policía* who looked like he lived on *churros* and bribes.

El capitán smiled nervously. "Are you sure? Perhaps there was an accident. Things happen sometimes." He shrugged expressively.

"Are you calling the colonel a liar?" one of Pepe's men demanded.

Capitán Ibarra licked his rubbery lips. "Of course not. I meant no disrespect." His eyes darted left and right. "Personally, I think it was animals."

"You're calling us animals?" another of Pepe's men said. He couldn't tell if the outrage in his voice was real. The men were stressed and had been bottling it up or drowning it in beer and tequila.

The police chief held up his hands. "No, no. We have had several animal attacks on the edge of town. Have you seen any large animals? Jaguars, perhaps? The two men who were most recently killed, we never found their bodies."

"Then how do you even know they are dead?" one of Pepe's men asked. "Maybe they just ran off."

"The blood," one of the townsmen said, looking at the guerrillas with both fear and anger.

Pepe slowly shook his head back and forth. "That's got nothing to do with us, but thank you for stopping by."

Capitán Ibarra couldn't decide whether to be offended or relieved that he was being dismissed. He opened his mouth, not sure what he was going to say, then paused when he heard an engine, distant, but growing louder. "Cristobal," one of the men before him said. Ibarra didn't know who Cristobal was, but when he'd spotted the men and vehicles under the trees, he'd put out a radio call to his officers helping with the search. It was a black and tan *Policia de Xicotepec de Juarez* pickup truck that bounced into view.

Pepe frowned when he saw it. "Are we going to have a problem?" he asked the fat, sweating cop.

"No, no problem," Ibarra said. He wondered if perhaps he'd made a mistake, as the pickup containing two of his men pulled up in the grass beside his SUV. As it did, even more *Fuerzan* walked out from the trees. Even with six people, they were outnumbered more than five to one.

"What do you mean? Of course there's a problem," one of the townspeople said. The man stomped up next to Ibarra and pointed at the leader of the guerrillas. "Why aren't you arresting him? Taking him back to the station for interrogation? You know they killed Ruggerio and Raul."

"If you don't shut up, I'm going to arrest you," Ibarra said as his men got out of their truck. They were warily eyeing the thirty-plus men under the trees, most of them carrying rifles. There was no question about who and what they were. The officers made sure to keep their hands clear of the pistols on their belts. "*¿Capitán?*" one of them asked. "*¿Necesitas ayuda?*"

"Now, why would he need help?" Pepe asked, deciding to have a little fun with the situation. At least it was better than being bored. He'd been bored since arriving in the valley, stuck in the barn most of the time to avoid the rain.

Ibarra lifted his hands, palms out. "No, no, I don't need help. You're fine. People are just upset over the two dead men. I'm sure you had nothing to do with that. You have not seen any large animals? Tracks? I'm sure that's what it was, an animal attack. Jaguar, or maybe a dinosaur."

Many of Pepe's men laughed at that. "Dinosaur?" several of them scoffed. None of them had seen any, and most of them didn't believe the animals even existed, not outside a few parks reserved for rich, evil capitalists.

"We'll just leave right now. Sorry to have disturbed you," Ibarra told Pepe, obviously some sort of officer in *La Fuerza*. He was in his mid-thirties and had clearly seen a lot of war, enough to use a nickname so the Mexican military would have a harder time tracking down his family for reprisals. There was a deadness in his eyes that Ibarra usually only saw in the worst criminals, the sociopaths. That wasn't a problem when they were locked in a cell, but this commander had three dozen armed men with him.

Pepe held up a hand, now smiling. "No, hold on. Let me hear about these dinosaurs. Have you seen them?" Ibarra couldn't help but notice the man's smile didn't reach his eyes.

Ibarra shook his head. "No, no one has seen them. The animal attacks, they happen at night, usually, on the edge of the city. In fog. Personally, I think it is a big cat, maybe a jaguar, but some people, they have said dinosaurs. They claim to have seen tracks…"

"It sounds like they have overactive imaginations," Pepe said.

Ibarra nodded vigorously, his chins wiggling. "Yes, yes, but they are worried, and scared."

"What kind of detective are you, that you can't find a Tyrannosaurus rex?" one of Pepe's men demanded of the police chief, which got a lot of laughs.

"Most of the dinosaurs, I've heard, are small," Ibarra said, "the size of dogs or horses."

"Have you seen a lot of dinosaurs?" Pepe asked him.

"No, just on the internet. People post videos. The ones from Chichén Itza last year…" Ibarra took a breath and tried to get back on topic. "Like I said, we are sorry to have bothered you. Obviously your men were not involved in… whatever happened. We'll just…" He stopped talking as he saw the guerrilla commander had stopped listening to him, and was instead looking past him. Ibarra realized he could hear more engines. Another search party, obviously. He wasn't sure, but he thought that was probably a good thing. The more civilians, the more even the odds, the more witnesses, the better chance there was of this Pepe letting them head back to Xicotepec.

That was a lot of noise. A lot of engines. How many vehicles were in the search party? Ibarra turned to look. He caught glimpses of them over the coffee trees bouncing up the road. A truck, a van, another truck... when he saw the fourth vehicle, he finally realized it was no local search party.

The lead vehicle, a large pickup carrying four men, pulled up beside Ibarra's police vehicle, and the passenger window rolled down. The man inside looked at Ibarra, the marked SUV, then Pepe. "Problem?" he asked, one eyebrow raised.

Pepe smiled at Cristobal. "No, Sergeant. We're just having a conversation with *Capitán* Ibarra here, the local police chief. Why don't you park your vehicles over there and join us?" Cristobal smiled and waved at his driver.

As the engines growled, the vehicle swayed over the thick grass around the parked vehicles and into the trees. One of his men walked up beside Pepe and leaned in.

"*¿Jefe?* If I may say something?"

"Yes?" Pepe asked, smirking at the police chief a dozen feet away. The man was sweating through his uniform.

"*El puerco policía.* Maybe he radioed out to everyone, telling them exactly where they were. Maybe just to the other car. But those *policía* in the second car seemed surprised to see us, so I think he just radioed his location. Do you agree?"

"It did seem that way. What's your point?" Their conversation was lost under the growl of the newly arrived vehicles moving back and forth, trying to find parking spots between and behind the buildings.

"If they go back, there is no doubt everyone will know exactly where we are, and how many of us there are. There is supposed to be a ceasefire, so maybe he tells no one. Maybe none of these people tells anyone. Maybe they tell the military or *escaras* where we are, and they don't care. Maybe."

The man wasn't saying anything Pepe hadn't already been considering. Cristobal walked up, followed by half a dozen of his men, all carrying rifles. "So," Cristobal said, a gleam in his eye and a smile on his face, glancing from Pepe to the fat police chief and back, "what are we doing?"

* * *

Seamus knelt under a coffee tree 25 meters away, invisible in the dark shadows behind the branches and the tall grass. He had the Blackbird up, safety off, the tip of his triangle reticle dancing gently over Pepe's head, but his finger was nowhere near the trigger. As much as he would have liked to start dumping bodies, it would be sure suicide. With the new arrivals, there had to be 75 FRAP fighters. Against who? Him and six locals who would be somewhere between little and no use in a firefight. He'd likely be long dead before Corey, Torres, and Alvarez could race up to his rescue.

He was catching only snatches of the conversation between the guerrilla leader and the police chief, who was clearly in way over his head. He likely hadn't been expecting to run into FRAP at all, much less a company-sized element. Seamus' eyes darted back and forth between the two men and the others. He took a deep breath, lowered the Blackbird, and flipped on the safety.

After what felt like two lifetimes in combat zones, he was an expert at reading situations, reading body language, and he wasn't surprised at all when the conversation became shouts, the smiles became snarls, and the rifles of the guerrillas came up to point at the cops and locals. The six people were disarmed and marched away from the vehicles—straight toward Seamus. His eyes went wide, and he dove for the dirt just before the guerrillas opened up on full-auto, executing the six men. One bullet thumped into the ground near him, and several snapped over his head.

He heard laughing and voices that became clearer as men walked closer to him. "Drag the bodies into the jungle behind the buildings," he heard, and recognized the voice of the leader. He raised his head and saw the man less than ten meters away, looking down at the corpulent corpse of the police chief.

"*Sí, jefe.*"

The guerrilla leader shouted out to another of the men. Guerrillas tossed the bodies into the back of a pickup amid much cursing, and they drove into the trees between the two buildings. Then the men walked away, back toward the barn.

Seamus lay back down and clicked on his comm. "You catch that?" he murmured, lips almost in the dirt.

"*Yeah, shit,*" said Corey, who'd watched it live on the drone's camera. "*Nothing like a firing squad to start your day. You close?*"

"The bodies almost fell on me. Listen, I think I recognize the leader, goes by Pepe. Can't remember his actual name. Colonel, I think, one of the top FRAP officers still breathing. Looks like he still has a command."

"*I'll relay the info. You close enough to hear what they're doing? Why they're here?*"

"Negative."

"*All right. Drone is still on station, but I'm pulling it back, battery's about dead. I'll call upstairs and... shit, you see this?*" Seamus couldn't see anything with his face in the dirt to muffle the faint sounds he was making. He lifted his head, then carefully rose to one knee and peered out. The guerrillas were backing the white box truck through the big open doors of the barn. "*You think they're loading it up?*"

"Shite," Seamus swore almost silently. He peered at the barn, and once again examined it through the binoculars. He couldn't see much of the interior, and unless he wanted to sit out in the open grass and wave at the guerrillas, he wouldn't be able to see much more, at least not from the field out front...

"It'll be dark soon," he told the team. "I'm going to slip sideways through the field, and as soon as it's dark enough to not get spotted, I'm going to head into those trees, circle around, get a better look at what they're doing, and maybe peek into the barn."

"*Ahh... do you think that's a good idea?*" Torres asked.

"Dense as jungle across the way," Seamus assured him. "I've got night vision goggles. They'll never know I'm there."

Alvarez spoke for the first time. "*I believe those are called 'famous last words,'*" he said drily.

* * * * *

Chapter Twenty-One

Sadie ran into the rain, into the jungle, Hein at her side at first, then letting her draw ahead. She saw Luc and Michael in front of her, jogging awkwardly through the underbrush after Leo. There was a thick line of trees draped with vines keeping them just within sight of the R&D building. They paralleled the building, catching glimpses of it through the bushes and between the trees, everything glistening in the steady rain.

Sadie caught up to Michael almost immediately. The computer expert spent very little time out of a desk chair and ran awkwardly. "Where are we going?" he panted.

"Just keep moving," she said, waving him on with her free hand. In her other she held Hein's rifle, and it gave her a sense of comfort. Michael gave her a dirty look but began moving once again, walking as fast as he could, moving like his knees were built of jelly and string. Sadie looked over her shoulder and saw Hein there, half-turned, checking behind them. They were leaving a clear trail through the undergrowth.

As they drew even with the far end of the building and the parked Vaquero, the dense tree line moved away from the parking lot there. Leo crouched low and gestured at them to do the same. Then, moving more slowly, he took a path deeper into the vegetation. The Vaquero was no longer alone in the parking lot, it was surrounded by guerrilla vehicles. He could see a dozen men on foot talking and examining the armored personnel carrier.

"Why do you have a rifle?" Michael asked her, trying to distract himself from his fear and physical discomfort. He was scared and confused, and running through the jungle in the middle of a rainstorm, trying to evade enemy soldiers. Exactly the last place he wanted to be.

"*Ta gueule*," she growled at him and shoved him to keep him moving, but the truth was, she was tired of being frightened, with no way to deal with her fear, her memories, her nightmares. She was angry with herself at how she'd let the fear control her. She hadn't realized just how tight a grip the fear had around her heart until she'd followed the sudden urge, ran down the hall, and grabbed Hein's rifle.

She knew how to use a shotgun and a rifle. The weight of it in her hand, the confident, solid feel of wood and steel against her palm, didn't erase the fear—it allowed her to shove it into a corner where the fear would be out of the way, held at bay by well-armed anger. She didn't have time for fear. As Seamus liked to say, she had shit to do.

Michael was about to say something, or give her another dirty look, or both, when he caught a glimpse of the guerrillas clustered around their transportation. A tough-looking lot in worn clothes, ignoring the rain, rifles held casually in their hands. His face went pale, and he instinctively crouched, which was good, but froze, which wasn't.

Sadie grabbed his hand and pulled him along with her. She was just as terrified as he was, but she'd somehow locked that fear into a box off to the side, where it didn't affect her, and she wasn't letting it out. All she felt was irritation and anger. She knew what had to be done, knew what they had to do—get away without being spotted. The only problem was the jungle literally pressing up against the building, trees, vines, and bushes in a snarled tangle so thick, every time they tried to angle away from the building, it pushed them back in tighter.

They drew even with the parking lot, crouched nearly on all fours and moving slowly, the sound of their passage hidden in the rush of the falling rain. Leo, in the lead, saw a gap between two trees, almost an archway festooned with vines, and most importantly, heading almost directly away from the parking lot and building.

Leo paused beside it, making sure Luc saw him, then slipped through, disappearing on the far side. As Luc did the same, one of the guerrillas by the Vaquero saw something, movement or the outline of a head, jerked his rifle up, and fired a shot in their direction.

Michael yelped and fell to the ground in surprise. Sadie, next to him, thought he'd been shot, and it filled her with sudden fury, all her pent-up emotions boiling over. She stopped thinking. Screaming obscenities, she raised herself to her full height, shouldered the rifle, and fired, the noise of the big-game rifle like a bomb going off, the muzzle blast stripping leaves off the vines in front of her. It rocked her back, and she almost fell down.

She worked the bolt as the rifle came down out of recoil, the big brass case deflecting drops of rain as it arced to the ground. After the shot, she couldn't hear, and wasn't aware she was screaming in French, profanity that would have shocked even the war-weary guerrillas had they understood it. As soon as the sights came down on the guerrillas, she fired once more, blowing leaves and bark off branches.

Then Hein tackled her to the ground as the space above them was filled with wild return fire, the bullets snapping overhead.

Sadie was screaming with rage, trying to work the bolt of the rifle even as Hein lay across her, shielding her with his body. "Get off me, *enculé!*" she shouted reflexively, then Leo opened up on full auto from behind the cover of a tree, firing past them, emptying an entire magazine at the men filling the parking lot. They scattered and dove for cover behind vehicles.

"Go! Run!" Hein shouted in her face, shoving her forward before rolling back, lifting the shotgun, and emptying it in the direction of the guerrillas as he sat on the wet ground, thunder rolling across the parking lot as he filled it with clouds of tungsten buckshot, firing blindly through the underbrush. Then he was up and running after Sadie, flying past Leo, who was changing magazines behind cover.

Return fire whipped past and over their heads as Leo fired another long burst at the guerrillas, then he pulled back behind the tree and broke into a run. "Go, go, GO!" he shouted at Michael as he caught up to him. "Follow Luc!" Luc was up ahead, throwing himself bodily through the greenery. Leo didn't know where the man was going, but at the moment, it didn't matter—all that mattered was putting distance between them and the guerrillas, who were sure to give chase.

Hein was moving as fast as he could while he stuffed fresh shells into the Benelli. Leo posted himself behind a tree and let Hein go past. He thought he saw movement and fired a three-round burst, the G3 bucking in his hands like a wild horse. Full-auto was bad for hitting anything, but good if you were trying to discourage pursuit. He fired another burst, then sprinted after Hein. They were trampling a clear trail through the wet vegetation, but luckily it was so dense he couldn't see more than a few meters in any direction. That meant the guerrillas couldn't see to shoot them.

Hein stopped beside a tree and shouldered the shotgun, covering Leo as he ran by. His ears were warbling from the gunfire, but he thought he heard shouting from the guerrillas, getting closer. He fired once down their trail, then ran after Leo, stuffing a fresh shell in the gun, wondering if this was the day he died. He looked up and put on speed, then did a doubletake at the sight of Sadie, positioned on one knee behind a fallen tree, his rifle at her shoulder, covering him, murder in her eyes.

"No, no!" he said in a panic, eyes wide, jumping over the tree to her side. He reached for her as she fired, the blast of the .300 Winchester Magnum rocking both of them back. In the distance, a man screamed. "You're going to get killed. Come on!" He grabbed the back of her shirt and pulled her to her feet as she worked the bolt again. Return fire hammered the vegetation around them and thudded into the downed tree. Fist full of her shirt, he dragged her with him into the jungle.

* * *

It was a nightmare, blindly running through a dark, wet jungle as bullets whipped by over their heads. Luc was in the lead, and didn't know where he was, didn't know where he was going, but that didn't seem to matter. Every time he slowed down or stopped, gasping as he fought for breath, Leo or Hein, or even Sadie, inexplicably carrying a huge rifle, would catch up to him and yell at him to keep running, shove him forward. He fell over and over, knees and elbows green, grimy, and bruised, but fear kept the lawyer going.

Michael was having an even worse time of it. He never exercised and was carrying twenty extra pounds. Luc grabbed him by the arm and dragged him along, both of them panting and wheezing as they fought for air. After what seemed like forever, the guerrillas stopped shouting, maybe because they were having to fight for air as well. The shooting died down to occasional random shots far behind them, then those stopped as well. And still they ran, until Luc could run no more.

Leo jogged up behind them. Luc and Michael were bent over, fighting for air. "Don't stop, keep going!" he urged them.

Luc didn't have the breath to talk, he just pointed. There was a wall in front of them. A low wall, waist-high, concrete, but designed to look like molded earth. Leo looked left and right and couldn't see where the barrier ended. "Climb it," he told them in a low growl.

Wheezing and trading a look, Luc and Michael climbed over the wall and fell to the ground on the far side, which was several feet lower. Leo, Sadie, and then Hein jumped down behind them, then they ran as a group across even ground covered with ferns and low bushes.

Luc felt exposed, out in the open for the first time since they'd started running, so it took him a few seconds before he realized where they were. "Hey!" he said, pointing around them.

"Yeah," Hein said. "Keep moving."

They'd climbed over the wall into one of Pangaea's animal exhibits. On the inside, the concrete wall was two meters high. There were a few low hills in the center of the big oval habitat, but mostly it was even ground that was now covered with a thick layer of low vegetation, horsetail grass, ferns, and paleolithic plants, cycads, benettites, and a few ginkgoes. Luc and Michael looked around, wide-eyed, but of course whatever animals had been penned in the enclosure were long dead or escaped. With a wall only two meters high to keep them in, the animals in this pen had to have been somewhat small, or unable to jump or climb.

The animal exhibit was roughly a hundred meters in width. Leo paused at the far side and lifted first Sadie, then Luc and Michael so they could climb over the wall. The rain was still coming down, and the far side of the enclosure, where they'd jumped down, was a fuzz behind the falling drops. He didn't see any pursuers. He hadn't heard any in several minutes either, but that didn't mean they'd broken off the chase. Leo hoisted Hein up, then the older man gave him a hand and pulled Leo over the wall.

They found themselves on a wide asphalt path bordered by overgrown shrubs and ornamental trees. It ran between two exhibits, and the bushes, growing wild for twenty years, had turned the path into a bit of a tunnel, the asphalt almost completely covered in years of dead and rotting leaves. For the moment, they were hidden from view. Hein pointed, and they started along the path at a slow jog.

The path wound back and forth, with trails branching off to either side, garbage bins every fifty steps. Hein tried to keep them heading in a constant direction, as he didn't want to accidentally circle back. At the intersection of three wide asphalt walking paths, they found a long-dead electronic kiosk. Hein looked at the dark digital display and frowned.

"I think I know where we are," Sadie said between pants. She'd been in the park once and had studied the maps of it endlessly. She pointed. "That heads to the Promenade, the front of the park, and that—" she pointed at the path leading off to the left, "—heads to the north side of the park, toward the hotel."

"Then that way," Hein said, nodding at the path north, following a sudden impulse. It seemed a less likely route for fleeing people to follow; the path was a bit narrow and darker as it curved out of sight.

"I'll take the rear," Leo said.

Hein nodded, then looked at the group. They were soaked through, dirty, and smeared with grass and leaves. Luc and Michael looked miserable. Sadie, gripping the rifle, looked determined. With the rain falling, it was dark as dusk. "Come on. We can't stop." The sound of the rain would muffle their noises, but it would also hide the sound of any pursuers until they were dangerously close.

Hein started up the north path at a fast walk, wiping the rain off his face with a hand, then glancing down at the shotgun in his hands. He'd burned through almost all his ammunition trying to create distance between them and the pursuing FRAP. There were three, maybe four shells left in the Benelli, and that was it. He wasn't sure how many magazines Leo had left for the G3. Maybe he was on his last one. They'd broken contact with the guerrillas, and what they needed to do now was create distance.

Hein walked fast, jogged a short distance, then fell back into a quick walk, going as fast as he thought his tired companions could manage. The path wound back and forth, walled animal enclosures appearing to either side. Some featured overhanging platforms. Once they passed underneath a glassed-in walkway, the windows fogged over. It stretched from a three-story building in the distance to some sort of observation tower with an exterior railed deck. Twice they hurried by small buildings made to look like cabanas, "SnackShack" still visible in red-edged fat yellow letters on their faded marquees. Near each one were square, unadorned structures slowly being swallowed by shrubs and vines—bathrooms for the park guests.

They passed through an open play area meant for small children, with cartoonish dinosaurs small enough to climb on and a low fountain styled of roaring baby T. rexes that was now filled with weeds and a few wildflowers dancing in the heavy raindrops. Not far beyond that they crossed over train tracks for the line that circled most of the park and provided great views into several of the animal exhibits.

Ahead, Hein saw metal gates, the north entrance to the park. He paused at them and waited for the rest of the group to catch up. Behind him, past the gates, was a narrow parking lot, then a wall of evenly spaced pine trees, obviously planted. Past the trees, he could see the top half of the park hotel. Somewhere on the far side of it, if he remembered correctly, there was a narrow river that bordered the park property to the north.

"Where are we going?" Michael asked him, water dripping from his nose.

Hein pointed across the parking lot. "Get to the trees, then we'll talk. Go. Run."

Michael scowled at him but broke into a halting jog across the parking lot, which was a riot of grass sprouting from ragged cracks. Leo stood on the far side of the gates as their clients jogged across the parking lot, and the two men watched the path. Hein had been checking, and the asphalt paths hadn't shown much sign of their passing. The rotting leaves layering the asphalt looked darker and bruised from being trod on, but he wasn't sure if the guerrillas were sharp enough to spot it. He nodded at Leo, and they moved through the gate and walked backward slowly across the parking lot, jogging the last ten meters. Only once they were hidden from view inside the thick belt of trees, narrow red pines with some sort of flowering bushes gone wild planted at their bases, did Hein allow himself to relax a little bit.

"Okay, so?" Luc asked him.

"I think we've lost them, but I can't be sure," Hein said. He looked up, realizing the pines were shielding them from most of the rain.

"So what do we do, hide in the hotel?" Michael asked, glancing at the nearby hotel visible through the trees.

"No, we want to get back to civilization; there's no telling how long they plan to camp out in the park—or how long they might search through it, looking for us," Hein said. He pointed east. "We walk out to 85, and then we flag down a ride."

"What, 85 the highway?" Michael said incredulously. He waved his arms. "That's ten kilometers." He was already exhausted, soaking wet, covered in mud…

"Keep your voice down," Leo growled.

"Are you okay?" Luc asked Sadie. His eyes flicked from her face to the rifle in her hands and back up.

"*Oui. Êtes-vous?*" She cocked an insouciant eyebrow at him. In truth, she had no idea what she was feeling, and wouldn't have been surprised if she was in shock.

He had to smile and shook his head. "My wife is going to kill me for this." He fought equally strong urges to laugh and vomit.

Hein patted the lawyer on the shoulder, then looked at the group. "Less talking, more walking." He pointed. On the far side of the copse they were hiding in, away from the park, was a wide expanse of overgrown grass. In the distance, the grass merged with thicker undergrowth, and then more trees.

* * *

They were tired before they started the cross-country walk from the park to the highway. The dark and rain cut visibility, but they relaxed even more when they pushed into a thick patch of near-jungle not quite a kilometer east of the park hotel and disappeared from sight. It was at that point Hein figured they were safe—he could have tracked their party, but he doubted the guerrillas were capable, even if they found the trail where they'd entered the open land between the park and the highway.

"Are you going to get fired?" Michael asked Hein.

"For what? He did nothing wrong," Sadie said in his defense.

"For abandoning the Vaquero," the computer expert said. "I can't even imagine how much it cost."

Hein chuckled. "It's insured, and it has a kill switch. It's not going anywhere."

"Unless they hotwire it," Luc said. "Can they hotwire it?"

Hein shook his head. "I have no idea. I guess I'll find out tomorrow. Get you back to the hotel, see you off to the airport, then head back with whoever's willing to go, considering the FRAP might still be there." He looked at Luc and Sadie. "There might not be any police willing to accompany me back there for a few days, if then. Maybe Raven? I don't know." He looked at Leo, who shrugged.

"I don't think I left anything in the Vaquero," Luc said. He looked at Sadie, and she shook her head. A change of clothes, that was it.

Half an hour later, after trudging up and down heavily wooded hills that never seemed to end, Michael looked at Hein. "Are you sure we're going the right way?"

"I have a good sense of direction. If we go too far north, we'll run into the river. If so, we can follow it to Llera de Canales."

Michael was soaked through from the rain and pushing through dripping plants, yet he was dying of thirst. "Anyone have anything to drink?"

"In the cooler. In the Vaquero," Hein said with a smile. "We'll be back before you know it, don't worry."

They broke through a tree line and found a field before them, the grass and bushes glistening with drops. Hein found a narrow game trail and took that through the grass, as it was easier walking. They were halfway across the field when a branch snapped loudly off to their right. Everyone stopped, and Hein and Leo dropped to their knees. Sadie planted her feet on the trail and planted the butt of the rifle against her shoulder, the sights on the thick wall of bushes before her.

Her finger tightened on the trigger, taking up the slack. She heard a low sound she couldn't identify. It repeated, and she realized it wasn't coming from a human, but an animal. Her heart began hammering in her chest. A shape pushed through the bushes right in front of her, and she almost fired, thinking, assuming, it was a Coelophysis.

But the shape was all wrong. The size was all wrong.

Stomach acid burning her mouth, breath loud in her ears, she watched over the sights of the rifle as the angular, distinctive head fully emerged from the underbrush. Sadie took a deep breath and dropped the rifle butt from her shoulder, hands shaking, as the Stegosaur snuffled back and forth, and then took a leisurely bite of leaves. The animal took a slow step forward, then another, and its body emerged from the undergrowth, gently shoving bushes aside.

Its head was tiny in comparison to its body, and that was even more evident up close. It nosed at bushes as it slowly walked along, stripping leaves off branches, occasionally sniffing at the ground. It had to have seen them, smelled them, but it paid them no mind.

The five of them watched silently as the Stegosaur glided through the clearing, taking a bite of this, sniffing that, grunting and snorting quietly, its tail with its giant spikes swaying gently back and forth with every step. This had to be the same animal they'd seen the day before from inside the Production building, but their elevated position had prevented her from realizing just how large it was. It had to outweigh an elephant. The plates on its back stretched far above her head, and nose to tail, it was nearly as long as a bus.

The big dinosaur was in no hurry, and they watched until it disappeared into the next patch of trees. "*Putain de merde*," Luc finally breathed.

"So big," Michael said. "I didn't realize."

Sadie laughed, relieved the Stegosaur hadn't been a Coelophysis, or a guerrilla. It had just been... magnificent. Beautiful.

Hein stepped up next to her. He held out the shotgun. "Hold this a second," he told her and took the bolt-action rifle out of her hands. Frowning, she watched him lift the bolt and carefully pull it back. He caught the round that was in the chamber, and held up the big brass cartridge for her to see. He used it as a pointer to show her it was the only one left in the gun.

She nodded, suddenly serious. "*Oui*."

"We should be clear, you shouldn't need it, but... one and done," he said as he slid the cartridge back into the chamber and closed the bolt on it. Then he handed the rifle back to her and touched her shoulder. He didn't know if she was aware of it, but he'd clearly seen her first shot drop a guerrilla like an automobile had fallen on the man.

"Come on, we've got to go," Hein told them.

* * *

"How do you want to do this?" Leo asked Hein, frowning. They were crouched in a deep culvert beside Highway 85, which they'd reached without incident after more than two hours of walking. The rain had finally stopped, but everything, including them, was soaked. They were exhausted and covered head to toe in mud and grime. They collectively poked their heads up like a flock of birds and saw a pair of headlights approaching from the south, perhaps heading to Llera de Canales, but more likely Ciudad Victoria.

Sadie shook her head. "Men," she said with a snort. She scrambled up the wet bank and walked out into the middle of the two-lane highway. She pulled out her flashlight and waved it back and forth, then shone it on herself, on her face and the wet shirt clinging to her chest.

She heard the sound of something big downshifting before she was able to make out any details of the vehicle behind the headlights. It stopped a few meters before her, and she saw it was a commercial bus. The uniformed driver stared at her curiously. No doubt she was quite a sight, a pale Frenchwoman, wet and dirty like she'd been wrestling in a ditch, in the middle of the road after dark in the middle of nowhere. Of course he would stop.

The driver opened the door as Sadie walked around to the side of the bus. The driver hit her with a flurry of rapid Spanish. Sadie swung out the rifle, which she'd been hiding behind her leg, and held it casually at her side, pointed downward. The driver made a small sound, his eyes bulging. *"Un momento, por favor,"* she said and gestured out the windshield.

The man's eyes went even wider as four men, two of them armed, appeared and walked across the road to the bus. Sadie stepped aside for Leo, who hit the driver with a flurry of Spanish. The driver's eyes kept getting wider. Sadie recognized a few words, including *La Fuerza.*

"Sí, sí," the driver said, gesturing toward the back of the bus.

Leo, smiling, inclined his head toward Sadie. She climbed the stairs, and as she passed the driver, told him, *"Gracias."*

There were a dozen passengers, and they stared silently at the five fantastical figures as they boarded the bus. One old woman dressed in black was frowning at Sadie and the big rifle beside her as she sat on a bench seat. She had one hand around the forend, the rifle's butt on the bus floorboards, muzzle pointed at the ceiling. Sadie nodded at her. *"Buenas noches,"* Sadie said politely, as if she was at a dinner party, as the driver set the bus back in motion. The woman's frown deepened.

A man dressed in dirty coveralls, who looked like he wasn't sure he if he was having a weird dream, happily moved from his seat to allow Hein to sit directly behind the driver. Hein laid the shotgun across his thighs and handed the driver two $100 bills for his trouble. The man's eyes bulged once again, and he stuffed the bills into his shirt pocket. "Thank you, thank you," he said with a heavy accent.

Luc and Michael were sitting together and looked ready to fall asleep at any moment. They were so dirty, it was almost comical. Michael looked over at her sitting there, hand on the big rifle planted in the middle of the aisle, as tall as she was when sitting down, and he nodded and smiled.

"What?" she said.

"Badass," he said, nodding at her. "*Dur à cuire.* I told you."

She cursed in French.

"What?" Luc said blearily.

"All that, and for nothing. We never found anything. Well, never found what we were looking for."

Michael shook his head and dug in a pocket. He pulled out something and held it up. It was gray and rectangular, the size of a deck of playing cards.

"What's that?" Sadie asked.

"The hard drive from the MacLeod-Weiss biomedical computer in the Fertilization room. You told me to pull it. If anything has the data you want, it's this, provided it didn't get too wet in my pocket…"

Sadie laughed with delight, leaned over, moving the rifle out of the way, and gave Michael a kiss on the cheek. "Look who saves the day," she said, and he turned bright red. She fought the sudden urge to break into tears. She'd cry later when she was alone in her hotel room.

At the front of the bus, the driver glanced at Leo, who was leaning in the well beside the accordion door, G3 held loosely in his hands in case they ran into any other surprises on the road. "They are probably heading to Tampico," the driver said in rapid Spanish to Leo.

"*¿Las Fuerzan?* What's in Tampico?" Nothing especially came to mind.

"The Cubans."

Hein and Leo traded a look. "What Cubans?" Hein asked in fluent Spanish, surprising the driver.

"Well, I guess they are not there yet," the driver observed with a shrug.

"There for what?"

"*Alto de fuego*," the bus driver said and repeated it in English loud enough for them all to hear. "The ceasefire."

Hein, Sadie, Luc, Leo, and Michael all traded looks, then stared at the driver. "What ceasefire?" they said in unison.

* * * * *

Chapter Twenty-Two

The road leading into the valley wound along the base of the low south ridge from one end to another. At the east end of the valley, it climbed a saddle before disappearing from view. The coffee field was situated three-quarters of the way along the valley, and on the far end of the field, the two-track ran north off the road to the two buildings.

The space between the two-track and the east end of the valley wasn't huge, maybe two hundred meters wide and three hundred long, but like the other end of the valley, it was dense with green: tropical and temperate trees laden with vines, below which were thick shrubs, lacy ferns, and long grass. Beyond the two buildings, the foliage was dark and impenetrable.

The foot and vehicle traffic around the two buildings had matted down the undergrowth. While Seamus couldn't see further in, he suspected that beyond where the vehicles were parked, the undergrowth was just as dense in every direction, and he should be able to sneak up right to the edge of the guerillas' encampment without being spotted. Keeping close to the cliff face on the north side, he suspected he could get all the way to the big barn unnoticed.

He slowly and carefully worked his way southward through the coffee field, staying beneath the fruit-laden trees, but sticking close to the overgrown two-track. When he was within sight of the connecting dirt road, he stopped and looked back toward the buildings. He could see bits and pieces of a few vehicles through gaps in the vegetation, but he couldn't see the buildings themselves, or any of the guerillas unless they stepped out from underneath the trees. Theoretically, he could walk right across the two-track unseen. The jungle was a thick green wall just a few meters away, and he'd only be spotted if somebody happened to wander out and look in his direction right at that moment. The guerrillas seemed to be keeping a lower profile since the shooting, and their leader had pulled everybody underneath the trees.

* * *

Corey called Kresge to update him on the situation, including the execution of half a dozen locals. The colonel cursed under his breath. "So you're telling me we have the highest-ranking officer in *La Fuerza* and seventy-five troops right out in the open? No cover, no heavy weapons?"

"Yes, sir," Corey said.

"And of course we have a ceasefire," Kresge growled.

Corey licked his lips and traded a look with Torres, who could hear everything. "I thought that was, well…"

"What?" Kresge said.

"Kinda flexible," Corey said with a shrug.

Kresge snorted. "'Kinda flexible' means I have latitude to clean up a mess if something happens on the ground. It doesn't mean I can order an airstrike in clear violation of a ceasefire issued by the president of our host country, even if, privately, he's okay with it."

"Oh," Corey said, while Torres nodded.

"Not when my men aren't under fire," Kresge added pointedly. Corey didn't miss the caveat.

"Well, sir…"

"What?"

"As soon as it gets dark enough, O'Malley is going to attempt an infil, see if he can get eyes on that package, confirm its presence, since we now have a box truck on site."

Kresge didn't say anything for a while. Then he sighed, long and hard. "Keep me updated every hour, at a minimum," he finally said.

"Yes, sir." After disconnecting the call, Corey got on the radio. "Delta, I'm thinking you should displace, move to our position, in case we have to act as QRF for Alpha."

"*Agreed. Oscar Mike,*" Alvarez said.

"Oscar Mike? QRF?" Torres asked.

"On the move and Quick Reaction Force," Corey told him, reminded that the man had no military background. "Rescue team for when Seamus gets into trouble."

"When? Not if?"

Corey snorted. "You have met him, haven't you?" He grabbed his Raven-issued, satellite-linked radio. "Viking 23, Whiskey 7."

Chris Evers grabbed her radio out of her breast pocket. "*Viking 23.*"

"Viking, we've got a man going in close to the tangos, doing recon," Corey told her. "Once the sun is down, we'd like you in the air and on station nearby, just in case. Running dark, out of sight, out of hearing, but close enough to respond ASAP."

"*Copy that,*" she said. She jogged over to her cockpit and looked at the notepad she kept taped to her center display. "*Sunset is in fifty-two minutes,*" she said, glancing up at the cloudy sky. "*So… maybe an hour, hour fifteen to ensure the sky is dark enough we're not silhouetted.*"

"I'll take your word for it," Corey said with a smile. He'd been in regular contact with her ever since they'd spotted the guerillas. She knew the exact location of the valley and the strength of enemy forces. "I think I'd like you somewhere north of their location, away from the city," Corey said. "Fewer eyes to spot you."

"*Understood.*"

* * *

"What's up?" Hatch asked her, walking up as she put the radio away.

"They want us airborne after sunset. Let everyone know. Hit the head, do whatever you need to do, but I want to be hitting pre-flight checklists in forty-five minutes."

"Finally," he said. "I've been losing my mind sitting here." Miller Station had been empty when they'd arrived, then filled up with full-size drones and aircraft, most of which had proceeded to head out again to monitor the inbound Cuban fleet and seemed to be cycling back and forth from Victoria Base, which had much larger fuel tanks. He flashed a smile at Chris. "Maybe you can get a little more action in before you retire to that fat corporate gig."

She shook her head at him. "You know better than to say shit like that out loud."

"What? You don't have the shakes, do you?" He glanced at her hands. Nope, steady as rocks. "So we're cool."

* * *

H is plan was to wait until after sunset, but the sky was so overcast, if Seamus hadn't known which direction was west, he wouldn't have known which of the thick granite-colored clouds hid the sun. As the sky began to darken even further, he got tired of waiting.

"Commencing recon, going radio silent," he ducked his head to murmur into his comm.

"*Copy that, Alpha,*" Corey said, not sounding very happy.

Seamus pushed through wild sheaves of long grass and low-crawled across the two-track into the jungle on the far side. The undergrowth was as thick as it looked, and he barely made any noise as he crawled deeper inside on a thick bed of rotting ferns and leaves. It was dark as dusk under what wasn't, quite, triple canopy jungle. Seamus climbed to a knee and listened. There were the sounds of nature, birds and insects. If one of the guerrillas shouted, he'd been able to hear it while sitting out beneath the coffee trees, but the jungle around him now seemed to absorb all sound.

He didn't want to head straight toward them, paralleling the road, but circle around and come in behind them, where they'd be less likely to be on their guard and looking for visitors. He estimated he was at least 50 meters from the closest vehicle, and the men seemed to be hanging around the vehicles and buildings rather than wandering through the trees, but still, he was wary of being spotted.

Where the trees weren't so thick as to block the light from reaching the ground, ferns sprouted up, forming a waist-high layer so dense and even it looked solid enough to walk on. Thick bushes grew up between the tangled trunks of trees that stretched their roots above the ground like bones. Vines hung from everything.

Seamus moved through the jungle like a ghost, sliding from tree trunk to bush to tree trunk silently, in open spaces dropping to all fours or to his belly to crawl unseen beneath the ferns that hung above him like a layer of verdure clouds. Everything was damp or dripping with water, and the jungle smelled of wet earth and vegetation, fresh and decaying. The sun, wherever it was, continued sinking, and the jungle shifted from dim to dark.

Seamus paused and dug out his Raven-issued night vision goggles. They weren't quite the latest-generation models used by military Special Forces, but they were close, and the true-color, AI-enhanced goggles were far superior to the previous bulky units. They truly weren't much larger than safety goggles and barely extended past his nose. He secured them around his head with the elastic strap and turned them on.

The jungle around him, which had faded to shades of gray and charcoal, sprang back brightly. He fought back a smile—while the goggles provided a full-color image, it seemed as if he was wearing 30-year-old NVGs, as everything around him was shades of green. Turning his head very slowly left and right, he saw nothing but green, green, and more green. He dug the military radio out of the backpack as well and positioned it in a pouch just behind his arm, just in case. He slung his backpack over his shoulders and lifted the Blackbird. The tritium in the optic made the triangle reticle glow fiercely bright through the goggles.

He'd been keeping track of his progress, counting his paces whether he was walking or crawling, and after he'd traveled sixty meters into the dense foliage, he figured that was enough and turned left. Another fifty meters or so, and he should be directly behind the buildings and all the parked vehicles. And then, as slow and quiet as he'd been, stealth would be doubly important, as he'd be right on top of seventy-plus guerrillas. As dark as the jungle was, and as loud, drunk, and oblivious as they'd been for the past day, he doubted they'd ever know he was there.

He was staying on his feet, though crouched, as much as possible, simply because it allowed him to see a little bit further. He took one careful step at a time, ensuring there was nothing under his boot to snap or otherwise make a sound before placing weight on it. His progress was maddeningly slow, but as dusk turned to dark, he was both silent and invisible.

"*Alpha*," he heard in his ear, Corey reaching back out. "*I'm getting air support up as soon as it's full dark and will have it orbiting near your location just in case. I'll let you know when they're on station, but I'm estimating forty mikes from now. Delta and I are going to be moving a little closer to you, also just in case.*" Seamus clicked his comm twice to acknowledge receipt of the message.

After traveling twenty meters in their direction, the sounds of the guerillas, which had faded out, became audible again. Talking, very faint, and occasional laughter broke through the background noise of the jungle, the constant drip of water mixed with the hum of insects. After five more slow, careful paces, Seamus caught a glimpse of light through the leaves sooner than he was expecting.

He froze, then slowly sank to his knees and elbows, and began crawling in that direction. The raised roots of a tree were murder on his joints, and he bit back a curse as he clambered over them in slow motion. Beyond that was a more open area densely packed with ferns. He crawled underneath them, their pungent, almost herbal scent filling his nostrils. At the far end of the patch of ferns, he pushed between two big bushes. He found himself at the top of a gentle slope and followed that downward for several body lengths.

The bottom of the depression wasn't just muddy, it seemed to be filled with standing water, and he felt it soaking through his shirt and pants. He crawled forward once again, and that was when he smelled it, the odor breaking through the pungent reek of the ferns still in his nose. Rot, and not the rot of vegetation, but of meat. The unmistakable smell of death. The rich, coppery odor of blood. He stopped moving, nearly stopped breathing. The smell of blood was... *everywhere*.

The jungle was dark, but the depression he found himself in was blacker than night. Seamus raised himself to his knees and looked around, the goggles automatically adjusting the gain to show him as much detail as possible. What he'd thought was a small rise ten feet away wasn't earth, but a pile of bodies. The half-dozen townsfolk the guerrillas had executed had been dragged deep in the jungle and tossed here to rot. The blood had leaked from their bodies, run down the slope, and pooled in the small depression, mixing with the mud. Seamus wasn't wet with rainwater and mud from hands to feet, he was soaked with the blood of Pepe's victims.

* * *

The Nissan was parked next to the Toyota, and Corey and Alvarez were putting on their combat gear. Torres was eyeing them, not sure how to feel about their preparations. "He's just supposed to be trying to get a look inside the barn, see if there's any money in there."

"He was just hitching a ride from one base to another, and the FRAP ended up trying to feed him to their pet T. rex," Corey said.

He gave the inspector a look. "He's got that kind of luck. Prepare for the worst, hope for the best." They hadn't brought armor, but he, Seamus, and Alvarez had brought simple chest rigs to hold gear and spare magazines if they found themselves in a combat situation. Corey checked that his radio and magazines were in place, then chambered a round in his AK and looked at Alvarez. "He might not need help at all, but if he does, we're over five minutes away here, driving over muddy roads in the dark. I'd much rather have eyes on in case this goes sideways."

"You want to move closer? I think there is a spot along the road in the valley that works in the dark. You remember, from the drone?" He finished loading his FX-05 and slung the rifle across his chest. "We could park there. At night, we could move through that coffee field, be right across the road from the barn if we needed to, and they'd never spot us. They don't have any sentries out."

Corey considered it as he grabbed his radio. "Alpha, I'm getting air support up as soon as it's full dark and will have it orbiting near your location just in case. I'll let you know when they're on station, but I'm estimating forty mikes from now. Delta and I are going to be moving a little closer to you, also just in case." He heard two clicks in his ear as Seamus acknowledged.

"And me?" Torres said.

Alvarez looked at him. "You stay here. Someone at least should act smart."

Corey snorted. "You ready?"

"Yes. Night vision goggles on, no headlights. Cut the engine as soon as we crest the ridge; we should be able to coast down to that spot. Then... leave the vehicle and move on foot?"

"Let's see when we get there." He looked at Torres. "We'll check in when we've got the pickup stashed."

Torres frowned and shook his head, but took the Bren off the back seat of the Toyota and loaded the rifle.

* * *

B lake, her copilot, was shaving in the mirror when Chris Evers pushed through the door into the locker room. The small building only had one unisex room for crew, and they'd done what they could to keep from walking in on each other naked, so Blake was surprised when Evers walked in without even knocking.

"'Sup?" he asked her. He had his flight suit unzipped and was cleaning up a bit before they started their pre-flight checklists. He still had time before she expected them in the bird.

Chris blinked at him. "I don't..." she said and frowned.

Terry Lister looked around an open locker door at her. "I thought we had another fifteen minutes. You need us to clear out so you can use the john?"

At that question, the sound of a flushing toilet echoed around the room, and Hatch stomped out of the toilet stall at the far end of the room. "I apologize in advance," he said with a smile. Then he saw his pilot. "Evers, what's up?"

"I'm not..." she said, then shook her head, looking confused.

Hatch saw the look on her face and nearly ran over to her. He peered into her eyes, then grabbed her hands and lifted them up between them. They looked just fine, but he could *feel* them. They were quivering, then suddenly they were shaking.

"Son of a…" he said and then dropped her hands and shoved her back out the door. "Go!" he told her, and she turned and broke into an uncertain run. He spun back around to the two surprised faces. "Get the bird in the air!" he shouted.

Blake looked confused. "Pre-flight?"

"No pre-flight," Hatch said. "Turn and burn. Get your ass in that cockpit, now! Move!" He looked at Lister. "Get on your goddamn mini-gun!" he roared, pointing out the open door.

Lister was even more confused than the copilot. He frowned at his crew chief. "What are you—?"

Hatch didn't give him time to finish. He balled up his fists and took a step toward the man. "Get on that mini-gun and get it hot, now!" Terry Lister saw the look in his eyes and abandoned all thought of asking why or what. He jogged out the door behind Blake.

Hatch ran after the two men, scanning the skies in every direction. The heavens were a mottled charcoal above them. He didn't hear or see anything, but that didn't matter. Evers was in the cockpit, helmet on, flipping switches. Blake jumped in beside her. "There's nothing on the scopes," he said, scanning the screens as he grabbed his helmet. "What are we doing?" But even as he asked, he had his helmet on and was strapping in.

"Earning your fucking money today," Hatch said, jumping into the bird as the engines whined to life.

Lister had his helmet on and was clicked onto his safety line. His mini-gun was hot, and he was scanning the skies and the property beyond the fence line, swinging the muzzle of the big gun to follow his eyes. "I've got nothing. Anybody see anything?"

"Evers, what are we doing?" Blake asked, his hands dancing over the controls as he got the Peregrine ready to fly.

"Airborne in thirty!" Evers announced over the crew channel.

Hatch strapped in and got his helmet on. Then he jerked, they all jerked their heads at the loud radio transmission. Someone shouting, the words indecipherable over the sound of full-auto weapons fire, an explosion, more than one man screaming, and in the background, screeching, oscillating, whistling roars for ten full seconds, then the transmission abruptly cut off.

"What the fuck was that?" Blake said, his eyes wide, voice cracking.

"Who accepted the collect call from hell?" Lister said, and he was only half joking. It had sounded exactly like that.

"Whiskey 7," Evers said, nodding at the ID that had accompanied the digital broadcast. Plus, she'd recognized Seamus' voice, even if she hadn't understood the words. So had Hatch. "Hang on."

Hatch had his knees bent and felt the weight as Mad Sweeney took to the air. Evers increased the RPMs as fast as possible, rotating the nacelles downward as they gained airspeed. "Whiskey 7, say again," she said, lips pressed tightly together. "Going dark," she told everyone and flipped the switch. The display in front of her seemingly went dark, but she slid down her night vision visor, and her controls were brightly lit again.

"Verify all indicator lights are out."

Blake looked left and right. "Indicator lights are dark, check."

Evers nodded. "Whiskey 7, say again your last transmission," she said tersely. They waited, but there was no response except a brief, staticky warble the computer couldn't identify as a signal. The Peregrine shook as the rotors fought the air for speed.

"Time to call it in. Boss, may I?" Hatch said with exaggerated politeness.

"Yeah, go ahead," Evers said through clenched teeth. She knew how far past the redline she could push Lucille. Mad Sweeney, on the other hand, was a new bird, and she'd never pushed it past 90 percent. "ETA… fourteen minutes if I don't blow an engine."

"Raven Command, Viking 23," Hatch drawled lazily. The wind through the open door was buffeting him, and the engines were roaring overhead.

"*Viking 23.*"

"Whiskey 7 is a ground team now in active combat with enemy forces, requesting help at the coordinates we are sending now. Not responding to radio calls. Viking 23 en route to that location, ETA fourteen minutes, repeat one four mikes. Enemy combatants and multiple dinosaurs." Those screeching, bone-chilling roars couldn't have belonged to anything else on the planet.

"*Uhhh… did not copy, Viking 23, say again.*"

Hatch smiled as he spoke calmly and clearly. "Whiskey 7 is a lightly-armed, four-man team in active combat with an estimated seventy-five enemy dismounts and an unknown number of dinosaurs." He turned his head and leaned back to get a look inside the cockpit. Evers' hands gripping the controls were still vibrating. "Please be advised, *La Bruja* got a good case of the shakes to start us off before the call even came in, and her hands are still going like hummingbirds, so I'd recommend sending everyone you can to what might be the last decent fight of this war. Anybody remember Oaxaca? Plus, you know, dinosaurs. Seriously. Not fucking kidding. We all heard them. *Them*, plural. Just sayin'. Over."

Blake turned around in the cockpit and gave Hatch a look. The veteran crew chief just shrugged.

There was no response for three seconds, then a voice they recognized came over the air. "*Raven Command, Raven 2 Actual,*" Kresge said.

"Go for Command, 2 Actual."

"*My authority, divert half the aircraft monitoring the Cuban fleet to Whiskey 7's location, priority tasking, and anything else already in the air within two hundred klicks of them that's got fuel and fucking ammo. Do it now. Do it right* now."

* * * * *

Chapter Twenty-Three

The blood at the bottom of the depression had mixed with the mud and rain, and it had to be six inches deep. Seamus was soaking in it like a spa treatment in hell. He crawled out of the blood-mud soup up the slope toward the bodies.

The obese police chief was at the bottom of the pile of corpses, but his face was uncovered and turned toward Seamus. His eyes were open, a surprised look on his slack, waxen features. It was sad and horrible, yet one more inhumane brutality in a war that had seen so many. Too many. Seamus wondered if the man had a wife at home, confused and worried why he hadn't yet returned. A wife or children.

He heard a sound, something out of place, not part of the background music of the jungle, and he straightened up just a bit more. Past the sprawl of awkward limbs and staring faces, gaping mouths and stiff fingers, something was snuffling at the bodies, tugging at them. Seamus saw a fuzzy shape about the size of a large possum. His goggles tried to highlight its outline, but the enhanced AI couldn't make sense of the animal's profile. Seamus raised his head another inch, frowning.

The animal suddenly noticed Seamus moving beyond the corpses and jerked to its full height, hissing in surprise and anger. What Seamus had thought was a small animal was in fact the head of a Utahraptor, startled, angry in defense, claws up, towering over him. Behind the animal were three more, all of them larger than the first.

The startled raptor issued an angry, screeching, oscillating, hissing roar of challenge, its head jerking and weaving, a shockingly loud, terrifying sound like nothing Seamus had ever heard before, a steam whistle mixed with the screams of tortured souls. The other animals ran up beside it, standing on the bodies, shrieking the same deafeningly loud scream-whistles at him, waving their claws in a show of aggression at this potential threat. Standing on the rise above him, they looked even larger than they were—massive, deadly, nightmarish creatures. Four of them almost right on top of him, and past them he saw the undergrowth shaking as even more animals responded to the alarm.

The closest raptor darted its head toward Seamus, and he flung himself back, the serrated teeth snapping right where his face had been. He flipped the selector on the Blackbird to full auto and fired a long burst at the bird. He clearly heard the bullets hit it, even saw the impacts in the feathers covering its chest, but they seemed to have no effect on the animal, which weighed as much as three men. It launched itself at him, and he rolled to the side, then he was up on his feet and sprinting through the jungle.

He was knocked to the ground almost immediately and felt a piercing pain in his thigh. The injured leg was pinned to the ground as he felt his upper body lifted into the air and jerked back and forth. The raptor had bitten down on his backpack and was trying to chew through it and shake him hard enough to snap his neck. Sheamus managed to twist around and fired another burst over his shoulder at the animal. It let go with an injured howl, and he was up, running flat out toward the lights and men ahead of him, ignoring the incredible pain in his leg, hearing the animals behind him, to either side of him. Belatedly, he realized he was covered head to toe in blood, and that was all they could smell of him, fresh, wet blood. The blood of easy prey.

He dove between two parked cars. One of the cars rocked as a raptor hit it. Two others easily hurdled the sedans, landing beyond

Seamus as he rolled and popped up to his feet. He heard the warble of sheet metal buckling as another raptor leapt atop one of the cars. The raptors were taller than him, heavier, faster, and far stronger, and he knew he was going to die. But not without a fight.

He ran at the closest raptor, screaming, and emptied the rest of his magazine toward its head as it swung its claws at him. He felt searing pain in his arm as its razor-sharp talons cut him to the bone, and he spun as he fell, which allowed him to see that he was being pursued not by four raptors, but at least twice that many.

His rounds hit their target, and the raptor fell with him. Seamus rolled over its body, came up again, then ran past two guerrillas leaning against the fender of a pickup truck, smoking, staring open-mouthed not at him, but past him. Before him were a dozen vehicles parked randomly, between and past them a dozen men on foot, just starting to turn toward the strange noises.

Seamus zig-zagged between the densely packed vehicles, and he heard human screaming behind him, then one of the guerrillas opened up on full auto. Some of the vehicles were parked too closely for the Utahraptors to fit between, and they leapt from hood to roof to hood, following the smell of blood and meat. Eight of them, nine, a dozen, the entire jungle around them seeming to come alive with animals, running, leaping, screaming their roars that were like no other sound on Earth.

The guerrillas ahead of him went bug-eyed and whipped up their rifles... those that didn't turn and run. They didn't care about Seamus—they didn't know who this blood- and mud-smeared man was—they only had eyes for the monsters coming behind him, flowing between and over the automobiles. A dozen rifles opened up as the raptors roared in challenge, their vibrating, hissing, whistle-screams somehow louder than the gunfire. Seamus grabbed one of his grenades, pulled the pin, and threw it blindly behind him, then dove over the hood of a pickup. More guerrillas ran up, following the sound of violence and terror.

The wild-eyed guerrillas came running right at him, shooting, but they only had eyes for the monsters behind him. Seamus ducked to keep from being shot as five men ran past him, shooting from the hip. Even over the sound of gunfire, Seamus clearly heard a meaty *thud* right behind him that he knew, somehow, meant a man had died. The grenade went off with a muffled *crump*, and someone screamed.

He couldn't get through—the haphazardly-parked vehicles blocked his way—and Seamus rolled into the bed of a pickup. He startled the drunk man sleeping there, and the guerrilla sat up, blinking, and peered in confusion at Seamus. Then a raptor leapt in from the side, digging its claws into the man's chest and pulling him bodily from the pickup bed.

Seamus dove backward out of the truck without looking, and landed badly, almost atop two sets of worn boots. The guerrillas reached down and grabbed his upper arms to pull him up. Just as they realized Seamus wasn't one of them, he stitched them across their chests with the Blackbird, close enough to feel the spray of blood in his face, pushed past their falling bodies, dove underneath a truck, and crawled to the far side.

Seamus pulled the pin on another grenade and threw it toward the jungle, reloaded his Blackbird, then grabbed his radio. "Alpha's in some trouble!" he shouted over the sound of gunfire, screaming guerrillas, and indescribably terrifying raptor attack howls. He jerked as the grenade he'd tossed went off somewhere behind him. He heard shrapnel hitting vehicles. One of the men running past saw Seamus sitting on the ground and realized he wasn't *La Fuerza*, but before he could swing his AK around, Seamus put a burst into his face. The sound of the suppressed gun was lost in the chaos.

"I'm trying to get clear!" Seamus shouted into his radio, then gasped in awe as a raptor sailed over him, an animal twice as large as any he'd seen before, as long as the truck he hid behind, leaping twenty feet and landing on a running man, knocking the rifle out of his arms. With one snap of its jaws, it bit through the man's throat and ripped his head completely off.

Seamus shouted reflexively at the sight, shouldered his Blackbird, and dumped the rest of his magazine into the animal's side behind its arm. It jerked, shuddered, and screamed in outrage and pain, dropping the dripping severed head, then looked around for something to kill, not sure what had hurt it. It spotted Seamus, its eyes glittering in the light.

"Shite," Seamus gasped and was off and running again. Wild gunfire snapped past his head as men and confused, angry Utahraptors—everyone and everything both terrified and mad with bloodlust—raged back and forth. Seamus pulled out another grenade as he darted around the back of a small SUV and threw it toward the huge raptor as it lunged at him, half a second too slow. He felt its breath as its teeth snapped onto him, tearing a bit of his kit and flesh, but Seamus jerked free. It lunged again, but he was past the vehicle, and the SUV rocked from the impact of its body. The animal tried leaping over it after Seamus but was injured from the bullets. Instead, it climbed over the vehicle, claws digging into and through the sheet metal, windshield cracking loudly.

Seamus slammed into a running guerrilla, and they both went down. Seamus was up a fraction of a second before the other man. He kicked the guerrilla between the legs, then shoved him back, right under the fifteen-hundred-pound raptor as it jumped down from the SUV. Then the grenade went off under the vehicle's gas tank, flipping the vehicle in a massive fireball. It landed on both man and raptor, the raptor's feathers exploding in flame as it flailed under the

Chevy, the crackling orange-ruby tongues close enough to crisp Seamus' hair.

The change in illumination blew out the auto-gain in his night vision goggles, and they went black. Seamus ripped them off, ran three steps, then bounced off something big and black. He blindly ran along the edge. He reached a corner and spun around it, finding himself inside the big barn. A burst of rifle fire from outside splintered the wood above his head, and Seamus ducked so violently, his feet went out from underneath him. Then he realized he heard an engine and looked up to see the big white box truck right before him, a man behind the wheel putting the truck into gear.

Seamus raised the Blackbird and pulled the trigger, and—nothing. Swearing, he dropped the Blackbird, drew his pistol, and fired half a dozen shots, but the angle was wrong, and the bullets smacked into the steel behind the driver's head, but didn't penetrate. Snarling, he reholstered his pistol, struggled to his feet, and shoved a fresh magazine into the Blackbird. By the time he had it loaded, the truck was out of the barn and out of sight. A quick glance around the barn showed him two pickups, one large and one small, and no money. He darted to the open door and flinched back, then held up a hand to block the heat and glare of the burning car. Several more vehicles raced off after the truck.

The guerrillas were running everywhere between and past the parked vehicles, firing wildly and shouting. He caught only one glimpse of a raptor, and it was disappearing into the surrounding jungle. One of the guerrillas spotted Seamus at the front of the barn, lit up brightly by the flames, and fired a long, wild burst at him. Seamus ignored the bullets snapping by him and fired once, dropping the man with a headshot, then grabbed his last grenade. He jerked the pin and tossed it over the burning wreckage into the middle of the chaos, then took off in a limping run down the two-track after the box truck.

* * *

Corey and Alvarez were in the little Nissan pickup, coasting silently down the slope into the valley, when Seamus came on the radio, shouting, gunfire, screams, and explosions behind him.

"Shit!" Corey said. He restarted the truck's engine and stomped on the gas, knowing the noise would no longer matter. The truck fishtailed down the muddy road, and he fought the wheel. He'd barely understood Seamus' words, but the fear in his voice had been clear. They could just see the edge of the coffee field ahead of them when Corey hit a rough patch of road. The light truck bounced hard, swerved violently, and then was into the deep underbrush.

"Shit!" Corey said again. He threw the truck into reverse, but the tires just spun.

"*Whiskey 7, say again,*" they heard, the calm voice of the pilot of their air support.

The two men bailed out of the vehicle. They ran down the dirt road as fast as their gear allowed, then Alvarez pointed, and they jumped into the long grass and ran into the coffee field. Gunfire raged ahead of them, too many rifles to count. They heard no response from Seamus over the radio.

"*Whiskey 7, say again your last transmission,*" they heard. There was again no response.

"Alpha, inbound to your location," Corey said into his radio as he ran. "Viking 23, do you copy?" Radio silence. "Shit, maybe the valley walls? Or the cloud cover?" Alvarez shook his head.

They made no attempt at stealth as they ran, side by side, between rows of coffee trees. There was an explosion ahead of them, and fire lit up the night sky, flaring out their night vision goggles before they auto-corrected. They neared the end of the field and crouched between the last set of trees. The guerrillas' virtual parking lot was right before them. One of the vehicles was upside down and on fire right beside the large barn, and there, right at the door of the barn, neatly silhouetted in flame, was Seamus.

A long burst of rifle fire seemed aimed right at them, and Corey and Alvarez dove to the ground as bullets thudded into the dirt and whipped through the tall grass nearby. Corey ate dirt, but when no additional fire was sent their way, he popped his head up. He wasn't sure if anyone had even seen them; the guerrillas were running and shooting in every direction. It looked like Seamus had kicked an ant-hill. Another explosion—one of Seamus' grenades, had to be—sent a body in two pieces flying over one of the cars, but Seamus himself was no longer in sight.

"Alpha, what's your status?" Corey said into his radio, but there was no response.

"He must have pulled back inside the barn," Alvarez said.

"Yeah. Shit." There was no question they were there to back him up, and for every guerrilla they saw sprawled on the ground, there were another five still on their feet. "You ready?"

"Go."

They climbed to their feet and ran across the two-track. They almost made it before they were spotted, and one of the guerrillas shouted. Then they were inside.

"Seamus!" Corey shouted. Rifles up, they ran through the barn. There were two pickups parked inside, and some old farm equipment, but nothing else. No Seamus. The burning car had caught one side of the barn on fire, and the flames were licking through the wood planks. "Shit, do you see him?"

"Negative, negative," Alvarez said.

"Where the fuck is he?" Corey grabbed his radio. "Alpha, what's your location?" Then several guerrillas appeared at the open door of the barn and fired at them. Corey and Alvarez dove behind the vehicles and returned fire. They were pinned down, and the wall beside them burst into flame, the orange tongues stretching toward the roof beams and toward the wall at the back of the barn. They had flames spreading in front of and behind them.

Corey fired a burst at the open door, then ducked back down as return fire shredded the truck's windows and sprayed him with glass. "Alpha, do you copy? What's your location, over?" Alvarez leaned out past the truck he was hiding behind and fired short bursts from his Fire Snake. One guerrilla fell with a cry, and his fellow soldiers dragged him out of the line of fire. Alvarez performed an impressively fast reload and then was up and firing again. "Goddammit!" Corey cursed. He tried the radio again. "Viking 23, do you copy?"

Finally, he got a response, but it was scratchy. "*Affirmative, Whiskey 7, what's your status?*"

"Two friendlies, pinned down in a building at the east end of the valley. Building is on fire, repeat, building is on fire. Unknown location on other friendlies, but we've got hostiles all around us." He fired a long burst, emptying the rest of his magazine, through the near wall of the barn, stitching a waist-high zipper through the burning wood. He was rewarded with a scream. "What's your ETA, over?" he asked as he reloaded.

"*Ten minutes, Whiskey, estimate ten mikes, copy?*"

Corey ducked as several FRAP opened up on his truck. He felt the body vibrate under the hits, and a round skipped under the frame, off the cement floor, and took a small chunk out of his calf. Corey swore. He'd thought he was behind the wheel. He and Alvarez both fired bursts toward the front of the barn as it grew brighter and hotter. Corey tore the goggles off his eyes as they shut down, emptied half a magazine through the open door, then ducked down to reload. He was trying to keep the guerrillas from charging in. But was that the smart move?

The wall beside them was orange rolling flames. Most of the back wall behind them was on fire, even as it was being heavily splintered by incoming rounds going between and over the trucks. The flames were spreading across the rafters above them, and the rafters themselves were disappearing as the thick layer of smoke drew closer to the ground. He traded a look with Alvarez, an unspoken agreement, and they'd each taken a step to charge out the door—and maybe die in the attempt, rather than get burned alive—when nearly a dozen guerrillas opened fire on full auto, and Alvarez fell back with a curse. He'd been hit in the thigh, and he scrambled back behind the truck, trying to put pressure on the wound and return fire.

Corey stuck his AK above his head and fired off half the magazine above the truck, then darted across the open space to Alvarez' side. "Well, this was stupid, and we're going to die." He cursed. He clicked the radio. "Copy that, Viking, don't think we're going to last that long." He risked a peek past the edge of the truck, as the enemy fire had died off. "But we appreciate the effort."

* * *

Inside the Peregrine, Evers clenched her teeth, fighting the urge to scream in frustration. Her eyes scanned the dials and gauges. She was pushing it as hard as she dared, and still she might only shave those ten minutes down to eight.

"Whiskey 7, does your team have IFF transponders?" she asked. "Whiskey 7, do all the members of your team have IFF?"

"*Yes, Viking, affirmative. We have IFF.*"

She nodded. Well, that was something. "Hatch!" Evers yelled.

"On it. How many?"

"All of them!"

"Copy, robot apocalypse ready when you are."

* * *

"**Y**ou want the good news or the bad news?" Corey panted. It was becoming hard to breathe inside the barn. He handed Alvarez a tourniquet.

"There's good news?" Alvarez said with a grimace, sliding the tourniquet up his leg.

"They've pulled back. I can see them, but…"

"Why?" Alvarez gasped.

Corey got down on one knee. "Well, it looks like they'll shoot us if we try to run out, but otherwise they seem happy to let us burn to death." He shook his head, then looked around. The big, wide, heavily guarded door at the front was the only exit from the barn. It was wreathed in gold and orange, as the fire had reached it. He looked over his shoulder. The rear wall of the barn was engulfed in flames, reaching nearly to the blazing rafters. The wall was shredded from the guerrillas' automatic weapons fire, and through some of the holes he could see the gray rock of the cliff behind the barn.

Corey caught Alvarez' eye and nodded toward the door. "You want to Butch and Sundance this bitch?"

"*¿Que?*"

"Run out the front door, guns blazing, and whatever happens, happens?"

Alvarez finished ratcheting the tourniquet around his leg. "I will not be doing any running. They will shoot me as I limp like an old woman, and I do not want to give them that, the *pendejos*. I would rather let the fire take me, have them choke on the smoke from my burning body. They say fire, it's not so bad. You die from smoke inhalation before you burn." The smoke was getting thick. Their eyes were watering from it, and they were starting to cough, and the heat grew so intense their hair began twisting and curling. Alvarez kicked at some flaming straw that threatened to ignite his trousers. The heat was like a weight, pressing in from every direction.

Corey darted around the side of the truck and looked in. Then he checked the other truck. "Shit, no keys." He sat down beside Alvarez, defeated. The air was a little clearer, closer to the floor. "Well, that was my last idea." He stared at the burning back wall of the barn. The raging fire was eating through the splintered wood. Soon the roof would collapse. A few minutes, and it would all be over.

The moisture around his eyes was drying up, and he could barely blink. It was like dragging his eyelids through glue. "Hey." He looked around. "Where's the truck?"

"What truck?"

"The big white truck. Wasn't it in here? It was in here. Son of a bitch." In frustration, he grabbed a shovel and flung it at the back wall of the barn. It hit in a blinding explosion of sparks.

* * *

Seamus jogged down the two-track after the column of vehicles led by the white box truck. The farther he ran, the less the injury in his leg hurt, adrenaline and endorphins killing the pain, and he took the turn from the two-track onto the road at a full run. The vehicles were already a quarter mile ahead of him and almost out of sight, but for the occasional flash of a brake light. They'd turned left, the shorter leg of the road heading for the low saddle at the near end of the valley. Another chorus of brake lights, and they were up and over the ridge.

He staggered to a stop and reached for his radio to call in, wondering why he hadn't heard anything, assuming it had just been too noisy, and discovered his radio was gone, both of them, along with his backpack, shredded by the raptor.

"Ah, shite," he gasped. He wiped his face on his sleeve, but only managed to smear more half-dried blood across his cheeks and forehead. He couldn't see it on his face, but he could smell it, and it was all over the backs of his hands.

Standing in the middle of the road, Seamus looked from the escaping vehicles, now out of sight down the narrow road, back to the barn, which was out of sight behind the trees, but throwing a huge, flickering glow into the cloudy sky. He was alone in the night. Where was the rest of his team?

He heard a faint sound, and just had time to turn before a gray shadow leapt at him from the tangled bushes beside the road. The Utahraptor was nowhere near full-grown, barely four hundred pounds, but being young made it foolish. It was also angry, scared, and hungry, and nearly mad with the smell of blood all around. As a hunter, it wasn't that experienced, and didn't expect its prey to fall backward and kick outward and upward with both feet.

Seamus' boots impacted the animal's ribcage, and it flipped over him. Seamus had barely gotten to his knees when the animal charged in again, the attack completely silent. Seamus fell back and reflexively shoved his Blackbird sideways into the raptor's snapping mouth. The claws on its feet and hands raked his arms and thighs, digging deep, and he fought the urge to scream. It was heavy and impossibly strong, mouth chomping at the gun, lunging at Seamus' head. His arms were forced back against his chest, the raptor's rank breath in his face. The raptor was too strong; Seamus was losing the fight, and quickly. He had to do something.

In a panic and last-ditch effort, Seamus shoved the Blackbird, and the raptor's head, off to the side, let go of the Blackbird, and grabbed for the handle of his knife that he knew to be right there on his chest. Seamus blindly found the handle, yanked the knife out of its sheath, and drove it into the side of the raptor's neck, right underneath its long skull.

He buried his knife in the creature's neck, twisted it, yanked it out, and buried it again. Blood gushed from the wounds all over Seamus' face. The raptor dug its claws into him deeper and fought to get away from the pain. It reared away from him, lifting him half off the ground as the Blackbird, still in its mouth, was slung around Seamus' body, but then the sling snapped. Seamus scrambled backward and fought to his feet. He was surprised to find the knife somehow still in his hand.

He crouched, half in the weeds on the side of the road. The raptor stood in the center of the road, towering over him. It was in severe pain, maddened by it and the smell of blood, and it focused on Seamus as the cause of it all. It worked its claws, opened its mouth wide, and screamed its death-whistle roar at him.

This was every nightmare Seamus had ever had come true. He could feel the deep claw wounds all over his body, weakening him. Whether he'd already been fatally injured or not, he knew the raptor was going to kill him, and all he could hope to do was take it with him.

He screamed back in its face and waved his knife, urging the carnivore to come at him. The creature at first was little more than a dark silhouette, eyes glinting. Blood from the two knife wounds was gushing out of the animal's neck, darkening its feathers. In the moonlight, the blood was black against the charcoal of the raptor's feathers. Then the Utahraptor was revealed to be clad in blue-gray feathers, its eyes a glittering amber. Before Seamus had a chance to wonder why he could suddenly see it so well, it turned its head to address this new threat, and Torres slammed the Toyota Land Cruiser into the creature at thirty miles an hour.

The Toyota slid sideways down the road with one headlight shattered. The raptor bounced off the crumpled front end, flew through the air, and hit Seamus with a glancing blow, knocking him back down. The raptor landed in the ditch next to Seamus, where it lay, unmoving. Torres opened the door and climbed out, numb and shaking. He stared at the raptor, in disbelief at what he'd seen, and then at what he'd done. He looked back and forth between the animal and Seamus, on his back beside the creature and covered in blood. Profanity tumbled from Torres' mouth like water over a cliff, then he asked, "Are you okay?" He held a hand out to Seamus.

Seamus shook off the man's hand, realized he'd lost his knife, and crawled over to his Blackbird. The raptor's serrated teeth had gouged bright, ugly lines in the aluminum receiver and handguard. He couldn't tell by looking at it if the weapon was damaged, so Seamus pointed it at the raptor's still body and pulled the trigger. It fired with a quiet cough, and the animal didn't twitch at the impact. "Right, where were we?" he mumbled. He made it to his feet, swaying a bit. He looked around and saw Torres staring at him with concern. "Go," he told Torres, pointing down the dark road and trying not to fall down. It was surprisingly difficult.

"¿Que?"

"Truck… took off… cars," he panted, spitting the Utah's blood out of his mouth, stumbling around the far side of the Toyota, and climbing into the front passenger seat. Sitting was much better. He pointed. "Box truck," he panted. "Cash. Catch it."

The inspector finally figured out what Seamus was trying to say. With one final look at the raptor, making sure it hadn't moved, Torres got back behind the wheel.

He raced down the road, the Toyota bouncing and skipping, mud flying. He kept glancing over at Seamus, who by the light of the dashboard was covered with blood from hair to boots. Seamus felt the eyes on him. "Watch the road," he croaked. He was in too much pain to be dead, so there was that. The raptor's claws had sliced his arms and legs deeply, in some places to the bone, and he'd already lost a lot of blood. He looked down at himself, not thinking too clearly. What he needed was four or six tourniquets, maybe some pressure bandages, perhaps a month in the hospital. He was soaking the seat with blood, and it was dripping on the floor. His hands still seemed to be working. Mostly.

"Where are the lads?"

"They went after you," Torres told him. Frowning, Seamus looked over his shoulder, but of course there was nothing to see. Well, nothing to do about it now. They had a mission. They couldn't let the box truck escape with the cash.

Torres pushed the Land Cruiser to the limit. The narrow road twisted up over the saddle, then curved down a steep slope into a narrow valley, not a single light to be seen. It zig-zagged back and forth, up the opposite slope to the crest of a ridge, and back down. They drove through jungle so dense the branches scraped both sides of the SUV, then broke through into a wide field. There in the distance, they saw taillights—the box truck and the three trailing vehicles heading southeast. "Catch them!" he shouted at Torres, surprised at the reedy sound of his own voice.

"And then what?"

In response, Seamus rolled down his window and stuck the Blackbird out.

* * *

"Raven Command, Viking 23." Evers' voice was calm and even. The background was an even screaming roar of engine noise.

"Go, Viking, you've got priority across channel."

"One minute to contact. ETA on other air units?"

"*I've got three inbound soonest, the closest fourteen minutes out at current speed, which seems to in excess of the manufacturer's listed maximum speed. All Raven aircraft inbound to your AO appear to be redlining it.*" Command didn't sound surprised.

"*Viking 23, Viking 17, that's us in the lead,*" a male voice came across the air. His voice was flat and tense. "*Making all possible speed your location. Save some for us if you can.*"

Chris Evers' eyes darted back and forth across her control panel, out the window in front of her, then back down. Mad Sweeney was roaring and vibrating. Her airspeed indicator read 512 KPH. Top speed of an empty Peregrine was supposed to be 485 KPH. Interesting.

"Evers," Blake said warningly.

"I see it." One of her indicator gauges was bouncing in and out of the red.

"Seriously," her copilot said.

She ignored him. "Thirty seconds out," she growled into the comm. "Weapons free." Her hands were finally rock solid on the controls. "There's thick tree cover; everyone make sure they're on hybrid optics." The combination night vision and thermal optic lenses in their helmets, the AI switching automatically back and forth between them, would be the best in this situation.

"You still got the shakes?" Hatch asked, both hands on the big mini-gun in front of him. The sliding door before him was all the way open, and he hung from the ceiling in a three-point harness, buffeted wildly by the wind. He couldn't keep the smile off his face.

Blake glanced over. "Negative," he told Hatch. Was that good or bad? He still wasn't sure if he believed in her "voodoo hands," as a lot of guys called them, but he was still haunted by what he'd heard in that radio distress call, by which time they were already nearly in the air.

Hatch chuckled. "Ohhh, this is gonna be *good*." He looked over his shoulder at Lister behind a second mini-gun pointed out the opposite side of the fuselage. "Lister, you fucking kill everything not fucking blinking green, you got me?"

"Yeah, yeah, this isn't my first rodeo," the younger specialist said.

"You don't know shit until you've ridden into battle on *La Bruja's* broom!" Hatch shouted, already riding an adrenaline high, and then they were roaring over the valley, five hundred feet above the ridges at 515 kilometers per hour. The barn was fully engulfed in flames reaching thirty meters into the air, a brilliant orange cube almost too bright to look at, scorching all the trees around and over it. And there, on three sides of the burning building, outlined by the targeting computer, were dozens of men, not one of them blinking the green of a friendly IFF transponder.

"Hang on," Chris said and banked the Peregrine, hard. They felt the blood pooling in their legs from the G forces, and Hatch and Lister sagged in their harnesses. Hatch found himself staring straight down at the ground. Chris used the turn to kill their forward speed. By the time she'd come around, the valley lined up ahead of her, she'd bled off half their airspeed. "Whiskey 7, Viking 23 has arrived. If you've got IFFs, last chance, light 'em up now, we're coming in." She flipped over to the crew channel. "Going straight at them, this first pass," she said through clenched teeth as they roared toward the valley. "Hatch! You dump 'em when I call out."

"*Copy that!*" Hatch moved to the side as he felt the nose of the Peregrine dip for their first attack run.

"Can they take a drop at this speed?" Blake asked her.

"We'll find out."

The valley was less than two kilometers long. Blake fired rockets, and Chris pulled and held down the trigger for the nose-mounted mini-gun as soon as they entered the valley, targeting everything with a human or vehicle profile. The sound of the mini-gun was like God's electric zipper, fifty rounds a second, a ten-second burst that seemed to last forever. The recoil slowed the Peregrine. A dozen small rockets hit in and around the vehicles parked beside the burning barn, and the bullets from the mini-gun shredded running guerrillas and vehicles alike.

"Hatch!" Chris shouted, finger still on the trigger, and the crew chief pounded his fist on the big red button on the wall. With a loud *THUNKA-THUNK*, the WarDogs, folded into compact steel cubes, were spat out the bottom of the Peregrine, one on each side, but not quite at the exact time. The first WarDog impacted near the middle of the coffee field and bounced and rolled. The second released a bit late and slammed into one of the burning vehicles, flipping it over. It was damaged, but the other one unfolded, ran a systems check, and then began prowling, programmed to engage any heat sources larger than half a meter in length without IFF tags.

Then Mad Sweeney was past, fourteen seconds from one end of the valley to the other. Chris banked it into an even harder turn, fighting the Gs, the tunnel vision, and the urge to pass out, hearing the grunts of her crew in her headphones.

"Command, 23," she spit out through her teeth. "The computer tells me it's got in excess of fifty targets on the ground, multiple vehicles. Taking fire. Two WarDogs deployed. No sign of friendlies." She switched channels. "Lister, you're up," she gasped as the Peregrine came out of the bank, and the east end of the valley was below them. She wasn't sure her newest crew member had heard her—maybe he'd passed out from the high G forces—then he opened up with his minigun, and she saw him work a long burst back and forth across the wrecked vehicles.

There was an IR laser on the mini-gun they used when wearing night vision, and it was almost like cheating. Put the beam on the target, pull the trigger, target destroyed. Men were still moving between the burning vehicles, and he targeted several with long, sweeping bursts, the empty cases falling like brass rain out the bottom of the big gun. There was a pause, and then he fired shorter bursts into the trees, picking out individual men, the muzzle of the mini-gun flaring like a dragon spitting electric flame.

Chris did a full, tight orbit five hundred feet off the ground, with Lister cutting down running men left and right, then she broke off and came back, flying in the opposite direction over the valley, putting Hatch on target. Hatch saw a vehicle driving away from the crowd and stitched it from tailgate to engine with a long burst. He fired at individual targets under the trees, and a few running down the road. Some of the guerrillas were shooting at them, but they couldn't see the Peregrine, only hear it, and were shooting at the trailing sound of its exhaust. It wasn't fair, which was the point. Meanwhile, Chris kept trying to raise Whiskey 7 on the radio.

* * *

"I lost my radio; where's yours?" Seamus asked as Torres raced after the vehicles. The Land Cruiser was gradually drawing closer as they raced up and down the ridgelines. Their one working headlight was little help.

"There, right there on the seat."

Seamus found it. He saw the radio had an earpiece plugged into it, and he yanked that out. Immediately the cab of the Toyota filled with urgent radio transmissions. *"Whiskey 7, Viking 23, repeat, do you copy? Whiskey, please respond."*

"Viking, Whiskey. Where are you?"

Chris Evers sounded both relieved and annoyed. *"Where are we? Where are you? We've been orbiting over the target location for five minutes."*

"Must have just missed you. We're in pursuit of several vehicles from that location. Get up close!" he shouted at Torres as the Toyota weaved back and forth on the dirt road, and briefly became airborne after an unseen bump. The vehicles they were pursuing were just ahead, one sedan trailing two pickups, and beyond that the white box truck. "Right on his ass."

"Don't tell me how to drive," Torres growled. He had twenty years' experience chasing *pendejos*.

The vehicles before them suddenly became aware they were being chased, but they weren't sure how to respond. The road was narrow, and the box truck was slow. Torres roared up right behind the sedan.

Seamus leaned out the window, flipped his selector to full auto, and dumped a long burst through the back window of the sedan. The driver slumped over the wheel, and when the road curved, the car went straight, sailing off into thick trees. The sound of the Blackbird was lost over the laboring engines, but the passenger in the next truck figured out what was happening. He leaned out and fired at Seamus and Torres, the shots going wild as both vehicles bounced and swerved over the rough road. And then the bumps instantly stopped. Seamus looked down, then up. They were on pavement on the outskirts of Xicotepec de Juarez. He steadied his aim and took out the truck's passenger with a burst. The man dropped his rifle and slumped over the door.

The road widened to two narrow lanes, and both the pickups in front of him began to weave back and forth, tires howling. A man in the lead pickup leaned out a window and fired at them. Cursing,

Torres jerked the wheel back and forth. Several holes appeared in their windshield, and Torres flinched as flying glass cut his cheek.

"*Are the other Whiskey elements with you? The ones who were in the barn?*"

Seamus frowned as he reloaded the Blackbird. His last magazine, and it was already coated with blood, which seemed somehow unfair. "Don't know what you're talking about, luv. Is it just you up in the air?" The box truck took a corner fast enough to go up on two wheels for half a second. The pickups followed, their back ends sliding. Seamus braced himself as Torres took the corner like the veteran cop he was, closing distance effortlessly. Seamus ducked below the dash, and a guerrilla sprayed wildly at them, then he sat up and fired several bursts through their windshield, which was rapidly disappearing from both incoming and outgoing fire. He blew out a window on a pickup, but that was it. Firing from a moving vehicle at a moving vehicle wasn't easy.

"*We've got other aircraft inbound, but they're ten minutes out.*"

"Copy that. You need to break contact and head this way."

"*I've got multiple enemy contacts here, over.*" Seamus could hear the unmistakable sound of a mini-gun behind her, and it made him smile.

"They're not the mission. *This* is the mission, in pursuit of a big white box truck, and it can't be allowed to escape. Copy?" He bounced off his door as Torres swerved around a parked car. They were in a more crowded area of the city now, with terrified faces flying by. A woman shouted and shook her fist at them as if they were drag racing teenagers. "Hold it steady," he bellowed, and when Torres did, he leaned out and fired a long burst, the Blackbird vibrating nearly silently in his hands. Seamus had been aiming for the driver of the trailing pickup, and missed him entirely, instead hitting the passenger in the lead pickup. Both pickups remained on the bumper of the box truck as it roared down the narrow streets of Xicotepec.

"*Copy. What's your location?*"

"What's our—I don't feckin' know! We're a bloody racing convoy, aren't we, four vehicles now, led by a big white lorry at the north end of the city, lookin' to be in the downtown area." He drew his pistol and fired the remainder of the magazine at the pickup weaving in front of them. He blew holes in the back window and in the tailgate, but that was it. Swearing, he reloaded with the one spare pistol magazine he had in his vest.

The box truck took another corner, banging against a light pole, the impact costing them some speed. The two pickups slowed down as well, bottling up at the corner, and the one right in front of them seemed to pause at an angle. Seamus couldn't get a bead on the driver, but the rear tire was right there in front of him. He fired half a dozen shots, and the tire blew out with a loud *pop*. The spinning rim shredded the tire in just a few seconds, and then there was a shriek of metal as the pickup began riding on the rim. It slowed down noticeably.

"See if you can—"

"*Sí,*" Torres said. The pickup in front of them had been weaving back and forth, but now it was slower. As it swung back to the right, Torres headed left, floored it, and drew alongside the struggling truck. Seamus emptied the rest of his magazine into the driver, and the truck veered off, crashing into the front of a vacant business.

"Ha!" Torres shouted.

"That's great, but now I'm out," Seamus said, holding up his pistol. The slide was locked back.

Torres frowned. "My rifle is in the back."

Seamus blinked dully. "What?" He turned and lunged over the seat with a wordless shout, coming back with Torres' Bren 805 in his hands. The movement had hurt him terribly, though, and he had to take a moment, leaning against the door. His belly and thighs were slick with fresh blood, and he could see raw meat through long cuts in his trousers. A lot of raw meat. Maybe a bit of bone peeking out at the bottom of those gullies in his flesh. He was no doctor, but he didn't think that was good. Blood was practically running off his hands from the cuts to his upper arms, and he stared at them stupidly. He was suddenly very tired, and the darkened streets seemed even dimmer.

"Whiskey, 23, we're a minute out from the city limits, what's your location? Can you call out any landmarks?"

Hearing her confident voice gave Seamus a burst of energy. He stuck the Bren through the ragged windshield and fired at the remaining pickup truck, the sound of the rifle deafening after the suppressed Blackbird. The pickup wove left and right even more aggressively as Seamus blew out windows and pounded sheet metal. It followed the box truck around a corner, and the pickup's driver leaned out his window and fired a pistol at them, emptying the magazine before ducking back inside and correcting a skid.

Seamus jerked and grunted as one of the pistol bullets slammed into his chest. With all the noise, Torres wasn't aware he'd been hit. Torres reached over the seat and grabbed a spare magazine for the Bren. "Here," he told Seamus.

Seamus grunted and took the magazine with blood-slick hands, but he was having trouble focusing. He struggled to get the fresh magazine in the rifle, then looked around dazedly. What was...? Oh, right. He planted the rifle butt against his shoulder and fired. The pickup weaved violently back and forth, but Seamus managed to hit the driver in the shoulder. Injured, the man slumped over the steering wheel, but kept after the box truck.

"*Whiskey 7, Viking's over the city, what's your location, over?*" Her voice seemed distant, echoing. Seamus looked out the windshield, then leaned forward and peered upward. He grabbed the radio.

"The cross," he croaked. "Look for the cross."

Seemingly in slow motion, Seamus watched the driver of the pickup through the blown-out back window raise a grenade into view and twist out the pin. He moved to stick his arm out the window, perhaps to toss the grenade back at them, and Seamus fired, pulling the trigger over and over. The rifle was very quiet. Everything seemed so quiet. He saw the blood fly, saw the man drop the grenade and slump over. He tried telling Torres, about it, it seemed important, but he was tired. So tired.

The grenade blew with a soundless flash, and as pieces of the truck came at them, Torres twisted the wheel and locked up the brakes, and suddenly the world was a spinning kaleidoscope of blood and broken glass.

Seamus found himself on his back in the middle of the street surrounded by twisted, smoking metal and the smell of diesel fuel. He blinked slowly, seeing the stars above him. Then he turned his head. The buildings to either side of the two-lane street made it seem even narrower and longer than it was. The white box truck looked so far away, about to escape. Then there was a sound of the sky ripping apart, and golden, bouncing metal rain fell all around him as a giant bird raced overhead.

The long burst from the Peregrine's nose cannon nearly cut the box truck in half, killing the driver instantly, and it flipped over in the middle of the road and slid for some distance, sparks flying. The Peregrine came looping back around and hovered over the flaming wreckage of the two vehicles, directly above Seamus. The wind from the rotors was warm. He was smiling as he looked up at it. It seemed almost like an angel hovering above him. And just past it, above it, the giant bright blue cross floating in the night sky.

* * *

"I've got nowhere to land!" Chris shouted, looking down at the street below. Even if it hadn't been filled with flaming wreckage, it was too narrow for Mad Sweeney.

"Put it on the roof!" Hatch shouted at her. He looked over his shoulder. "Lister, you're with me."

Chris swung the Peregrine over to one of the nearby commercial buildings with a flat roof, avoiding electric lines. Hatch was cross-trained as a paramedic. He unhooked from his harness, grabbed a first aid kit with one hand, a carbine with the other, and hopped down, Lister right behind him.

The Peregrine slid back over the street and covered the two men with its nose cannon as they hopped from the tall roof to a lower one, and from there to an awning, and then to the ground.

Hatch saw a man crawling out of an overturned vehicle. He was bleeding from a head wound and pressed a palm against it. Hatch wasn't sure whose team he was on—with all the blood covering his face, he didn't recognize him—but when the man saw the two contractors running toward him, he shook his head and pointed a bloody hand at O'Malley, lying a few feet away. That was enough for Hatch.

Lister stood behind him, carbine in hand, as Hatch went to work on the contractor, who was fading in and out of consciousness. "Guard the truck," Seamus wheezed.

"Don't worry about that," Hatch said, busily putting on a second tourniquet. O'Malley's arms and legs were shredded, and he lay in a pool of his own blood. "Lister! I'm going to need you to hold an IV bag!"

"Keep it safe," Seamus croaked, pointing a bloody, dripping finger down the street at the overturned truck, then passed out.

Lister let his carbine hang from its sling, took the IV bag, and held it above the man as Hatch worked frantically. There was blood everywhere. There was nothing but blood. Lister knew a lost cause when he saw it and looked away, down the street at the box truck. Blake's well-aimed burst from the mini-gun in the nose had stitched the truck from tailgate to headlight, killing the driver, who was alone in the vehicle. It also tore a ragged line through the box in back, which had split wide open as the truck tipped over and sledged down the street, knocking over garbage cans. The back of the truck was clearly empty, so he wasn't sure what O'Malley was talking about. Maybe there was some valuable intelligence in the cab or on the driver.

* * *

Pepe had been angry that some of his men had jumped into vehicles and driven away instead of fighting off the military attack. *Pinche pendejos*, violating the ceasefire, but it didn't surprise him, not at all.

He'd caught a glimpse of one of the men, but there had to be others. His men were firing in every direction, over and between the vehicles. Then there were the dinosaurs! Leaping through the air, screaming like demons, driven mad to attack for some reason he didn't understand. The sight of them panicked even his most seasoned men, and they fired at them, and shadows, and each other, for several minutes until he got things under control. They trapped the other two *escaras* in the burning barn, waiting for them to start screaming. The barn was completely engulfed in flame, nowhere to escape—and then cars exploded from rockets, and bullets fell like rain, and a dozen of his men fell. One car flipped sideways through the air, crushing one of his men. Then, with a growling blast of noise and wind, an unseen aircraft went racing by overhead.

"¡*Escaras!*" Pepe shouted, pointing toward the sky. "When they come for another run, shoot them out of the sky!" He clenched a fist, but even as he did, he looked around. Twenty of his men were dead, maybe more. Almost all their vehicles were destroyed, and those that weren't were blocked in under the trees by the others. He was a veteran of the war, and he knew you couldn't outrun an aircraft—that was simple suicide, especially at night. They could see in the dark. Their only chance, *his* only chance, was to slip away on foot.

"I need a rifle!" he shouted. "We will fight! We will show them!" He ran past several burning vehicles, looking down as if he was searching for a dropped weapon, headed into some thick bushes—and kept running through the trees, fighting his way through unseen vines and roots that wanted to trip him. He could hear the aircraft in the distance, its engines howling as it banked to come at them again.

The jungle was fighting him at every turn. He forced his way off to one side, to the edge of the driveway leading to the barns, and looked in both directions. None of his men were visible, and he took off running across the two-track and between the coffee trees, into the deep grass. He was fifteen paces into the field, racing through the grass between dark rows of plants, when one of the dinosaurs leapt up in front of him, startled. It was mortally wounded and had laid down to die, but it wasn't dead yet, and it reacted to this new threat. Then a long burst of automatic fire stitched across the chest of the animal. Pepe dove to the ground as the Utahraptor fell sideways, dead.

"*¡Amigo! ¡Soldado!* Well done!" Pepe said, climbing back to his feet. He looked around to see which of his men had saved his life and caught just a glint of firelight reflecting off the eyes of the War-Dog as it prowled through the orchard before it fired another burst, cutting him down. It paused, sensed no movement from either of the bodies, then continued patrolling.

* * * * *

Chapter Twenty-Four

When dawn slowly broke over the mountains to the east, Chris Evers was still orbiting the valley in slow circles a hundred meters above the ridgelines. There were two V-22 Ospreys on station at five thousand feet, but all the other aircraft that had responded to the scene had returned to base or monitoring the Cuban fleet, which was now less than a hundred nautical miles from Tampico. There were a dozen contractors on the ground, securing the scene and counting bodies. The surviving WarDog was patrolling the perimeter.

"*Viking 23, Cobra 5.*"

"Viking 23."

"*Inbound to your AO, five minutes out. You got any spots nearby big and level enough for a Hydra?*"

Chris looked out the cockpit window. "Affirmative, at least two spots in the road next to the field. You'll see them."

"*Copy that. Meet us down there.*"

"Affirmative."

Blake looked at her. "Who was that?" Chris shook her head. She hadn't recognized the voice.

She landed the Peregrine in the open spot in the field beside the coffee trees that looked like an overgrown helicopter LZ. The rotors were winding down as a Hydra jumpjet screamed in from the west. It made a wide circle around the valley, bleeding off speed, then came in slow, exhaust vents tipping down as it slid in over the dirt road. The pilot found a spot he liked, slid the Hydra above it, put the jet into a hover, and then slowly eased the jet to the ground, the exhaust flinging water and mud from the road.

"Finish shutting her down," Chris told Blake.

"You got it." She glanced back into the fuselage reflexively, but it was empty—Hatch and Lister had loaded O'Malley onto a stretcher and carried him down half a block to an intersection, where they'd loaded him into a Blackhawk, which had then screamed off to the closest trauma center.

Chris pulled her helmet off and left it on her seat, then grabbed the Blackbird out of the cockpit holster. It had been hours since any enemy combatants had been seen in the area, but it was still considered an active combat zone. She chambered a round and carried the suppressed carbine in both hands as she walked through the thick grass toward the jet.

The jet's engines were still cycling down as Chris approached. The cockpit opened, pivoting up. The pilot gave her a salute, then continued shutting down his bird. The man sitting behind him pulled off his flight helmet and worked his neck. It was stiff. He hadn't slept all night, but no one in the valley had, so he had nothing to complain about. He leaned forward, said something to the pilot, then climbed down from the cockpit using the short ladder that deployed.

"Captain," he said, nodding at her.

"Colonel," she replied. She was a bit curious at his presence, but didn't say anything.

"Walk with me," Kresge told her and didn't wait for a response.

They walked down the muddy road before the jet. Kresge looked around the valley, seeing it in person for the first time. "So, I hear you went bowling with a half-million-dollar WarDog and killed nothing but a car? And, of course, the Dog."

"It appears so, sir, but the other one took out over a dozen guerrillas according to its telemetry."

"Hmm. Apparently, two hundred and fifty kph is too fast for deployment. Remind me again, what's the max recommended airspeed for safely deploying a WarDog?"

"Fifty kilometers per hour, sir."

"Fifty. You're sure? Not two fifty?"

"No, sir."

"Hmm." They walked for a bit. "What's the latest on O'Malley?" he asked.

"It's bad. Shot, some burns, but his worst injuries are cuts all over his arms, legs, and abdomen. He nearly bled out. To be honest, from what I hear... I'll be surprised if he makes it. Got into a knife fight with a big raptor." They reached the two-track and turned onto it. Their boots swished through the grass.

Kresge snorted and shook his head. Seamus and his stories. "Is that what he said?"

Chris shook her head. "No, the guy with him. Older, Mexican *fédérale*. He flew back to the hospital with O'Malley."

"Torres?"

"That's it."

"Torres said he was knife-fighting a raptor?"

"Yes, sir. Why?"

She couldn't read the odd expression on the colonel's face. He sighed, then told her, "Because if Inspector Ramon Torres told you that... it's true." He stopped in the middle of the two-track, put his hands on his hips, and stared at the sight before them.

There were at least a dozen civilian vehicles under the trees, although the exact number was hard to determine, as many of them had been blown apart by rockets, in addition to being shredded by the mini-guns. Most of them were still burning, black, acrid smoke trailing into the sky. The trees, which had provided concealment, had withered under the heat and flame. There were a few contractors nearby in full armor, wearing helmets and carrying carbines, and those who spotted Kresge saluted him. A few were still picking through the vehicles, their hard-shell armor helping to protect them from the heat.

Past the vehicles was the remains of the barn. It had collapsed in upon itself hours ago, and while it was no longer burning, the blackened, charred beams were still smoking. Fifty feet away, Kresge could feel the heat on his face.

"Fifty-two enemy KIA, at last count," Evers told him, "although that's likely to go up; the WarDog chased a number of them into the jungle."

Kresge was listening to her as he looked at the destruction. Then he cocked his head and walked toward the scattered wreckage that had been the guerrillas' parking lot. He stopped before the burned-out frame of a vehicle that was upside down. Not lying on the grass, but... Kresge pointed a finger. The contractor standing nearby in full armor walked up on one side of him, and Chris the other. Raven was a bit like a small town in the number of people it had in-country, and Chris recognized the man from various missions—Carter.

"I mean, holy shit," Kresge said. Even completely burned and partially flattened by a vehicle, the Utahraptor's corpse was *huge*, nearly as big as the vehicle atop it. Even with its skull half-charred, it seemed to be staring malevolently at them. He squatted down. Its teeth were as long as his thumb with tiny serrations, and it had dozens of them. The claws on its hands were longer than his fingers. Kresge had seen dinosaurs before. This didn't look like a dinosaur. This looked like a... demon.

"Yes, sir, that was my thought," Carter said. "Looks like it crawled out of hell." He pointed. "Most of the rest are deeper under the trees."

Kresge's eyes grew wide. "There's *more?*"

"Yes, sir, but that looks to be the largest. Utahraptor is what I think we've agreed on; they're too big for any other kind. Not sure what the fuck happened here." He looked around, shaking his head. "I'm half sorry I missed it." After a pause, he said, "But only half."

Kresge took half a step back and pointed at the carcass. "O'Malley won a *knife fight* with one of these? Without armor?" Muttering to himself, Kresge turned and walked to the front of the barn, or what had been a barn, and now was little more than a black square on the ground. The walls were mostly gone, with a few thicker beams still smoldering, leaned up against the cliff face at odd angles. There'd been a steel roof, but it had fallen off to the side in sections buckled from the heat. There were two pickups inside the barn, and they'd burned through. Their windshields were cracked and frosted from the heat, and they sat on bare rims after the tires had roasted off.

"Two men were inside?" Kresge asked, just to be saying something. He knew the answer.

Chris nodded. "Yes, sir, we believe so. John Corey and..."

"Sergeant Miguel Alvarez. Mexican Special Forces. On loan. Shit." He peered into the charcoal landscape. "Did we recover the bodies?"

Chris shook her head. "No sir, not yet. Been waiting for the heat to die down. It looked like it was going to rain earlier, but..." She looked up. Only a few clouds in the sky now. The rest of it was a beautiful, brilliant blue.

Kresge growled low in his throat. "Never ask anyone to do something you're not willing to do yourself," he muttered and walked into the barn. He could feel the heat through his boots almost immediately and wondered how long it would take before the rubber soles started melting. He'd lost men before—it went with the job—but now he was hoping these were the last men he lost in this war.

There wasn't much at the front of the barn; the fire had burned the floor clean. Kresge walked around the scorched trucks, looking at their melted dashboards, and wrinkling his nose at the noxious smell of burnt plastic. On the far side, he stopped and scanned the floor for bodies. He didn't see anything, and he wondered if maybe the men had climbed inside the trucks and died there, and he just hadn't spotted their roasted corpses. There was a scraping sound, and he looked up.

John Corey stepped into view, appearing out of nowhere. He was covered with black smudges, some of his exposed skin red and splotchy from burns, but was otherwise apparently, impossibly, uninjured. More than that—alive. He held a rifle down along his leg. "What took you so long?" he asked Kresge, a hint of a smile on his face.

Kresge stared at the man in shock, thinking he was dead, killed in one of the worst ways possible. "What?" he said, his voice cracking. Several of the contractors nearby stopped dead and stared at Corey as if he was a ghost.

Corey coughed harshly, then said, "I've been waiting for a face or voice I recognized. Do you have any water? Wait, hold off on that, I've got something to show you. Just you," he said, pointing at Kresge, his eyes darting past him to the handful of armored contractors in view.

Kresge blinked twice, then said, "Captain Evers!" He stuck a finger at her, then jabbed it at the ground by his feet. "Post yourself here. Nobody else in the barn."

Chris had no idea what was going on, but she did as she was instructed, ecstatic to see Corey somehow alive. The heat in the middle of the barn immediately had her sweating, but she stood there, hands on her Blackbird, and turned her back to the cliff.

Corey, limping slightly, led the colonel toward the rear of the barn, which was a jumble of half-burned boards, precariously-leaning beams, and one L-shaped section of roof. The floor was littered with ancient metal farm implements. Corey ducked between the section of roof and a half-burned stretch of wall, stepping over a shovel, and Kresge followed. He couldn't see a thing until Corey clicked on his flashlight, then he found himself in a cave. The mouth of it was ten feet high and nearly as wide, the stone various shades of gray.

"Natural," Corey said, his voice echoing, "although I think they leveled the floor, maybe widened the mouth."

Kresge followed him deeper into the cave and looked at the man sitting on the stone floor, propped against the wall. "Colonel," Alvarez said with a nod, then went into a coughing jag. There was a bandage wrapped around his thigh spotted with blood.

"Sergeant," Kresge said, trying not to laugh at the surreal surprises that kept coming.

"His leg wound's not too bad," Corey said. "We had a tourniquet on it, but I took that off after I got a look at it. We've got a few burns, but mostly it's the smoke inhalation. I'm trying not to cough with every breath." He shone his flashlight around at the rough walls. "There are a lot of cracks, and I think at least some of them go all the way through to the cliff face. Enough to let in some air, apparently. I was worried the fire was going to suck all the oxygen out of here, but no. Or maybe the cave was just too damn big. Come on, this is what I wanted to show you."

Corey kept walking, his flashlight beam leading the way. Kresge thought the tunnel-like cave ended ahead of them, but as they drew close, he realized the cave just had a sharp bend. He followed Corey around it, and then the young contractor stopped and shone his light ahead of them.

Kresge blinked at the bright light shining back at him. The flashlight beam reflected off the white plastic, throwing light everywhere. Kresge stepped up. There was already a large hole torn in the plastic through which he could clearly see a wall of densely packed American $100 bills.

"Couldn't just assume, had to see what was inside. Shrink-wrapped," Corey announced, "for long-term storage, I guess."

Shrink-wrapped in tight, white plastic, the pallet of cash reached to the middle of Kresge's chest. Kresge took the flashlight from Corey's hand and played the beam over the pallet of cash. Then he stepped back and shone the light down the length of the cave, which stretched deep into the mountainside and beyond the reach of the flashlight beam. The pallets of cash, all wrapped in thick, white plastic, looked like a row of teeth in a giant's mouth. Tooth after massive, square tooth, stretching into the dim distance.

"Pretty sure that's why they built the barn there," Corey said, "to cover up the opening. I'm assuming there was a hidden door in the back wall of the barn they could swing out and drive through."

"How many?" Kresge asked in wonder, staring at the pallets. He couldn't tear his eyes away from them.

"Sir, I was a Marine," Corey said, his voice echoing hollowly. "Once I ran out of fingers and toes to help keep count, I was lost."

Kresge barked out a laugh, then swore. "How the hell am I going to get all this out of here?" Without it becoming public knowledge, he meant. He handed the flashlight back to Corey, put his hands on his hips, and stared at what, undoubtedly, was billions of dollars.

Corey coughed lightly, then said, "With all due respect, sir, that sounds like a *you* problem, not a *me* problem."

* * * * *

Chapter Twenty-Five

"Señor O'Malley, 'sta bien for a visitor?"

Seamus cracked an eye and looked at his nurse. "I don't remember you asking before sending in Gordito and *el presidente* yesterday, Esmerelda," he said, raising one eyebrow. His voice was very weak, and he was under the influence of the best painkillers in the world, but he was alive. He'd been in the hospital for five days, and conscious—technically—for three. She gave him a dirty look and disappeared out the open door. He smiled. Even half-dead, he still had a way with the ladies.

He must have drifted off again, because the next time he opened his, eyes Kresge was at his bedside.

"Sir," he said weakly. "Give me a moment, I'll get up and salute you properly."

"O'Malley, for once, would you just shut up?" Kresge said, but the smile on his face was genuine. Kresge gestured at Seamus' injured limbs. His arms were above the sheet and wrapped with bandages. His legs were wrapped, too, bulky under the sheet. The gunshot wound in his chest, from a pistol, was actually his least serious injury, according to the doctor. "They tell me you're going to need a few more surgeries. Sliced down to the bone, likely some nerve damage. Record number of stitches for this hospital."

"You should see the other chap."

"I did." Kresge barely suppressed a shudder. Even in daylight, the raptor was fearsome. "Carter recovered your knife, by the way. Thought you might want it for sentimental reasons."

Seamus made a noncommittal grunt. "I'm sure the scars will remind me."

"Yes, well." Kresge cleared his throat. "Xicotepec de Juarez. I think we solved their animal attack problem. We found the bodies of seven raptors around that barn, big ones. One of them had to be over a thousand pounds."

"Utahs," Seamus told him, nodding. "The biggest."

"Yeah."

"Aye. Led them straight into the FRAP bastards, didn't I? Only thing that saved me arse, giving them a few others to chew on, but I saw more than seven. At least ten, maybe over a dozen." Not to mention the nest full of eggs, which he was now convinced had hatched baby Utahs. He sighed. "Still, they're likely to be more cautious around humans."

"Didn't you say they'd killed a lot of people? Women and children."

"Yes, and now they know who the culprit was. So there's that."

Kresge nodded and looked Seamus over again. He cocked his head. "What's your intention if—excuse me, when—you get back in shape? You coming back to Raven?"

"That question has been on my mind," Seamus admitted.

"You're the oldest man I've got still pulling combat tours," Kresge told him, "and the doctors tell me it's going to be at least six months if not a year before you're combat effective, which will make you that much older."

"I'm not so drug-addled I've forgotten how time works, sir," Seamus said. The two men shared a look, and Kresge had to shake his head. Neither said anything for a while. In fact, the doctor had told Kresge that O'Malley would need a year to heal, he'd always have a limp, and likely would never fully recover. "In that case," Kresge had told the doctor, "I expect he'll be back on his feet and limp-free in eight months." To the doctor's dirty look, he'd said, "You simply don't know the man."

"*Señor El Presidente Magnifico* and Gordito dropped by yesterday, wishing me well. They didn't say anything specific, of course, lots of ears here, but a little bird," Corey being the name of that bird, "told me that we did find what we were looking for, and not in that fecking truck Torres and I were chasin' up hill and dale, which really chaps my arse. I trust it's been relocated somewhere safe and under government control? After all, who's more trustworthy than a government?"

"I'm sure I have no idea what you're talking about," Kresge told him.

"Shame," Seamus said. "I would've liked to at least see what that much quid looked like, maybe rolled around in it a bit in the altogether."

Kresge pulled out his palm, tapped it a few times, and turned it toward Seamus without a word. He'd taken a photo inside the cave just before they'd started moving the pallets out. From the photo, you couldn't see what was under the plastic, just that there was a seemingly endless row of heavily laden pallets.

Seamus blinked a few times. "Shite," he finally said.

"That's been everyone's reaction." Kresge put the palm away. "Torres just had a few cuts and bruises and walked out the same day.

Alvarez is due to be released tomorrow, Corey as well. Their main issue was smoke inhalation, but they should be good to go in short order. Corey's thinking of signing on to a new contract we just picked up in Europe."

"That's what he says. Just training, isn't it?"

"Yes, but you know how these things sometimes bloom into something bigger."

Seamus couldn't shrug, it hurt too much, so he moved his head from side to side. "Well, even if it doesn't, it's not like he hasn't already seen his share of action. The change of scenery will do him good. Get himself a nice Polish or Czech girl."

"I don't know how long I'm for Mexico," Kresge admitted.

Seamus was surprised to hear that. "Really? Things have quieted down that much, have they?"

His colonel shrugged. "The temporary ceasefire expired, but we really haven't seen any more fighting. Eight hundred and change guerrillas showed to take the Cubans up on their offer. I don't know whether that's more or less than they were expecting, but all that was remarkably trouble-free. Which, honestly, was not what I was expecting. It didn't hurt that the sky over the ships was filled with armed aircraft."

"Not even a thousand? That's nary a drab compared to their numbers when I signed on. What of the rest?"

Kresge shook his head. "Went home, disappeared into the countryside. Don't know, and don't much care, especially if it means they're done fighting. Our Mexican friends probably won't leave it at that, they'll spend a few years tracking some notables down in the dead of night, but…" He shrugged.

"So Mexico can finally start trying to rebuild? That's going to take a bit of cash," Seamus said, a smirk on his face as he looked at Kresge.

Kresge shared the smirk. "My guess is they've got some lying around."

"Yes, but how much cash is the question," Seamus said, giving Kresge a direct look.

Kresge gave an elaborate shrug. "I wouldn't be surprised if they found an extra fifteen billion sitting in their treasury," he finally said.

Seamus closed his eyes. Kresge thought the man might have fallen asleep, but then he heard him mutter, "Fifteen bloody billion, and I didn't get one flippin' cent."

He opened his eyes, and Kresge was still there. "I've got to head out; the paperwork doesn't stop just because the war's over. I'd shake your hand, but..." He nodded at Seamus' bandaged arms, then straightened to attention and saluted him. "I'll be back in to check on you before you're discharged. Try not to get into any trouble."

Smiling, Seamus nodded and said, "I always *try*, sir."

* * *

He kept dropping off, so he wasn't sure whether it was one or two days later that his palm rang when he was conscious, and he was bored enough to answer a call when he didn't recognize the number, hitting the speaker button so he didn't have to hold it up to his ear, which he really couldn't.

"O'Malley."

"Sergeant! Good to hear your voice again. It's Randy Max."

"Aye, sure it is. Let me guess, you need a dance partner for the next episode of *Dancing for Quid*."

The man on the other end of the line laughed. "Honestly, I get that reaction a lot."

"That's what I get for mentioning I met the man; it's me own damn fault," Seamus grumbled. "Now it's the lads having a go at me when I'm down. Who put you up to this, that bastard Carter?"

"No, seriously, O'Malley, it's really me."

"How about you seriously piss off so I don't have to reach over and hit the button again?"

The man chuckled. "You told a few people you met me? Did you tell them we recited the entirety of Henley's *Invictus* together? To be honest—and I'll deny I ever said this—it sounds much better in your accent than mine."

Seamus blinked three times, swore silently, then politely said, "Mr. Max, so nice to hear from you again. This is unexpected. Are you looking for an autograph? I do usually charge for those."

Randy snorted, then had to laugh out loud. Seamus was just as he remembered, which was good, and not interested in kissing his ass, which he found refreshing. He cleared his throat. "I've nearly finished a screenplay. There... might be a character in it who resembles you." He paused. "No might, and more than a little resemblance. It's a slightly fictionalized treatment of the excitement we had down in Mexico last summer. In part, I started it to help me work through a few things, get them out of my head and into a computer, but in truth, it's good. It's really damn good if I do say so myself. I'd like to have you sign a release. Just so there's no... confusion."

"Confusion."

"Well, lawsuits you know, but I'd like you to do more than just sign a release. I'd love to have you involved in pre-production, helping to educate and work with the actors as a technical advisor. In production, on the set, helping to make things as accurate as possible. Maybe give you a little background cameo, for which you'd get a modest payment up front, and a small percentage of the gross. If you were thinking of retirement from actual combat and wanted to try your hand as a technical advisor, this would open all the right doors for you. Hell, I'd love to use you for future projects."

Seamus gave a long sigh. Retirement was something he'd been giving a lot of thought to. He hated the very sound of the word, but he wasn't getting any younger, or less battered. This sounded, at the very least, interesting. He looked down his body, bulky with bandages. "When might this be?"

"Well, I'm going to be starting principal photography on another film next month. Then there's the reshoots, the editing… but I'd want to do this next after that. Pre-production would be maybe, eight, nine months out, and that's when I'd like you to start working with the actors."

"Eight months." He looked down at his body. "I should be available, depending. How small is this small percentage of the gross?"

"As your character—the character based on you—would be one of the main supporting roles, and I really would need your assistance fleshing out the film, and likely you have some very interesting contacts who could help with military equipment and the like, as I want to film as much of this practical, in camera, not CG, maybe even in Mexico itself… say, a million up front, and 3 percent of the gross?"

Seamus cleared his throat and went to sit up. The sharp pain all over his body helped clear his head, and he was proud he didn't scream, not even a little. The machines by his beside pinged loudly, however. "A million?" he said with as much nonchalance as he could muster. He didn't trust himself to say anything for a few seconds. He made good money working for Raven, but that was three years' salary. "Three percent?" Esmerelda poked her head through the door, frowning at the electronic alarms, and Seamus glared back at her. She rolled her eyes and left.

"I know it doesn't sound like much, but people have been begging me for the Oman story for years. They're primed, and this is even better, at least by Hollywood standards—famous actor playing himself, professional hunters, private contractors, war-torn country, rampaging dinosaurs, the beautiful, sandy beaches of Cancún, the smart young daughter of a billionaire with world-class breasts—"

"They are that," Seamus agreed.

"Factoring in the production budget I'm aiming at, the world-wide appeal of the story line, and the fact that it really fucking happened, it should net you ten million even if it flops. I've been doing this a long time; I don't think it will, especially since I'm writing, starring, and executive producing it. Everything but directing; that's a bridge too far. Remember, we're talking gross receipts, not net, worldwide, so that 3 percent should get you another ten, but maybe as much as sixty million. I'd say that's a decent nut for your retirement, if and when."

Seamus didn't say anything for a long while. "Enough for a nice apartment in Paris," he mused.

"A nice apartment *building* if this hits like I think it will, and likely sequels. That's more money than you're likely to see in your life, otherwise."

Seamus smiled and laughed hard enough for it to hurt. More alarms pinged. "You'd be surprised."

* * *

Eddie Echevarria had likely tattled, as after he'd been visited by the Mexican president, thanking Seamus for his service and discretion, he'd gotten calls from Tina Echevarria, Roger and Michael Rudd, even Beni Trujillo, Echevarria's taciturn chief of security. Gordito's wife, a lovely former actress, had sent a massive bouquet of flowers and a heartfelt Get Well card.

But as for outgoing calls... he'd been waiting to call her until he got his mind right, answered a few pressing questions he'd posed to himself. He had a long conversation with Corey after the visit from Kresge. He'd been in the hospital for ten days before he finally called Sadie. She'd left him several messages, but had assumed he was still working in the field.

"Sorry it's taken me a bit," he apologized. "Longer than I thought it would. I did speak with Peter Hein. He had a tale to tell."

Sadie laughed in his ear, the sound sweet and clear. "We definitely had a little excitement. We ran into some guerrillas. Well, actually, we ran *away* from some guerrillas. It was after the ceasefire, but that didn't seem to matter. Other than a few bruises and scrapes, we made it home safe."

"Maybe a few more nightmares?" he asked quietly. Hein had told him about the running gunfight through the jungle.

"Maybe," she agreed. "Likely. But I... truly, after thinking about it... think it was for the best. I mean going to Mexico."

"Did you find what you were looking for?"

"Yes," she said with sudden excitement, "and so much more. The hard drive we found was filled with most everything we were looking for, as well as a few surprises. This prion, it's going to completely change medicine they think. To be honest, much of it—much of the potential—is beyond me, beyond my imagination."

"As long as they spell your name right on the Nobel Prize check," he said. "Isn't there a prize with the prize?"

She laughed. "Yes, but I'm not going to be winning it. That's for other people."

"But you're going to get a piece of it, right? If they can figure out how to make it work on people? Make money off of it?"

"Yes, maybe, someday, but I don't want to get my hopes up. It's going to be years away. I'll be old and gray." She paused for a bit. "I'd love to talk to you about what we discovered." She paused again. "What we saw," she said quietly. *What we did*, is what he knew she meant. What *she* did.

"I would like that," he said, "but I've got... well, I don't know if it's good news or bad news. I've got news. I'm back in the hospital," he told her. She made a small sound of dismay that he felt in his heart. "I'll live," he assured her. "Just a little dust-up. A minor little gunshot wound. I did a little wrestling with a few dinos, just some Raggedy Andy between friends. They say I'll recover, more or less, with a few more colorful scars to add to me catalog. We'd be a matching pair, strolling along the Champs-Élysées. But..." He let the word hang in the air for a long time. She seemed to sense that it was better not to interrupt him.

"I think I'm done," he said finally. "Between the Paras and Raven, I've been doing this for twenty years. I've got more gray hair than my father had when he died. By the time I'm in good enough shape to go back on active duty, I'll be... well, far older than I ever thought I'd be." His age was a number that started with 4, a fact he found very upsetting. "I won't retire completely," he said quickly. "I couldn't bear the thought of just sitting around, but I think I'm done doing *this*. War's a young man's game."

"Okay," she said slowly.

"I've got a nugget put away," he continued. "Not quite a princely sum, but they pay us lads very well, and I haven't seen fit to spend hardly any of it over the past decade. And a job offer came up that, if it pans out, would set me up quite right. So I can afford to relocate… anywhere. In thinking about all the places around the world I've visited, at the moment, I can't think of anywhere I'd rather relocate than Paris." He cleared his throat. "But I thought I'd check with you first, seeing as you're a local." He found he had to clear his throat again; for some reason it was quite tight. "Do you recommend it? Or should I look elsewhere? It wouldn't be right away. Not for a few months. Maybe April." He stopped talking and waited.

She didn't answer for ten long seconds, but it felt like forever. Then gently, softly, she told him, "Paris is lovely in the springtime."

"So I hear," he said, a big smile on his face.

# # # # #

Author's Note

Writing the *Echoes of Pangaea* series has been an absolute blast. Not only because I get to envision what it would be like interacting with dinosaurs in the wild, but because a near-future novel set in war-torn Mexico has afforded me the opportunity to do research, and educate myself, about so many odd and wonderful things, from next-gen night vision optics to coffee farms, from Chichén Itza to, of course, dinosaurs. Hopefully my enthusiasm has made its way onto the pages.

Seemingly every month we learn new things about dinosaurs, and every fact and detail in this book is technically accurate to what we know now. Of course, I'm not alone in my semi-technical wild speculation about what these animals might have been like when alive, even scientifically-based properties such as *Walking With Dinosaurs* are filled with SWAGs (that's Scientific Wild-Ass Guesses.) No one knows what a Utahraptor sounds like, how smart they were, or how they socialized in groups, but I did my best to make things realistic based on how we know living creatures behave.

The discovery of dinosaurs is, from a historical perspective, a very recent thing. America is a young country, and yet still, the Founding Fathers were dead and buried before the first dinosaur was discovered and named. Who knows what additional treasures the ground will give up in coming years?

I'm not sure about future sequels, but I definitely have a prequel planned, set around the FRAP attack on Pangaea. People always want to know how everything began, and I plan to eventually start back at the beginning, because Pangaea is not done giving up its secrets.

I have to thank a few people. My sons Harrison and Barrett were my initial readers and editors, and as usual, they made this a better book with their observations and critiques. Rob Reed is an excellent author in his own right, and he thought enough of *Bestiarii* to put me in contact with Chris Kennedy of Chris Kennedy Publishing/Theogony Books. Chris liked *Bestiarii* and *Fire and Bone*, but like editors and publishers everywhere, he wasn't satisfied and demanded a third. "Everyone loves trilogies," he told me. I hate to admit it, but he was right. *The Ghosts of Xicotepec* is the direct result. I hope you've enjoyed the ride.

* * * * *

413

About the Author

James Tarr is a regular contributor to numerous outdoor publications and has appeared on or hosted numerous shows on The Sportsman Channel cable network. He is also the author of several books, including **Failure Drill**, **Whorl**, and **Carnivore** (with Dillard Johnson), which was featured on The O'Reilly Factor. He lives in Michigan with his fiancée, two sons, and a dog named Fish.

* * * * *

The following is an

Excerpt from Book One of Abner Fortis, ISMC:

Cherry Drop

P.A. Piatt

Available from Theogony Books

eBook, Audio, and Paperback

Excerpt from "Cherry Drop:"

"Here they come!"

A low, throbbing buzz rose from the trees and the undergrowth shook. Thousands of bugs exploded out of the jungle, and Fortis' breath caught in his throat. The insects tumbled over each other in a rolling, skittering mass that engulfed everything in its path.

The Space Marines didn't need an order to open fire. Rifles cracked and the grenade launcher thumped over and over as they tried to stem the tide of bugs. Grenades tore holes in the ranks of the bugs and well-aimed rifle fire dropped many more. Still, the bugs advanced.

Hawkins' voice boomed in Fortis' ear. "LT, fall back behind the fighting position, clear the way for the heavy weapons."

Fortis looked over his shoulder and saw the fighting holes bristling with Marines who couldn't fire for fear of hitting their own comrades. He thumped Thorsen on the shoulder.

"Fall back!" he ordered. "Take up positions behind the fighting holes."

Thorsen stopped firing and moved among the other Marines, relaying Fortis' order. One by one, the Marines stopped firing and made for the rear. As the gunfire slacked off, the bugs closed ranks and continued forward.

After the last Marine had fallen back, Fortis motioned to Thorsen.

"Let's go!"

Thorsen turned and let out a blood-chilling scream. A bug had approached unnoticed and buried its stinger deep in Thorsen's calf. The stricken Marine fell to the ground and began to convulse as the neurotoxin entered his bloodstream.

419

"Holy shit!" Fortis drew his kukri, ran over, and chopped at the insect stinger. The injured bug made a high-pitched shrieking noise, which Fortis cut short with another stroke of his knife.

Viscous, black goo oozed from the hole in Thorsen's armor and his convulsions ceased.

"Get the hell out of there!"

Hawkins was shouting in his ear, and Abner looked up. The line of bugs was ten meters away. For a split second he almost turned and ran, but the urge vanished as quickly as it appeared. He grabbed Thorsen under the arms and dragged the injured Marine along with him, pursued by the inexorable tide of gaping pincers and dripping stingers.

Fortis pulled Thorsen as fast as he could, straining with all his might against the substantial Pada-Pada gravity. Thorsen convulsed and slipped from Abner's grip and the young officer fell backward. When he sat up, he saw the bugs were almost on them.

* * * * *

Get "Cherry Drop" now at:
https://www.amazon.com/dp/B09B14VBK2

Find out more about P.A. Piatt at:
https://chriskennedypublishing.com

* * * * *

The following is an
Excerpt from Book One of The Last Marines:

Gods of War

William S. Frisbee, Jr.

Available from Theogony Books

eBook and Paperback

Excerpt from "Gods of War:"

"Yes, sir," Mathison said. Sometimes it was worth arguing, sometimes it wasn't. Stevenson wasn't a butter bar. He was a veteran from a line infantry platoon that had made it through Critical Skills Operator School and earned his Raider pin. He was also on the short list for captain. Major Beckett might pin the railroad tracks on Stevenson's collar before they left for space.

"Well, enough chatting," Stevenson said, the smile in his voice grating on Mathison's nerves. "Gotta go check our boys."

"Yes, sir," Mathison said, and later he would check on the men while the lieutenant rested. "Please keep your head down, sir. Don't leave me in charge of this cluster fuck. I would be tempted to tell that company commander to go fuck a duck."

"No, you won't. You will do your job and take care of our Marines, but I'll keep my head down," Stevenson said. "Asian socialists aren't good enough to kill me. It's going to have to be some green alien bastard that kills me."

"Yes, sir," Mathison said as the lieutenant tapped on Jennings' shoulder and pointed up. The lance corporal understood and cupped his hands together to boost the lieutenant out of the hole. He launched the lieutenant out of the hole and went back to digging as Mathison went back to looking at the spy eyes scrutinizing the distant jungle.

A shot rang out. On Mathison's heads-up display, the icon for Lieutenant Stevenson flashed and went red, indicating death.

"You are now acting platoon commander," Freya reported.

* * * * *

Get "Gods of War" now at:

https://www.amazon.com/dp/B0B5WJB2MY.

Find out more about William S. Frisbee, Jr. at:

https://chriskennedypublishing.com.

* * * * *

The following is an

Excerpt from Book One of Chimera Company:

The Fall of Rho-Torkis

Tim C. Taylor

Now Available from Theogony Books

eBook, Paperback, and Audio

Excerpt from "The Fall of Rho-Torkis:"

"Relax, Sybutu."

Osu didn't fall for the man steepling his fingers behind his desk. When a lieutenant colonel told you to relax, you knew your life had just taken a seriously wrong turn.

"So what if we're ruffling a few feathers?" said Malix. "We have a job to do, and you're going to make it happen. You will take five men with you and travel unobserved to a location in the capital where you will deliver a coded phrase to this contact."

He pushed across a photograph showing a human male dressed in smuggler chic. Even from the static image, the man oozed charm, but he revealed something else too: purple eyes. The man was a mutant.

"His name is Captain Tavistock Fitzwilliam, and he's a free trader of flexible legitimacy. Let's call him a smuggler for simplicity's sake. You deliver the message and then return here without incident, after which no one will speak of this again."

Osu kept his demeanor blank, but the questions were raging inside him. His officers in the 27th gave the appearance of having waved through the colonel's bizarre orders, but the squadron sergeant major would not let this drop easily. He'd be lodged in an ambush point close to the colonel's office where he'd be waiting to pounce on Osu and interrogate him. Vyborg would suspect him of conspiracy in this affront to proper conduct. His sappers as undercover spies? Osu would rather face a crusading army of newts than the sergeant major on the warpath.

"Make sure one of the men you pick is Hines Zy Pel."

Osu's mask must have slipped because Malix added, "If there is a problem, I expect you to speak."

"Is Zy Pel a Special Missions operative, sir?" There. He'd said it.

"You'll have to ask Colonel Lantosh. Even after they bumped up my rank, I still don't have clearance to see Zy Pel's full personnel record. Make of that what you will."

427

"But you must have put feelers out…"

Malix gave him a cold stare.

You're trying to decide whether to hang me from a whipping post or answer my question. Well, it was your decision to have me lead an undercover team, Colonel. Let's see whether you trust your own judgment.

The colonel seemed to decide on the latter option and softened half a degree. "There was a Hines Zy Pel who died in the Defense of Station 11. Or so the official records tell us. I have reason to think that our Hines Zy Pel is the same man."

"But… Station 11 was twelve years ago. According to the personnel record I've seen, my Zy Pel is in his mid-20s."

Malix put his hands up in surrender. "I know, I know. The other Hines Zy Pel was 42 when he was KIA."

"He's 54? Can't be the same man. Impossible."

"For you and I, Sybutu, that is true. But away from the core worlds, I've encountered mysteries that defy explanation. Don't discount the possibility. Keep an eye on him. For the moment, he is a vital asset, especially given the nature of what I have tasked you with. However, if you ever suspect him of an agenda that undermines his duty to the Legion, then I am ordering you to kill him before he realizes you suspect him."

Kill Zy Pel in cold blood? That wouldn't come easily.

"Acknowledge," the colonel demanded.

"Yes, sir. If Zy Pel appears to be turning, I will kill him."

"Do you remember Colonel Lantosh's words when she was arrested on Irisur?"

Talk about a sucker punch to the gut! Osu remembered everything about the incident when the Militia arrested the CO for standing up to the corruption endemic on that world.

It was Legion philosophy to respond to defeat or reversal with immediate counterattack. Lantosh and Malix's response had been the most un-Legion like possible.

"Yes, sir. She told us not to act. To let the skraggs take her without resistance. Without the Legion retaliating."

"No," snapped Malix. "She did *not*. She ordered us to let her go without retaliating *until the right moment*. This *is* the right moment, Sybutu. This message you will carry. You're doing this for the colonel."

Malix's words set loose a turmoil of emotions in Osu's breast that he didn't fully understand. He wept tears of rage, something he hadn't known was possible.

The colonel stood. "This is the moment when the Legion holds the line. Can I rely upon you, Sergeant?"

Osu saluted. "To the ends of the galaxy, sir. No matter what."

* * * * *

Get "The Fall of Rho-Torkis" now at:
https://www.amazon.com/dp/B08VRL8H27.

Find out more about Tim C. Taylor and "The Fall of Rho-Torkis" at:
https://chriskennedypublishing.com.

* * * * *

Made in the USA
Las Vegas, NV
11 September 2022

55106257R00236